Praise for the
CAT CRIMES series!

Cat Crimes
"Scary, funny, clever and traditional, each story has its own special flavor. . . .This is a grand collection indeed."

—*Mostly Murder*

Cat Crimes 2
"Offers an even livelier selection of cat tales for reading and rereading pleasure."
—*Mystery News*

Cat Crimes 3
"Tales from some of the best writers in the business."
—*The Washington Times*

By Martin H. Greenberg and Ed Gorman
Published by Ivy Books:

CAT CRIMES
CAT CRIMES 2
CAT CRIMES 3
DANGER IN D.C.: Cat Crimes in the Nation's Capital

By Martin H. Greenberg
Published by Ballantine Books:

THE MICHAEL CRICHTON COMPANION*
MUMMY STORIES

By Ed Gorman
Published by Ballantine Books:

THE SHARPSHOOTER
WOLF MOON
NIGHT KILLS
DEATH GROUND

Forthcoming

DANGER IN D.C.

Cat Crimes in the Nation's Capital

Martin H. Greenberg and Ed Gorman

IVY BOOKS • NEW YORK

Ivy Books
Published by Ballantine Books
Copyright © 1993 by Martin H. Greenberg and Ed Gorman

Library of Congress Catalog Card Number: 93-70900

ISBN 0-8041-1277-0

This edition published by arrangement with Donald I. Fine, Inc.

Manufactured in the United States of America

First Ballantine Books Edition: September 1995

10 9 8 7 6 5 4 3 2 1

Contents

Author Notes

John Lutz's *Single White Female* was both a smash novel and a smash motion picture last year. But Lutz also writes two fine mystery series, one about a rather hapless man named Nudger, the other about a more demonstrative character named Carver.

Carole Nelson Douglas excels in several genres but her Irene Adler mysteries and her novels about a cat named Midnight Louie have brought her special prominence.

Barbara Collins may well become the Roald Dahl of her generation. She has a great appreciation for the sardonic and the ironic, and puts them forth with admirable panache and zeal. Her stories can be very, very sweet and very, very nasty—often at the same time.

Barbara Paul is one of the true masters of the detective story. She has written virtually every type of suspense story possible, and done so with enormous skill and deadly wit. She is especially good on the subject of cats.

Jon L. Breen is not only the world's preeminent mystery critic, he's also a first-rate author of mystery novels. His *Touch of the Past* was one of the best books of the eighties.

Author Notes

Richard T. Chizmar's stories have started to appear in a variety of anthologies and magazines. He writes in an easy-going style that very subtly takes its toll on the reader. He is a good candidate for much greater fame.

Carolyn Wheat is both an attorney and an author. She frequently uses the former to inform the latter, turning out a type of contemporary crime fiction all her own.

Max Allan Collins has won the Shamus Award for his series of mainstream novels about a 1940s private eye named Nate Heller, who finds himself investigating such cases as the Lindbergh kidnapping. The books are a major contribution to the literature of private-eye fiction.

Larry Segriff has sold several short stories in the past year, and is on the verge of selling his first novel. While his first love is science fiction, he is already a masterful spinner of mystery yarns.

Dan Brawner is a young writer who is just now directing his energies toward the suspense field. This is his first published story.

Gary A. Braunbeck writes stories in his own quiet and individual voice. His characters are real people and his plots dazzling. He will be a major name in popular fiction.

William J. Reynolds writes a private-eye series about a colorful guy named "Nebraska." What makes the books notable is the sly fun they poke at the entire genre.

Bruce Holland Rogers is a name to watch for, his forceful use of the mystery story presaging an important career.

Author Notes

Bill Crider's *Blood Marks* was recently designated one of the best serial-killer novels of the past decade. But Crider writes everything, from traditional mysteries to westerns, and writes them all very well.

Wendi Lee is an accomplished western writer who is just now starting to write mysteries. She is also a journalist and occasional writer of graphic novels.

Peter Crowther burst on the scene several years ago with a few dozen brilliant tales of life in contemporary England. He is just now starting to be known in America.

Billie Sue Mosiman is a recent Edgar nominee whose excellent dark suspense novels have already won her comparison with the legendary Patricia Highsmith.

Barbara D'Amato's series about Cat Marsala is proving to be one of the big hits of contemporary mystery fiction. Her latest is *Hard Luck*.

Kristine Kathryn Rusch is not only a fine short-story writer and novelist, she is also editor of the *Magazine of Fantasy and Science Fiction*. She writes with remarkable clarity and feeling and depth to give each one of her stories a memorable twist.

Introduction

Being somebody who hates both American political parties with equal ferocity, I can think of no more suitable fate than for the crooked and decadent members of our Congress to be replaced by felines.

A) Felines are honest.

B) Felines are smart.

C) Felines never go on junkets.

D) Felines have never driven anybody off a bridge.

E) Felines have never run Willie Horton–style TV commercials.

None of the above can be claimed by any congressperson I've ever heard of, especially those who sanctimoniously insist they're paragons of American virtue.

But, appealing as the notion of cats running the country is, we are left with drab glum reality in the person of those folks who actually run the good old U.S. of A. these days.

So we thought we'd have a little fun by bringing Cat Crimes to Washington, D.C.

God knows nobody knows more about crime (and from firsthand experience) than congresspeople.

We hope you enjoy these tales (I'll resist the obvious "tails" pun) as much as we did.

DANGER IN D.C.

Because face it, some subjects are so overwhelming, all you can do is laugh about them.

So has the kitty litter box been freshened? Clean cool new water put in the bowl? Yummy snacks set out for good little kitties?

Good.

Now that all your duties have been discharged, you can sit back, relax and travel with us to the sin capital of the United States . . .

Washington, D.C.

—Ed Gorman

The President's Cat Is Missing

•

John Lutz

There are some people I owe money, but I'm square with the law and with my Aunt Amanda. Which is why she said it was okay if I stayed at her secluded little farmhouse outside Washington, D.C., while she spent the month in Europe. I figured a month was all I needed for some bets I had on some sporting events to pay off, and I would be out of the mess I was in. I didn't count on Roy showing up.

Aunt Amanda's farmhouse has got nothing to do with farming. It's a three-room cottage that used to be a farmhouse until Aunt Amanda bought it and sold all the land around it to somebody who wanted to make it into a bird sanctuary. A condition of the deal was that Aunt Amanda, who's not a rich woman but is comfortable, would be able to live in the farmhouse for the rest of her life. So she fixed it all up and called it a cottage and moved in her precious antique furniture and knickknacks and spent her time there writing her children's books in seclusion. It was the seclusion that she liked about the place, and that I liked right now, with certain parties actively seeking me.

How Roy Smathers found me I'll never know. I woke up one morning and heard somebody tromping around outside on the porch. My heart jumped against my ribs and I was already on the way out the back door in my pajamas when it occurred to me that the folks looking for me wouldn't be knocking on the door, which was happening now, or calling my name. If they'd found me, I no doubt wouldn't have awoken at all.

"Norman! I know you're in there! C'mon, open up! It's Roy! Your old pal Roy!"

Now, let me tell you about Roy. He's an old pal, true. But I don't like being around him because he's mostly trouble. Roy is a guy with more energy and ambition than brains. That's something Aunt Amanda once said about me, and it stuck in my mind because it fit Roy so perfectly. He's a guy that'll rush in where even fools and angels fear to tread. The thing is, it's impossible to stay mad at Roy, even if he gets you furious. That's what makes him dangerous. His charm, which I admit he's got, gets him out of scrapes sometimes, and sometimes not. He's done two stretches behind walls that did about as much to rehabilitate him as a hyperactive two-year-old. Aunt Amanda had often given me strict orders to stay well away from Roy, and here he was, on the front porch of her cottage.

I opened the door. What choice did I have?

Roy, all right. Looking like a young Will Rogers, with his amiable smile and friendly blue eyes, the lock of straight black hair flopped down on his forehead where it usually was. He was wearing a suit and tie, like always, looking ready for any funeral or wedding even if his clothes didn't quite fit. He grinned at me and said, "How you been, Norman?"

"Sleeping is how I've been. I'm not now, though."

"Well, ain't you gonna—?"

"Invite you in? No."

His bright grin stuck like it was plastered there. "I'm here to help you, Norman," he explained. "You're here because you need money to get certain people off your trail."

I stepped back to let him inside. He was coming in any-

4

way, so I figured at this point I might as well be cooperative.

Squeezing past me, he sniffed the air and said, "Got any coffee made?"

"No. How'd you find me?"

"Doesn't matter. If I found you, so can the Belinski brothers. Hey, this is a nice place, except for all the old stuff."

Roy had my predicament figured right. And he no doubt knew who was paying the dangerous and merciless Belinskis to look for me. Knew why I needed money. Knew why I always needed money. Question was, what did he want from me in return? I asked him that question.

He began to pace back and forth over Aunt Amanda's antique Persian rug, faster and faster. I sat on Aunt Amanda's dainty rose-colored Victorian sofa and watched him.

"I need this place for a very short time, Norman. For a thing I got planned."

"No."

"There's big money in it, Norman, and I'll cut you in for twenty percent. That'll be a lot more money than you owe."

"My aunt warned me about you. And she made it clear when she said I could stay here—"

"Sure, sure," Roy interrupted, "but she didn't know I had the means to make us both rich. And that this would be just the spot I needed to make it happen."

"What's so special about this place?" I asked.

"It's off by itself, can't be seen from the road. And it's near D.C., but not too near."

"D.C.? As in Washington?"

"Sure. Our nation's capital." He said it as if it were the answer in a quiz. "You had breakfast yet, Norman?"

"No, I was sleeping." Visions of federal men ran through my mind. They had badges and guns. "You're not planning some kind of political scam, are you, Roy?"

5

"Nope. Simple kidnapping. You got any eggs or sausages out in the kitchen?"

I stood up. My worst fears were confirmed. "Roy, there's nothing simple about kidnapping, even if it begins that way. I want out, even though I was never in."

He looked puzzled, then grinned. "You don't understand, Norman. I guess I used the wrong word. All I'm gonna do is snatch a cat."

"You're going to hold a cat for ransom?"

"You got it. But not just any cat. Boots."

"I never heard of—" Then it hit me. Boots was the name of the First Daughter's cat. The daughter of the President of the United States. "Not *the* Boots?"

"No other. *The* Boots is the only cat worth half a million dollars."

"And the only cat that lives in the White House and is guarded by the Secret Service and that'll bring down all of Western civilization on you if you so much as harm a hair on him."

Roy waved a hand as if shooing away a fly. "No harm's gonna come to any cat, Norman. I love cats. It's just I love money more."

"What about the Secret Service, the FBI, the Marines, Navy, Army and Air Force?"

Again he waved his hand. "I got a way to get around all that."

Now I raised a hand, like a policeman halting traffic. "Don't tell me!" I said. "I don't want in. In fact, I want as far out as possible."

He sighed and propped his hands on his hips, all the time smiling as if he'd just had his teeth cleaned and wanted to show them off. "You know, Norman, I would never rat on you, but like I said, the Belinski brothers can follow the same trail I did. They might not be far behind me. You're going to need money and distance."

6

"You saying I've got two choices? It's you or the Belin-skis?"

"Is that what *you're* saying, Norman?"

He was right. I wasn't saying it, but I knew it. And I'd already figured that after paying my debts from twenty percent of half a million dollars, I'd have more than fifty thousand left for myself.

Thinking, Forgive me, Aunt Amanda, I said, "Tell me the plan, Roy."

He began pacing even faster, his chest puffed out, talking louder. He was as confident as he was dumb. He was known for that. He said, "I got more than a dozen cats in heat, Norman."

I didn't think I'd heard right, but I was afraid I had. This was going to be worse than I'd thought. I stood up and went into the kitchen to put on some coffee, knowing he'd follow.

Walking right behind me, yammering in my ear, he said, "It's how I'm gonna lure Boots off the White House grounds. I got these cats in wire cages in a van. It'll be parked in a spot I picked out not far from the White House, with all its windows and doors open. If the wind's right, male cats like Boots can tell from miles away if there's a female cat in heat. It don't happen to cats real often, like with humans. Remember my ex-wife Trixie? Never mind. Think how Boots'll react to more'n a dozen frisky females in heat!"

Spooning coffee into a filter, I said hopefully, "Maybe Boots has been neutered."

"Nope. I checked that out. President knew he was gonna run for the top office years ago and didn't want the animal rights people on his case. Boots is a normal male cat that's gonna react in the normal way when confronted with a cathouse on wheels, Norman. Trust me on that. What about pancakes? Anything around to make pancakes?"

"And after you have Boots?"

"I bring him here and hold him hostage, wait for the First Family to decide to pay ransom. That twelve-year-old daughter, Soho, you think she's not gonna pressure mom and dad to fork over a measly half million to get the cat back? Heck, Congress diddles that much away every day before lunch. You recall the time I pretended to be a university and got that federal grant to study the odds in blackjack?"

I said, "Aunt Amanda would kill me if she knew I let a cat into this place. You gotta promise me you'll clean up after it."

"Sure, I promise. You won't regret this, Norman."

"When's it going to happen?"

"Tomorrow morning."

"Tomorrow!"

"Hey, put a pinch of salt in with those beans. It'll make the coffee less bitter."

I added a lot of salt.

I didn't sleep well that night, and the next morning it seemed that Roy's visit had been a dream. He'd arrived out of nowhere, told me his insane plan, gone through the kitchen food supply like a giant locust, then departed. I wasn't sure he'd really been there at all.

Until I walked over to the TV and turned on CNN.

It was all over the news. Against a backdrop of black sedans, police cars with flashing lights, all kinds of cops in suits and in uniforms scurrying around in front of the White House, Bernie the anchorman was solemnly describing how a catnapper (that's what Bernie said) somehow lured Boots the presidential cat from the grounds and made off with him.

The First Family was enraged. Soho, the daughter, was devastated.

I switched channels and found the story on network news, too. Sam Davidson the journalist was trying to elbow his way through a phalanx of Secret Service agents. He had a forlorn-looking cat beneath one arm that somewhat resembled Boots and he was yelling, "Is this the cat? Is this the cat? Let me talk to Soho! Let me speak with Bill!" Bill was the President. There was a brief tape of Soho sobbing, not about to talk even to the persuasive Davidson.

I switched off the TV. I didn't want to see anymore. My heart was banging away like an MTV drummer. I said, "Good Lord!"

Just then I heard the sound of a vehicle approaching, its engine racing. I looked out the window and there was a red van speeding and bucking along the road to the cottage. I could see Roy bouncing around behind the steering wheel.

The van screeched to a halt outside the cabin and Roy jumped out. He was grinning maniacally, his hair tousled and his eyes wide.

I went to the cottage door and opened it.

That was when Roy opened the van's sliding side door, and what seemed like fifty cats raced out. Some seemed to be chasing others. The ones being chased headed for the shelter of the cottage. The others followed. The screeching and hissing was deafening.

As Roy followed the cats into the cottage I recovered my senses enough to shout, "I thought they were in cages!"

"They were, some of them," Roy said, still grinning crazily and pacing back and forth the way he always does when he's hyper, somehow ignoring the earsplitting turmoil. "Boots left the White House grounds and came into the van, just like I planned. What I didn't plan was all the other male cats around the White House showing up. Over a dozen of them arrived all at once and got in the van. They raised such a fuss trying to get to the females, all the cages came open. But I got Boots!" His grin was gleaming and triumphant.

"So keep him!" I said angrily. "Get rid of the others! Now!"

For the first time since he'd returned, Ray stopped grinning. "I can't, Norman. I don't know which one he is."

I stood there astounded. "You don't know what he looks like?"

"I seen newspaper photos and seen him on TV, just like you." He pointed vaguely at the racing and yowling cats. "*You* pick him out!"

Roy had a point. I couldn't tell males from female cats, even at a slower speed than they were all traveling. They were wrecking Aunt Amanda's cottage, darting over the furniture, climbing the curtains, doing other things.

Roy scratched his head and said, "They look like they're all related."

"If they're not related now, they soon will be," I said. "My aunt's gonna kill me. Get them out of here! All of them!"

"Aw, Norman! If I do that, Boots'll run away."

He had another point. Guys like Roy always had just enough of a point to keep themselves and everybody around them in trouble.

"Then at least get them all in one room!" I shouted.

Roy started yelling and waving at the cats, scooping them up and shoving them toward an open door. When a valuable Chinese vase hit the floor and shattered, I began helping him.

It took us fifteen minutes, but we got them all into Aunt Amanda's bedroom and slammed the door. The yowling and hissing from inside the room came in waves.

Roy slumped on the sofa, gasping. "I'm sorry, Norman. Really! . . . But you're gonna be rich, just like me. Not quite as rich as me, maybe, but still rich. Did we eat all the eggs yesterday?"

I couldn't believe it. "Are you bonkers? This thing didn't work. All you've done is turn an entire country against you, make a nice young girl sad, and set us up for life in prison if the jury doesn't recommend putting us in a sack and drowning us!"

Roy shook his head as if I was the dumb one. "They don't know where I am or where Boots is, Norman. My plan's working fine so far. I've just got some extra cats. You make coffee this morning?"

We both froze at the sound of someone moving around on the porch.

Roy and I exchanged terrified glances.

The door burst open and banged against the wall.

The Belinski brothers swaggered in.

They were huge, paunchy twins with marble-slab faces and slashes for mouths beneath little hooked noses. Their suits were cheap gray and probably bought at a two-for-one sale. Their porcine little eyes were like laser beams. They were identical twins; neither looked meaner than the other. No one could.

"Gotcha!" the one on the right said, staring straight at me. They were both staring at me. Every part of me went limp with terror, yet somehow I remained standing. I tried to plead for mercy but something square and with thorns seemed to be lodged in my throat.

The twin on the left said, "What're *you* doing here, Roy?"

Roy shrugged. "Just leaving, actually."

"Actually not," the twin on the right growled. "Seems you're in the wrong place at the wrong time, Roy. Don't matter none to us, though. We never liked you much anyway. Cheap con like you, nobody'll miss you."

"We'll do Roy right after we finish with Norman," the other twin said, smiling with anticipation. In unison, they drew ugly blue-steel revolvers from beneath their wrinkled suitcoats.

Just then the cats let out an awful yowling and the twins both looked at the closed door to Aunt Amanda's bedroom.

11

Something inside the room hit the floor hard. Glass shattered.

"What's all that?" the Belinski on the right asked, leveling his revolver at my heart.

"We have cats," I managed to squeak.

One of the Belinskis said, quite seriously, "Most people got mice."

I hoped the Belinskis hadn't been listening to the news. The odds were that they hadn't heard or read about Boots yet. They weren't the type to keep up on current events, and I doubted if they could read. If they knew about Roy's latest stunt, they'd kill us both slow and twice over for even getting them near it.

One of the twins edged over to the bedroom door, rotated the knob, and eased it open half an inch to peer inside.

He closed the door and turned around, an expression of disbelief on his cruel face. "Cats," he confirmed. "A thousand of 'em."

But he hadn't closed the door quite all the way. It hadn't latched. Suddenly dozens of cats came streaming out and were racing and yowling around the room.

The Belinskis cursed and swatted and kicked at them but the cats were too fast. One of the twins yelled "Ow!" and made a face, holding up a scratched hand.

Roy chose that time to run for it. He crossed the room in two giant strides and had the front door open.

More cats streamed in, from outside. They came in a torrent of fur. There was no way to have so many females in heat in one place and not attract every male cat within five miles. The masses of cats met in an explosion of yowling and hissing and motion. I'd never seen so many cats. Never dreamed there were so many cats in one place. And that one place was Aunt Amanda's cottage.

"Freeze!" one of the Belinskis screamed.

I thought he was yelling at the cats, but I froze anyway. The only warm-blooded creatures motionless in that whirlwind of a room were Roy, the Belinskis and me. The cats were everywhere, in constant turmoil and raising a terrific din.

"Let's do it and get outa here!" the other Belinski yelled. He'd dropped his gun in the uproar and was stooping down groping for it on the floor. A cat ran across his back.

He'd straightened up to stand next to his twin, and guns and nasty smiles were aimed at Roy and me, when we all heard another sound.

It took us a few seconds to realize what it was.

Barking.

The Secret Service was using dogs to track the cats.

Dogs—bloodhounds, I think—roared into the cottage at top speed and began skittering around on the floor and yapping in bewilderment at all the cats.

Roy, me, the Belinskis, stared at each other.

All hell broke loose.

The cats continued chasing each other. And doing other things. The dogs had never seen anything like it and started chasing the cats. Roy, me and the Belinskis got out of there, bursting onto the front porch.

I wiped my eyes to make sure what I saw was real. What looked like a thousand men with guns, half of them in uniform, were advancing across the field toward the cottage. A division of cars with flashing rooflights were lined behind them. The whole scene was peppered with TV crews carting cameras and other equipment. Half a dozen helicopters thrashed in the air above the cottage. Above them, a formation of jet fighters roared across the sky.

The Belinskis stood stupefied, their arms at their sides and their guns dangling.

One of them blinked. "What kinda pull have you *got*, Norman?"

I grinned at Roy, who was grinning at the advancing army.

"We're FOBs," I said.

13

Both Belinskis looked puzzled. The one nearest me said, "Fobs?"

"Foes of Bill," I explained.

The Belinskis still looked confused.

Then the army was on us.

We raised our hands high.

I make license plates now, and will for the rest of my life.

Roy works in the laundry, way over on the other side of the penitentiary. That's the way I requested it, and the warden, who hates cats, granted my wish.

Still, while I don't want Roy near me ever again, I have to admit I owe him something. I mean, I wouldn't be here if it weren't for Roy. I don't mean *here*, in prison, I mean anywhere. The Belinskis would have killed me if he hadn't come on the scene. Aunt Amanda would have killed me if Roy hadn't convinced the feds the whole Boots thing was my idea, so they kept me safe in custody without even a thought of bail. And my shirts are always soft, with exactly the right amount of starch in the collars.

It's impossible to stay mad at Roy.

Sax and the Single Cat

•

Carole Nelson Douglas

The day I get the call, I am lounging on Miss Temple Barr's patio at the Circle Ritz condominiums in Las Vegas, trying to soak up what little January sunshine deigns to shed some pallid photosynthesis on my roommate's potted oleanders.

Next thing I know, some strange tom in a marmalade-striped T-shirt is over the marble-faced wall and in my own face.

It is not hard to catch Midnight Louie napping these days, but I am on my feet and bristling the hair on my muscular nineteen-pound-plus frame before you can say "Muhammad Ali." My butterfly-dancing days may be on hold, but I still carry a full set of bee-stingers on every extremity.

Calm down, the intruder advises in a throaty tone I do not like. He is only a messenger, he tells me next; Ingram wants to see me.

This I take exception to. Ingram is one of my local sources, and usually the sock is on the other foot: I want to see Ingram. When I do, I trot up to the Thrill 'n' Quill bookstore on Charleston to accomplish this dubious pleasure in person.

15

I look over my yellow-coated visitor and ask, "Since when has Ingram used Western Union?"

Since, says the dude with a snarl, he has a message for me from Kitty Kong. The intruder then leaps back from whence he came—Gehenna, I hope, but the city pound will do—and is as gone as a catnip dream.

A shiver plays arpeggios on my spine, which does nothing to restore my ruffled body hair.

This Kitty Kong is nobody to mess with, having an ancestry that predates saber-toothed tigers, who are really nothing to mess with. They would make Siegfried and Roy's menagerie at the Mirage Hotel look like animated powder-room rugs.

Though the designated titleholder changes, there is always a Kitty Kong. Long ago and far away, in Europe in pre-New World days, this character was known as the King of Cats, but modern times have caught up even with such a venerable institution. Nowadays Kitty Kong can as easily be a she as a he, or even an it. Nobody knows who or what, but the word gets out.

Supposedly, a Kitty Kong rules on every continent, the seven-plus seas being the only deterrent to rapid communication. Even today, dudes and dolls of my ilk hate to get their feet wet. If the aforementioned saber-tooths had been as particular, they would have avoided a lot of tar pits, but these awesome types are legend and long gone. Only Midnight Louie remains to do the really tough jobs, and at least I resemble an escapee from a tar pit.

I follow my late visitor over the edge to the street two stories below and am soon padding the cold Las Vegas pavement. Nobody much notices me—except the occasional cooing female, whom I nimbly evade—which is the way I like it.

Ingram you cannot miss. He is usually to be found snoozing amongst the murder and mayhem displayed in the window of the Thrill 'n' Quill. Today is different. He is waiting on the stoop.

"You are late, Louie," he sniffs.

Such criticism coming from someone who never has to go anywhere but the vet's does not sit well. I give the rabies tags on his collar a warning tap, then ask for the straight poop.

"And vulgar," he comments, but out it comes. A problem of national significance to catkind has developed and Kitty Kong wants me in Washington to help.

No wonder Ingram is snottier than usual; he is jealous. But his long, languorous days give him plenty of time to keep up with current events.

I am not a political animal by nature, but even I have noticed that the new Democratic administration in Washington means the White House will be blessed with the first dude of my ilk in a long, long time, one Socks (somehow that name always makes my nose wrinkle like it had been stuffed in a dirty laundry basket). However, I am not so socially apathetic as to avoid a thrill of satisfaction that one of Our Own is back in power after a long period when the position of presidential pet had gone to the dogs.

This First Feline, as the press so nauseatingly tagged the poor dude, is not the first of his kind to pussyfoot around the national premises. I recall that a polytoed type named Slippers was FDR's house cat and the White House's most recent First Adolescent, Amy Carter, had a Siamese named Misty Malarky Ying Yang. Come to think of it, Socks is not such a bad moniker at that.

Anyway, Ingram says the inauguration is only two days away and a revolting development has occurred: The President's cat is missing; slipped out of the First Lady's Oldsmobile near the White House that very morning. We cannot have our national icon (Ingram uses phrases like that) going AWOL (he does not use expressions like that, but I do) at so elevated an occasion. The mission, should I choose to accept it (and there is nil choice when Kitty Kong calls): Find this Socks character and get him back to the White House lawn doing his doo-doo where he is supposed to do it.

The reason Midnight Louie is regarded as a one-dude detection service is some modest fame I have in the missing-persons department. A while back I hit the papers for finding a dead body at the American Booksellers convention, but I also solved the kidnapping of a couple of corporate kitties named Baker and Taylor. Things like that get back to Kitty Kong.

You would be surprised to know how fast cats like us can communicate. Fax machines may be zippy, but MCI (Multiple Cat Intelligence) can cross the country in a flash through a secret network of telecats who happen to look innocent and wear a lot of fur. These telecats are rare, but you can bet that they are well looked out for. I have never met one myself, but then I have never met a First Cat, either, and it looks like I will be doing that shortly.

After I leave Ingram, I ponder how to get to Washington, D.C. I could walk (and hitch a few rides along the way), but that is a dangerous and time-consuming trek. I prefer the direct route when possible.

Do I know anyone invited to the shindig? Not likely. Miss Temple Barr and her associates are nice folk but neither high nor low enough to come to this particular party. I doubt any of the Fifty Faces of America hails from Las Vegas (though several million such faces pass through here every year). I would have had better odds with the other guy and his "Thousand Points of Light."

But *que será, será*, and by the time I look up my feet have done their duty and taken me just where I need to be: Earl E. Byrd's Reprise storefront, a haven for secondhand instruments of a musical nature and Earl E. himself.

If anyone from my neck of the wilderness is going to Washington, it will be Earl E., owing to his sideline. I scratch at the door until he opens it. Earl E. stocks a great supply of meaty tidbits, for good reason, and I am a regular.

Of course, when I visit Earl E., I have to put up with Nose E.

I do not quite know how to describe this individual, and I am seldom at a loss for words. Nose E. resembles the product of an ill-advised mating between a goat-hair rug and a permanent-wave machine of the old school. Imagine a white angora dust mop with a hyperactive hamster inside and a rakish red bow over one long, floppy ear. Say it tips the scale at four pounds, is purportedly male and canine. There you have Nose E., one of the primo dope-and-bomb-sniffing types in Las Vegas, even the U.S. You figure it.

Earl E. has a secret, and lucrative, sideline in playing with bands at celebrity dos all over the country. The lucrative part is that Nose E. goes along in some undercover cop's grip, ready to squeal on any activities of an illegal nature among the guests, including those so rude as to disrupt the doings with an incendiary device.

Dudes and dolls of my particular persuasion are barred from this cushy job for moral reasons. Our well-known weakness for a bit of nip now and then supposedly makes us unreliable.

Oh. Did I mention Earl E.'s instrument of choice? Tenor sax. Will Earl E. be at the inauguration? As sure as it rains cats and dogs (that *look* like dogs) in Arkansas.

Commercial airlines are not my favorite form of travel, but with Earl E., I and Nose E. get separate but equal cardboard boxes and a seat in first-class. (Actually, my box is bigger than Nose E.'s, since I outweigh this dust-mop dude almost five to one.)

Getting here is not hard—after I gnaw on the heavy cream parchment of Earl E.'s invitation for a few minutes he gets the idea and says, "What is happenin', Louie? You

19

want to go to D.C. today with Nose E. and me and boogie?"

I look as adorable as a guy of my age and weight can stomach, and wait.

"All right. I am paying for an extra seat anyway for the sax and Nose E. A formerly homeless black cat like you should have a chance to see history made."

See it? I make it. But that is *my* little secret.

As per the usual, there is little room at the inn in D.C., but Earl E. has connections due to his vocations of music and marijuana sniffing. My carrier converts into a litter box for a few days in a motel room not too far from the Capitol with a king-size bed I much approve and promptly fall asleep on for the night, despite the company. I also plan to use most of my facilities outdoors, reconnoitering.

Naturally, Earl E. has no intentions of letting me out unchaperoned, though he takes that miserable Nose E. everywhere. Imagine a Hostess coconut cupcake sitting on some dude's elbow and squeaking every now and then. But there is not a hotel maid alive who can see past her ankles fast enough to contain Midnight Louie when he is doing a cha-cha between the door and a service cart.

I am a bit hazy on dates when denied access to the Daily Doormat—otherwise known as the morning paper—but I discover later that we arrived on the day before the inauguration.

Washington in January is snowless, but my horizon is an expanse of gray pavement and looming white monuments, so the effect is wintry despite a delicate dome of blue backdropping it all.

I stroll past the White House unobserved except by a pair of German shepherds, whose handlers curb them swiftly when they bay and lunge at me.

"It is just a cat," one cop says in a tone of disgust, but the dogs know better. Luckily, nobody has much listened to dogs since Lassie was a TV star.

Socks is not officially resident at the Big White until after the swearing in, so I do not expect to find any clue in the vicinity. What I do expect is to *be* found. When I am, it is a most unexpectedly pleasant experience.

I am near the Justice Building when I hear my name whispered from the shade of a Dumpster. I whirl to see a figure stalking out of the shadow—a slim Havana Brown of impeccable ancestry.

"You the out-of-town muscle?" she asks, eyeing me backwards and forwards with a dismaying amount of doubt.

"My best muscle is not visible," I tell her smugly.

"Oh?" Her supple rear extremity arches into an insulting question mark.

I sit down and stroke my whiskers into place. "In my head."

That stops her. She circles me, pausing to sniff my whiskers, a greeting that need not be intimate but often is. Then she sits in front of me and curls her tail around her sleek little brown toes, paired as tightly as a set of chocolate suede pumps in Miss Temple Barr's closet.

"You know my name," I tell her. "What is yours?"

"You could not pronounce my full, formal name," she informs me with a superior sniff. "My human companions call me Cheetah Habanera for short."

Cheetah, huh? She does look fast, but a bit effete for the undercover game.

"You sure you are not a Havana Red?" I growl.

She shrugs prettily. "Please. My people fled Cuba more than thirty years ago with my grandmother twelve-times-removed. I am a citizen, and more than that, my family has been in government work ever since. What have you done to serve your country lately?"

Disdain definitely glimmers in those round orbs the color of old gold.

"They also serve who stand and wait," I quip. An apt

21

quote often stands a fellow in good stead with the opposite sex. Not now.

She eyes my midsection. "More like sit and eat. But you managed to get here quickly, and that is something. Do you know the background of the subject?"

"What has grammar got to do with it?"

"The subject," she says with a bigger sigh, "Socks, is a domestic shorthair, about two years old; nine to ten pounds, slender and supple build." She eyes me again with less than enchantment. "He has yellow eyes; wears black with a white shirtfront, a black face-mask, and, of course, white socks."

"Yeah, yeah. I know the type. A Uni-Que."

"Uni-Que? I never heard of that breed."

"It is not one," I inform her brusquely, "just a common type. That is what I call them. Street name is 'magpie.' I know a hundred guys who look like that. If this Socks wants to lose himself in a crowd, he picked the right color scheme for the job. You, on the other hand—"

"Stick to business," she spits, ruffling her neck fur into a flattering, chocolate brown frill.

I refrain from telling her that she looks beautiful when she is angry. The female of my species is a hard sell who requires convincing even when in the grip of raging hormonal imbalance, and I do mean moan. This one is as cold as the Washington Monument.

"Fixed?" I ask.

"Do you mean has he had a politically correct procedure? Of course," she answers, "is not everybody 'fixed' these days?"

"Not everybody," I say. "What is the dude's routine?"

"He is not a performing cat—"

"I mean where does he hang out, what jerks his harness?"

"Oh. Squirrels."

"Squirrels?"

"He is from Arkansas. They must have simpler sports there."

"Nothing wrong with a good squirrel chase," I say in the absent dude's defense, "though I myself prefer lizards."

Her nose wrinkles derisively. "We D.C. cats have more serious races on our minds than with squirrels and lizards. Do you know how vital to our cause it is that an intelligent, independent, dignified cat with integrity inhabit the White House, rather than a drooling, run-in-all-directions dog, for the first time in years? The four major animal-protection organizations have named 1993 the Year of the Cat, and the year is off to a disastrous start if Socks does not take residence ASAP."

"Huh? What is ASAP, some political interest group?"

Her lush-lashed eyes shudder shut. "Short for 'As Soon As Possible.' Do Las Vegans know nothing?"

"Only odds, and it looks like Washington, D.C., is odder than anything on the Las Vegas Strip, and that is going some. Okay. We got a late-adolescent ex-tom who is a little squirrelly. Any skeletons in the closet?"

"Like what?"

"Insanity in the family?"

For the first time she is silent, and idly paws the concrete, all the better to exhibit a slim foreleg. I cannot tell if she is merely scratching her dainty pads, or thinking.

"Family unknown," she confesses. "Could be a plant by a foreign government. Odd how neatly he became First Cat of Arkansas. The Clintons had lost their dog Zeke to an auto accident—"

I nod soberly. "It happens, even to cats."

"The First Offspring, Chelsea, saw two orphaned kittens outside the house where she took piano lessons and begged for the one with white socks. The President and his wife are allergic to cats, but okayed Chelsea taking the male."

"Now that is the most encouraging sign of presidential timber I have seen yet," I could not help noting. "Ask not

23

what you can sacrifice for your country when your own President and spouse will suffer stuffy noses so their little girl can take in a homeless dude. Kind of makes your eyes water."

"Mine are bone-dry," Cheetah answers with enough ice in her tone to frost her brown whiskers white.

"What about the female?" I ask next.

"What female?"

"You said 'the male.' There were two orphans. Ergo, the other must be female."

She blinks, impressed by my faultless logic and investigative instincts, no doubt. Then she sighs.

"Taken in too, by a friend of the piano teacher who read about Socks and also had lost a pet dog. A Republican lady." She sniffs, whether at the political or former pet leanings of the other kit's adoptive family, I cannot tell.

"Another Uni-Que?" I ask.

"No." Cheetah Habanera is proving oddly reluctant to reveal Socks's family connections. I soon discover why. "Jet black. All over. Now called 'Midnight.' "

All right! Methinks a small detour to Arkansas on the way home might become necessary. I am not politically prejudiced. Republican cats are still superior to Democratic dogs. Midnight, huh. Nice name. At least Little Miss Midnight is not missing.

"She is also fixed?" I inquire.

"Who knows? Or cares? Listen, Mr. Midnight, better keep your nose to business. Without Socks found by tomorrow, your name will be *Mudd*night Louie. I do not know why Kitty Kong wanted out-of-town help anyway."

"To catch a thief, send a thief. To find a disoriented, disaffected out-of-towner—"

"Right. If you get a lead on Socks, you can find me here."

She sidles back into the Dumpster shadow like she was

born there, and I start looking around Washington. My plan is serendipitous, which is to say, nonexistent.

I pace the terrain, sniff the chill winter air and generally observe how this place would strike a fellow from the country's heartland. Like a monumental chip off the big cold white berg on an iceman's truck.

Miles of hard pavement and towering buildings as white and bland as the grave markers in the National Cemetery would not seem welcoming to a junior good ole boy squirrel-chaser from Little Rock.

One other thing is clear. Not many cats hang out in these sterile public corridors. Even a down-home Uni-Que would stick out like a sore throat.

Naturally, I do not expect to stumble over the absent Socks on my first tour of the place, so I amble over to the Arkansas Ball hotel for some forced-air heat and human company.

The place is a mess of activity, a snarl of hotel minions and party organizers in both senses of the word, a veritable snake pit of electrical cables and audiovisual equipment. Even the Secret Service wouldn't notice a stray cat in this mayhem and I make sure I am not noticeable when I want to be.

Earl E. is jamming onstage with the other boys in the band. (How come there are never girls? Even we cats make our night music coed.) He is rehearsing for the big Arkansas Ball tonight, where you can bet Clinton, Inc. will be even if Socks is missing.

Nose E., wearing a Scotch-plaid vest to protect him from the winter chill, is lying like a discarded powder puff near the Earl E.'s open burgundy-velvet–lined instrument case, eyes the usual coal black glint behind the haystack hairdo, and black nose pillowed on furry toes. I presume the thing has toes.

I have been out pounding pavement all morning while

this fluffpuff has been supine posing for a Johnnie Walker Red ad.

Nose E. gives an obligatory growl of greeting, then admits that he has nothing to do. It seems that Earl E. and his buddies are too busy jiving and massaging their glittering brass saxes onstage to pay Nose E. any mind. Or is that saxi?

That is the trouble with a prima donna dog, whatever the gender: they get addicted to being the center of attention. So would I if I were carried everywhere, wore bows on my ears and was called "Sweetie Pie" by celebrities who never would dream that I am really a cross between a bodyguard and a snitch. Me, I like being Mr. Anonymous and underestimated.

Nose E.'s litany of ills goes on. Nothing is doing until six o'clock or so, he says. He has met his handler of the evening, and it is not the usual scintillating doll in rhinestones, but a former football player who holds him like a dumbbell, with one hammy hand around his rib cage.

Besides, Nose E. notes morosely, so many federal security types decorate the building, and indeed the entire town—they even seal the manholes along the Inauguration parade route—that not even a speck of fairy dust could escape notice. Nose E., in short, is redundant. For such a spoiled squirt, that is indeed hard to take.

So sunk is Nose E. in his imagined troubles that he does not think to ask about my mission; besides, to a dude after cocaine and TNT, normal, ordinary canine pursuits, such as finding and harassing cats, is low priority.

This is fine, for my observations during my meander, in which I have seen Socks's puss peeking out from every newspaper-dispensing machine, has given me an idea—not that anybody outside the Clinton inner circle knows that Socks is missing.

What is obvious, if not the whereabouts of Socks, is that this dude's overnight fame has made him a hard slice of salami to hide, no matter how commonplace his appearance. Now I know where to look.

I wander toward the river. I am not much for rivers, but I avoid the public portions bordered by leafless trees and bare expanses of brown green lawn, heading for the fringes where I know I can find a population that inhabits every city—the homeless.

Even the homeless are hard to find in D.C. right now. Panhandlers know better than to haunt the populated areas when a major network event is unfolding; besides, half of them are dressing and duding up like the rest of the inauguration influx, to play Cinderella and Prince Charming-for-a-day at the Homeless Ball.

At last I find a motley group wearing their designer hand-me-downs from Salvatore Arme. In their battered trench coats and tattered sweaters and mufflers, they resemble a huddle of war correspondents.

I do not expect any revelations as to the whereabouts of the missing Socks from these folks, but where the homeless gather, so do their animal companions of choice: dogs. And no one on the city streets knows the scuttlebutt like a dog that associates with a transient person.

Sure enough, I spot a Hispanic man in a cap with numerous news clips safety-pinned to it, surrounded by a bark of dogs, doing same. I look for the unseated Millie of White House fame among them, but these dogs' only visible pedigree is by purée. They are as awkward a conjunction of mutts as I have ever seen, and are barking and milling and twining their leashes until they resemble one of those seven-headed monsters of antiquity, but they are at least talkative and really rev up when I stroll into view.

I sit down, making clear that I will not depart without information. The people present view me with alarm, but I am used to being considered unlucky and even dog bait. Besides, should the pack lose their leashes, I have already spied the tree I would climb like a berserk staple gun.

"Cat," these morons yap at me and each other, growing evermore excited. (I do not speak street dog, a debased and monosyllabic language, but I understand enough to get by.)

"Yeah," I growl back, "I suppose you are not used to seeing such fine specimens of felinity."

They claw turf as their whines go up a register. The poor dude in the cap now has his arms twisted straitjacket-style as he tries to control his entourage, all the while yelling, "Scat!"—only he pronounces it "Escat!"

The other homeless watch in hopes of some action entertainment shortly.

"Black cat," the dogs carol in chorus after rubbing their joint brain cell together.

"Bingo." I yawn. "See any black-and-white cats lately?"

They go berserk, baying out cats of all colors that they have seen and pursued. Not one is a magpie.

After a few more seconds of abuse, I am convinced that the street dogs have not sniffed hide nor hair of Socks, luckily for him. Further, I also learn that the humans present are not as ignorant of Socks's newfound celebrity as I had hoped.

A woman with a face as cracked as last year's mud edges toward me, a bare hand stretched out in the chill. "Here, Kitty. Stay away from those dogs. Come on. If you walked through whitewash you'd even look like that there Socks. Here, Kitty," she croons in that seductive tone of entrapment used upon my ancestors for millennia, "I got some food."

I remain amazed that people who have nothing, not even the basic fur coat my kind take for granted, are so eager to take kindred wanderers under their wings.

These homeless individuals may be sad, or deficient in some social or mental way, but they share a certain shrewd survival instinct and camaraderie also found among the legion of homeless of the feline and canine kind. Of course we all need and want a home, but most are not destined for such bounty and are not above appealing to the guilt of the more fortunate in making our lot more palatable. At least the homeless of the human kind are not corralled into the experimental laboratories or the animal-processing pounds that ultimately offer little more than the lethal injection or the gas chamber in the name of mercy.

So I look upon this sweet old doll with fond regret, but I am a free spirit on a mission, and too well-fed (if not well-bred) to take advantage of a kind face despite the temptation of a free meal. I scamper away, leaving the battlefield to the dogs, and trudge back downtown, much dispirited.

If even the homeless have seen enough discarded newspapers to know about Socks, it will prove harder than I thought to turn up the little runaway. Will Socks vanish into the legions of homeless felines from which he came? Will the country and the Clintons survive such a tragic turn of events? Will Midnight Louie strike out?

I picture Cheetah Habanera's piquant but triumphant face as I trot back to Hoopla Central. The sun is shining; the brisk air hovers pleasantly above freezing. For some reason mobs of people are thronging down Pennsylvania Avenue. I manage to thread my way through a berserk bunch performing calisthenics with lawn chairs. People do the strangest things.

Still distracted, I return to the hotel that will host the Clintons' triumphant Arkansas Ball. Everybody in this town has something to celebrate, except for Socks and me.

The stage area is temporarily deserted; even Nose E. is gone, and I shudder to find that I miss the little snitch's foolish face. Earl E.'s instrument case is still cracked open like a fresh clam. I curl up on the burgundy velvet lining—an excellent background for one of my midnight-black leanings—and lose myself in a catnap. Maybe something will come to me in a dream.

* * *

29

The next thing I know, I am being shaken out of my cushy bed like a cockroach out of a shoe.

Earl E. Byrd is leaning over me, his longish locks pomaded into Michael Jackson tendrils and his best diamond earring glittering in one ear. I take in the white shirtfront and the jazzy black leather bolo tie with the real live dead scorpion embedded in acrylic in the slide. Earl E. looks snazzy, but a little shook up.

"The case is for the instrument, dude," he thunders, brushing a few handsome black hairs from the soft velvet. "Behave yourself or you will be ejected from the ball. How did you get here, anyway?"

Of course I am not talking, and I can see by the way the lights, camera, action and musicians are revving up that Earl E. has no time to escort me elsewhere. He has other things on his mind as he lays his precious sax back in *my* bed. Does a sax feel? Does a sax need shut-eye? Is a sax on a mission to save the First Feline? Is there no justice?

Nose E. comes up to sniff at me in sneering rectitude, and I know that the last question was exceedingly foolish. Before Nose E. can really rub it in, a humongous man in a structurally challenged tuxedo swoops up the little dust bunny and moves into a room that has now filled with women in glitz and glitter and men in my classy colors— black with a touch of white about the face.

Let the ball begin.

Earl E. and the boys swing out. Although Earl E. is essaying the licorice stick at the moment, several musicians bear saxophones that shine brassy gold in the spotlights and wail, I'll admit, like the Forlorn Feline Choir in the darkest, bluesiest, funkiest alley on the planet. Folks foxtrot. The hip ... hop. I settle grumpily next to the sax case from which I was so rudely evicted. All is lost. On the morrow the nation will wake to the news that it has a new president and a former First Feline. Bast knows—Bast is the Egyptian cat deity and my purrsonal favorite—what Kitty Kong will do.

While I am drowsing morosely, I start when the case beside me jolts. A burp of excitement bubbles just offstage. Someone knocks into Earl E.'s sax. So what. A pair of anonymous hands rights the big, shiny loudmouth thing. I see enough black wingtips to shoe a centipede cluster onto the stage from the wings. When the phalanx of footwear suddenly parts, the First Couple stands there like a King and Queen in a Disney animated feature—Bill and Hillary dancing.

No doubt this is a festive and triumphal scene, and the First Lady's hair is rolled into a snazzy Ginger Rogers do, and they got rhythm and all's right with the world and I could go out in the garden and eat worms ...

As my bleary eyes balefully regard the hated sax that has usurped my spot, I spy an odd thing. Inside the deep, dark mouth of the instrument something shines—not bright and gold—but whitish silver.

A snake of suspicion stirs in my entrails until it stings my brain fully awake. Why is Earl E. not playing the sax, when he brought it especially for that purpose?

Even as I speculate, Earl E. slips offstage and heads toward me. I expect another ejection, but he ignores me and reaches for the sax, his eyes on the stage where the First Couple has stopped dancing. The President is edging over to the band and microphone. He's going to talk, that is what presidents do, only when they do it, it is an address. He's going to address the crowd ... my big green eyes flash to the approaching Earl E. The President is going to talk, then Earl E. is going to give him the sax and the President is going to *play it*!

The President is going to play a doctored sax in front of millions of TV-watching citizens.

Even as Earl E. grabs the sax I leap up, all sixteen claws full out, and sink them into his arm.

He jumps back and mouths an expression that luckily is drowned out by all the bebopping going on, but it rhymes with "rich" if that word had a male offspring.

I can tell I drew blood, because Earl E. drops his precious sax and it hits the case sideways and something falls out of the mouth like a stale wad of gum.

Earl E.'s eyes get wide and worried. He whirls back to the stage, runs over to appropriate a sax from a startled fellow player and hands it to the President with a flourish.

Everybody plays. Saxophones wail in concert. Everybody laughs and applauds. Something rustles behind me. The Meat Locker has returned Nose E. to the vicinity. The creature stiffens on its tiny fuzzy legs as its nose gives several wild twitches. Nose E. rushes toward the fallen sax, sits up and cocks an adorable paw as he tilts his inquisitive little noggin one way, then the other.

Earl E. is over in a flash. This nauseating behavior is Nose E.'s signal that he has smelled a rat. Being an undercover canine, he can resort to nothing obvious like barking. (Besides, he squeaks like a castrated seal.)

Then Earl E. upends the sax to shake out a windfall of plastic baggies, containing a substance that much resembles desiccated catnip. I come closer for a look-see, but am rudely shoved aside.

"Good dog," Earl E. croons several sickening times.

What about my early warning system? Except for rubbing a hand on his forearm, he seems to have forgotten my pivotal role in exposing the perfidy. Probably puts it down to mysterious feline behavior.

Two of the wingtips come to crouch beside Earl E., taking custody of the bags, the sax and the case. There goes beddy-bye.

"Marijuana. Whoever did this," one comments softly, "wanted to make sure that this time the President would inhale."

"Saxophones don't work that way."

"Does not matter," the other wingtip says. "The idea was to embarrass the President. The dog yours?"

"Yeah," Earl E. says modestly.

"Sharp pup." The wingtip pats Nose E. on the cherry red bow.

Sure, the dog always get the credit.

So I sit there, overlooked and ignored and Sockless, as the party goes on. The President surrenders the sax and the stage and leaves for another inaugural ball. I cannot even get excited at this one when Carole King comes on to sing "You've Got a Friend." Name one.

The band plays on. I recognize a couple tunes, like the ever tasteful "Your Mama Don't Dance and Your Daddy Don't Rock and Roll," and the ever inspirational "Amazing Grace."

I'll say inspirational. I rise amid the postinaugural hubbub and make my silent retreat. Nobody notices.

Outside it is dark, but I have already reconnoitered the city and I know where I am going. There is only one place in town where a dude as overpublicized as Socks Clinton could hang out and be overlooked.

"I once was blind but now I see." I see like a cat in the dark, and I see my unimpeded way to a certain street on which stands a certain civic building. Around back is the obligatory Dumpster.

I wait.

Soon a curious pair of electric green eyes catches a stray beam of sodium iodide street light. The dude's white shirt-front and feet look pretty silly tinted Mercurochrome pink as he steps out into the sliver of light. He looks okay, for a Uni-Que.

"Why did you do it?" I ask.

"How did you find me?" he retorts instead of answering. Then I realize that the poor dude *has* answered me.

"I figured out that there was only one place you could hang out and beg tidbits without being recognized: The Society for the Blind. Midnight Louie always gets his dude. You have to go back."

"Where? Home? I live in Little Rock."

"Not any more. You are a citizen of the nation now."

"I didn't ask to be First Cat."

I search through my memory bank of clichés but only find "Life is no bed of Rose's." (I do not know who this Rose individual was, but apparently she knew how to take a snooze, and that I can endorse.) I decide to appeal to his emotions.

"It seems to me that your human companion, Miss Chelsea Clinton, faces the same dislocation," I point out. "I would hate to see my delightful roommate, Miss Temple Barr, face a barrage of public curiosity and a new and demanding role in life without my stalwart presence at her side."

"You would move here?" Socks asks incredulously. "Where are you from?"

"Las Vegas."

"Oh," he nods, as if that explains a lot. "I bet you do not even chase squirrels. Did you know the White House squirrels may be . . . rabid?" he adds morosely.

"No!" I respond in horror. There is nothing worse than tainted grub. Poor little guy . . . no wonder he split.

"And," Socks adds in the same spiritless monotone, "you have not had the press shooting pictures down your tonsils for weeks, or getting you high on nip so you'll spill your guts to the press and embarrass your family. Then they dug up some rumor that my father was a notorious tomcat—"

"Shocking! But so was my old man."

"You are not First Feline," he spat glumly. "There's that instant book about me by that name, and all those T-shirts, then menu items named after me in places where I would not even be allowed to lap water. Can you believe that a local hotel concocted a Knock Your Socks Off drink?"

"Sounds like incitement to riot to me. What is in it?"

34

"Frangelico, Grand Marnier, half-and-half and crème de cacao."

"Does not sound half bad."

"I do not even know what most of those ingredients are. Now if they had made it from Dairy Queen ice cream—"

"Forget Dairy Queens. You are on a faster track now."

"I guess. They dug up some love letters I scratched in the sand to a certain lady named Fleur before I was fixed; I'm only an adolescent, for Morris's sake—I should be allowed some privacy."

"Sacrifice of privacy is a small price to pay considering what you can do for the country and your kind. We need a good role model in a prominent position. You owe your little doll and cats everywhere to stick in there for four years."

"Eight," Socks says, a combative gleam dawning in his yellow eyes.

I swallow a smile (my kind are not supposed to smile or laugh, and I like to keep up appearances) and trot out my more grandiose sentiments. I begin to see that what this dude needs is a campaign speech.

"Remember, Socks, you represent millions of homeless cats, crowded masses yearning to breathe free of the pounds and the lethal streets. We are a transient kind in a world that little notes nor long remembers our welfare. You may not have chosen prominence, but now you can use it to do good. Some are born great," I add, preening, "others have greatness thrust upon them by circumstance. You are one of these . . . circumstantial dudes. Do you want to drive your little doll into such loneliness at your defection that the First Kid goes turncoat and gets a dog to replace you? Do you want to be known as the first First Feline in history to abdicate?"

"No-o-o."

I have him. I brush near, give him a big brotherly tap of the tail on his shoulder. "What is really troubling you, kid?

What made you snap and take off just as you got into town?"

Socks sighed. "I have been offered a book contract."

"Hey! That is good. I dabble in that pursuit myself."

"The book is to be called *Socks: The Untold Story*."

I am nudging him down the alleyway and into the full glare of the streetlight. The bustle of inaugural traffic rumbles in the distance along with faint sounds of revelry. D.C. could be the Big Easy tonight.

"What is so bad about that?" I ask.

Sock stops. "There is nothing untold left to tell! The press has squeezed every bit of juice out of my own life. I have nothing to say."

"Is that all? Big-time celebrity authors do not let that stop them from penning shoo-in bestsellers. You just think you are not interesting. What you need, my lad, is what they call a 'ghostwriter'—someone discreet and more experienced who can help you bring out the most interesting facets of your life."

"Squirrels?"

"No. We must create a feline 'Roots.' We can call it 'Claws.' What do you know about your mom and dad? All cats in this country are descended from the Great Mayflower Mama, of course, but I have heard on good authority that your forebears were mousers around Mount Vernon. Did not Martha Washington herself have a cat-door installed there for somebody's ancestors? Why not yours? Obviously, there is a long tradition of presidential association in your family . . . speaking of which, how about your sister, Midnight—nice name—where in Little Rock did you say she hung out?"

By now I have the dude heavily investing in his new career as raconteur and idol of his race. We reach the White House in no time, and I push him in. He admits that he could use the litter box in the engineering room. Aside from a few distraught aides—and aides are used to being distraught—no one need know of Socks's little escapade.

I trot back to my hotel, anticipating informing that snippy Cheetah Habanera of my success, and contemplating the fifty-fifty book deal I have just cut with Socks. Somebody has got to look out for a naive young dude in this cruel world.

Even though it is late, I have to wait outside the motel room door for at least an hour before Earl E. and Nose E. arrive, both a bit tipsy: Earl E. high on jamming and celebrity, Nose E. on all that marijuana he sniffed out.

I am in like Flynn and ensconced on the king-size before either of them gets a chance at it. Earl E. phones home before he retires, with news of his big adventure, which is how I learn who planted the weed in the presidential saxophone.

"PUFF," Earl E. explains to a benighted buddy on the phone while Nose E., half zonked, tries to curl up near me. I cuff the little spotlight-stealer away. "They called to claim responsibility. Can you believe it, man! PUFF is a radical wing of the prosmoking types. I do not know what it stands for—People United For Fumes? Whatever, they were ticked off when Clinton made such a big deal about not inhaling once long ago and far away! They think it is un-American and namby-pamby to smoke anything without inhaling. Weird. We have had a weird time in this burg, man. What a gig. I cannot wait to get back to someplace normal like Las Vegas."

Amen.

That Damn Cat

•

Barbara Collins

The silver sorrel Somali walked in the gutter along Pennsylvania Avenue, its bushy red foxlike tail dragging in the dirt, a miniature streetsweeper.

Suddenly the cat stopped, and jumped up on the low wall separating the street from the sidewalk. To the cat, the three-foot-high reinforced concrete barrier was just another wall—that it was erected after 240 Marines died in Beirut when a dynamite-laden pickup truck smashed into their barracks was beyond its comprehension, highly intelligent though the Somali was. The obstacle was meant to protect the north end of the White House from a similarly explosive fate—not to keep out a cat.

The Somali crept along the wall, its graceful, elongated body moving lithely, then it jumped down and padded across the wide sidewalk, which was free from tourists and protesters in the early morning hour on this unseasonably cool summer's day.

Carefully, cautiously, the animal approached the black wrought-iron fence embedded into more concrete, and stuck its head through the spearlike rods. With almond-shaped eyes the cat gazed out across the expansive, immaculate White House lawn. Dew sparkled on the grass like millions

38

of diamonds thrown carelessly out onto endless bolts of green velvet.

Quick as the rising deficit, the cat shot upward, over the concrete base and through the fence.

With powerful legs, summoning athletic ability accountable to its Abyssinian ancestry, the Somali darted across the lawn, oblivious to any pressure sensors or motion detectors it might be setting off.

From around the northwest corner of the White House, two burly men in dark suits and sunglasses came running, machine guns in hand.

Immediately the cat saw them and froze, a lifelike lawn ornament.

The two men fanned out and approached the animal from opposite ends, their machine guns pointed at it.

The cat didn't move.

"Nice kitty kitty," one said. He was smiling, but the smile was nasty.

"Come to poppa," the other one said. He had an ugly scar on his cheek. Under his breath, he murmured, "Fifteen years with the Secret Service, and I wind up chasing a damn cat off the lawn . . ."

As the two men dove to capture the animal, it shot out between them, and they cracked their heads together in a bone-crunching effect. With a Chaplinesque pratfall, the man with the scar keeled over, knocked out cold. But not before his machine gun went RAT-A-TAT-TAT, across the other man's foot.

The wounded agent howled and grabbed that foot and joined his partner on the grass, writhing in pain.

The cat seemed unaware of all this, however, continuing its forward assault on the White House.

Now another Secret Serviceman appeared—a bigger and even meaner looking man. He had a snarling canine on a leash—the vicious dog, mouth peeled back showing sharp teeth, pulled the man along as it ran toward the cat.

Once more the animal stopped. Calmly the feline sat on its hindquarters, and waited for the dog to draw near.

When the yapping canine had almost reached it, the cat took off, circling around the man, one, two, three times. The dog followed, and in a matter of seconds the cursing Secret Serviceman found himself tied up in the dog's heavy chain.

The cat, a comet now leaving its orbit, blazed out again for the White House.

The dog, too stupid to know what had happened, tried to continue the chase, even though his master called out, "Heel!"

And the Secret Serviceman, legs bound by the leash, hit the lawn with a *whump!*

"Somebody get *that damn cat!*" the fallen man hollered.

But the Silver Sorrel Somali had already reached the north portico, and was triumphantly climbing the White House steps.

Up on the portico, the cat turned its head and looked back casually at the shambles it had left behind.

It almost seemed to smile.

"Cut!" yelled Christopher Hughes, a wide grin splitting his bushily bearded face. "Fan-tastic!" To himself he muttered, "If only every actor could hit his mark like that damn cat."

The slightly overweight director in gray sweats and baseball cap looked like he belonged at a Redskins game, not standing behind a movie camera.

Out on the lawn the actors began to pick themselves up, joking and laughing. A thin, thinning-haired young man wearing jeans and a navy windbreaker was ascending the White House steps where the cat sat waiting patiently. This rather anemic-looking man had a silver cat-carrier, into which the animal placidly allowed itself to be placed.

Christopher Hughes turned to the assistant director, a pretty, bespectacled dark-haired woman wearing a white silk blouse and short black skirt. She was holding a clip-board.

"That's a wrap," he said to her, pleased. "Tell everyone we'll see them back in L.A. on Monday."

"Right," she responded. Then hesitated. "For the Oval Office scene . . . ?"

"No, the state dinner scene," he answered, faintly irritated. "Keep up with the changes, Lisa, and for God's sake make sure all those pies are delivered and kept refrigerated. I want to do it in one take . . . otherwise, it's gonna be one hell of a mess to clean up for a retake."

"I thought the prop master recommended shaving-cream pies . . ."

"I don't give a damn what he recommended. I told you three days ago I wanted *real* pies. We're in the business of selling *believable* lies—got it?"

"Got it," she said, nodding, making notes.

A Secret Service agent approached them—a real one. He looked no less mean than the actors had.

"Finished?" the agent asked the director.

Hughes nodded. "We're outa here," he smiled at the man. "And again, please convey our thanks, and the studio's, to the president for allowing us to shoot here this morning."

The agent frowned. "Frankly, we advised him against it," he said, "but he's such a big fan of your movies . . ."

He'd said it like he couldn't for the life of him understand why.

"I bet he's screened *That Damn Cat Goes to Vegas* a dozen times," the agent continued. "We have a theater here, you know." He nodded toward the White House.

"Ah!" Hughes said. "Then, please, tell the president I'll send him his own personal print of *That Damn Cat Goes to Washington*, as soon as it's edited. Sixteen or thirty-five?"

The agent cocked his head, apparently confused. "Pardon?"

"Sixteen- or thirty-five millimeter? I'll need to know what kind of print to have made up."

"Uh, I'll have to find out, sir."

"Well, do it quickly, if you would, and tell that young woman over there." He pointed to Lisa.

The agent nodded, and stepped closer. He took off his sunglasses; his eyes were tiny black marbles.

"It's too bad someone didn't tell you," he said, lowering his voice.

"Tell us what?" Hughes raised his eyebrows.

"Secret Service doesn't carry machine guns. Unless we're in a presidential motorcade, that is."

"Really?"

"Really. And," the agent continued in a hushed voice, "*we* don't patrol the grounds. The Uniformed Division does. They're more like regular cops." He paused, then added, "But we do use canines, you got that part right."

Hughes smiled at the man. "Well, thanks for the info," he said, "but we knew all that. But seeing some poor cop get shot in the foot with a pistol can't compare to some pompous jerk in shades and a suit getting his toes blown off with an Uzi. Now *that* will make the kiddies laugh." Hughes reached out and patted the taken-aback agent on the arm. "That's entertainment!"

Not far from Pennsylvania Avenue, north of the Capitol Building, Todd and Julie sat on the white leather overstuffed couch in the deco-modern living room of their charming little brick townhouse.

Outside, dusk had settled in.

Todd was a darkly handsome man in his early thirties, with slicked-back Valentino hair, and sensuous eyes surrounded by long thick lashes. His lips were pressed against the rim of a crystal goblet as he sipped red wine—Château Latour. The jacket of his tan Armani suit lay neatly folded on the back of the sofa, next to him.

Julie was a beautiful blonde so buxom she approached a parody of pulchritude, though she by no means looked cheap in her red Kamali suit. A handsome thirty, but looking it, she was slouched down on the couch, her shapely legs up on a glass coffee table, where art books of Dali, Rousseau and Parrish lay carefully arranged. Her red-painted pedicured toes showed through sheer nylons. Delicate fingers clutched her nearly empty wineglass, resting it on her stomach as she stared into the fireplace, its flames dancing a hot little number.

Todd stared at the orange glow, too, knowing how badly they needed money, knowing that—in the short-term—Julie was the one who could get it for them. But bringing up the subject would be . . . difficult.

"What are we going to do about the car payment?" she asked.

He almost smiled, but repressed it; she'd opened the door. Good. Now he had a chance . . .

"Don't sweat the small stuff," he answered. "First priority, babe, is the mortgage."

She frowned. "But I'll *die* if we lose the BMW!" she moaned, then brightened. "There's always plastic . . ."

He shook his head. "Maxed out."

She sat up, dropping her feet off the table, and turned to him, looking at him with an expression that was part pout, part scowl. "You just *had* to have that Rolex!" she said sharply.

He said nothing. He was looking at the painting on the wall above the fireplace.

That would get her going, he thought.

"I suppose we could sell the Nagel," he sighed.

The strikingly beautiful nude blonde, hugging her long legs, stared accusingly back at them. The modern pinup in its sleek black-and-gray frame had bold lines, bold colors; a sophisticated symbol of the now distant '80s.

"No!" Julie said. "She looks too much like me. It would be like selling myself!"

He raised an eyebrow. "Sorry," he said. "I should have thought of that."

But, of course, he had.

She crossed her arms on generous breasts and huffed, "Besides, we'd never be able to afford another one."

They sat in brooding silence. Flames hissed on the fake logs in the fireplace. He waited for her to take the conversation another step . . .

Then she lowered her voice, as if the place might be bugged. "I don't dare 'borrow' any more money from the inactive accounts. Those bank examiners could show up at any time . . ."

"And," he added in a hushed tone, "I can't 'shift' any further funds at the brokerage. Not now. Not again."

"Damn! Is there *anything* we can do?"

They fell silent again. Then he turned and gazed meaningfully into her eyes.

They went wide. "Oh, no!" she said, "Not *that*."

He leaned close to her, pressing his body against hers. "Just this one more time, to tide us over," he pleaded. "Until I can think of something *big*, to really get us back on our feet."

"But I *hate* it!"

"Nobody's asking you to sleep with anybody, babe. Just a little powder in a cocktail, some sexist lech takes a little nap, and you take his money." He said this casually, as if describing shopping for a specific flavored coffee.

"But you *promised* me I wouldn't ever have to do that again!"

He pulled away from her. "You're right," he said, shaking his head as if ashamed of himself. "I did. Tell you what . . . I ran into that senator's wife the other day . . . the one that couldn't keep her hands off me at the Crawford party? She made it perfectly clear she'd be willing to pay for my . . . company."

Julie glared at him; flames now danced in her eyes. "All right, all right!" she snapped. "I'll do it, damnit! But this is the last time! I mean it, Todd."

He put an arm around her. "Sure, babe," he said, nuzzling her soft, perfumed neck. "I just want you to have nice things."

And he kissed her, passionately enough, but when the kiss had ended Julie pulled away.

"Not now," she said, obviously punishing him. "I have to go get us some money, remember?"

She rose from the couch and picked up her red shoes and padded off across the white carpet toward the bedroom.

Todd smiled to himself and poured himself another drink, and sat back on the couch. That hadn't been so tough . . .

After a few minutes, Julie came back, her blonde hair hidden beneath a lovely, flowing black wig. She was wearing a tight, low-cut black designer dress, dark nylons and black patent-leather heels; a white fur wrap caressed her bare shoulders. With her white skin and full red lips, she looked like a twentieth-century vampire about to crash an inaugural ball.

Julie extended one hand and jingled her car keys.

"Drive me," she said. "I don't want to leave the car on the street."

He felt a little woozy; he didn't know if it was the wine, or this suddenly incredibly beautiful wife of his.

They went out into the cool summer evening, to the silver BMW convertible parked in the driveway. He opened the door for her.

"Got the powder?" he whispered.

She nodded, and slid inside.

He went around to the driver's side and got behind the wheel. "To the Watergate?" he asked.

"No," she answered, eyes focused straight ahead. "I can't

45

go back there—not after the last one almost died on us. Make it One Washington Circle. And put the top down. I need some air."

He backed out into the street, then followed it to Pennsylvania Avenue, which was pulsing with traffic. They drove in silence. The scent of her Chanel No. 5, borne by the wind, teased his nostrils.

A few blocks from the posh hotel, Todd pulled into a loading zone. Julie started to get out.

"Be careful," he said, leaning over, grabbing her hand.

"I will," she whispered. "I'll call you when it's safe to pick me up."

"I love you," he said, as earnestly as he could.

She didn't answer for a moment. Then, sadly, said, "I love you, too."

He watched her for a few moments, as she walked toward the hotel. Then he pulled away from the curb, and drove back to the townhouse.

Inside, he finished off the wine, then stretched out on the couch to wait for Julie to call.

He hoped she'd come through. Otherwise, he'd have to dump her.

The thought gave him no pleasure; it wasn't as if he'd be leaving her for a younger woman. To continue living in the fashion he craved and deserved, a wealthy widow would be his ticket. Unfortunately.

Feeling a chill, he rose to turn up the flame on the gas fire, sat near it, huddled there, waiting for the phone to ring.

At first, entering the hotel lounge, she thought she was out of luck: everywhere she looked, in the dimly lighted bar, were couples. Except for one man, sitting on a bar stool, and he looked like a bum! Bearded, in sweats and a baseball cap, he was hardly the sort of prospect she was after.

She decided to play a waiting game, taking a small round

table for one against a mirrored wall. Somebody would wander in, looking for a little singles action. Some married man, perhaps . . .

An attractive black waitress in a frilly white blouse and black skirt brought Julie the 7-Up with cherry she'd ordered. Julie had already had enough wine; she needed to keep a clear head.

"Letting the riffraff in?" Julie asked the waitress smirkily.

"Him? He's hardly riffraff, miss. That's Chris Hughes."

Julie sat up straight. "The movie director?"

"That's right."

The waitress smiled, shook her head and wandered off.

Julie carried her tall glass of soda with her when she took the stool next to Hughes. She didn't look at him. She could feel him looking at her. Crossing her legs, she began to wiggle her right foot, letting her high heel dangle on her toes.

She looked at her watch, sighed, shook her head.

She repeated this action, every thirty seconds or so, for five minutes.

Finally she smiled at Hughes, looking at him as if she realized for the first time that he was there, and said, "I guess I've been stood up."

A smile peeked out of the bushy beard. "Beautiful woman like you? Seems unlikely."

"Washington is full of surprises."

"You're not an actress, are you?"

"Actress? No, why?"

Hughes smiled again, swirled a glass of dark liquid that was probably bourbon. "Just wondering. I get . . . hit on by actresses a lot."

"Why's that?"

"I'm a movie director. Christopher Hughes?"

He extended his hand and she took it. "Sally Davis. I'm

47

a secretary for a lobby group here in town. Would I have ever seen any of your films?"

"You might. *That Damn Cat*, perhaps?"

"That was yours? Well. I have to admit I may be the only person in the United States who *didn't* catch that one."

He laughed. "Believe it or not, that's a refreshing answer."

"But I did see the sequel . . . the one about Las Vegas? I loved it when that cat chased Siegfried and Roy's tiger off the stage! That animal is a wonder."

"I'd like a hundred actors like him. What sort of lobbying group do you represent?"

She thought fast. "The A.R.I.—Animal Rights Institute? We're trying to stop animal testing in cosmetics."

She hoped that would work: between Hollywood and *That Damn Cat*, maybe Hughes would be sympathetic to a cause like that.

"Admirable." He leaned in. "But isn't that a fox fur around your lovely shoulders?"

"Fake fur. Uh, that's our point . . . why should a woman bother with the real thing, when the imitation is cruelty-free? And less expensive."

"Good point. But you also seem to be wearing Chanel. I believe *they* use animal testing . . ."

"It's an off-brand that smells exactly like the real thing. But absolutely *no* animal testing. I could send you a bottle for your wife, or your girlfriend . . . ?"

"I don't have either. Have you had supper?"

"Why, no. That's what I was supposed to have, before I was stood up."

"You know," he said, grinning, "there's something you might like to see. Knowing your interest in animal rights."

Soon they were standing at a door on the seventh floor of the hotel. Room 714. The director was knocking.

"Stan? Are you in there?"

No answer.

"I have a key," Hughes said. He was just a little drunk. "Come on . . ."

He opened the door and they were in a nice room—though not a suite—and on the bed was an unconscious man in his underwear. He was snoring loudly.

"Stan's the best trainer in the business," Hughes said, "but he's got a little problem with the bottle."

"Should we keep our voices down . . . ?"

"Don't bother. You set an atomic bomb off in here and Stan would saw logs right through it. Look at this!"

He was gesturing to a beautiful bushy-tailed foxlike cat, who had also been slumbering, but now raised its head to cast bored almond-shaped eyes upon these intruders.

"There's 'that damn cat,' " Hughes said.

She smiled. She bent over to have a better look; the cat cocked its head and purred lazily. "I never met a movie star before. It's amazing, in the one film I saw, the things this cat could do!"

"Amazing. Truly amazing. Now . . . may I invite you to my room, for a late-night room-service supper?"

"You certainly may."

She talked him into letting her serve them a cocktail from the elaborate suite's wet bar before he could phone in a room-service order, and he was slipping an arm around her, risking a peck of a kiss, when the knockout powder kicked in.

He dropped to the floor like he was curtains and the rods had broken. She dug into his pocket and found the key to Room 714.

The shrill ring of the phone woke Todd. He looked at his Rolex. It was a little past midnight.

"Todd!" It was Julie, out of breath.

"Where are you?" he asked.

"In a hotel room at One Washington Circle." Her voice sounded strange.

"Did it go all right?" he asked.

"Yes!" she said, then, "No! I'll tell you when you get here . . . take an elevator up to the seventh floor."

"What?"

"Just hurry up. I'll be waiting. I've found that 'something big' to get us back on our feet."

The phone clicked in his ear.

He put down the receiver, frowned at it, then smiled, and ran out to the car.

Todd walked casually through the lobby of the hotel—not too fast but not too slow. He didn't want to be noticed. Which was no trick, the lobby being relatively empty this time of night.

He stood at one of the large, bronze elevator doors and pushed the UP button. He patted his pockets, then fished around in them as if looking for his room key, in case anyone at the registration desk was watching, or some security guard in a back room somewhere had picked him up on a monitor.

The elevator door opened and he got on, and pressed the seventh-floor button. He faked a yawn—just a tired exec going back to his room after a boring evening with a client. The elevator door swished shut.

But on the seventh floor, when he got off, only long stretches of corridors greeted him. There was no Julie.

He stood there wondering what to do next, when a door opened about four rooms down, and Julie's black-wigged head popped out.

She beckoned to him animatedly with one hand.

Christ, he thought as he hurried along the plushly carpeted corridor, what the hell was this all about? Had she gone too far? Was he going to have to look at some dead guy's body?

Todd stepped inside the dimly lit room. Julie shut the

door behind him. She looked gleeful, and almost satanic, the way the shadows fell across her pretty face.

Todd shivered, then noticed the man sprawled across the bed. He was wearing ugly boxer shorts.

"Is he *dead*?" Todd whispered.

"Dead drunk's more like it," Julie smirked.

Todd moved toward the bed and looked more closely at the man.

"Jeez, babe," he whispered, "you're slipping . . . I can't imagine *this* geek's got much money."

"Never mind him," she said, "*there's* our ticket to paradise."

He followed her gaze to the head of the bed, where between two plump pillows lay a cat.

"What?" he asked, confused. "*That* damn cat?"

"Then you *do* know!"

"Know what?"

"About *That Damn Cat*."

"What *about* that damn cat?" He raised his voice, irritated with her.

Suddenly the drunken, slumbering man on the bed gave out a quick snort. Todd and Julie froze. But the man returned to his labored breathing.

"Todd," Julie said in a hushed voice, "that damn cat is *That Damn Cat*!"

Somewhere in his head, a light bulb popped on. "The *Washington Post* did a feature on that cat," he said. "And how they were going to get to film at the White House . . ." He paused and looked at the animal, which looked back at him as if understanding what he was saying. "But are you sure that's *the* cat?"

She told him about her encounter with the director.

He smiled, and started to reach for the cat, but quickly pulled back. "Isn't it dangerous?" he asked his wife. "Remember that scene from the second movie when it practically bit that guy's finger off?"

Julie just laughed and bent over to pick up the cat, which went limp in her hands. She held it against her bosom. It purred.

"I think it only responds to the trainer's commands," she said.

They both looked at the drunken, snoring man.

"Then let's get out of here," Todd said, "before he comes to and starts giving some."

Julie tucked the cat beneath her fur jacket.

At the door, Todd stopped. "You know," he told her, "that article said Lloyd's of London insured that cat for a million dollars!"

"Good," Julie said with a wicked little smile, "now we know how much money to ask for!"

Todd and Julie drove back down Pennsylvania Avenue in their convertible, with Todd behind the wheel and Julie next to him. The cat seemed content to be held in her arms, its face peeking out of her coat.

The street was nearly deserted now. Several limos streaked by, windows darkened, hiding some VIP no doubt, and a few cabbies were on the lookout for late-night customers. At a stoplight, Todd turned to Julie. "Maybe I should put the top up," he said.

She shook her head. "That might scare the cat," she replied.

He nodded, studying her; never had she looked so beautiful. Holding a million bucks worth of cat did wonders for her.

"We're going to be so rich!" he grinned.

"We can trade the BMW for a Jaguar."

"And the townhouse for a mansion across the river."

"I love you," he said, meaning it.

"And I love you."

A car horn blared behind them.

"The light's turned green," Julie said.

"My favorite color . . ."

Todd drove, the wind riffling his hair. He glanced over at Julie again. Her luscious lips were pursed in the sweetest smile . . . but Todd thought the cat looked strange.

Its head stuck farther out of her jacket, ears now pointing forward, eyes narrowed to tiny little slits.

Suddenly Julie shrieked as the cat clawed its way out of her coat, and leapt from her arms into the air, flying like some goddamn Super Cat, and disappeared over the side of the car.

Todd slammed on the brakes, tires squealing, and brought the car to a halt.

"There it is!" Julie shouted, pointing, looking back over her shoulder.

Todd could see the cat walking along in the gutter, then springing up on the reinforcement wall and running along it.

By the time Todd got out of the car, the cat had already jumped down from the barrier and was padding across the wide sidewalk, which was free from tourists and protesters in the early morning hour.

"Get it! Get it!" screamed Julie.

But Todd wasn't quick enough, and the cat disappeared through the White House fence.

"You *idiot*!" snapped Julie as she joined him on the sidewalk.

"Me?" he shouted. "If you'd let me put the top up on the car, this never would have happened!"

"Quit wasting time! Go over the fence and get it!"

"Are you *nuts*? I can't go in there!"

"Look!" she said, lowering her voice, pointing out onto the lawn. "It's just sitting there . . ."

In the dark Todd could see the cat, not too far inside the fence.

"Go!" Julie said between clenched teeth. Then, almost

spitting out the words, she said, "Do you want to lose a *million* bucks?"

Cursing, Todd grabbed the iron rods and began hauling himself up. The bars were cold and slippery. And at the top he had trouble getting over, and caught his Armani trousers on one of the sharp spear tips. *Rippppp!* went his expensive pants as he fell to the ground, cursing some more.

From a crouched position on the grass, Todd could see the cat, still sitting motionless. Good, he thought, he hadn't scared it. In the distance the White House looked dark and quiet.

"Hurry up!" Julie said from the other side of the fence.

Todd was rising to stand, when out of a bush stepped a uniformed cop. The officer had a mean, nasty look on his face, and a gun in one hand.

Startled, Todd jumped, then automatically threw his hands in the air.

"You're in a lot of trouble, pal," the cop said, and with his other hand threw the beam of a flashlight in Todd's face.

"Ah . . . look, officer," Todd stammered, squinting from the glare, "I was just trying to get my cat . . ."

The cop flashed his light across the lawn, catching the animal in a circle of white. It sat almost bored.

"I don't care what your excuse is," the officer said gruffly, "this is restricted property, and you're under arrest."

Julie called out from the fence. "Oh, please!" she said. "Don't arrest him! It's all my fault . . . I made him go in there."

Now the cop shone his light on her.

She had hold of the fence, like a prisoner behind bars, pleading her innocence.

"The cat belongs to Senator Hartman," she explained convincingly. "We promised to take care of it for him. Please, officer, won't you help us? The senator will be so upset if anything happens to his pet."

Todd, hands still in the air, nodded sincerely. The cop seemed to vacillate. "Oh ... all right," he finally said roughly, and lowered his gun.

"Thank you," Todd said gratefully, putting his hands down, "and I promise you, you'll never see us again."

The cop grunted, and put his gun away in his belt and motioned with his flashlight toward the cat, which still sat.

"Get it," he ordered.

"Can you help me?" Todd asked. "I'm afraid the cat doesn't know me very well."

The officer sighed irritably, but complied.

And the two men approached the animal from opposite sides.

The cat didn't move.

"Nice kitty kitty," the cop said. He was smiling, but the smile was nasty.

"Come to poppa," Todd said, arms outstretched.

As the two men dove to capture the animal, it shot out between them, and they cracked their heads together in a bone-crunching effect. With a Chaplinesque pratfall, the cop keeled over, knocked out cold. But not before the gun in his belt discharged, sending a bullet flying into Todd's foot.

He howled and grabbed that foot and joined the officer on the grass, writhing in pain.

The cat seemed unaware of all this, however, continuing its forward assault on the White House.

Now another uniformed policeman appeared. He had a snarling canine on a leash, and the vicious dog, mouth peeled back showing sharp teeth, pulled the man along as it ran toward the cat.

Once again, the feline stopped, and waited for the dog to draw near.

When the yapping canine had almost reached it, the cat took off, circling around the man, one, two, three times, and in a matter of seconds the cursing officer found himself tied up in the dog's heavy chain.

"Heel!" the cop hollered. But the dog tried to continue the chase, and the officer, legs bound by the leash, hit the lawn with a *whump!*

"Somebody get *that damn cat!*" the fallen man yelled.

But the Silver Sorrel Somali had already reached the north portico, and was triumphantly climbing the White House steps. At the top, it turned its head and looked back casually at the shambles it had left behind.

It almost seemed to smile.

Christopher Hughes sat on the edge of the bed in his hotel suite, still wearing the sweat suit he'd worn the preceding day. He held a cold washcloth to his forehead.

The director looked over with lidded eyes at the trainer, who sat on the couch nearby. The man, now in T-shirt and jeans, had an ice bag balanced on his head. The director wasn't sure who felt worse, on this morning after.

"I'm surprised at you," said the Secret Service agent who stood in front of Hughes, looking down his nose at him.

"A big Hollywood director like you," the guy continued with a smirk, "falling for a gag like that. I thought you were a city boy."

Hughes looked up at the agent—the one he had called a pompous jerk in shades—and opened his mouth to say something witty and cutting, but the thought never materialized in his still-doped brain, and the director closed his mouth again.

"You're lucky we recovered the cat," the agent said, gesturing to the animal that lay curled next to the trainer on the couch. "It was the president that recognized it ... woke him up in all the commotion." The agent laughed. "I think that damn cat would have sat on the portico waiting for its next cue until hell froze over!"

Hughes just sighed.

"And," the Secret Service agent continued, "it didn't take much for that couple to turn on each other—and turn each other in . . . their kind always does."

The agent frowned and stepped closer to Hughes. "Well?" he said. "You don't seem very grateful your cat was recovered. The paper said that cat's worth a million dollars."

Hughes looked up at the agent and smiled slowly. "And here I thought *you* were a city boy . . ."

"What do you mean?"

"I mean that's Hollywood hype."

"Hype?" the agent asked, confused.

Hughes grinned. "That cat's not insured for a million dollars. And there's not just *one* cat, there's a dozen of the damn things . . . maybe two." The director raised both hands and started checking off fingers. "One that does the cute closeup shots, one that climbs a ladder, another that high-dives into a pool . . . hell," he gestured to the slumbering cat on the sofa, its back rising and falling peacefully, "running berserk on a lawn is all *that* damn cat can do!"

Close, But No Cigar

•

Barbara Paul

"Here, kitty! Come here, you stupid cat. I'm not going to hurt you! Why does he think I'm going to hurt him?"

"Stop screeching at him, Richard—you're frightening him."

Feeling insulted, Richard gave Justine his best villainous glare. "I do not," he said, "screech."

The cat opened his mouth and gave him a loud hiss.

The third member of the group spoke up. "Just keep quiet, Richard," Lyle said softly. "Your voice is aggravating him."

Richard rolled his eyes. "Et tu, Lyle?"

"Oh, look!" Justine exclaimed in alarm. "Come down, kitty! You'll hurt yourself!"

The yellow tom had leaped up to the balustrade and was crouching there uncertainly, looking for a way to escape from these three noisy and insistent humans.

Lyle approached the cat cautiously. "C'mon, kitty, no one's going to hurt you. Come here."

The cat glowered at Lyle's approaching hand, and after a moment's hesitation launched himself away from the theater box. His three pursuers watched in awe as he sailed through the air, landed on the stage, and scampered away into the wings.

"My god, did you see that?" Richard asked, dumb-founded. "Just like John Wilkes Booth!"

"And from the very same spot, too," Lyle added, equally impressed.

"But John Wilkes Booth broke his leg when he landed," Justine said anxiously.

"Nothing got broken this time. You saw him run away," Richard pointed out. "Cats aren't like people—he's all right."

"What the hell are you doing up there?" They looked down to see Mona Armstrong standing on the stage and glaring up at them. "Nobody's supposed to go into that box!"

"We were trying to catch a cat," Justine explained. "And, Mona, he jumped! All the way from here to about where you're standing. Did you see him? Is he all right?"

"Oh, is that what that yellow blur was?" Mona asked. "Don't worry. Anything that can run that fast can't be in-jured. How did a cat get in here anyway?"

No one knew. The three actors left the private box where Abraham Lincoln had met his untimely end and went down to join Mona. Ford's Theater was to see the debut of a new play called *Inchmeal*; the buzz had it that the dark comedy was a winner and would prove a career boost to everyone appearing in it. The hiring of Mona Armstrong to direct upped the odds even more; Mona was on a streak, having directed four successful productions in a row.

When all fifteen actors had arrived for the day's re-hearsal, Mona told them what she wanted. "We're going to walk through the blocking for the first scene of the second act. Something's not quite right and I want to fix it now. When you—" She broke off to look at a young man chew-ing on a hamburger. "Sammy, you know the rule. No food onstage."

The young actor stopped in midchew. He swallowed and said, "Oh, right. I forgot." Sammy dropped the rest of his hamburger into its paper bag and trotted offstage. He set his lunch on a folding chair and never saw the yellow paw that darted out to snag the paper bag the minute his back was turned.

The director finished giving the cast its instructions. As the actors moved to their places, Lyle stopped Richard. "When we get to the newspaper bit," Lyle said to him, "if you pick it up with your left hand instead of your right, you won't look so awkward to the audience."

Richard gaped at him.

Mona had heard. "You don't look awkward, Richard," she said hastily. "Just keep on doing it the way you've been doing it."

Lyle shrugged and moved away.

Mona put them through their paces. When she was satisfied that they'd got their stage movements right, she called a break and motioned Lyle aside. "I want you to stop it, Lyle," she said. "No more of this 'friendly' advice to Richard."

"Oh, hey," Lyle replied, all sympathetic concern. "I didn't mean to step on your authority."

"Cut the crap," she snapped. "We both know what you're doing, and I'll not have you undermining Richard's confidence with all these little helpful suggestions that have him thinking he's doing everything wrong. Ever since Day One you've been 'helping' him. I've watched you giving him little exercises to get rid of what you call the abrasive quality to his voice and—"

"His voice *is* abrasive," Lyle interrupted.

"To you it is. He got the role *you* wanted. That's what this is all about, isn't it?"

Lyle nervously twisted the ring he was wearing on his left hand, round and around. It was a Thespian Society ring, the preferred article of jewelry of an organization whose main order of business seemed to be thinking up things to complain about to Equity, the actors' union. Lyle saw Mona staring at his ring-twisting and put both hands in his pockets. He also saw that further protest would be useless and opted to play it straight. "Richard's wrong for the role, Mona. He has no presence, no stage weight—"

"Whereas you do? Forget it, Lyle. Richard's playing the lead and that's that."

"I know the role. Every word. I could step in for him on a moment's notice."

Mona took a deep breath. "I should hope so, since you're understudying him. Look, I'm sorry you're feeling frustrated, but you're right for the role you're playing. And I meant it about your making no more suggestions to Richard. None at all. If you keep it up, I'll have to replace you."

He smiled icily. "Threats, Mona?"

She nodded. "Threats, Lyle. Now behave yourself. Concentrate on your own role."

Mona left him standing there and headed toward the ladies' before resuming rehearsal. On her way she passed Justine and a woman named Ginger sitting on the floor; Justine was cuddling a big yellow cat in her lap. "Is that the cat you were chasing?"

"This is the guy," Justine said happily. Mona nodded and moved on.

The cat licked his lips, belched politely, and snuggled down for a nap.

Ginger stroked the cat's head. "Wonder where he came from? He must be a stray."

Justine shook her head. "He's too sociable for a stray. He has to be somebody's pet."

The cat purred.

"I doubt it," said Ginger. "People are pretty good about getting their cats altered these days. But this one—well, he's still all boy."

Justine perked up. "Then he doesn't belong to anybody?"

The other woman laughed. "You want to keep him."

"I think I'll call him Abe."

Ginger looked surprised, she'd heard about the cat's flying leap to the stage floor. "Not John Wilkes Booth?"

Justine made a face. "I'm not going to name a nice innocent cat after an *assassin*. His name is Abe."

Mona returned and called everyone back onstage. She should have told Justine and Ginger to get rid of the cat; but she was a sucker for felines herself so she let him stay. Lyle, she noticed, was keeping to himself, brooding and playing with his ring. Richard, as usual, was champing at the bit. "Okay, everybody," she called out, "act two, scene one. Full out, this time. Remember your new blocking."

"Somebody stole my hamburger," Sammy complained.

It was Abe who found the body.

The next day, the minute Justine let him out of his new carrier, the cat crouched low to the floor and began to growl.

"What's the matter with him?" Ginger asked.

"I don't know." Justine bent down and tried to stroke Abe's back, but he slunk away from her touch.

Sammy wandered up. "What's with Abe? Why's he gone into attack mode?"

"That's what we're trying to figure out," Ginger replied. "Oh—where's he going?"

The three actors followed as the cat assumed a stalking posture and crept slowly to the head of a stairwell leading to the substage area. There he stopped, growling low in his throat.

Ginger was the first to look. "Oh, my god—it's Richard!"

The other two joined her. "Shee-ut!" said Sammy.

The play's leading man lay in a heap on the first landing of the stairwell. His head was bloody, and there was blood on the brass handrail where he'd hit. Richard's feet were tangled in the coil of lighting cable that had evidently tripped him.

"Sammy—go get Mona," Ginger said. She put her arm around Justine, who was trembling violently. "He must have been there all night."

Abe's growl turned into a high whine. They waited.

Sammy came back with Mona, who took one look and went down the cement steps two at a time. Although Richard was clearly dead, she felt for a pulse. She looked up at the others and shook her head. Justine began to cry.

"Shee-ut," Sammy said again.

Mona was fingering the lighting cable. "Who the hell left a coil of cable at the top of the steps? Anybody with half a brain could see that's a safety hazard! Some stagehand is going to get fired," she muttered, "union or no union."

"Shouldn't we call someone?" Ginger asked.

"Yeah." Mona came back up the steps. "I'm going to do that now."

"Poor Richard," Justine said between sobs.

It took the D.C. police twenty minutes to get there, with an ambulance not far behind. The medical examiner's guess was that Richard had been dead at least fifteen hours, probably a little longer. The police took statements.

The director and cast of the new play *Inchmeal* said their rehearsal had broken up shortly before six the day before. They'd drifted out singly and in pairs over a ten- or fifteen-minute period. Spread out like that, no one had given any thought to not having seen Richard leave. Mona told the police that Richard's official residence was in New York and that he'd lived alone in Washington; he'd been using the apartment of a friend who was spending the next few months in London. She didn't know about next of kin, so she gave the police the name of Richard's agent.

While the police were questioning the cast, Mona spent the better part of an hour on the phone with various Ford's Theater officials. The PR office wanted a statement. Even though she hadn't completely absorbed the shock of Richard's death, Mona knew she had to think ahead.

Lyle was going to get to play the lead in *Inchmeal* after all. Sammy had been understudying Lyle, so he'd take over Lyle's old part. The only problem was that Sammy was a bit young for that role. But he was a good actor, and it would be easier to find a replacement for Sammy's old role than for Lyle's. So Lyle would move into Richard's role, Sammy would move into Lyle's, and Mona would make some unemployed actor deliriously happy by calling him in to take over Sammy's small role. She had a long list to choose from, actors who'd auditioned but who had not been cast. Then tomorrow they'd start rehearsal earlier than their usual hour to make up for lost time. Mona felt callous treating Richard's accident as an obstacle to be worked around, but it had to be done.

The police were finally finished; they started leaving, taking Richard's body with them. Members of the cast were standing around helplessly, not wanting to linger but not wanting to go, either; Mona was going to have to say something to them. After she'd seen the last police officer out, she started back toward the stage. But her eyes were drawn to the stairwell as if by a magnet. Abe was down there where Richard had been, playing with something that made a light metallic sound as it rolled over the cement landing.

The others were waiting for her on the stage, the fourteen who were left of a fifteen-member cast. They'd fallen into the informal half-circle they adopted when listening to their director. Mona took her usual place, facing them, back to the empty auditorium. She cleared her throat.

The damned cat was playing with something right where Richard had died.

"Wait here," she told her numb-looking actors.

She ran back to the stairwell. Abe was still on the landing, but now lying on his side and looking bored. Mona approached him cautiously; when she stroked his throat for him, he let her pick up his toy. It was a Thespian Society ring.

Mona clenched her fist around the ring, trying desperately to think what to do. She took her time getting back to the stage. Lyle was staring gloomily at his feet, a scowl on his face. Stumbling over her words and having trouble finishing her sentences, Mona told the actors there was no point in trying to rehearse today. Go home, she said, do something to take your mind off Richard. You need time to catch your breath.

And I need time to think.

Mona had spent a sleepless night, trying to decide what was the best thing to do. She ought to call the police and give them the ring. But if they arrested Lyle, *Inchmeal* would close before it even opened; where was she going to find a leading man at this stage of the game? Sammy wasn't experienced enough to carry a lead. Oh, maybe someone was available; but finding him could take weeks and they didn't have weeks.

But she couldn't let Lyle get away with murder. No way. She thought about calling a lawyer. She thought about calling the chairman of the board of Ford's Theater. She thought about calling her mother.

And what if she was jumping to conclusions? There could be some perfectly innocent reason Lyle's ring was on the landing where Richard's body had lain. *Yeah, sure.* But shouldn't he be given a chance to explain? She thought about confronting him privately, hearing what he had to—

Whoa. A private meeting with a man who could be a killer? Good god, what was she thinking of! No, that kind of thing happened only in dumb movies. She would *not* talk to him alone.

So what was the opposite of a solo confrontation? A group confrontation. A group like the cast of the play. Safety in numbers. The more she thought about that, the more she liked it. She, Mona Armstrong, would call everyone together, explain what had happened, and finger the killer. Straight out of Agatha Christie. Only this time the suspected killer would be given full opportunity to offer his explanation. If he had one.

So the next morning she told the actors to find a place to sit; they had something to talk about. Mona herself was seated behind a card table that held a copy of the script and her usual notes, but for once she ignored them. As the actors found seats, Abe wandered in from the wings, sat down in exact stage center, and cocked his head at her. Mona noted that Lyle was to her left, sitting between Ginger and Justine. He was slumped in his chair, both hands jammed into his pockets.

"I have reason to believe," she started out, "that Richard was murdered." She was expecting an outcry at her announcement, but she didn't get one; they all sat staring at her blankly. "You know . . . *murdered?*"

Finally Sammy responded. "You mean, like, on purpose?"

Mona sighed. "Well, yes, Sammy, if it's murder it would have to be on purpose. I'm telling you Richard didn't just trip and fall. Somebody pushed him down those stairs. Then whoever did it must have put that cable around his feet to make it look like an accident."

"No!" Justine gasped.

Mona got the general outcry she'd been waiting for. She waited for the hubbub to die down, but it never really did.

Finally Ginger shouted, "Why, Mona? What makes you think so?"

They fell quiet to hear her answer. "Before I tell you that," Mona said, "I have to ask a question myself." She turned to Lyle. "Lyle, just how badly did you want to play the lead in *Inchmeal?*"

He sat up straight, his eyes wide. "What?"

"You'd been doing everything you could think of to demoralize Richard and make him appear incompetent, in the hopes that I'd kick him out and give you the lead. What else did you do to him that we don't know about?"

Lyle swallowed and said slowly, "Mona, that sounds very much as if you're accusing me of murder!"

"Did you push him down those stairs?"

"No! Goddammit, Mona! Where the hell do you get off, asking me a thing like that!"

Mona took out the ring and held it up so everyone could see. "A Thespian Society ring. It was on the stairwell landing where we found Richard's body."

Every eye in the place turned toward Lyle.

His look of astonishment grew even greater. He shook his head incredulously and pulled his left hand out of his pocket. He was wearing his Thespian Society ring.

The hubbub broke out all over again. Mona buried her head in her hands. Her one chance to play Miss Marple and she blew it.

Salvage what you can. "Okay, I was wrong," Mona said, waving the others to silence. "I'm sorry, Lyle. I'll apologize more adequately later. But right now, who else here belongs to the Thespian Society?"

"Not me," said Sammy. "Dues are too high." The others were shaking their heads.

"Lyle, you must know," Mona insisted.

"I have no idea," he said. "It's a national organization, big membership. And we come from all over."

Ginger turned to him. "Don't you have a membership directory?"

Lyle's face lit up. "Yeah! Mine's back in L.A., but we shouldn't have any trouble getting hold of one!"

"Good!" Mona exclaimed happily, feeling like a detective again. "And whichever member of this cast is listed in that directory—"

"Never mind," Justine said in a high, choked voice. "It's my ring."

There was a startled silence. Then:

"Yours!"

"Justine?"

"Shee-ut."

No one knew what to say. They were all staring at Justine in disbelief. Abe jumped up on her lap and started butting her with his head.

"*You* killed Richard?" Mona finally asked.

"It was an accident," Justine said unhappily, absently stroking the cat. "Just what it looked like. And I didn't put the cable around his feet, he really did trip, and I couldn't do anything, I just had to stand there and watch . . ."

Mona sighed. "Start at the beginning."

"Well, he was teasing Abe," Justine said. "And he was being really mean about it, real nasty. Richard kept poking at him with a ruler, and poor little Abe thought he was being attacked and was hissing and swiping at Richard with his claws. I told Richard to stop it, but he said they were just playing and he went on poking and poking. Anyone could see the cat was traumatized."

She stopped to wipe the tears off her face with the palm of her hand. Ginger handed her a Kleenex.

"Anyway, Richard was *enjoying* it—tormenting an animal! I'd never seen that side of him before and it scared me. I kept telling him to stop, but he wouldn't listen to me. Finally I got myself in between Abe and him, and I pushed him, like this." She demonstrated, thrusting both hands forward, palms out. Abe growled at the sudden movement and jumped down from her lap.

"And that's when he fell down the stairs," Mona said.

"No," Justine replied, "that's when he pushed me back. So I pushed him again and he pushed me again and we were pushing and shoving and not looking where our feet were going and Richard got all tangled up in that lighting cable . . . and, and down he went." She took a long breath, let it out. "It was an accident."

"And the ring came off your finger during the tussle?"

"I wore it on a chain around my neck." Justine reddened at the high-schoolishness of it. "Richard must have hooked a finger in it. I found the chain caught in my bra when I got home."

"So what did you do when Richard fell? Did you go for help?"

"For a dead man? I did the same thing you did, Mona. I went down and felt for a pulse. I even put my ear against his chest to listen for a heartbeat. He was *dead*. I was scared. I'd been kind of fighting with him, and I was afraid of being accused of . . . you know. Murder." She shivered. "It was just a stupid accident. Abe had taken off, and it took me some time to find him. Then I, er, I went home."

The actors were all exchanging startled looks. Ginger said, "You should have told someone. Right then."

"I know," Justine wailed. "I can see that now. But I was so upset with Richard and when I saw what happened to him . . . aw, my brain just turned itself off."

Lyle patted her clumsily on the shoulder. The entire cast proceeded to analyze Justine's emotional state at the time of crisis and draw conclusions as to whether her own trauma excused her subsequent behavior or not. "Are you going to tell the cops?" someone asked Mona.

"Oh, why?" Ginger interposed. "They'll just let her go after they hear her story. Why put her through all that?"

Lyle said, "I agree. But I feel I must point out you were all ready to turn me in when you thought I did it."

"That's when we were still thinking murder," Ginger told him. "Big difference between murder and accident."

"Besides, Richard started it," Sammy said judiciously. "If he hadn't been tormenting Abe, Justine would never have given him that first push."

Yes, that's true. Heads were nodding sagely in agreement.

"Mona?" Justine's voice was tiny. "What are you going to do?"

Pin-drop time.

They all seemed to be holding their breath. Mona let the silence build and then said, speaking slowly: "Richard's death is on the police books as an accident. We now know for certain that that's exactly what it was. I see no reason to cause the police more paperwork."

A cheer broke out among the actors. Justine rushed over and hugged Mona, knocking over the card table. Abe scooted off the stage to get away from all the dancing feet.

Mona watched the actors with a smile, shaking her head. Fourteen of the original cast—fourteen extroverted, gregarious, talkative people. How long could they keep a secret like this?

Long enough for the play to open.

"Do you suppose we could get in a rehearsal sometime today?" Mona shouted over the clamor.

Good-naturedly, they made the effort to settle down. Playscripts were located, the rehearsal furniture rearranged, places taken.

Mona gathered up her spilled notes and folded the card table. As she was carrying them offstage, she glanced toward the auditorium and caught a glimpse of Abe, who was comfortably ensconced in one of the seats in the first row.

She could have sworn the damned cat was laughing at her.

Rachel and the Bookstore Cat

.

Jon L. Breen

One evening in Vermilion's bookshop, Rachel Hennings
was eating pizza with Stu Wellman, book columnist of the
Los Angeles News-Canvass, and trying desperately to
change the subject. In recent months, Stu had become more
and more worried about the safety of the L.A. streets and
was spending an inordinate amount of time and energy trying to convince Rachel to move her business to a safer
neighborhood. Tonight he was in full cry, crime statistics at
his fingertips, police sirens unwittingly abetting him with
dramatic background noise. Rachel, of course, knew she
could never move Vermilion's, the home of so many literary traditions and authorial ghosts. Besides, she felt safe
there.

To get him off this tiresome hobbyhorse, Rachel mentioned offhandedly that she was thinking of getting an animal for the store, a sort of combination companion and
mascot.

"Get a dog," said Stu instantly. "The bigger and louder-
barking and more vicious-looking the better."

"I don't need a watchdog. And I certainly don't want an
animal that will scare off business. I was thinking of one of
those Vietnamese potbelly pigs. They're intelligent. They
like people. They wag their tails like dogs."

"I thought they were out of fashion now," Stu grumbled.

Rachel waved a hand at the ranges of shelves. "So are most of these authors. That's why I love them. But maybe a bookstore animal shouldn't be quite that energetic. Maybe an iguana would be better."

"An iguana? You're kidding."

"No, really, they're very placid and pleasant animals. They just sit there munching their lettuce leaves and waiting for you to stroke them."

"Maybe so, but they look like prehistoric monsters. Some people would find them at least as scary as a pit bull."

Rachel thought about that. "What then? I think a mynah bird would be too messy . . ."

"Why such exotic ideas? If you have to have an animal, why not get a cat? Aren't bookstore cats sort of traditional?"

Rachel smiled and shook her head. "No, not a cat. Anything but a cat."

"You don't like cats?"

"Sure, I do, but I made a vow some time ago I would never have a bookstore cat. Didn't I ever tell you about that?"

She knew she hadn't. Before Stu could reply with the latest commercial burglary rate, she hurried into her story.

Rachel had been in Washington, D.C., on a combination vacation and business trip. A former Vermilion's customer who had taken a job as speechwriter in the current administration wanted to sell off some of his modern first editions, which included most of the works of Saul Bellow, Norman Mailer, and John Updike. It was a collection valuable enough to justify a flying visit to appraise the books and make an offer. While in Washington, she stayed in Georgetown with a couple of friends in the rare-book trade. Gus and Emma Ordway operated Ordway's Bookshop, located on D Street, an easy walk from the Capitol and the Congressional office buildings. They could boast any number of legislators, political staff members, and lobbyists among their customers.

Gus was a tall, lean, bearded man of about fifty, an occasionally published poet who dressed with the drab casualness of a fifties beatnik. Emma, who had been a classmate of Rachel's at Arizona State, was not quite thirty, lacked any literary talent or aspiration, and invariably dressed like a *Vogue* model. Despite their odd-couple appearance and the difference in their ages, the Ordways had in common a love of books and literature, and their marriage seemed a singularly happy one. They had become a fixture at art gallery openings and bookish events in the Washington area, he dressed in garb that suggested proud homelessness, she in gowns fit for an inaugural ball. They had a sense of humor about it: at one Malice Domestic mystery convention in Bethesda, he had shown up in white tie and tails with a Lord Peter Wimsey monocle, she in torn jeans and an Elmore Leonard T-shirt. Once they got their laugh, though, the reversal was never repeated.

For all their seemingly idyllic relationship, Emma and Gus had one strong point of disagreement: cats. Gus loved them. Emma hated them. She wasn't allergic, but she was uncharmed by their standoffish personalities and felt loose cat hair put a crimp in her fashion statement. It was a measure of her love for Gus that she managed to tolerate the fat feline named Oswald who was allowed the run of Ordway's. Emma vowed that once the elderly Oswald went to his reward no other cat would browse among their stacks. It was only fair to give Oswald a special dispensation, she realized, since his tenure at Ordway's antedated hers, she having joined the staff only a few months before she married the boss.

Then, too, Oswald was beloved of the Ordways' customers, and Emma, who had a better business head than Gus, knew the cat had sometimes attracted lucrative commerce. That helped her maintain her tolerance, but she still referred to Oswald as the Capitol Rotundo in reference to his girth. Gus, of course, claimed the cat's corpulence was exaggerated, being an illusion created by his lush gray-and-white coat.

One compromise Emma demanded and Gus agreed to: Oswald never set foot in the couple's Georgetown home. He spent his nights in the store. One morning during her visit, Rachel inquired over breakfast whether that wasn't somewhat risky.

Gus shook his head. "Not a bit. There's plenty of room for him to roam around in, nothing fragile for him to knock over, and his toilet habits are immaculate. We've got the best commercial security system available, so he's safe from catnappers."

"Who'd want him?" Emma said. She glanced at her watch. "Have to open on time today. Congressman Petrie's coming by to pick up that Dortwiler book."

"Amos Cosgrove called yesterday and asked me about that."

"He's too late. The congressman's first in line."

"That'll really frost Cosgrove. Those guys hate each other."

"Rival collectors?" Rachel asked.

"Well, that, too, but they have other reasons. Amos used to be CIA and Petrie is on the House Intelligence Committee. They had a heated exchange in a hearing once over some blown operation or other and ever since they've been don't-invite-'ems. I can't imagine their altercation could have hurt either of them too much. Petrie's still a rising star in the party, and Amos seems to have nothing but time and money on his hands, but those guys would do anything to best each other or embarrass each other or inconvenience each other. In a more civilized time, they might have settled their differences on the duelling ground." After a thoughtful pause, Gus asked Emma, "What are we charging the congressman for the Dortwiler book?"

"Fifteen hundred."

"A steal. Ask for bids and I'll bet Amos would pay two thousand or more. Set them against each other and there's no telling how high we could run up the price." Gus leered greedily.

"Gus, you know we don't do business that way. We really don't, Rachel, he's just being silly. Besides, Cosgrove talks a good game, but the congressman's a steady customer."

Her buying activities concluded, Rachel was now playing full-time tourist. She intended to continue her walking tour of the capital: yesterday, the White House; today, the Library of Congress; tomorrow, the Smithsonian. Emma would give her a ride as far as Ordway's and she would continue on foot from there.

As Emma aggressively navigated the Washington streets, Rachel said, "I'm ashamed to ask, but who is this Dortwiler? You're getting fifteen hundred for one of his first editions and I've never heard of him."

"Join the club. I'd never heard of him either until Jim Petrie asked us to search for his books. Gus claimed he had, but I think he was snowing me. Gus has to give the illusion he knows everything. Once he spent all evening ridiculing me for not knowing the contribution to American politics of Senator Claghorn, and it turned out he was a character on some radio show." Cutting in front of a limo with diplomatic plates, Emma went on, "Let's see now. Rudolph Dortwiler was a political theorist who held a minor post in the Lincoln and Andrew Johnson administrations. His books apparently had some influence on later politicians, but they were issued in very small editions, and today they're scarce, to say the least. This one's called *Lectures on the Essentials of Political Economy*, published in

1872, and the contents look even more boring than the title. But the book's a hot item to these two guys. Amos Cosgrove wants it for his Lincoln collection."

"A completist, is he?"

"You could say that. He's got things with a lot remoter Lincoln associations than this Dortwiler book. Not that he ever buys anything from us. He just comes in a couple times a week to talk big to Gus about what a great collection he has. He and Gus are old friends."

"How do they happen to know each other?"

"I'm not sure," Emma said, adding with an amused smirk, "I think Gus may have been a spook in an earlier life. I don't much like Cosgrove, but we have one thing to bring us together."

"What's that?"

"He hates cats, too. I can't say I like Congressman Petrie much either, but at least he's done several thousand dollars worth of business with us over the last few years. We've helped him build his Dortwiler collection, and this is the one item he lacks."

Emma pulled her BMW to a screeching stop behind the shop. She unlocked the back door into the stockroom, setting off a loud alarm. Opening a panel inside, just next to the door, she entered a code to disarm the security system.

"If I don't do that in thirty seconds, the D.C. police *and* the security firm are here on the run."

Rachel nodded. "So you've told me every morning." The Ordways really loved this security system.

"Absolutely foolproof," Emma said. "With this in place, you can relax. And you have to have some extra protection in Washington. Or any big city nowadays. I guess you have the same thing in L.A., huh?"

Rachel shook her head. "No, I never felt the need. Of course, I live above the store, so . . ."

"Rachel, that's all the more reason," Emma said, opening

76

the door from the stockroom into the store proper. "You should look into—"

As Emma opened the door, she broke off and furrowed her brow. Unlike the other mornings Rachel had come to the store with Emma, Oswald did not appear at once with a meowed greeting. Emma had ignored him those other times, but Rachel had kneeled down to stroke him and inquire about his night's rest. This time, Oswald was nowhere to be seen.

Emma walked a few steps into the store, sniffing the air. Rachel sniffed, too, but her nose didn't detect anything but the pleasant mustiness of old books. Emma obviously smelled something else. She flicked a light switch and marched purposefully to the front of the store. Rachel followed her, and by the time they reached the counter, the unpleasant stench was obvious to her, too.

"I'll kill that cat!" Emma shrieked. "I'll kill him!"

"What happened?" Rachel asked, then saw the source of the odor: a soggy-looking old book sitting on the counter in a puddle of liquid.

"He peed all over the Dortwiler. It's ruined."

At that instant, Rachel heard a noise behind her, and she watched the bulky form of Oswald scoot across the floor from under a table of cookbooks to the shadows of the military history shelves. The usually placid cat was certainly agitated, whether out of guilt or for some other reason.

"Well, you should hide, you . . . you . . ." Emma was quivering with rage, too angry to think of an appropriate insult.

There was an almost apologetic tapping on the front door of the shop. Emma walked to the door, turned the OPEN sign outward, and let in the first customer of the morning, while Rachel helpfully switched on the rest of the lights.

The customer was a tall, elegantly dressed man in his forties with the vapid good looks of a Ken doll. Had to be a politician. Rachel wasn't surprised to learn he was Congressman Jim Petrie, Democrat of Illinois.

"I, I don't know how to say this," Emma said, almost tearfully. "The book's ruined. It was sitting here on the counter and I guess Oswald . . ."

"Do you know how long I looked for that book?" Petrie exploded. Rachel was surprised his face was capable of that much animation.

"I know, I know," Emma said. "We'll just have to find another one, I guess. I'm devastated."

"*You're* devastated?" the congressman snapped back.

"If you want it for the text, it will probably dry out reasonably well, and of course we would adjust the price . . ."

"Forget it! I don't want it for the text." Petrie threw her a withering look, as if the idea of wanting a book for its contents was alien or even obscene. "Don't you understand collectors at all?"

Before the flustered Emma could say any more, the door swung open and a second customer entered the store. He was a short and stubby man with an amiable smile offset by the coldest eyes Rachel had ever seen. He looked at Petrie somewhat sardonically. Assessing the animosity level in Petrie's return look, Rachel figured this must be Amos Cosgrove.

"Something wrong, congressman?" he said. "Oh, Emma, I won't be needing that Dortwiler book after all. Picked up another copy over in Arlington. A real nice find. Even though they doubled the price on me."

"You found one?" Petrie said, his curiosity overcoming all other emotions for an instant. "For how much?"

Cosgrove shook his head in mock dismay. "You won't believe this. The Salvation Army store now sells hardcovers for two bucks instead of one. But in this case, I decided I'd pay it."

The congressman stormed out of the store, and Rachel

wondered how long it would take him to reestablish his
bland political face.

Emma introduced Cosgrove to Rachel, then said sarcas-
tically, "That was a big help, Amos. You know we weren't
going to sell you that book. Jim Petrie's mad enough already, and now he'll think we're offering you books we
found for him."

"No, he won't," Cosgrove said unconcernedly.

"Did you really find a copy of the Dortwiler at a Salvation Army store?" Rachel asked.

"No, I was just having a little fun with my pal the congressman." He added, as if in explanation, "Jim and I go
back a long way."

"Well, now *I* can offer you a copy for two dollars,"
Emma said. "That's about what it's worth after the Capitol
Rotundo got through with it." She gestured at the counter.

Amos Cosgrove seemed to find it all very funny, but his
laughter seemed forced to Rachel.

"No, thanks," he said. "Fine condition only."

Amos Cosgrove browsed through a few shelves in desul-
tory fashion while quizzing Rachel about her own business,
but within a few minutes he was out the door.

"Emma," Rachel said, "is there anything I can do to help
out?"

Emma shook her head. "No, thanks, there's nothing. The
damage is done. We're out a two-thousand-dollar sale."

"If the book's that rare, you'd think one of them would
buy it, even if it's, ah, slightly damaged."

"I don't think so," Emma said. "Not after that little scene
this morning. Neither would give the other the satisfaction
of knowing he bought a book soaked in cat piss."

"Well, if there's nothing else I can do, I'll just go about
my sightseeing and see you tonight. I don't know how long
I'll be, so I'll get a cab back to Georgetown. I may look at
some other bookshops while I'm at it. Do you have a local
directory of them?"

* * *

That evening Rachel returned from her capital explorations to witness an embarrassingly loud domestic argument between the Ordways.

"If it weren't for that damned cat of yours—"

"Who says it was Oswald? You didn't see him do it."

"I left the store secure last night, and it was secure when I opened up this morning. Who else was in the store to deposit cat piss on that book, Gus?"

"Oh, yeah, and who says it was cat piss? Did you get a lab analysis of it?"

"I don't think the mice or the cockroaches hold that much, do you?"

Rachel said, "I wonder if I could offer something. I don't want to take sides or anything, but I've been thinking."

Both of them looked at her, their natural courtesy to a guest warring with exasperation.

Gus said, "I should apologize, Rachel, for subjecting you to this—this discussion."

"Don't worry about that. I think I know what might have happened. Emma, didn't this morning seem a little too neat and convenient to you?"

"What do you mean?" Emma said, a note of impatience in her voice.

"Amos Cosgrove just happens to drop in to witness the congressman's dismay. Doesn't that seem like too much of a coincidence?"

"I don't know. They're both in the shop quite a bit."

"At the same time?"

"No, but—"

"Amos almost always comes in in the afternoon," Gus said thoughtfully. "It's very unusual for him to turn up in the morning, and I think if he saw Petrie there, he'd turn around and walk the other way."

Emma nodded grudgingly. "Okay, you're right. So what?"

Rachel went on, "I understand Oswald had no history of dirty tricks in the store at night. Am I right about that?"

"Absolutely," Gus replied.

"Up to last night," Emma said.

"Doesn't it seem a little too good—or, I guess, bad—to be true that when he finally turned incontinent he just happened to jump up on the counter and pee on the most valuable item in the store?"

"Couldn't happen!" Gus agreed.

"It could and it did," Emma said. "It's just the kind of thing I'd expect from him. He was just waiting for his chance."

"You're irrational!" Gus snapped. "You have a blind spot about cats."

"Can I say one more thing?" Rachel said. "This whole thing has all the earmarks of a setup. Cosgrove hates Petrie. Enough so he will destroy something Petrie wants. But Cosgrove wanted that book himself, didn't he? I mean he's a serious collector, right? He didn't just want that Dortwiler book because Petrie wanted it too?"

"No, he's a real collector all right," Gus said. They both looked at Emma, who nodded in irritable stipulation.

"So I figured Cosgrove might have been the one to destroy the book, framing Oswald. But he wouldn't do that as long as there was some possibility of getting the book for himself. Unless—" She broke off and looked at her hosts expectantly.

"Unless he found another copy," Gus said.

"And he did!" Rachel pronounced.

"Rachel," Emma said, "that story about getting a Dortwiler at the Salvation Army store was just something he made up to torment Petrie. He admitted it himself."

"Right. He didn't get a copy at the Salvation Army store, but that doesn't mean he didn't get a copy somewhere else. This afternoon I put off my visit to the Library of Congress and checked out a few of the city's rare-book dealers. I enquired about the Dortwiler book to see if any of them had sold one recently. If I hadn't found one, I was going to try some of my other contacts in the trade to see if one could have been sold by mail order or at auction in the past few days. But I didn't have to go that far. There was a copy of Dortwiler's *Lectures on the Essentials of Political Economy* sold in Washington, D.C., yesterday, and by a little mild subterfuge I was able to get the dealer to confirm Cosgrove was the buyer. He has his copy. He doesn't need yours, so he decided to make sure Petrie doesn't get it either."

"A dog in the manger," Gus said, flashing a look at his wife that said, *They don't blame that on cats.*

"He got into the store somehow. How he did it with your security system is the one thing I can't figure out. If he stole the book or mutilated it in some way, you'd know someone had broken into the store. But if he poured urine all over it, he would implicate Oswald, and there would be no reason to look for a burglar. You told me, Emma, he hates cats as much as you do, so the idea of putting the blame for his crime on Oswald would appeal to him. It may or may not have been cat urine. I like to think it was from his own personal supply."

"Can you prove this?" Gus asked.

"Of course not," Rachel said with a laugh. "But you have to admit it fits the circumstances. It explains Cosgrove just happening to turn up in the store the morning after he got a copy of the book in question. It explains that Oswald's inexplicable behavior never happened."

"Gus and Emma finally agreed my theory must have been the true one," Rachel told Stu, as she reached for the next-to-last slice of pizza. "They confronted Amos Cosgrove with it, and he immediately confessed, laughing all the time. He thought it was a great practical joke, though Emma and Gus never did see the humor of it even after he paid them for their loss on the sale to Petrie. Oswald was vindicated and still roams the shelves at Ordway's, and they all lived reasonably happily ever after. But since going through all that, somehow the idea of a bookstore cat has never appealed to me."

Stu said, "Great story, but there's a loose end."

"Oh, is there?"

"Of course there is. How did he get in the store past that vaunted security system? You saw Emma disarm it before you went in that morning. She was sure she'd secured the store the night before. She would have had a code presumably only Gus would have known." After a moment's pause, Stu said, "Don't tell me Gus was in on it with Cosgrove."

Rachel shook her head. "No chance."

"I suppose the fact Cosgrove used to be with the CIA suggests he could have known something about security systems, but still—"

Rachel said placidly, "Gus and Emma cleared that up. As I fretted on about how Cosgrove could have gotten in, I saw them looking at each other, not mad any more but like people sharing a secret. Gus gave this embarrassed smirk and said to Emma, 'You want to tell her or shall I?' "

"Tell you what?"

"Cosgrove sold them the security system."

A Capital Cat Crime

•

Richard T. Chizmar

CLASSIFIED MATERIAL (File #33)

The following transcript contains excerpts from the tape-recorded interrogation of suspect Michael Lee Flowers, conducted on April 12, 1994. Interrogation duties handled by Special Agent Jay Ryan (#A3323) and Special Agent Frank Cavanaugh (#A4194). Side B of the first of two tapes (Files #31 and #32) begins with the following statements:

RYAN: State your name again.
FLOWERS: Michael Flowers.
RYAN: Age?
FLOWERS: Forty-one.
RYAN: Occupation?
FLOWERS: I told you . . . I'm unemployed . . . I used to be a sixth-grade teacher, but that was a long time ago.
RYAN: Residence?
FLOWERS: (*laughs*) Washington, D.C. Downtown mostly.
RYAN: Okay, then let's get back to where we were before the tape ended. I'd just started to ask you who else you'd shared this information with. Can you tell me exactly how many people you told about the cats?
FLOWERS: Humph, that's kinda tough to answer. Maybe six

... seven ... ten people. A dozen if you count the two cops who caught me this morning.

RYAN: *(directed at Agent Cavanaugh)* Jesus, that many.

FLOWERS: I don't know for sure. Maybe more, maybe less. Spend a few years out on the street and you become a storyteller. Everyone out there's got a story to tell—

RYAN: Names. We'll need the names of every person you told in case we need to talk to them later. When we're finished here, we're going to give you some paper and a pen, and what we need for you to do is this: write down the names and where we can find each and every person you told about this. If the senator decides to press charges, it'll be a damned sight better for you, if we can verify your story. A couple of witnesses who'll swear you told them this same story *before* today's events will prove that you didn't make up the whole thing on the spot just to save your ass ... or as an excuse for what you were doing to those poor cats.

FLOWERS: *(pounds fist on table)* Christ, a city full of the damned animals and I have to pick a senator's daughter's cat. *(Several seconds of silence.)* Do you really think he'll press charges?

RYAN: Relax, Mr. Flowers. It's like I said, if you cooperate with us, tell us the complete truth, we'll do our best to make sure there are no charges. Agent Cavanaugh has known the senator for many years; if anyone can take care of you, he can.

FLOWERS: Well ... I can give you the names, but it won't be easy to find these guys. Most of them are like me; they have to move around a lot.

RYAN: That's okay. It's really just a precaution we're taking for your own protection. Hopefully we won't have to bother with any of them. Now, listen, what we need to do right now is go over your story one more time.

FLOWERS: And then can I get something to eat?

RYAN: *(nodding)* When we're finished here we'll get those

names down on paper and then you can eat anything you want.

FLOWERS: Do I start from the beginning again?

RYAN: Yes, from the beginning. But this time, instead of listening to the entire story at once, we're going to run through the short version. We're going to ask you specific questions and we'd like for you to answer each question to the best of your ability. We understand that the day in question took place almost a year ago, but remember, we're looking for details here. The more you remember, the better. So take your time and think carefully about everything you say.

FLOWERS: Not really much more to remember, but I'll tell you again just the same.

RYAN: Okay, let's go back to that day again.

FLOWERS: One more time, huh? *(Clearing his throat)* Let's see . . . it was a Monday, the day after Easter. I remember that because my stomach was still full from the big dinner we'd had the night before at Patterson's Shelter over on L and Tenth. Fresh Virginia ham, potato salad, hot rolls, the works. It was one helluva feast. Don't remember the exact date—

CAVANAUGH: Did you have anything to drink that night?

FLOWERS: Don't drink alcohol. Never have. I told the police they could test me but—

CAVANAUGH: Drugs?

FLOWERS: Never have.

RYAN: Are you certain about that—?

FLOWERS:—was early in the morning, somewhere between six and seven. I remember it was raining. A breeze was blowing in from the Potomac and it was cold. Real cold for April. I had just come from the wall . . . the Vietnam Memorial, you know? I go there a couple of times every month to visit some old friends of mine. I spent one tour in Vietnam . . . and I know maybe fifteen, twenty of those names on that wall. I know too many of them. Also know that I was damned lucky to come home from there, so I go and see my friends as often as I can.

The workers and guards don't like it when we come around during the day, though, because the tourists don't like to see us close up. It's the same way all over this city. Go right ahead and live and die on our streets, but for Godsakes, don't come near our national monuments, and whatever you do, don't do it when someone else can see you. You're too dirty, you stink, you're animals, you're dangerous. They've got plenty of reasons. Not too many good ones, though. The volunteer workers are a whole lot nicer, but they don't start up until the summer.

Anyway, back to the story. After I finished at the war memorial, I cut across the recreation fields near the river and walked over to one of the abandoned row homes over on Preston. You know, the ones they closed down last winter? Some of us used to go there from time to time to play cards or to get out of the cold. The basement was too messed up to be of any good use and was usually flooded anyway, but the top floor wasn't so bad. Corner unit had a sofa and a table and some old chairs. We tried to keep the place in decent condition and keep it quiet so that not too many others would find out about it. But it didn't work. A few months ago, a bunch of crackheads burned the place down, fried themselves in the process.

So, anyway, that's where I was—on the top floor of that old rowhouse on Preston Street, reading a paperback next to the window—when it happened . . .

RYAN: There were how many men?

FLOWERS: There were two men and—

CAVANAUGH: And you're sure they didn't come together?

FLOWERS: Positive. I watched them pull up on opposite sides of the street. I only read for about an hour or so that morning, and then I got tired and put the book down on the windowsill, checked out the view. It was still pretty early and the rain was getting heavier, so the streets were empty. I know what you're thinking . . . Preston Street is never empty, but it was that morning.

Both cars pulled up within a few minutes of each other. First, one of those long dark sedans with blacked-out windows circled the block, then parked across the street. I couldn't tell how many people were inside, but the man got out of the back door, so there was at least someone else inside the car doing the driving. The man who got out was black. Black skin, black coat, black pants, black umbrella. That's the best look I got of him and that's all I can remember about the way he looked. That and the fact that he was tall, very tall.

A minute or so later, a green van pulled up almost directly beneath my window, and the second man got out.

RYAN:—so you're certain that you never saw a third person?

FLOWERS: Yeah. I never saw the driver leave the limousine, and I don't think there was anyone else inside the van.

CAVANAUGH: Why do you say that?

FLOWERS: Well, the guy driving the van wasn't very big and he didn't look very strong, either. After he opened the van's back doors, he struggled with that box for quite some time before he got a good hold on it. The black guy was still standing across the street, and I just figured that if someone else was inside the van, the little guy would've asked them for some help—

FLOWERS:—almost had myself a heart attack when I heard their footsteps on the stairs. I thought for sure that they were coming all the way up to the top floor, and I swear, I've never been so scared in my entire life. I didn't know what was going down—big-time drugs, a payoff, something—but I didn't think they'd be real happy to find me waiting up there. So I crawled into the corner behind the sofa and tried my best to stay real quiet. When they stopped on the second floor, I thanked the Lord and sat perfectly still, praying that they'd take care of their business in a hurry and be on their way.

But what I'd forgotten about that particular corner was that there were two holes—one about four inches across and one about half that size—in the floor behind the sofa where pipes used to run up from the basement. Not only could I hear most of what they were saying, I could actually *see* a small portion of the room.

CAVANAUGH: You say you saw only one of the men clearly?
FLOWERS: That's right. The man who was driving the van stopped right in my line of sight, at a perfect angle for me to see through the big hole, and that's where he put the box down. They talked for a minute or so, they might've shook hands, and then he started pacing back and forth as they spoke ... so I could only see him for a few seconds at a time before he disappeared from my sight, but I must have glimpsed his face twenty or thirty times.
RYAN: Okay, one more time, what did he look like?
FLOWERS: Well, he sure wasn't anything special to look at. That's what I remember most about him. He was no taller than me and probably just as skinny. And he had white hair. I remember that real well. I'd thought he was blond when I saw him outside, but it must have been the rain and the window glass, because his hair was as white as snow—

FLOWERS: Christ, I've already told you all of this!
RYAN: I know this is terribly repetitive, Mr. Flowers, but that's the idea here ... to see if we can help you to remember something you forgot about the first time. Now,

please be patient with us. This next part is extremely important. What else can you tell us about the box he was carrying?

FLOWERS: *(Several seconds of silence.)* I'm telling you the truth, I don't remember anything else. The box just about came up to the man's waist. It was covered with a cloth or a blanket or something, which the man removed once they were inside. The box or cage or whatever it was looked like it was made of glass and metal, and it looked like it must have been pretty heavy. When I saw it, I remember thinking: no wonder he'd had so much of a problem getting it out from the van. And when the man removed the blanket, I got a clear view of what was inside that box—

FLOWERS: That's right. There were cats inside the box. Nothing else, I'm certain. The glass looked thick and heavy and practically bombproof, but it was crystal clear. The box was divided right down the middle by a clear partition and there were two cats inside one section and a third cat inside the other. I saw them clear as day. No question about it. And all three cats looked the same; I remember thinking that they looked like Halloween cats because they were orange and black—

CAVANAUGH:—and you're absolutely certain you heard them use those exact words?

FLOWERS: I told you, I couldn't hear everything clearly because it was raining so damned hard and the rain was making too much noise on the roof. But I heard enough. Snatches of conversation here and there. Words. Sentences.

The black man spoke kind of softly, so I didn't hear him much. I don't think he was American, though. He spoke pretty good English, but the words came out slow and stiff, like it was a learned language. The man from the van had a surprisingly strong voice, though, and I could hear him talk the majority of the time. I think he might've been nervous because—

CAVANAUGH: But let's be perfectly clear here, you do submit that you heard them talk about some type of rabies and you heard them mention those particular countries by name?

FLOWERS: Yeah, I heard all of that. I swear to it. I didn't hear the specifics, but I heard a word here, a word there, and it all fit together. They were talking about some kind of disease, some kind of new rabies strain or virus or something or other, and how dangerous their business at hand was. I remember they kept pointing and leaning down and looking at the cats, and the man from the van made a big show of explaining that the single cat was pregnant. Then they started talking about all those medical terms and foreign countries and they lost me in a hurry—

CAVANAUGH: But you recognized the names of those countries, huh?

FLOWERS: Sure did. I taught history for two long years before switching over to social studies, so I knew exactly what countries they were talking about, knew where they were located too. But it all happened so fast . . . I just couldn't piece everything together . . . until I read that newspaper last month—

RYAN: And you came to this conclusion as soon as you read the newspaper article?

FLOWERS: No, not *the* newspaper article; there were many articles. You see, papers are easy to get around here, even for the homeless, because so many people throw them away, leave them in the park, on the subway, wherever they please.

I read the first article last month in the *Washington Post*. The second story a week later. Then, two more ran last week, in both the *Post* and the *Washington Times*. Each story almost identical. Two tiny countries across the Atlantic, nearly a quarter of Central America, even somewhere in Cuba for Christsakes ... all suffering from the same deadly virus. Thousands dead, thousands more dying, scientists and doctors baffled. A disease of unprecedented danger and unknown origin, the officials claimed. And the names of those countries ... well, I could have told you them almost a year ago. Jesus—

FLOWERS:—was scared and that's the how and the why I got caught this morning taking off with the senator's daughter's cat. I freely admit it ... I was gonna take that cat somewhere and kill it. Just like I did to all the others. All I can think about now is that I knew all this time. All those people dead ... and I knew.

I'm not sorry for what I did to those cats, either. I mean, maybe our cats *are* safe, maybe it was just those three in that glass box. Who knows? But, for Christsakes, Cuba's awful close to the coast of Florida ... and, besides, what if—

CLASSIFIED MATERIAL (File #34)

Confidential Memorandum

To: Royce Larkin, Commander-in-Chief
From: Jay Ryan, Special Agent
Date: April 13, 1994

Matters regarding the Michael Lee Flowers Case as of 10:30 A.M.—Immediately following his interrogation, Flowers identified (from an employee file photo) government researcher Jeremy Blevins as the man he observed in the green van. Blevins was apprehended at 4:54 A.M. and remains under guard at CIA Headquarters. After listing the seven names and approximate locations of other persons he'd shared this information with, Flowers was sedated and efficiently terminated. Special agents were dispatched immediately and as of nine this morning, only one of the seven persons remains at large. We are continuing to question the two police officers who brought Flowers in, although we have their full cooperation and the full cooperation of their home district. At this time, they appear to present no problem to this investigation. The senator is unaware of any problem other than that of the homeless catnapper. Please post further instructions at your convenience.

(The rather unusual structure of this tale evolved from two wonderful short stories—"The Interrogation" by Dean R. Koontz and "Love Letters" by Thomas F. Monteleone. I'd like to thank both authors for the inspiration.)

The Black Hawthorn

•

Carolyn Wheat

I love cats. And I like to help my friends, so when Mrs. Simpson-Phelps, my next-door neighbor, asked me to cat-sit for her, what could I say but yes? Little did I know that the job would entail the skills of a private detective—which I most decidedly am not, though I do read what my husband refers to as "those stupid mysteries."

I know her cats. Everyone in our Georgetown neighborhood knows her cats. We see the curious Tigger in her backyard, acting like his Winnie-the-Pooh namesake, all stripes and bounces, peeking under the fence, jumping at squirrels. We see Paddington, the Fred Astaire of cats, graceful, slender, impeccably dressed in a sleek black fur tuxedo with a white patch at his throat, walking along the back fence, delicately stepping over each picket. We see Arthur, the Mighty Hunter, stalk through the tall summer grass, on the prowl for a mouse, a bird, anything he can capture and crow over. Once he "caught" a charcoal briquette from my barbecue, and meowed as loudly and as proudly as if it had been the biggest rat in the world.

You have to be a very close neighbor of Mrs. Simpson-Phelps to see her fourth cat. Little Orphan Annie, who's very shy, likes nothing better than to bask in the sun, preferably on a self-made cushion of newspaper or a grocery bag. She views the world through grass-green eyes that see everything and register surprise at nothing.

Mrs. Simpson-Phelps and her feline family welcomed me to the neighborhood when I first moved in three years ago. I was a newlywed, she newly widowed. We started chatting over the back fence, the way neighbors do, and soon I was picking up one or the other of her straying pets and handing him over the fence. She handed me homemade scones, perfectly toasted crumpets dripping real butter, lemon-curd tarts—all the delicacies of her native England.

Mrs. Simpson-Phelps was Violet Simpson of London's East End till she met a handsome GI named Harry Phelps and became a war bride. Now she wanted to go home again. But what to do about the cats? That was where I came in.

". . . just couldn't trust an agency, so impersonal. And my dear niece, Wanda, lives all the way in Fredericksburg, so it won't do to ask her, though I know she'd oblige if she could. She's a doctor, you know, very busy. She suggested I board them with a vet, but I can't bear to think—"

"Of course I'll take care of them, Mrs. Simpson-Phelps," I said warmly. I'd said it once already, but my neighbor's anxiety about leaving her pets seemed to have affected her hearing. After all, I reasoned—already mentally making my case to Bud, my skeptical husband, who would no doubt call me a pushover—how hard could it be? I'd open cat-food cans, empty the litter pan, let them sit on my lap and purr for a while, and that would be that. Just because Bud called our neighbor's cats The Wild Bunch didn't mean they were really—

"*No*, Arthur," Mrs. Simpson-Phelps said firmly, as Arthur made a gigantic leap into the air, going after a low-flying blue jay. Arthur plopped down on the brick patio and licked his white paw furiously, as if to show he had no interest whatsoever in creatures of the avian persuasion.

We were in our usual conversational mode: standing on

either side of the whitewashed fence that separated our tiny backyards. Around us, forming a square, were the rear entrances of townhouses, their warm Georgian brick lit by early spring sun. My apricot tree was in full creamy bloom; Mrs. Simpson-Phelps's weeping cherry was just budding in pink.

"I'm so pleased, Nikki. Thanks ever so, love. With you looking after them, I know my darlings will be in good hands." She clasped her own beringed hands to her breast.

Mrs. Simpson-Phelps had one of the few clotheslines left in our rapidly gentrifying neighborhood. She did her own hand-washing and often hung lace dresser scarves and linen tea towels out to dry in the sun, proclaiming electric dryers the ruin of good Irish linen. I noticed a clothespin dangling from the line; whatever it had secured had fallen to the ground.

"Look, I think Annie has—" I began, but my neighbor had already noticed; she made a beeline for the white-and-tabby cat. Annie was busily kneading the tea towel into a cushion, getting it ready for her plump little body.

"Annie, love, please give me that nice clean towel," my neighbor cooed, deftly pulling the now-dirty scrap of linen from under the cat's white feet. Annie meowed indignantly and stalked, tail high, into the house through the open French doors.

"Oh, dear," Mrs. Simpson-Phelps looked at me ruefully. "They *are* rather a handful, aren't they?"

I was beginning to have second thoughts about cat-sitting The Wild Bunch, so I changed the subject. "When was the last time you were in England?" I asked.

"Oh, not for years and years. I believe little Prince Charles was just being christened the last time I was home. Oh, dear, I shall have forgotten everything I ever knew about getting round London, I know I shall."

"But why haven't you gone back?" I asked, my head filling with romantic stories about her family cutting her off without a shilling because she dared to marry an American soldier.

"Because of my kitties, of course. England has the *most* barbaric quarantine laws, and I just couldn't bear to leave my darlings home for so long." Mrs. Simpson-Phelps gazed fondly at Paddington, who glided along the back fence with the graceful balance of a tightrope walker.

"Before I had this lot, there were other cats in my life," she explained. "Let me see—there was Bunny Brown and his sister Sue, Alice in Wonderland—she was a sweet little thing, pure white and deaf as a post. And Mole and Ratty and Mr. Toad—the fattest ginger tom you ever did see. I never could bear to part with them, or to have them quarantined for six whole months. But now," she said, her face clouding, "with my sister Mavis ill, I really must go over. No more excuses."

"Oh," I said. I explained my melodramatic picture of family opposition to her American husband, and she laughed.

"No, it was nothing like that, love." Her chuckle was as rich as Devonshire cream. "My family adored Harry, really they did. The only thing my father wanted was that I keep the family name, which is why I go by Simpson-Phelps. As though my old dad was a duke instead of a pubkeeper. In return, he gave us The Black Hawthorn as a wedding present."

She said the words in capital letters. I had to ask what The Black Hawthorn was, and she responded by inviting me to "come round at once and be educated."

It was my first entry into my neighbor's house. For all our good-natured back-fence chatting, we had never been inside one another's homes. I had to admit I was curious; it's always instructive to see how others choose to live.

When she opened her front door to let me in, Tigger bounced at me and twined himself around my legs, mewing pitifully. "Shush, you awful Tig," my neighbor said, her voice tinged with a mixture of mock annoyance and shameless indulgence. "You'll have Nikki thinking I never feed you, when the fact is you're positively stuffed with tinned mackerel."

The front parlor—Georgetown houses have front and back parlors instead of living rooms—was a little piece of England tucked away in the capital of the colonies. A Victorian sofa of hideous proportions occupied the place of honor across from the fireplace, and vases of dried weeds with peacock feather accents sat in corners on dark, carved tables with marble tops. The walls were festooned with family photographs in oval frames, along with pallid watercolors.

"There," my hostess said proudly, pointing to the mantel, "that's The Black Hawthorn."

I had no trouble seeing why she spoke so respectfully of her heirloom. It was a Chinese ginger jar, slightly taller than a cat, of a deep rich black with a twisted-tree design on it. Very graceful, very old, very valuable.

"The Black Hawthorn was brought from China by Captain Hosea Simpson in 1869," my hostess explained. "My nephew, Gerry, says it's worth a small fortune, though it is only Ch'ing instead of Ming. Whatever that means," she added with a laugh.

"Such a shame I shall be going to England just when Gerry is visiting over here, but it can't be helped."

The words burst out of me before I could stop myself. "But, Mrs. Simpson-Phelps, Violet, you can't just leave a thing like that on an open mantel! What about the cats? Don't you worry that one of them will—"

"Nonsense, Nikki," my neighbor said complacently. "My darlings know how important The Black Hawthorn is to me. They would never knock it down. Would you, pets?" Since only Annie was in the room, sitting this time on a real cushion, the objet d'art, perched on the mantel with the Toby jugs and the seashell statue that said SOUVENIR OF

The Black Hawthorn

BRIGHTON 1943, was probably safe, at least for the moment. Wherever Tigger had disappeared to, his temporary absence gave the precious object a reprieve.

I stayed long enough to drink what Mrs. Simpson-Phelps proudly called "a proper cup of tea" and to eat two of her melt-in-the-mouth scones. Just as I was finishing the last few crumbs, Tigger bounced back into the room, dragging a shopping bag after him. I laughed as he shook his head from side to side, trying to free himself from the handle, which had wrapped itself around his neck.

"Nikki, it isn't a bit funny," my neighbor scolded as she caught Tigger and lifted the twine handle over his head while the cat squirmed and squealed with fright. "He might strangle on one of these carry bags. I should never have them in the house. And before I go, I intend to get rid of every one I have, even the lovely Christmas ones from Lord and Taylor's."

I apologized for laughing and promised once again to take good care of The Wild Bunch. I eyed The Black Hawthorn on my way out of the parlor. One more thing to worry about during the three weeks Mrs. Simpson-Phelps would be away. I wasn't just a cat-sitter any more; I was a ginger jar–sitter as well.

Still, The Black Hawthorn had survived The Wild Bunch and their predecessors for lo these many years; why should three more weeks put it in danger?

I put the ginger jar and my neighbor out of mind for the next week. It was getting closer and closer to April 15, when my office, the dreaded Internal Revenue Service, would be swamped with last-minute tax returns. I worked late every night and so waited till the last minute to shop for a birthday present for my sister in St. Louis. On my lunch hour, I crossed Constitution Avenue to the massive gift shop at the Smithsonian's Museum of American History. That's the home of the real ruby slippers and has more gift ideas than a whole raft of catalogues. Acres and acres of everything from replicas of Egyptian gold earrings to place mats with American advertising logos. Paper dolls of the First Ladies and Japanese playing cards. Rice-paper kites and Civil War soldiers and scarves with stained-glass designs and dominoes with pictures of presidents and make-it-yourself cardboard White Houses—and that's just the first floor.

The ginger jar sat on a glass shelf along with marble bookends in the form of lions. "Reproduction Ch'ing Dynasty ginger jar in unusual black lacquer with hawthorn pattern," the printed label read. "While primarily produced for the export market," it burbled, "these vases are among the rarest of their period. Add a touch of Oriental elegance to *your* home with this reproduction of the real thing."

I bought Susan a silk scarf with purple irises and a silver iris scarf pin. But I couldn't get the ginger jar out of my mind; its image followed me onto the bus for the ride home to Georgetown. Had Mrs. Simpson-Phelps made up the story about her sea-captain forebear, passing off a museum reproduction as a valuable antique? Did that explain her willingness to leave the ginger jar within easy reach of feline tails, or did she really own the genuine article—and have an extraordinary faith in the kindness of cats?

Either way, the ginger jar would become my responsibility in the morning. Should I leave it in its place of honor on my neighbor's mantel, or should I take it to my own home for safekeeping while she was away? I pondered both sides of the question as the bus made its way into the picturesque narrow streets of Georgetown. I continued thinking about it as I walked along the brick sidewalk toward my townhouse.

I had no clear answer as I rang the next-door bell the next day. I found Mrs. Simpson-Phelps in a state of pretravel panic. "Oh, dear, where *is* my passport?" she asked, rummaging through a kitchen drawer. "Do you think

I've bought enough cat food, love?" She pointed to a mountain of canned gourmet meals for felines.

I never had a chance to say yes. "And on top of everything, Gerry and Wanda—Harry's brother's oldest girl—have been quarreling over The Black Hawthorn. They've each asked me to leave it to them in my will. As if I could think about something as trivial as a will at a time like this!"

She was putting her hat on as we spoke, but that didn't stop her telling me, for the fifth time since asking me to cat-sit, how Annie hated liver but Paddy doted on it and how Arthur was not under any circumstances to be allowed outside.

"I'd worry myself sick thinking he might be lost, you see," she explained. "Which reminds me. At least Wanda has some appreciation of my feelings. She promised to take good care of my darlings if anything ever happened to me. In return for The Black Hawthorn, no doubt. But that's more than Gerry offered. He can't stand cats, made no bones about it when he came to see me. 'Keep them away from me, Aunt Violet,' he begged. 'Especially that black one!' As if my Paddy wasn't the gentlest creature alive," she finished indignantly.

The doorbell rang. I went to open it, since my neighbor was proving her point by cuddling the black cat, murmuring endearments into his oversized ears.

The woman at the door was about my age, tall, with blonde hair cut short and sculpted to her head like a cap. A Valkyrie with a Vidal Sassoon haircut. "I'm Wanda Phelps," she explained, offering me a hand to shake. The other hand held a handsome wine-colored doctor's bag.

"I'm driving Aunt Violet to the airport," she said. Ms. Phelps looked meaningfully at her aunt as she added, "I'll probably pop in on the weekends to see that everything's all right. I see patients at a free clinic on Saturdays and it's on my way. But I couldn't make the trip every day, so I'm really glad you're taking care of her cats."

"Oh, it's no trouble," I said lightly, noting that Tigger was about to make a giant leap from the back of the sofa to the top of the china closet. Arthur stood at the French doors, meowing to be let out into the sunny summer day.

Mrs. Simpson-Phelps put Paddy down and stroked Annie's white fur. "Oh, I must go, mustn't I?" she asked Wanda in a plaintive tone.

Turning to me, she said, "Here are the keys. *Do* pet them for me, will you?" Her eyes filled with tears.

"Yes, of course I will," I said, impulsively grasping her plump hand in mine and giving it a farewell squeeze.

It's hard to leave your children in someone else's hands.

As the door closed behind Wanda's hand-knit pink sweater and Mrs. Simpson-Phelps's good traveling hat, I looked at The Wild Bunch and said, "It's up to you, guys. You can be good kitties or you can break an old lady's heart. Which is it going to be?"

Despite the full bowls of food on the kitchen floor, all four felines ran to the mountain of cat-food cans and begged as though they hadn't eaten in a week. I sighed.

Nevertheless, the three weeks my neighbor was gone passed smoothly. I opened can after can of gourmet cat food, cooked liver for Paddy, changed litter box after litter box, picked up hairballs, and generally made sure things were all right in the Simpson-Phelps menagerie. Each Saturday morning Dr. Wanda Phelps's white Volvo pulled into a parking space on our narrow street and the tall blonde navigated the cobblestones, her wine-colored medical bag in her hand.

The day before Mrs. Simpson-Phelps was due to arrive home from her native land, I opened the door to chaos. I looked first at Paddington, perched on the mantel licking his paw. Then I saw what lay on the floor beneath him. I looked at Arthur, batting something around the floor while

Tigger poked his head out from inside a shopping bag with twine handles. Finally, I looked at Annie, curled up on a bundle of pink stuff she'd managed to knead into a cushion.

Any other cat-sitter would have gotten out the broom and cleaned up the mess.

I called the police.

"Just what is it you think happened here?" the stalwart, skeptical, just-the-facts-ma'am detective—who also happened to be my husband—asked for the third time.

I took a deep breath and started in again. "Bud, I've already told you. We're supposed to think Paddy broke The Black Hawthorn," I explained. "When I came in, he was on the mantel, licking his paw. And, as you can see, the jar's in pieces on the floor."

My hand waved at the shards of black lacquered porcelain that lay on the parquet. "But Paddy's the most graceful cat I've ever seen. There's no way he could have been clumsy enough to knock that thing down."

Detective Bud Parker raised a single eyebrow. Apparently the gracefulness of cats didn't qualify as admissible evidence.

"If your men do a thorough examination of the mantelpiece," I went on, "I think they'll find traces of liver. Cooked liver that someone put up there to lure Paddy onto the mantel."

Now the other eyebrow went up. I'd seen this expression before, and it did not denote acquiescence to my point of view.

"Liver," he said. He sighed. "Was this on 'Murder, She Wrote' or something?"

"And then there's Tigger," I said, ignoring the comment. The fact that the hour between eight and nine on Sunday evening was as sacred to me as the Super Bowl was to him had no bearing on the facts at hand.

I pointed to the colorful shopping bag with the dangerous twine handles Mrs. Simpson-Phelps had been so concerned about. "It's from Harrods. That's in London," I added help-fully. "A place our neighbor hasn't visited in donkey's years. Which means that someone who *had* been in London recently came and left it here. What's more," I said, going for the clincher, "I know Mrs. Simpson-Phelps got rid of all her shopping bags because she was afraid Tigger would get his head caught in the handles. So that bag was brought here while she was away."

I sat back on the velvet-covered sofa, which was just as uncomfortable as it looked, waiting for Bud to catch up with my thinking. "Mrs. Simpson-Phelps has a nephew who lives in England. He's here in Washington right now—and he had his eye on his aunt's valuable antique."

Bud nodded. His eyebrows were back in their normal position; he was clearly more comfortable discussing human rather than feline psychology.

"Look at Annie," I continued, pointing to where the green-eyed cat sat in sphinx-like pose on a hand-knitted pink sweater. Even the arrival of several heavy-footed police officers hadn't moved her from her comfortable seat.

"See what she's sitting on?" Without waiting for an answer, I went on. "I last saw that sweater on Wanda, Mrs. Simpson-Phelps's niece. You remember, I met her just before Mrs. Simpson-Phelps left. And she had designs on the vase, too. That's why she came every Saturday, to show her aunt how much she cares for the cats, so Mrs. Simpson-Phelps will leave her the ginger jar in her will."

"So you think Wanda is behind all this?" Bud asked. "You've seen her enter the house; the pink sweater is hers—maybe she tried to steal the vase and broke it instead."

"No," I answered. "It was Gerry who stole the real vase. Then he broke this reproduction so his aunt would think it was destroyed forever."

"How do you know it was him instead of the niece?"

"Because of Arthur," I replied.

"Arthur? Who's he?" Bud demanded. "Another nephew?"

I laughed, then pointed at the gunmetal-gray cat with the white peninsula on his clown face. "That's Arthur," I said. "And if you'll look at what he has between his paws, you'll see what I mean about Gerry."

Bud hoisted his bulk out of the blue velvet sofa—which clung to its sitters like the sea to its dead—and walked to where Arthur guarded his captured prey. "Hey," he said, picking up the object, "this is a charcoal briquette. What's this cat doing with—"

"That's what I mean," I said triumphantly. "Arthur's been outside. Mrs. Simpson-Phelps specifically told me he wasn't to go out while she was away. Somebody disobeyed her and let him out. You remember the Adzakians' barbecue last Sunday—Arthur must have captured a briquette from their grill."

"So why couldn't Wanda—"

"Because she loved the cats," I said triumphantly. "She wouldn't have let Arthur go outside. And she'd never have left a shopping bag where Tigger could get his head caught in the handles. It's my guess Annie made a cushion of her sweater and Wanda left it so that her aunt would see it and be touched by her kindness."

Again Bud gave me the two-eyebrow treatment. I plunged ahead anyway. "But Gerry, unlike Wanda, dislikes cats. In fact, he's afraid of them. So it's natural he'd open the French doors while he was here in hopes that at least Arthur would go out and leave him alone. He brought the bag because it contained a replica of The Black Hawthorn from the Smithsonian gift shop. He took the real vase, then smashed the replica and put liver on the mantel so Paddy would climb up and get blamed for the broken ginger jar. He figured his aunt would never know he'd taken the real one. If you move quickly," I suggested, "you can probably catch him at Dulles Airport. He'll have to go through customs, after all."

I allowed myself to preen a little when Bud called an hour later to say that Gerry Simpson had been arrested. I may have allowed references to Jessica Fletcher to pass my lips when Bud reported that Gerry had declared a black hawthorn ginger jar as a souvenir.

I lost my complacency when Dr. Adzakian, chairman of the Chinese Art department at the Smithsonian and unofficial advisor to the D.C. police department, declared the ginger jar a fake.

The only thing that made up for my chagrin was what Bud described as the very real dismay on the face of Gerry Simpson.

"He really thought we were putting him on," Bud said, tucking into the leftover goulash I'd microwaved for him. "He thought he had the real thing, I'm sure of that."

"Which means," I began slowly, wary of making another blunder, "that somebody substituted ginger jars before Gerry made his move."

"I still think the old lady did it herself," Bud said. This was a theory he'd propounded more than once during my three weeks of cat-sitting. "I know if I had a valuable ginger jar and a houseful of cats, I wouldn't just leave the thing on the mantel."

"But you aren't Mrs. Simpson-Phelps," I argued. "She loves her cats and she loves her vase and she doesn't see any problem with—"

"Okay, so what happened, Sherlock?" Bud challenged.

"Wanda."

"When and how?" This was said through a mouthful of goulash.

I remembered the wine-colored doctor's bag. What reason could she have had for carrying it from her car into her aunt's house—except as a convenient receptacle for The Black Hawthorn?

Bud woke up a District of Columbia judge, got a search warrant signed, and had the ginger jar—the real one, this time, according to Dr. Adzakian—before Mrs. Simpson-Phelps's plane landed the next day. Since Wanda was in custody, I drove to Dulles Airport to meet my neighbor's plane.

After she'd heard everything, she leaned back in the bucket seat of my little red Honda and said, "Thank goodness you were there, Nikki. I can't thank you enough for what you've done for me. I don't know how I can ever show my gratitude."

"Oh, there's no need—" I began, but Mrs. Simpson-Phelps cut me off with a sudden cry of inspiration.

"I know," she said triumphantly, "I shall change my will and leave *you* The Black Hawthorn!" She turned to me, her face radiant. "And the cats, too, of course."

Catgate

·

Max Allan Collins

Senator Jim Rawson, Democrat, Iowa, forty-five years of age, pulled the sleek red sports car over along the edge of the gravel road. Virginia farmland, washed in moonlight, surrounded him, a fertile and yet desolate landscape, serene in its isolation. Not a farmhouse in sight; certainly not a car. And the only other human being present was a dead one.

Vicki.

The busty young woman wore a pink T-shirt and jeans and running shoes—though she was in her late twenties, she might have been a college girl. Her features were cute—big long-lashed eyes (shut now), pert nose, pouty puffy lips. She was slumped against the other window of the Jaguar. He'd have to move her.

Leaving the driver's side door open, Rawson—in University of Iowa yellow-and-black sweatshirt and black jeans and black leather gloves—came around and carried her from the rider's side of the vehicle. It was as if he were carrying a bride across the threshold, although the only threshold Vicki Petersen had crossed was death's, and she'd done that several hours ago.

Rawson—tall, rawboned, with blond-brown hair touched at the temples by distinguished gray—had a Marlboro Man look that boded well with his conservative constituency. Iowans rarely voted Democrats to the Senate. Rawson had maintained the office for three terms (with dead-certain reelection coming up next year) by balancing his own slightly left-of-center politics with country charm.

As he gently conveyed the shapely and very dead body of the woman who had been his mistress for three years, he was bitterly aware of his own reputation as a champion of women's rights, a battler for ERA, a vocal defender of Anita Hill. This irony left a bitter taste in his being as he arranged the corpse behind the wheel of the sports car, which had been purchased by him, in cash, with PAC money a little more than a year before.

"I loved you, Vicki," he said, and could hear his voice waver; tears were blurring his vision, if not his mission. "But you betrayed me."

Could she have really believed he would marry her? A Catholic in a predominantly Protestant state, Rawson knew the good people of Iowa would never stand for him divorcing, childless marriage or not, particularly not with a wife who was bedridden back home, wasting away with MS.

And then to threaten him with exposure—"How would you like to see our story on 'A Current Affair,' or maybe 'Hard Copy'? Maybe I could play myself in the TV movie!"—truly contemptible.

You little bitch, he thought, and raised a hand as if to slap her, but the beautiful, eternally slumbering woman behind the wheel was past feeling any such sting, and he immediately felt a flush of shame.

He sighed. A summer breeze riffled a nearby field of wheat, and his own wheat-colored, dead-dry hair. The moon was like a hole punched in a black starless sky, letting in too much light. He looked at his watch, shut the girl's car door with a *thunk* that echoed across the world. Where *was* Edward, anyway?

It was highly unlikely this dead girl would ever come

back to haunt him. He knew that. The only nervousness he felt was immediate—once Edward had arrived, and he was back safely in his townhouse on P Street in Georgetown, Jim Rawson would be secure, with his best and only true friend—the big gray mixed-breed cat, Tricky Dick—settled on his lap.

He wondered if Dick would mourn the missing Vicki—the cat and the girl had taken to each other from the start . . .

A little over ten years ago, Vicki Petersen had been a cheerleader at the University of Iowa, a small-town girl with a big future—until she flunked out in her sophomore year, and found her way to New York, where an acting career seemed to beckon. Naturally top-heavy, her high, soft yet firm silicone-free breasts became tickets to stardom on the strip-club circuit.

This had been prior to the more recent influx of upscale topless nightclubs, venues in which she might have made some real money. But a few years ago, stripping was less lucrative, and when Rawson met her in a D.C. bar called the Gentleman's Club, she was at a low ebb.

He had encouraged her to quit her job as a stripper and get back to pursuing her acting career; as a senator, he'd met and maintained personal relationships with any number of Hollywood celebrities and could certainly help her make some connections.

She had been drawn to him immediately, he could tell—after all, not only was he a senator, and as handsome as Robert Redford, but a superstar celebrity back in their home state. Their affair had begun that first night.

Rawson didn't like risking motels—you never knew when some sleazeball reporter was lurking in the bushes, waiting to make a Gary Hart out of you—so early on in the relationship he had ensconced the girl in a suite at the Watergate. Irony was second nature to Rawson, and he relished having his mistress spirited comfortably (and handily) away in the hotel and apartment complex where a break-in had once led to that sleazeball Richard Nixon's downfall.

Vicki had been a private person. Her family back in Iowa—farm folk—had been kept in the dark about her stripping career. She would hardly have told them about an affair she was having.

Nor did she have any female friends among the strippers on the topless circuit—her aspirations toward acting had made her a snob toward them. They were sluts, tramps, lowlifes; she, on the other hand, was an actress reluctantly taking on this demeaning "role" on her way to a real career on stage or screen.

He knew she had made a few friends with other single women tenants at the Watergate—secretaries and such. But he had been adamant about her not sharing any secrets with them—after all (as he had drilled into her), these were women who swam in the same dirty Washington waters as he, working for this lobbying firm or that political action committee; the wrong word to the right one of them, and he'd be sunk. And, so, he felt confident, she'd protected him.

Even if she had mentioned him to a woman friend (and he doubted it), he knew they had never been seen together; no photographs of them, as a couple, existed to become a nasty surprise on the *Enquirer* cover.

She invariably would be picked up by Edward in the limo with its dark windows and brought into the townhouse from a garage in the alley that connected with an underground passageway that connected all of the homes on his block. Only Rawson knew about it, however, and that allowed Edward to bring Miss Petersen into (and out of) the P Street townhouse undetected.

"If people see us together," he would tell her, "it will taint our eventual marriage. When Marge passes away, we'll 'meet' for the 'first time,' and you'll be a senator's wife with all the respect and attention you deserve."

111

He could see how much she liked the sound of that, and knew she wouldn't risk such a future. But she had grown impatient of late, saying, "That woman is *never* going to die! Divorce her! No one will blame you."

She didn't understand that she was asking him to commit political suicide.

And now, thanks to the cocktail she'd sipped at the townhouse, laced with a deadly, tasteless and thankfully painless poison, she had committed literal suicide.

Not intentionally, of course, but the world wouldn't know that. They would find a frustrated would-be actress and ex-stripper, an empty pill bottle beside her lifeless form, a poor dead girl who wound up along the country roadside in a Jaguar purchased for her by some unknown gentleman friend who had, perhaps, dumped her, sending her into this fit of final despair.

If this sort of tragedy was not unknown to Washington, neither was it unique to that city.

For this once, he had invited her to drive directly to him; Edward was off tonight, he told her, so there would be no chauffeured limo ride from the Watergate.

But Edward was not off. Edward—the towering, discreet manservant with the faintly British accent and long, blankly cruel face, a combination driver/cook/valet highly recommended to him by a senator friend of his from Massachusetts—was waiting in the wings for Miss Petersen's cocktail to kick in, after which he would carry her to the garage where the Jag waited.

The limo, parked on the street for this once, was to follow Rawson and his deceased passenger to this prearranged spot, and Edward was overdue. Just by two minutes, but that was not typical for Edward, and it unnerved Rawson, who was not thrilled to be standing on the roadside near a sports car with his own murdered mistress in it.

But then the limo rolled into view, kicking up some gravel dust, and soon Edward—uniformed, formal, so elegant and proper—stepped out, opened the back door of the black Lincoln Continental, and Rawson crawled into the secure, leather-smelling womb of it. Edward even had a drink waiting on the extended bar tray—a Dewar's on ice.

"Unexpected traffic, sir," Edward said, as he took off.

"Thank you, Edward," Rawson said. "I'd like some privacy if you don't mind."

"Not at all, sir," the driver said, and closed off the compartment.

Rawson gulped greedily at the drink; he could not keep from looking back out the smoky glass window at the receding sight of the red Jag and the slumped blonde figure behind its wheel. When it was but a small red drop of blood on the moon-washed country landscape behind them, the limo took a hill, and the girl and the car were gone.

The following December, on a very cold lightly snowy night in Washington, D.C., against the advice of Edward (whose salary had been doubled after the "incident"), United States Senator Jim Rawson found himself, once again, drawn to the topless bar where he had met Vicki Petersen.

The Gentleman's Club, on M Street N.W., had been remodeled into a glittering chrome and mirrored wonderland, in the upscale fashion that was the current trend. Three stages, connected by runways, were being stalked by a trio of bare, bosomy beauties under disco-style flashing lights.

Rawson found a table against a mirrored wall and sat alone, away from the stages; he neither wanted to be noticed, nor to participate in the vulgar ritual of stuffing bills into dancers' G-strings. But watching these women was a hypnotic drug to him. He couldn't help himself . . .

He was working on his second Dewar's—he'd been drinking too much lately, and he knew it, but that was another compulsion he couldn't control of late—when he noticed the girl on the center stage.

But for her black hair—a long flowing mane trailing clear down to the dimples of her perfect behind—she could have been damn near Vicki's twin: a heartbreakingly cute, pug-nosed thing with full high breasts and endless legs. She was graceful like Vicki, too, and sensual, swaying with the music.

His eyes were tearing up; it was smoky in there.

He called a waitress over—the shapely blonde wore a tuxedo-like outfit, except her legs were exposed in fishnet hose. They had to shout at each other to communicate: some mindless Madonna song was blasting, the beat a pulsing thing.

"Please ask that dark-haired dancer to have a drink with me," he yelled. He gave her two twenties and told her to keep one for herself.

"Why, thank you, sir!" she hollered with wide-eyed appreciation.

Half an hour later, the young woman approached his table; she seemed to float to him, like an apparition of Vicki—albeit a dark-haired one. That hair was piled up high now, an ebony tower, and she was in a low-cut black gown, breasts pushed up by an engineering wonder of a brassiere, one long supple leg exposed by a slit up the side to her hip.

She extended a black-gloved hand. "Charmed, senator."

That threw him. He had hoped not to be recognized. But such was the price of fame.

"What's your name, dear?" he asked, rising, getting her chair.

"Brandi," she said. "I'm a big admirer of yours, senator."

Her voice was surprisingly cultured; it was also a low, catlike purr. Vicki had never seemed catlike to him, but this woman—who otherwise resembled Vicki so—was truly feline. Part of it was the black hair. Part of it was an almost oriental cast to the eyes, which wasn't like Vicki at all, though the China blue color of them was.

His tongue felt thick as he responded. "Admirer of mine?"

"Women's rights issues are important to me. So are issues of censorship. Any thinking person in my profession wants to see the arts protected."

"A wise point of view. You, uh . . . you're a very graceful dancer, Brandi."

"Thank you. I apologize for the surroundings."

"Why . . . this is downright elegant, here."

She averted his gaze. "I feel ashamed, working in a 'titty bar.' Glitz or not, that's what this is."

"I suppose. But I'm the one who should feel ashamed . . . I'm a patron, after all."

"A patron of the arts," she said, and her smile was white and dazzling, her lips transfusion red. "I *am* a dancer, and an actress. I'm only here because the money is good, and other opportunities just aren't there, right now."

"Times are difficult. Show business is a . . . challenging profession, in the best of times. Of course, I do have certain connections . . ."

She brushed his open palm with her fingertips; even with the gloves on, her touch seemed warm. "Oh—I wish I knew you better, senator. I could use a well-connected friend."

"Brandi, I . . . have to be honest with you. I'm a married man."

"I know. I've read about you. I know about your . . . tragedy."

He swallowed. "Pardon?"

Her expression seemed genuinely compassionate. "Your wife's illness. You have to stand beside her. Do the right thing by her. But still and all . . . a man needs companionship."

Her hand was on his thigh, under the table.

"And a real man," she said, "needs even more."

115

* * *

He walked with her through the underground passageway, saying, "If you come again, my dear, you'll have to allow Edward—my chauffeur—to pick you up and bring you here. I can't risk being seen . . ."

"I understand. Your reelection campaign."

He nodded. "Next year's going to be a busy time for me."

"Even so, you'll need to relax, now and then."

Her arm was in his; she was snuggling against him.

In his study, on the leather sofa, basking in the glow and warmth of the fireplace, over which hung a serene Bingham landscape, they lay locked in an embrace. His hand was on her breast and her lips were nuzzling his neck.

"Senator," she said. She seemed to be fighting her own urges. "Please . . ."

He drew away. "Is something wrong?"

She sat up and he settled in beside her, looking at her curiously. "Senator, I . . . I had hoped we could get to know each other."

"Well, I thought that was what we were doing."

She smiled; leaned in and kissed him, quickly. "You're a rogue."

It seemed an odd, almost archaic choice of words to him, even if apt.

"What did you have in mind, Brandi?"

"First of all, my real name is Sheila. Sheila Douglas." She presented her hand, in mock formal fashion, and he grinned, shook his head, then the hand.

"Hello, Sheila. You're not a reporter, are you?"

"No! No. Brandi's just my stage name. I'm a dancer at Gentleman's Club, with pretensions toward a show business career. Just as you thought. But I truly do want a friendship with you . . . well—I want more than a friendship. I want a relationship."

"I see."

"I felt . . . some chemistry between us, at the club. In the limo. In that passageway downstairs. Didn't you?"

"Frankly," he admitted, "yes."

"I know I can't ever be your wife. But I would like to be your . . . woman. The only woman in your life."

"Well, Brandi . . . Sheila . . ."

"Maybe you don't want to make that commitment. I understand. But just because I have the body of a whore doesn't mean I am one. After all, topless clubs are popular because sex isn't safe, anymore."

"Interesting piece of sociology."

"Thank you. What I'm saying is . . . if you're interested in me, as a person, as a friend, as a potential long-term relationship . . . a loving one, I think, possibly . . . I have to demand a . . . a period of courtship."

He laughed a little. "You're from the Midwest, aren't you?"

"Minnesota. Brainerd. We're both a couple of farmers, Jim. You mind if I call you 'Jim'?"

"Please. Have you had dinner?"

"No."

"Edward grills a mean steak."

"I'm a vegetarian."

"Well, he tosses a hell of a salad, too. Shall I put that in motion?"

She smiled, nodded; touched his knee.

They ate in the small, dark-wood–dominated dining room, under the miniature but intricate crystal chandelier. There was an elegance to it, and the mood of a . . . date. Much as he might want to get laid, he had to admit he liked the romance of this.

They retired to the study where the fire was dwindling; they sat and kissed and nuzzled. Tricky Dick came bounding in and jumped up, straddling them.

She squealed, but it was a squeal of delight.

"What a beautiful big tomcat! Mixed breed?"

Rawson scratched Dick's ears. "Yes. I took him in off the street."

The cat was standing on her lap, now, staring right at her, as if searching out a secret.

Sheila smiled at him. "We're one of a kind, Mr. Kitty, you and me. Strays this Good Samaritan here brought in off the street."

Then Tricky Dick curled up on her lap and she stroked him; he purred orgasmically.

"He's doing better than I am," Rawson said wryly.

"He likes me. Cats aren't always this affectionate."

"Dick's pretty easygoing, for a cat, but he seldom takes to strangers like this. I knew someone once who . . ."

He stopped short.

"What is it?" she asked.

He rose; went to the liquor cart and poured himself a tumbler of Dewar's. "Nothing." he said.

Tricky Dick had taken to Vicki just like that. Just that way . . .

"Where's his collar?" she asked.

He sat back down beside her. "He doesn't have one. He's a fat lazy old boy who never leaves the house. His litterbox is as close to the great out-of-doors as he gets."

"Poor poor kitty," she said, petting him. "How can you be so cruel, senator? I'm going to buy you a collar," she said to the cat. "You mind if I do that, Jim? Buy your kitty-cat a collar?"

"Not at all—if you can get him to wear the damn thing."

She was scratching the cat's neck; it purred rapturously.

"I think he'll love the attention," she said. "He's a male, after all. Males do love attention . . ."

"Sir," Edward said, later, "do you know where Miss Douglas lives?"

"No," Rawson admitted. He was still in the study, seated

on the couch, Tricky Dick curled up next to him, now; another tumbler of Dewar's in hand.

"The Watergate."

Rawson shrugged. Sipped. "A lot of people live at the Watergate."

"Miss Petersen once lived at the Watergate, sir."

"Your point being?"

"We know nothing about this young lady. Perhaps you should hire an investigator to look into her background."

"If anything serious begins to develop, I will. Is that all, Edward?"

"Yes, sir. Sir?"

"What is it, Edward?"

"About my raise . . ."

"You've had a raise."

"I'd like another, sir."

"I don't want to discuss this now, Edward."

"Fine, sir. But, sir?"

"*Yes,* Edward?"

"We *will* be discussing it, sir."

Three nights later, Sheila Douglas—wearing a baby-blue sweater and black ski pants and heels—was again a guest in Rawson's P Street townhouse. Edward prepared a seafood fettuccine (her vegetarianism, it seemed, pertained only to red meat), and the conversation was friendly. He prodded her about her show-business aspirations, and she talked about actresses she admired—Faye Dunaway was her favorite, but she also liked Debra Winger. Chitchat.

In the study, he sat on the couch, patted the spot next to him and she took it. She gave him a long, lingering kiss. Her tongue flicked at his teeth.

"Where's Tricky Dick?" she asked.

"My cat?"

"What other Tricky Dick do you have? Or should I ask?"

He grinned, laughed, said, "You want to make me blush,

young lady?" Then he whistled for the cat. When Dick wasn't curled up in the study, on the couch by his master, he slept in a little bed in a corner of the kitchen.

"He doesn't always come," Rawson said. "He *is* a cat, you know."

She called out, "Dick! Oh, Dick!"

And, soon, the cat came ambling in. The damn thing almost seemed to smile at her. It hopped up on her lap and began rubbing its head against her fuzzy sweater.

"He always gets a better shake out of you than me," Rawson said with a grin.

Her little purse was nearby on an end table. She reached for it and withdrew a sack with a pet-shop name on it; she took from the sack a heavy yellowish leather strap decorated with a few varicolored jewels.

"I hope Dick doesn't find the glitz effeminate," she said. "But it caught my eye at the pet store."

Rawson folded his arms. "Let's see if he stands still for *this* . . ."

The cat seemed to crane its neck yearningly as she fitted the collar about it; no protests. In fact, it was clear he liked the goddamn thing!

"You're a wonder, Sheila. But now I have something for you."

He rose and went to a drawer in the mahogany tambour secretary against the wall. He removed the simple strand of glittering diamonds and held it out gently as he walked over to her.

"It's not a collar, exactly," he said. "In fact, it's just a bracelet."

"Oh, Jim! It's lovely! A tennis bracelet . . . oh, I've always wanted one . . ."

She affixed it to her wrist and then held out her slender, red-nailed hand and gazed at the sparkling stones appreciatively. "Oh, Jim. How can I ever thank you?"

He sat down, slipped his arm around her. "There are . . . traditional ways I could think of."

She kissed him. The sound of the purring cat, as she stroked it, providing distracting background music.

"I think I could love you, Sheila."

"I feel that way about you, Jim. And I will thank you for this lovely gift. I want you to know I'll thank you the right way for it, too. But . . ."

"Still too soon? I can wait. I'm a patient man."

She smirked and shook her head. "It's not that. It's . . . you know. The wrong time of the month for me. I'm sorry."

"Don't apologize for biology. That's what this is all about anyway, isn't it? Biology."

"Partly," she admitted. She stroked his face with one hand, her other hand petting the purring cat.

A week later, Rawson was getting worried about Sheila. He had called her at the Gentleman's Club and she'd been warm, friendly, but hadn't made another date with him.

"Please understand," she said. "I . . . this is embarrassing."

"What?"

"I have really long, hard periods, okay? Cramps you wouldn't believe. And cramps or not, right now I have to keep this lousy dancing up, to keep the rent paid."

"Well, I can handle that. Quit! I'll take care of you."

"Jim . . . you're wonderful. But it *is* too soon to talk that way. Next week. I promise."

That had been almost a week ago; several similar but briefer conversations had followed. Last night, out of desperation, he had gone to the club, looking for her; he was told she no longer worked there. He had even risked going to the Watergate, personally, to her apartment, where his knocking at her door went unanswered.

Now, early the following morning, he sat in his silk robe, brooding in his study, staring at the unlighted fireplace, scratching Tricky Dick around his collar.

"Sir ..."

"Edward! I didn't hear you. Where the hell's my breakfast, man?"

"It'll have to wait, sir."

"Why in hell?"

"You should see the morning papers, sir. It's ... not good, sir."

"What are you talking about?"

Edward, looking solemn, and dressed in a dark suit with dark tie that represented his street clothes, handed him the *Washington Post*.

The headline shouted RAWSON SUSPECT IN MURDER INVESTIGATION, and above it a smaller heading said: POLICE SOURCES SAY. Just glancing, he took in his own picture, and another of Vicki, under which were the words SUICIDE OR MURDER?

Edward spoke in a whisper: "She is the girl's sister."

"What ..."

"Sheila Douglas."

"What the hell are you saying, Edward?" Rawson was transfixed by this front page from Hell.

"Sheila Douglas," Edward said slowly, as if speaking to a child, his barely audible voice nonetheless like a scream in Rawson's brain, "is Vicki Petersen's sister."

"Edward ... ?"

"She took a job where her sister had danced, hoping you would return to the scene of the crime. She had reason to believe you would. Apparently, the late Vicki had told her all about you."

"Oh, my God."

"When you take time to read that article, you'll discover that Miss Douglas ... actually, Miss Petersen, Sheila Peter-

sen . . . has given the authorities tapes of conversations between myself . . . your 'majordomo' . . . and you, sir."

"Oh. Oh, God. Just two nights ago . . . we negotiated
your latest raise . . ."

Edward continued in a barely audible, increasingly harsh
whisper. "And we mentioned Miss Petersen's murder, the
other Miss Petersen that is, as the motivation behind that
salary increase. Yes, sir. The little bitch has had this townhouse bugged."

"That's impossible! And this story is impossible. If this
had been brewing, my phone would have rung off the hook
last night with police and reporters . . ."

"Have you seen your answering machine, sir? The little
red light is blinking furiously."

Rawson's hand came to his face. "Oh, my God, Edward!
Where does that leave us?"

"I had hoped you might have some thoughts on that subject." Edward sighed. "But since you don't . . ."

Edward's hand came out from behind his back and
swung the wrench.

Rawson's surprised expression, below his caved-in skull,
remained frozen as he toppled off the couch onto the
parquet floor, where blood began to spill, then pool, glisten-
ingly.

Tricky Dick, the cat, startled, leapt from the couch, looking for safe haven. Edward didn't consider the cat worthy
of notice as he wiped the bloody wrench clean of his prints,
thinking, *For what good it will do me,* and made his escape
out the underground passageway.

His escape from the house, that is.

In the alley, the police were waiting. Edward sighed, put
up his hands; in the police car, nearby, sitting on the rider's
side in front, was Sheila Petersen. She was smiling like the
cat that ate the canary.

As for Tricky Dick, he was asleep in his bed in the corner of the kitchen. The only thing the tiny transmitter in his collar was picking up now was the deep, purringlike sound of the tom's breathing.

Photo Opportunity

·

Larry Segriff

There was a branch poking me in the face, but I couldn't squirm enough to get away from it. What made it worse was that I probably didn't have to be in the bushes. We'd done this enough times and never had any problems, but still, I guess one of the reasons we'd made it for so long was that we didn't take any chances we didn't have to.

I heard his low whistle then and relaxed. A few minutes longer and I could move. Grinning, I flipped the little lever and opened the cage. Tom streaked out, not even bothering to stretch. He knew what was coming. He was ready.

On the other side of the yard, Jamie was letting Tiger out. I grinned again, careful to keep my teeth from showing. The fun was about to begin.

I could feel them drawing closer to each other. Both cats were black as night, impossible to see in the nearly total darkness, but this was an old, familiar routine for all of us.

"Three ... two ... one," I counted silently. Right on cue, an explosion of sound rent the night.

Cat fight. At one o'clock in the morning, it was guaranteed to piss people off.

Tom and Tiger were giving it all they had, their yowls and screams sounding ferocious even to me. Within minutes, lights were going on all around us. Tom and Tiger

125

gave it a little bit longer, separating for a moment and then coming together again even louder than before. They split, then, each one vanishing once again into the darkness, finding his own way back to his waiting cage.

They were well trained, those cats. I smiled a third time as I bolted Tom in, but even as I did so I was taking careful note of which houses stayed dark. Later, when things quieted down, those were the ones Jamie and I would hit.

"Holy shit!" Jamie's voice cut across the silence of the room, but his words could just as easily have been mine.

This was the third house we'd entered since Tom and Tiger had done their thing. It was going on toward three o'clock in the morning. At this rate, we might have time to hit two more. A good night for us, if they all turned out like the first ones.

Now, though, we had to pause in our work and just stare at the photographs lining one wall of this den. It was dark in there, but our penlights were sufficient to illuminate an entire strata of our nation's history: there were maybe three dozen framed photographs, all showing the same guy, and all showing him with one or more political figures from the last twenty years. There were four different presidents, from both political parties, and more senators and congressmen than you could shake a federal indictment at.

"Jesus," I whispered. "Who is this guy?"

Jamie moved in closer, and in the shadows I could see him nod. "Yeah, I remember him. He was a big wheel in the Senate for a long time. Probably still would be if they hadn't passed all those term limitations."

This had me worried. I mean, D.C. was one of the cities on our circuit—we took our traveling cat fight to more than a dozen places before repeating, as a rule—and we'd broken into the homes of senators, congressmen, and even future presidents before. It was just that this was the first time I'd known about it while we were doing it.

"Should we leave?" I asked.

Jamie just turned and grinned at me. "Nah. Like I said, I remember this guy. If anybody deserves a visit from us, it's him."

"Are you sure you got all the alarms? He probably knows people in the defense industry."

That grin again. Jamie was nothing if not confident. "I'm sure."

It was a silly question, I guess. Jamie had about a dozen different ways to kill the power to an entire neighborhood. Sometimes, he did something to the electrical substation. Other times, like tonight, he took a bird that Tiger had killed—Tom was lousy at catching birds—and used it to short out a transformer. All things that looked accidental. On top of that, he also turned off the power at each house that we entered, and disconnected their phone lines, too.

He was cautious, competent, and thorough, and I shouldn't have been worried. I just didn't know enough about it to know if his precautions were enough. The electronics bit was his responsibility. I was lucky to know there was a difference between a green wire and a red one. Damned if I knew what that difference was. My job was to get us in after he'd done his thing. Well, that and finding all the best hiding places. I had something of a knack for that.

"What if he's home?" I asked. "He's pretty old. You can see that in these pictures. What if he didn't hear our boys out there? What if he gets up to pee and sees us?"

Jamie just shrugged. "What if he does? It's not like it hasn't happened before."

"Yeah." That was true, and we'd always gotten away. I didn't like it, though. Not like Jamie did. "But—"

"Christ," he interrupted me. "You're such a worrier anymore. Let's just do our thing and get out, all right?"

"Yeah. It's just that this guy is such a celebrity and all. I guess I'm a little intimidated."

127

He flashed me that famous grin again. "This guy's a crook, just like us. Now stop worrying about it, will ya? Where should I look?"

"The desk," I said, finally turning away from the rogue's gallery on the wall. "Lower right-hand drawer. Nine times out of ten, they'll have something there."

"Right. Now you do something, too."

I nodded, but he was turning away and didn't see me.

I started in on the bookcases. They lined every wall except the one with the photos. I didn't stay with them for long, though. Even in the dark, with only my penlight to guide me, I could tell that the books had never been read. They were free of dust, and all neatly aligned on their shelves, but they had that feel of newness to them. Leather bindings, like these, pick up oil when they're handled. They develop a certain texture, like well-worn gloves. These had probably been delivered by the case, and only handled when they were loaded onto the shelves.

All, that is, except for one shelf. This was near the desk, and down low to the floor. Handy for a guy sitting in that leather chair, and not conspicuous. They were paperbacks, not leather-bound books, and they'd been read a lot. Curious, I pulled one out and looked at it.

The Story of O. Flicking my light across the broken spines, I quickly saw a couple of other titles I recognized: *Fanny Hill* and the collected works of Anaïs Nin. There was even one large, metal-bound book that was just called, *Sex.* I grinned to myself in the dark. The old pervert, I thought.

I put the book back and went over to see what Jamie had found. He had the right-hand drawer out, and I tsked softly when I saw how he'd gouged the wood to force the lock. He should have had me open it. He knew how I hated to see things vandalized.

To make matters worse, the drawer had been empty, at least as far as we were concerned. There were some papers and stuff in there, and what looked like a large, leather-bound accountant's book, but nothing of interest to us.

I tsked again, shook my head, and turned back to the photos on the wall. Something about them was calling to me, and I wanted to know what.

Slowly I reached out and removed one that was near the center. It had this same guy—Clark, I suddenly remembered was his name—posing with a former president. One I'd liked, sort of.

The frame was nothing special, just a postmodern black-and-silver plastic thing done up to look like chrome and ebony. Or maybe it was supposed to be silver and jet. In the dim glow of my penlight, it just looked cheap.

The glass was nonglare and heavy. In fact, as I looked at the picture, it seemed to me that the whole thing was slightly deeper than normal. Turning it over, I slid the back out and removed both the picture itself and the padding.

Jamie came up about then. "What're you doing?" he asked in a low voice. "Looking for autographs?"

He'd never understood how I could find things the way I did. For that matter, I'd never understood it, either. He kidded me about it a lot, but he never, ever interfered.

The photo was a regular eight-by-ten glossy. There was an inscription on the front, but I'd been able to see that without taking the frame down. The back was unmarked.

Disappointed, I started to put everything back, ignoring Jamie's snort of derision—he'd have just tossed it on the floor—when I noticed that the cardboard backing was really two pieces stuck together. There was a slight gap between them that I might easily have missed, but Jamie's penlight had picked it up.

Slowly, I separated the two pieces. Sandwiched between them were several more eight-by-tens—four of them—of that same former president. These were much older, however, showing him a good twenty years younger than the photo in front, and they weren't nearly as professionally done. They were quite clear, however, leaving no doubt as to what the former president was doing, or who he was doing it to.

"Holy shit," I said. "Jamie, do you know what we have here?"

"Yeah," he said. "A golden opportunity."

I nodded. "Let's see what else this guy's got."

It turned out that every photo on the wall held secrets. Some were surprising. Some were almost comical. All were valuable.

"Jesus," Jamie whispered when we were all through. "This guy had dirt on everybody."

"Seems like it," I agreed.

"No wonder he's got so much money."

"Nah." I shook my head. "I seem to recall reading that he was born into a rich family. I don't think he was black-mailing these people for money."

"What, then?"

"Come here." I took the stack of glossies over to the desk and got out the leather-bound ledger Jamie had found earlier. Flipping it open at random, I glanced at the figures and started nodding.

"What?" Jamie asked.

"Look." I pointed at the first column. "These numbers are probably file numbers, or a coded reference for the people in the photos. We could probably figure it out, if we wanted, because these," I shifted my finger over to the remaining two columns of figures, "will tell us."

Jamie bent down and looked. "HR141," he read out loud, "S242. They don't make any sense to me."

"Me either," I said, "at least not for sure, but my guess is that these are legislative bills from both the House and the Senate. I'll bet you that each one of these represents a certain vote."

"Sure," he interrupted me. "One column is for yes votes, the other for no."

I nodded. "That's the way I see it."

Jamie reached out and flipped a few of the pages. He let out a low whistle as we saw just how many votes over the past couple of decades this guy had probably influenced.

"Explains a lot, doesn't it?" I asked.

He only nodded.

"What do you think we should do with them?" he asked.

"Use 'em. Hell, if nothing else, maybe we can force them to legalize burglary."

We grinned at that. Not too much later, Jamie went off to search the rest of the house. I should have gone with him, if only to keep the damage to a minimum, but I had a feeling there was something else in that den. Something I was missing.

I couldn't find it. I could hear Jamie as his search took him from room to room, but, unlike him, I was getting no closer to what I sought. Finally, in frustration, I went out to the truck and got Tom.

I had a knack for finding things. He had a nose for it. I swear, that cat could smell money, among other things. Over the years, he'd led me to a lot of well-hidden secrets.

Both cages were nestled in the back of the carryall, along with the half-dozen or so oversized backpacks we brought with us to carry things. We always kept the truck at least a block away from the houses we hit. We tended to hit up-scale neighborhoods, and the people who lived there tended to inform the cops when they were going to be gone for any length of time. A strange vehicle sitting in a supposedly empty driveway or in front of a vacationer's home was like a red flag to the patrolling officers. That was why we had the backpacks—so we could carry things relatively inconspicuously, and it was also why we always had to limit what we took to smaller, more portable items.

We could get away with carrying hiking gear down the street, even at three in the morning, but even the dumbest cop was bound to be suspicious if we were carrying framed artwork or expensive stereo equipment.

The bags we'd filled from the first two houses were near the cages, and I took a moment to look at them and smile. The cash we'd found would see us through a lot of lean times, and the jewels—even at the rates we had to pay to Three-Finger Mike—would buy a lot of beer.

Still smiling, I unlatched Tom's cage. "Come on, boy," I said. "There's work to do."

Tiger was at the door of his cage, and I could see his tail twitching. He hated to be left out of anything that included Tom. I grinned, and after a moment opened his cage, too.

"All right, Tiger. You can come, too." As far as I knew, he was no good at finding things, but at least he'd never gotten in the way.

The cats paced me as we walked, Tom on my right, Tiger on my left, and they stayed in perfect formation. I'd seen them do that before, but I still had to smile as I watched them.

My good mood didn't last, however.

I decided to walk around Clark's house once, just to try and get its layout firmly in my head. I was still convinced I was missing something, and if Tom couldn't find it, I wanted to be able to figure it out.

There was a silver sedan parked out on the street in front of the house. It was the only car parked out in the open like that, but I didn't pay it much attention. Over the years, Jamie and I had both learned to spot cop cars, marked and unmarked, and this one didn't send up any red flags for me. As I glanced over at it, however, I saw a match flare dimly within, and suddenly things didn't look so good.

As soon as I could, I cut between a couple of houses and started working my way back to Jamie. It was time to call it a night.

We didn't make it. I got back inside Clark's house all right, and found Jamie up on the second floor. When I told him what I'd seen, he agreed with me that we should leave, but then we'd learned years ago that anytime either of us felt uncomfortable we would knock off. The way we figured it, there were lots of houses to hit. No need to press our luck.

Besides, he'd made a pretty good haul. His backpack was full, but I didn't get a chance to ask what he'd found.

We were going down the stairs, Tom and Tiger invisible shadows at our sides, when a couple of figures stepped out of the darkness below. There wasn't much light coming in through the windows, but what there was glinted off the metal in their hands.

Shit, I thought.

Beside me, Jamie, who could sometimes think pretty quickly, snapped his fingers once. The men below us didn't say anything, so we continued moving slowly down the stairs.

When we reached the bottom, the two of them stepped back, out of range of any sudden lunges on our part, and motioned for us to precede them into the den. We didn't want to, but neither of us could see a way to avoid it.

We went.

My backpack was over by the desk, looking pretty empty. I wondered if the photos were still in it. They were all that I'd managed to stuff in there, those and that leather-bound ledger Jamie had found.

The men behind us gestured for us to go over by the desk. Once we were there, one of them spoke for the first time.

"You steal from Missah Clark, no? What you find?"

They were shorter than us, though their guns made them look much larger, and in the dim light I could see they were Asiatic, but that's all I knew about them.

Beside me, Jamie shrugged. "The usual. Some cash, a bit of jewelry, that sort of thing."

The other one hissed and said something in a fluent, sibilant language. The first one nodded and said, "We care nothing for that. You find pictures, you tell us, hey?"

"Pictures?" Jamie said, sounding puzzled. I let him talk. He was a better actor than I. Besides, he was the one with the plan. I had to let him set it up.

The second one spoke again, and again I didn't catch a word of it. I only knew he didn't sound happy.

"Yes," the first one said. "Pictures. Very—how do you say it?—*valuable* pictures. You give them to us, yes?"

"Who are you?" Jamie was playing a dangerous game, but it was for a reason. I thought I knew what that reason was, and I felt the skin on the back of my neck crawl as he gambled with our lives.

More fluid speech. The first one nodded, then said, "Let us say, we represent a foreign interest. These pictures will help us ease certain, ah, difficulties, between our governments. They will make for a better trade agreement, you see? It is no different than how these pictures have been used before, no? So, now you give them to us, and everybody win, okay?"

"Okay," Jamie said. "They're in my backpack. If I move slowly, can I get them out without being shot?"

All of a sudden, I was no longer sure what his game was. Sometimes—often, in fact—we found guns in houses like this. Had he found one upstairs? Was his whole intent merely to fish it out? God, I hoped not. I didn't think I would survive such a move.

Our friend was speaking again, the one I couldn't understand. We all listened, and then his partner said, "Of course. But, as you say, move very slowly."

Jamie nodded, slipped the pack off his shoulders, and started to kneel. It was then that he snapped his fingers again, and Tom and Tiger made their move.

He must have been waiting for them to sidle along the edges of the room, sticking to the shadows. Whether he knew they were in position, or whether he was merely hoping he'd given them enough time, I didn't know. I heard him snap his fingers and I started diving toward the floor.

The cats were quiet. They only made noise when we wanted them to. Out of the corner of my eye, I saw two black streaks launch themselves from the side, twin arrows aimed at those glinting gun hands.

Tiger was on my side, pitted against the one who'd spoken to us, and I saw his jaws lacerate the wrist. Blood spurted as the gun dropped to the floor, and I knew that both the artery and the tendons had been slashed.

Way to go, Tiger, I thought. Instinctively, I started moving toward the fallen gun.

Tom wasn't so lucky. He hit the Asian's gun, not the wrist, and for a moment I saw him hanging from the barrel by his jaws, his claws frantically searching for fingers or hand or anything.

He didn't find it.

Jamie was throwing his backpack; I was leaping for the gun; Tom was squirming for his life. None of us was in time. The barrel dipped, pulled down by the cat's weight, and then the gun went off. Even in the dark I could see how his side exploded outward, and I cried out in reaction.

A moment later Jamie's backpack hit the smaller man and then his partner's gun was in my hand. It almost seemed to rise of its own accord, turning to bear down on the man who'd killed my cat.

I fired once, but my anger made me jerk the trigger instead of squeezing it. My shot went wide, hitting him high in the shoulder, hurting him badly but not killing him as I'd intended.

That one shot was all I had in me. I tossed the gun at Jamie, and then went over to where Tom lay motionless on the floor. Tiger was already there, sniffing at his partner in crime, and letting out soft, plaintive mews.

Amazingly, Tom was still alive. Using my penlight, I

could see that his side was badly torn, but perhaps not as badly as I'd first thought.

I turned toward Jamie. "We have to go," I said. "We've got to get him to a vet."

"But—" he started, making a single, small motion with his gun to indicate the room around us: the photos, his bulging backpack, the foreign agents. There was a fortune there, waiting for us, if we knew how to use it. And if we had time enough to grab it.

I didn't say anything. I knew what he meant, but in my mind there was no choice to make.

He held my gaze for one heartbeat, then another, before he nodded.

As gently as I could, I scooped up my cat and headed for the door. I think Jamie might have looked back once, in curiosity or regret. I didn't.

Together, then, we vanished into the night.

A Taste for the Good Life
•
Dan Brawner

Henry probed delicately with the polished silver tines of
the fondue fork. This may be a sticky, messy business, he
thought, marveling at his own perversity, but it always
makes my mouth water. He chuckled giddily. Henry's great,
red, bulbous nose wrinkled autonomically at the pungent
wave that passed before it. He shifted his considerable bulk
and leaned forward, balancing on both knees and one dim-
pled hand, looking like a circus elephant about to perform
a headstand.

Suddenly, Henry let out a little cry of joy. The fondue
fork clattered to the floor, its ebony handle tapping out a
brief but lively African rhythm. With a flourish, Henry produced a monogrammed linen handkerchief, ceremoniously
dusted around a lump in the litter box and, with great rel-
ish, plucked it out and squeezed it between sausagelike fingers.

"Good boy!" Henry crooned. "Good boy, Carnegie!"

Carnegie, Henry's cat, so named for his uncanny ability
to win friends and influence people, rolled languidly on his
back and purred with abandon.

"See what you have here?" Henry said, now all flushed
and breathless. "See what you brought me?" He held the
object up to the kitchen light. "Well, I'll be blessed! Beryl-

137

lium aluminate. Chrysoberyl. A flawless, green cat's-eye!" Henry hefted the stone expertly. "I'd say eight—maybe ten carats."

To celebrate, Henry decided to treat himself to brunch at the Colonnade in the ANA Hotel. Even at thirty-four dollars per person, it wasn't the most expensive place in Washington, D.C. But he liked the elegant English decor and the thought of the steamed beef dumplings in their own little bamboo basket made him quiver with delight. And Carnegie was rather fond of the *coulibiac* of salmon.

As Henry was helping himself to his second macadamia-nut tart and listening to the ethereal strains of a Bach intervention played by the house harpist Holly Avesian, he fell into a reverie.

If Auntie Margaret could only see him now! Wouldn't she just bite her sharp, little tongue? Fat Henry! Clumsy, good-for-nothing Henry! You'll eat up all the profits, Henry! That miserable, greasy little bistro, Henry thought. His swelling disgust was suddenly ameliorated by the satisfying crunch of a macadamia nut. And yet, to think, he owed everything he had to Auntie Margaret. After all, she did give him Carnegie.

"You might as well take the cat," Margaret said the day she finally made good on her promise to throw him out. "It's the only friend you'll ever have."

And what a friend! Henry absently popped open the top two buttons on his waistcoat and smiled. Of all the cats in the whole world, his own dear Carnegie was probably the only one that ate jewels.

Henry discovered this astonishing fact quite by accident one day when he was mooning over a Rolex in Tiffany's. The rent was three days overdue but he felt he needed the distraction and nice things had always been a comfort to him. The clerk frowned when Carnegie jumped up on the counter but in no time at all they were fast friends. When a paying customer distracted the clerk for a moment, Carnegie slipped inside the display case and gobbled up two half-carat diamonds. By the time the clerk had turned around, the wily Siamese was rubbing against her elbow, purring for all he was worth—which, at the time, was about $2,500.

Henry sighed. The poor girl lost her job but from that time on, Henry and Carnegie were in business. Eight years and thirty-seven cities and still nobody had suspected them. Even that time in Scottsdale when Carnegie ate the 14-carat emerald and set off the alarm, the store owners finally had to apologize to the customers for the malfunction in the security system. The one tense moment was when one of the cops wanted to take Carnegie home with him. Henry knew that not having ID tags could mean a trip to the pound for Carnegie. But the alternative could mean a trip to the slammer for Henry. And Henry was sure he'd never get used to penitentiary fare.

However, the officer's captain talked him out of adopting the stray cat, and when the confusion was over, Carnegie gleefully bounded out to the parking lot where Henry was waiting with the air conditioner on high.

Henry dabbed the corners of his mouth and neatly folded his napkin. The high arches of the Colonnade and the colorful floor-to-ceiling windows rose up to meet his gaze. The elaborate crystal chandelier glinted off the sparkling swan ice-sculpture near the salad bar like some rare treasure fit for taking. Henry felt wise and rich as Solomon, basking in his righteous wealth. This was the life to which he was born. Had there ever been any doubt?

Carnegie purred like a well-tuned Model T. Remains of the cold salmon lay abandoned in his Chinese porcelain dish.

"Now how are you going to have the strength for our next adventure if you don't eat your din-din?" Henry rubbed Carnegie behind the ear.

DANGER IN D.C.

The cat closed his intelligent, almond-shaped blue eyes and leaned ecstatically into the pressure, clearly with no thought beyond the present moment. The future held no allure for him. He was happy.

Henry had tried suggesting to Carnegie what kinds of jewels he might eat. For days before a job, Carnegie was shown photos of diamonds. But he swallowed a garnet instead. If Henry put pictures of rubies by his dish, Carnegie would eat an amethyst. Lapis lazuli seemed to make him hungry for sapphires, and jade only reminded him of his fondness for creamy white moonstones.

Still, this one time, Henry figured it was worth a try. All around the hotel room were life-sized photographs of a 44.5-carat blue stone set in a relatively modest necklace.

"You see, Carnegie," Henry said, sounding as professional as he could, "the Hope diamond was in all likelihood, cut from the legendary French Blue which had been brought to France from India in 1668 to become part of the crown jewels of Louis XIV. Mysteriously, the French Blue was stolen in 1792 and never recovered. Poor Louis never got his hands on the Hope but we will, won't we, Carnegie?"

Henry realized this was a tall order, even for Carnegie. But the cat had been known to pry precious stones loose from their settings if he particularly liked them.

Shaking with anticipation, Henry bundled Carnegie into the rented Lincoln and headed off for the Smithsonian's Hall of Gems. Of course, his regular connection wouldn't know what to do with a diamond the size of the Hope. It would be the heist of the century. It would make headlines all over the world. He'd be rich and everyone would call him "sir."

Henry did not have to lead his cat through the doors to the National Museum of Natural History. Carnegie had a nose for jewels. A block away from Tiffany's and Carnegie would become animated and alert. His tail stood straight up like an antenna. For some cats, it's catnip. For Carnegie, it was precious stones.

Henry opened the passenger side of the sedan. Carnegie's sensitive eyes dilated at the sight of the museum. Clearly, his mission was already fixed in his mind.

Carnegie allowed Henry to stroke his back but the muscles were winding tighter, ready to spring.

"Good boy, Carnegie," Henry said, trying to soothe him. "There's no hurry. Take your time. Don't get caught. I'll be waiting just around the corner. And when you're through, I'll bring you back a nice piece of chicken Kiev from that place you like on M Street."

Carnegie settled into a crouch, his head resting between his front paws. Like a thoroughbred at the starting gate, he was trying to be patient.

"All right, all right, boy," Henry seemed to relent. "I'll make it for you myself with fresh basil and lots of butter. Just be a good boy and come home soon."

Carnegie turned his head toward Henry. Those piercing blue eyes now demanded an answer.

"Okay," Henry said softly. "Go on!"

Without even looking at where he was leaping, Carnegie jumped straight into the path of an old woman in a gray-and-purple jumpsuit. She had been muttering to herself, twirling her umbrella overhead in the bright sunlight.

"Oh!" the old woman shrieked. She managed to glance in the direction of the museum in time to see Carnegie streak up to the building and slip through the doors.

"That . . . that was a cat!" she stammered.

Henry nodded.

"It was your cat!" The old woman shook a bony finger accusingly at him.

Henry's cholesterol-coated heart pounded in his chest.

141

"My cat?" he said, trying to gain control of his voice. "You're mistaken."

A cruel smile crept over her thin lips. "I saw that cat jump out of your car. It was your cat!" The old witch twirled her black umbrella in the sunlight.

Henry blinked, momentarily hypnotized. "Cat?" he enunciated slowly. "What cat were you referring to, madam?" Henry held up two puffy palms in the "all gone" gesture.

The old harridan was still sputtering as Henry drove off to find a discreet parking place. He looked at his watch and sneered. It was a $28 Piaget copy. He made a mental note to go out and buy the genuine article first thing in the morning.

Henry slid the long black sedan into a narrow parking space. Almost immediately, a rusty 1972 Toyota pulled in alongside him. The driver, in fashionably ragged jeans, probably a student, hopped out and looked appreciatively at the Lincoln and gave Henry the "thumbs up." Henry raised his eyebrows in recognition. Even a cat can look at a king, he thought and smiled at his little joke.

Henry reclined in the luxurious seat and closed his eyes. This is the life, he mused, a getaway driver for a cat. The hours are good. The pay is terrific. Still, Henry thought, it was hardly respectable. What would he tell people at parties? What parties? Nobody ever invited him anywhere. Auntie Margaret was right. If it weren't for Carnegie, he'd have no friends at all.

Henry scrunched lower in the seat. So who cares? Money may not buy happiness but what a charming consolation prize!

And what better place to be consoled than Paris? He will eat his way through every five-star restaurant in the city. Maître d's will bow when they see him coming. They will call him by name and describe in detail the delicacies they have prepared for him. And when the meal is over, they will hover around, terrified that he is not delighted with their performance.

He will become a legend, known throughout Europe—a connoisseur's connoisseur. Royalty will invite him to dine with them, to pass judgment on their wine cellars. Perhaps, speculation will arise as to the source of his wealth. Although he will neither confirm nor deny it, rumors will begin to circulate that he was the mastermind who spirited away the Hope diamond. Perhaps . . .

Henry woke to a sharp rapping on his window. He looked up to see a uniformed police officer who smiled and gestured for him to roll it down.

Henry gasped. He fumbled for the electric window-opener and caught, out of the corner of his eye, the red expiration flag on his parking meter.

"I'm terribly sorry, officer. I must have dozed off and forgot to put money in the meter . . ."

The policeman waved away Henry's explanation. "That's not my department," he said cordially. "I just wanted to know if this was your cat."

The officer lifted Carnegie up to Henry's eye level. Carnegie, obviously happy to see him, jumped into Henry's car. Standing behind the patrolman, stood the old woman with the umbrella, leering at him.

"If this is your cat," the patrolman said carefully, "you'll be glad to know that he's feeling much better now."

Squad cars began gliding silently into position around Henry's Lincoln, lights flashing, blocking every possible exit.

"Was the cat ill?" Henry said, barely above a whisper.

The cop tipped back his cap with the end of his nightstick. "It seems something he ate disagreed with him."

Henry swallowed. "Was it the Hope?" he inquired weakly.

"No, sir." The officer shook his head. "It was the Rosser Reeves star ruby."

Henry beamed. "One hundred thirty-eight point seven carats of perfection!" Henry cradled his cat lovingly in his arms. "Carnegie," he said. "You have such good taste."

The Cat's-Paw Affair

•

Gary A. Braunbeck

Oh I am a cat that likes to
Gallop about doing good.
—STEVIE SMITH
"The Galloping Cat"

I watched the man pull himself and his bleeding nose up from the floor.

Already I could hear shouts and footsteps outside, followed by loud pounding—I'd locked the doors behind me when I forced my way in.

"I figure I've got about sixty seconds," I said, pulling the gun from my pocket and pointing it right between his eyes. "Now, goddamnit, you tell me where Winnie is!"

The shouts outside grew louder. Someone shot out one of the locks. My heart was trip-hammering and my hands were shaking because I figured I was going to be dead very shortly.

And here I'd thought this would be just another grooming job . . .

I had just entered my suite at the Georgetown Inn when the phone rang. I answered to hear the voice on the other end say, "Hello, Quixote."

145

"Aldonza!" I said.

"Uh-uh, watch it, buster. I'm *Dulcinea* these days."

"I'm confused, then—which one of you once urped in the backseat of my car when we were in high school?"

"Jerk."

"Strumpet."

"Geek."

"Liberal!"

"Okay, you win."

There's something about exchanging insults with the First Lady while standing in an expensive hotel suite that tends to make you feel that life doesn't bite.

"How are you, Tim?"

"Shaking from the flight."

"Not go well?"

"The flight was fine. You forget how badly I travel."

"No, I don't. *You* were the one who urped in the backseat of your car in high school. After the Jethro Tull concert, remember? I had to drive all the way back from Cleveland."

"Oh . . . yeah. It's all coming back to me now. So much for selling my tawdry tale to the tabloids."

"Nice alliteration."

"So pleased you noticed. God, Karen, it's great to hear your voice again." Karen Williams—before she'd married then-Lt. Gov. Jim Ryan—had been my closest friend in high school and college. And I'll state here for the record that, despite rumors, we never once did the Silk Sheet Samba.

"I'm glad you could come," she said. "Jim—excuse me—*the president* and I can't wait to see you."

"When can I expect you to bring Winnie by the hotel?"

"I've got a luncheon, a small dinner, and a contestants' breakfast to host. Whew! You know, I'll bet that I haven't seen Winnie for more than an hour in the last month. It's been . . . well, *Washington.* My assistant will bring her by in the morning."

"Complete with a Secret Service escort?"

"You betcha."

Winnie was the White House cat—a twenty-one-pound, long-haired black Persian the Ryans had adopted from a local animal shelter when Jim was governor of Ohio. Until Jim's landslide presidential victory eighteen months ago, I'd been Winnie's sole groomer. I had been "summoned" to Washington to prepare Winnie for her role of mascot in the opening ceremonies of the International D.C. Cat Show—an assignment I did not take lightly.

"So," I said, "when exactly will the First Family make time for *moi*?"

"We might squeeze in a few seconds before the opening of the show on Friday. I'll pat your head as I glide past you in the hall."

"You're an evil woman."

"And you're a wuss."

"Left-wing tramp."

"Nonpartisan dipshit."

"Hussy."

"Animal lover!"

"Okay, you win," I said. "I'll see you at the show, then?"

"In thirty-six hours. Afterward you're coming back to the White House with me."

"But—"

"No 'but,' thank you very much. Jim and I have a terrific evening planned for you—providing his address to the protesters doesn't go on for hours."

"Protesters? Is there some kind of trouble?"

"Nothing you haven't already read about. Animal rights activists are staging demonstrations on Constitution Avenue and at the cat show on Friday."

"I can understand the cat show—exploitation of animals and all that—but why in front of the White House?"

"Because Monday morning's the vote on FLT–82.

C'mon, Tim! You *have* to have gotten something about that in the mail."

I had. FLT–82 was a new (read: *experimental*) drug concocted in some lab in Geneva that supposedly was a miracle cure for FeLV—Feline Leukemia Virus, a deadly, contagious, and always fatal disease that strikes a full one-third of the cats in the U.S. and whose early stages are undetectable; by the time any warning signs *do* manifest themselves, it's too late. Even though one of the scientists who came up with the formula was an American who was in Geneva as part of a "scientific exchange" program, Jim Ryan—who'd gotten the animal rights people behind him early on in the campaign—had promised said activists he would not allow the drug to be brought into this country because of the "inhumane" methods employed in its testing.

"Do you think the vote will be in favor?"

"Sorry, Tim, but I won't talk politics over the phone. You understand, of course."

"Yes, sorry. National security, blah-blah-blah."

"Don't pout, it's annoying. If you behave yourself, Friday night I'll let you do spitballs off the East Balcony."

"No, you won't, but thanks for the thought."

"You never were any fun."

"Then why'd you hang out with me?"

"Because I wasn't any fun then, either."

I was smiling so widely when I hung up the phone I'm surprised my jaw didn't crack.

I fixed a drink at the minibar and stood looking out the window. It was a little after eleven Wednesday morning. I had a great view of the Potomac River and Key Bridge in the distance, with the austere architecture of Georgetown University as a plus. The sunlight made silvery glissandos on the water as a pair of the university team sculls slipped smoothly along. Traffic buzzed busily on the Whitehurst while joggers traversed the dried-out southerly bank of the C&O Canal.

When Karen had called the shop to invite me to D.C., she mentioned the name of the Georgetown groomer she used, so I was curious to check out my replacement. Groomers are a fiercely competitive lot (some almost viciously so) and I was no different; if I could pay a "professional" courtesy call on the shop and have their operation give me a few ideas on how to improve my own business, all the better. At least there was no question of a hidden agenda this way. Some groomers will go so far as to send in a cat's-paw (read: *spy*) to apply for a job at a rival shop, and after a couple of weeks the paw quits and goes back to the enemy camp with buckets of "inside" information, including copies of the files kept on clients' pets, making it easy to steal patrons. A startling number of grooming businesses have gone belly up because of such underhanded tactics. I hoped that Winnie's current groomer wasn't like that as I started on my way.

I walked up M Street for a while, turned right, and found myself staring up the seventy-five steps made famous in the film version of *The Exorcist*.

"Your sense of direction," I whispered to myself, "is, as always, for shit." I spent twenty minutes more roaming the tree-shaded cobblestone streets like some innocent simpleton out of a Kosinski novel before swallowing my pride and asking a street vendor for directions. Shortly thereafter I was standing in front of the magnificent brick building that housed the Cox's Row Grooming Salon.

The first floor was the grooming salon itself—four bathing areas, a large expanse of holding cages, each with its own gentle air-dryer unit, eight ideal grooming tables with attached harnesses (used when necessary), three supply closets, and an employee clean-up area that was nicer than my kitchen; the second floor was used to board animals whose owners traveled, and the third floor, which was still being remodeled, had as yet no designated purpose.

All this I learned from the receptionist—who had been getting ready to leave for lunch. She gave me a brochure describing the salon's services, then smiled and said: "You're Tim Welles."

"How did you know?"

She produced a copy of the society page from that day's *Post* and pointed to a slightly fuzzy reproduction of my college graduation picture; I'm happy to report I still have all of my hair, only a few of them gray, and my midsection is only one inch wider than the day the photo was taken: working with animals, some of them large and uncooperative, tends to keep you in good physical condition, gray hairs notwithstanding.

"Would you please wait?" she asked. "The owner will want to know you're here."

I said I'd be glad to and picked up the paper after she left, then sat in a chair next to a large toy chest. (Many grooming shops have these; basically, they're bribe boxes for children who suffer separation anxiety when they leave their pets.) The *Post* article was mostly about the cat show and the First Lady's "controversial" decision to call in a "non-Washingtonian" groomer for Winnie. I was just getting to the part where they mentioned my "successful by Ohio standards" business when I caught a whiff of five-hundred-dollar-an-ounce perfume.

"Mr. Welles. I'm Marian Lightle."

Her features were sharply defined—I know several women and a few men who'd have killed for her cheekbones—and were positioned to draw your attention to her jade green eyes: either God had been in a good mood the day she was born or some plastic surgeon had bought himself one hell of a Caribbean condo with her money. Before I had a chance to say anything she opened the front door and said, "I will not allow you to come into my shop and add insult to the injury I've already suffered."

Her tone could have frozen fire.

"Look, Miss Lightle, I didn't come here to—"

"To quote a famous Republican, sir, 'read my lips': get

150

the hell out of my salon before I call the police and have you arrested for trespassing."

I stared at her, shocked and awkward. She *was* angry, that was obvious, but there was something about her manner—maybe that her hands and midsection were shaking, or the trouble she was having breathing steadily—that betrayed her anxiety. She was nervous as hell—wait, scratch that; she was scared. Of me? I don't know why—it wasn't as if I was going to coldcock her or something.

I lifted my hands in acquiescence and began to leave her shop.

"And if you chance to speak with Karen Ryan anytime soon, please tell her for me that it was a pleasure to serve her." Rattlesnakes have less venom than did those words, and I couldn't help but suddenly feel that this was all an elaborate act, staged for the benefit of the employees—who watched, wide-eyed.

The door, though not slammed, was nonetheless closed behind me with a great amount of conviction.

Welcome to our nation's capital.

I was almost to the end of the street when a voice called out, "Mr. Welles! Please, wait!"

The receptionist came up behind me. "Jeez, but you walk fast!"

"Sorry."

"Don't be. I wanted to apologize for Marian. She's really not a vindictive person. In fact, you'll probably find a message from her when you get back to your hotel. She's already feeling bad about it, I can tell."

"Have you been with her long?"

"Ten years. We used to work out of a little place in Foggy Bottom before we moved over here a couple of years ago. She's worked really hard to get where she is today. She just felt . . . well, *hurt* when Mrs. Ryan announced she was going to have you come up and do Winnie. We just had her in a month ago. I think Marian feels betrayed."

"Well, you can tell her for me there're no hard feelings."
I smiled and started on my way again. She followed me.

"I'm Meg," she said. "Meg Simmons. I think it's sweet
that the President and First Lady remembered you. They
seem to have a real affinity for us 'everyday' folks. That's
the biggest reason I voted for Jim Ryan."

"He'd be pleased to hear that."

"Have you had lunch yet?"

"No."

"No wonder you're so skinny." She took my arm.

Meg turned out to be a virtual fountain of information
concerning the inner workings of the Washington elite;
from the rumors about new congressional pay hikes to
which senator's wife had the better eye for fashion, Meg
Simmons was proud to spout her opinions while flirting
outrageously with me. I found her absolutely enchanting.

"Marian knows just about everyone important," she said,
attacking her calzone with a vengeance. "I suppose everyone in Washington 'knows' someone, but Marian has . . . I
guess you'd call them 'connections.' "

"Sounds downright conspiratorial. Do go on."

"Well, take for instance the salon's new location. This
area wasn't originally zoned for our type of business, but
Marian somehow managed to get that changed." She leaned
closer, dropping her voice to a semi-whisper. "If you ask
me, it's because she and Senator Morrish are an item. He's
a great guy, even if he is a conservative."

"I'm guessing that's high praise, coming from an avowed
Democrat."

"Oh, you! I can see why Karen Ryan likes you. You've
got a dry wit."

"Wait until I whip out the repartee."

"Sounds kinky. Get that smirk off your face. Senator
Morrish smirks like that all the time. Probably why he and
Marian have been arguing a lot lately; she hates smirkers."

"I'm sorry to hear they're not getting along. Might have

something to do with the warm reception I got from her to-day."

"It's been nuts lately, what with her being so wound-up about the third floor."

"What's the story there, anyway? You seem to have more than enough space already."

Meg shrugged her shoulders. "Beats me. It's off-limits to the salon employees. Senator Morrish helped Marian get the money for the remodeling, and they've been doing a lot of work on it themselves." She giggled. "There's a rumor going around the shop that it's their private 'love nest.' I don't see why they'd need it; it's not like they're doing anything wrong, both of them being single and all."

Diverting as this gossip was (after all, who am I to comprehend the labyrinthine machinations of Washington politics and whatever affairs of the heart may subsequently result?), it wasn't until the next morning that everything Meg had said took on personal significance for me.

Karen's assistant, Antonia ("But please call me Gayle") Patrick arrived at 10:00 A.M. sharp with Winnie, who was not at all pleased with the cramped cat carrier in which she'd been forced to take up brief residence. I hadn't seen Winnie since before the inauguration, so I asked for a little time alone with her. Gayle gave me her beeper number, then Karen's, and introduced me to "Agent Paxton" (a six-one *Terminator* clone) who would be standing guard outside my room.

After they left I turned off the television. I had been watching a news report about the various rallies being conducted on Capitol Hill to urge the Senate to vote down the FLT–82 bill (the House had approved it by a very narrow margin). What really piqued my interest was discovering via the report that Sen. Tom Morrish was sponsoring the whole thing. There was some ersatz-dramatic footage of him and House Democratic Chairman Charles Thornton arguing over the bill at a banquet a few nights earlier.

Thornton, like Jim Ryan, was strongly opposed to allowing FLT–82 into the United States.

I found Washington power struggles more amusing than enlightening, and so was glad to turn off the barrage of political doublespeak for the soft purr of a cat.

I took Winnie out of the carrier and began petting her, saying hello and how nice it was to see her and my, my, it looked as if she'd dropped a little weight and—

—I know what you're thinking: *Get a life.*

It's important to acclimate a pet before you start the grooming process, even one you've done for years. So much time is spent dealing with the headaches of operation that it's nice to have a few minutes alone to establish a rapport with your animal before putting it under the spray.

I had set up my portable station in the bathroom; a special tank with hose attachment for bathing (I use only distilled water for baths), a bowled aluminum washbasin that attached to the rim of the bathtub and had four special filter baskets at each corner to catch loose fur (it kind of looks like a very small autopsy table that's been warped in the center), and the various soaps and ointments I would use to condition the fur. My small grooming table was next to the sink, along with my battery-operated clippers and the blades I would be using to layer the cut. I did a prebath cut with a #5 blade (standard procedure on both cats and dogs) and was using the #2 scissors to trim the hair from inside her ears when she stretched and yawned, pushing out her back claws.

My heart skipped a beat.

One of the things about Winnie which had originally melted Karen's heart was her handicap: she had been missing two toes on her back left paw.

The cat sitting so contentedly in front of me was not—I repeat, *not*—missing any toes from its back left paw.

There were other things, little things, things I doubt you would've noticed had you not been a groomer: the condition of the teeth, the pattern of the specks in the eye, the length of the tail, the texture of the fur around the shoulders ... details that are often lost on owners who can't or won't spend a lot of time with their pet, but ones that a seasoned groomer *will* notice. (Don't forget, I had groomed Winnie for seven years, and had spent a lot of time staring at her; you memorize a lot of details that way.)

I put the harness around the cat's neck, gave it a can of Tender Vittles to keep it happy, and went to make a call, remembering what Meg had said about the CRGS having had Winnie in just a month ago.

I punched in Gayle's number. She called back at once.

"What can I do for you, Mr. Welles?"

"Did you drive yourself over here?"

"No. There's a car and driver downstairs. Do you need for me to get something for you?"

"Uh, no. I need to make a quick visit to Winnie's regular groomer."

"Why's that?"

C'mon, c'mon, think quick. "I need to find out what sort of ointments and cleansing gels she's been using on the fur. It's important I don't counteract her conditioning treatment."

A laugh. "Sounds pretty technical."

"What you mean is boring, and you're right. I only brought a limited supply of things with me and I may need to purchase—"

"Would you like for me to come along?"

"No, that's all right. But you and Agent Paxton could keep Winnie company while I'm gone."

"You really take your work seriously, don't you?"

Goddamn right I do, especially when it comes to animal theft. "I guess I do at that."

Ten minutes later I stormed through the doors and almost collided with Meg.

"Whoa! Hey, Tim. Was I right? Did Marian call and apologize?"

"No, she didn't. I really need to see her right away, Meg."

"She's up working on the 'inner sanctum' with Senator Morrish. I'll have to call."

I pointed to a door at my left. "Are these the stairs?"

"Yes, but I—"

I didn't wait. I took the steps three at a time. Marian Lightle met me just as I rounded the third landing.

"Mr. Welles! I . . . you . . . what are you *doing* here?" She was even more flustered and nervous than she'd been yesterday, only now with dark circles under her eyes and a paleness that would have gotten her immediate attention at an emergency room.

"The Ryans may not have a lot of time to spend with Winnie these days," I said, "but did you actually think you'd fool a fellow groomer by switching cats?"

Her eyes narrowed. "I don't know what you're—"

"Spare me, will you? The only time in the last month that Winnie has been without some kind of security was when she was brought here. And it was about a month ago that Karen invited me to D.C."

"Why would I do something so . . . so *stupid*?"

"Because you're pissed off that some nobody from Ohio is doing Winnie for the cat show!"

She smiled. "I admit that I was angry. It's hurt my business and my standing amongst the grooming community—how good can I be if the First Lady won't trust me with her cat? That's what everyone's thinking, even if they don't say it."

"Did you switch cats?"

"I don't have to—"

"Tell him, Marian," came a deep, rich voice from behind her.

Sen. Tom Morrish stepped out from the third floor door.

156

A Sean Connery clone if ever there was one, he probably cut a charismatic figure on the Senate floor, but now he just looked tired. Part of it, I guessed, was because of the bumps his relationship with Marian had hit as of late.

He introduced himself and shook my hand after taking off the workman's gloves he was wearing. The heavy apron he had on must have been pretty uncomfortable. I wondered how much work had to be done up here.

Marian balked. "Tom, I just can't—"

"He already knows the cat isn't Winnie," said Morrish in an iron tone. "I warned you this might happen."

She blinked, looked at me, then at Morrish again. "Shit!" She sat down on the steps and produced a cigarette from her blouse.

"You did switch them, didn't you?"

"Yes," she whispered. "But it's nothing ... bad. I love that cat, I really do. I love all of the animals that come into this shop. Winnie is—well, hell, you groomed her for years, you know how sweet she is. Not aloof and arrogant like you expect a cat to be."

"Does she get up in your face and lick your cheeks for minutes on end?"

Marian smiled wistfully. "Yeah. Not a lot of cats do that. And the way she lets you hug her ..."

"Six months ago I hired a young man named Rodney Anderson as an assistant groomer. He came from a pretty poor section of the city. He was part of a community outreach program sponsored by Georgetown University. The staff and students there select a group of underprivileged teens and help them to find steady jobs. Father Martin Knight was the one who wrote Rodney's letter of recommendation.

"Last week Rodney and Winnie both disappeared. I felt like such an idiot."

"A cat's-paw?" I said.

"You got it. When it was announced that Winnie would

157

be the mascot for the cat show, every salon in the city made a play to groom her. Think of the status. They didn't care that I had been doing Winnie since the Ryans arrived in Washington. Some of them—I'm sure you've experienced this—started dropping ugly rumors in the right ears. That we were abusing some animals, giving them tranquilizers without owners' permission, that sort of thing."

I'd been down that road a few times myself.

"What salon hates you enough to do this?"

"That's easy," intoned Morrish. "The Capitol Grooming Emporium. It's off New Hampshire at the intersection of 18th and R Street."

"They were the biggest shop in the city until we moved here and began expanding," said Marian. "They'd love to see me fold."

"Did Rodney know you switched Winnie with the cat I've got?"

"He must have. That kid was always skulking around somewhere."

"Do you think he was copying your files?"

"That's what a cat's-paw does."

"So by stealing Winnie from you, he gives her to the Capitol Grooming Emporium so they can not only take credit for 'finding' her, but prepare her for the cat show as well."

"Yes. I'm amazed that Karen Ryan didn't notice the toes by now. That's what tipped you off, wasn't it?"

"Bingo."

"It wasn't easy to find a black Persian that was fat enough and goofy enough to pass for her."

"Do you suppose they're going to wait until just before the show to reveal the switch?"

"Dale wouldn't have it any other way. Dale Cummins, owner of the Emporium. It would be a supreme humiliation for me if he waited until the last minute."

"So you switched the cats for basically the same reason?

To groom Winnie and make me look like some Midwest amateur hick?"

She glanced at Morrish. The senator gave a short, firm nod.

"That was the idea," said Marian. "Sorry. It was nothing personal."

To reiterate: grooming can be a vicious business.

"I've got an idea. Come on."

She stood. "I am not going to Dale's shop."

"Neither am I."

"Then—"

"Georgetown University. Father Knight."

Morrish declined to accompany us, for all the obvious, politically prudent reasons. Besides, this wasn't his problem, it was mine and Marian's.

It took us a little while to track down Father Knight's office at the university, and when we did he could only spare us a few minutes. "I have a class to teach, you know."

Martin Knight was about fifty-six and put you in mind of Pat O'Brien until he opened his mouth. No watered-down Irish brogue for this priest; his speech was pure Ivy League.

"I'm sorry to hear that Rodney didn't work out," he told Marian. (We'd left out the part about Winnie. You think I'm stupid?)

"I just wanted to give him his last paycheck and ask him why he left us," said Marian, so sincerely I wondered if she'd ever been an actress.

"I'm curious, Father," I said. "What prompted you to write a letter of recommendation for him?"

"Rodney, despite his background, has vast potential. He was genuinely grateful to be given an opportunity to better his situation."

"Did you work with him exclusively?"

"Oh, my, no. Each of us is assigned four teens, all of whom are part of different programs at the community center. A large number of our alumni put up the money to build and maintain that center. That's how the teens find personal sponsors."

"Would you happen to recall who was Rodney's sponsor?"

"I would have to dig into my files for that, and as you can see"—he gestured to his cramped and cluttered office with its stacks of manila folders piled two feet high in some corners—"I am not the world's most organized person." He looked at his watch. "I really must be going. If you'd like to talk to Rodney, I believe this is his boating day."

"Boating day?"

"Yes. As part of the program's agenda we sponsor various activities in connection with the university's athletic department. On Thursdays several teens get to go rowing. You'll find the group down at the Potomac Boathouse. I really have to go. There's nothing uglier than a roomful of young Jesuits who've been kept waiting."

On the way to the boathouse Marian grabbed my arm and said, "Do you think Dale Cummins was his sponsor?"

"You said Cummins was a G.U. man. It makes sense."

"Then why on earth are we *here*? Shouldn't we have gone to the Emporium and—"

"Think about that for a second, Marian. If you were in Cummins's position, would you keep Winnie there?"

"No."

"What *would* you do?"

She was silent for a few moments, then said, "I guess I'd give her to someone I trusted—or someone who owed me a favor. I'd wait until the morning of the show to have her brought into the shop, then I'd do the grooming and go straight to the Convention Center."

"So it's not such a wild leap to think that maybe, since Cummins has an underprivileged teenager's future in his hands, that he would trap said teen into being part of his plan?"

"Rodney has Winnie?"

"That's what I'm thinking."

We arrived at the docks but the teens were already out on the water.

"Do you see him?" I asked Marian.

"I can't tell. They're too far out."

"You looking for someone in particular?" asked the boat-house manager.

Marian was quick. "Yes, my nephew, Rodney Anderson?" The name evidently didn't ring a bell with the man. "His mother has had a mild heart attack and has been taken to Georgetown General."

"Oh, my," said the manager, genuinely concerned. "That's too bad. Most of these kids have enough troubles without something like that to— Here, you folks climb in my launch. I'll take you out there myself, see if we can't spot your nephew."

We climbed into the small craft and headed out toward the teens. There were maybe seven two- and three-person rowboats out there, so it didn't take Marian long to spot Rodney.

"Rodney!" she yelled.

He turned toward us and blanched when he saw Marian. Looking frantically around, he saw no way to quickly ma-neuver himself from the semicircle of boats and so—much to the chagrin of his rowing companion—took a broad swan dive over the side and started swimming back toward the docks.

"Boy doesn't seem anxious to see you, ma'am," said the manager with more than a glint of suspicion in his eyes.

By this time the university team sculls were coming up behind us and not at all pleased we were in their way.

There was nothing else to do.

I tore off my jacket and jumped over the side, pumping for all I was worth. It had been years since I'd been in the water and it was a shock to my system at first, but four years on the O.S.U. swim team had left me more than capable of finding my center and my rhythm quickly, and it wasn't long—save for one near-collision with an abandoned oar floating in my path—before I was right behind Rodney Anderson. He seemed to be petering out but managed to beat me to the docks by about fifteen seconds.

He fell flat on his face, gulping for air, then squirmed around and saw how close I was. Cursing loudly and shaking his head, he fumbled to his feet and took off running just as I was pulling myself out of the water.

I was just about to start up the side of a hill where already he was scrambling over the top when a group of joggers came whizzing by, two of them slamming into Rodney as he pushed himself onto the path.

Arms pinwheeling, he fell backwards and rolled ass-over-teakettle to the bottom of the hill. I knelt next to him and said, "Hi, Rodney. I'm Tim Welles. I'm an animal groomer. I once had a pit bull take a chunk out of my leg, so don't think I can't handle your skinny butt."

"Don't hit me, please? I didn't hurt anyone. What the hell do you and her want, anyway?"

"Who was your sponsor, Rodney? Was it Dale Cummins? Did he put you up to stealing the president's cat?"

The kid just stared, terrified.

"Answer the question, Rodney."

"Why should I?"

"You can tell me, or you can tell the Secret Service. I'm nicer and I don't have a big gun."

"Pale Dale *tried* to get me to steal her, sure. He talked me into going to Marian's and being his spy. Told me he'd double my wages. But I didn't do it for him."

Uh-oh. "Then who'd you do it for?"

"My sponsor from the center."

"And that would be who?"

He told me.

"I don't know what's so great about that bony old cat, anyway," said Rodney.

162

And I got a sick feeling in my heart.

I was out of there before Marian and the boathouse manager were back at the dock. I hated leaving her like that but I didn't have time to wait, not if I was right about this—and God, how I hoped I wasn't.

Gayle's driver got quite an eyeful when I came bounding up to the car soaking wet. I leapt into the backseat and yelled at him to take me back to Marian's shop.

When we got there, I told him to pop the trunk.

"Mr. Welles, what's going on? You're getting me pretty worried."

"OPEN THE TRUNK!"

"But—"

I lunged over the seat and shot my arm across his chest, reaching down for the trunk release and popping it myself.

"Stay right here, and keep the engine going! I'm sorry that I yelled at you."

I ransacked the trunk until I found the tire-iron, then ran into the shop, still dripping wet, past a startled Meg, through the stairway door, and up the three flights to the 'inner sanctum.'

I have to tell you, under any other circumstances I don't think I could have done it, but I was scared, and I was mad, and I was running on pure adrenaline. It took five blows of the tire-iron to smash the padlock, then I kicked open the door and saw what was in there.

Back downstairs Meg was waiting with her hands on her hips, demanding an explanation. There was no time. On my way out I spotted the toy chest.

I grabbed it and turned it upside down, showering the floor with rubber balls, Barbie dolls, Teenage Mutant Ninja Turtles, and various other novelties, among which was a black squirt gun just big enough to pass for the real thing. I shoved it in my pocket, turned to Meg and said, "I need a smock with the salon's logo on it."

"What the hell is—"

163

I jerked open the door to a closet behind her and pulled out a smock, then said, "If I get out of this, you wanna go on a date?" But I was gone before she could answer.

I dove into the backseat of the car and told the driver where we were going. He looked unhappy about it.

As we pulled out into traffic, I snatched up the car phone and called the hotel, then had them connect me to my room. Gayle answered on the first ring.

"God, Mr. Welles! Where are you?"

"Listen to me, Gayle, I don't have time to explain but you've got to get in touch with Karen and tell her that Winnie's in trouble."

"I don't understand, she's—"

"That isn't Winnie. She's been stolen."

Her voice became measured and calm. "Do you know where she is?"

"No, but I think I know who does." I gave her the Foggy Bottom residential address.

"I don't believe it," she said.

"Believe it. You tell Karen, and both of you meet me there. And please bring Agent RoboCop with you."

For as much goddamn traffic as there is in Washington, it moves fairly fast. We arrived at the address in just under twenty minutes. I climbed out of the car and walked up the steps to the front door of the incredibly beautiful and expensive Federal House.

I knocked.

A lovely young woman in her early twenties answered.

"Hi," I said, making sure she got a good look at the salon's logo on the smock. "I'm from the Cox's Row Grooming Salon. I'm here to pick up your cat."

Her eyes grew wide. So did her smile. "A *cat*? Ohmigod! Daddy bought a cat for us?" She threw open the door and I stepped inside.

A door at the far end of the hall opened and a voice said, "Tiffany? Who is it, hon?"

"Oh, Daddy!" she shouted. "When were you going to surprise me with the cat?"

"The what?" And House Democratic Chairman Charles Thornton stepped through the doors of his study. "I don't know what—"

He saw me and said, "Oh, no, you tell that Marian Lightle that she's—" He froze halfway down the hall and blanched. "Wait a second, I know you. The *Post* story yesterday. You're— Jesus!" He started backing toward the doors. "Tiffany, call the police!"

"But, *Daddy*!"

"Do it!"

I shoved his daughter aside and ran after him, getting to the doors just as he was trying to close them. He was short and grossly overweight, so forcing my way in didn't take much effort. I locked them behind me.

He stood puffing a few feet away. "We have a private security force that patrols this neighborhood."

"Then you pay them too much."

"What the hell do you want?"

"You son of a bitch," I whispered. "You *knew* the whole time, didn't you?"

"I don't know what—"

"I'll bet you would have just let her die."

"I have no idea what—"

I slammed my fist into his face, spinning him around and dropping him to the floor. When he came up, his nose was bleeding.

"I figure I've got about sixty seconds," I said, pulling the gun from my pocket and pointing it right between his eyes. "Now, goddamnit, you tell me where Winnie is!"

We stared at each other for several seconds. Shouts and footsteps exploded outside. Loud pounding against the study doors. A lot of howling sirens coming close in a hurry.

Thornton stared at the gun, then my face. "You're not going to like prison very much, Mr. Welles."

"Maybe we'll get to be cellmates."

Someone shot out one of the locks, then began kicking at the center of the doors. Wood splintered outward. I didn't have long.

I grabbed Thornton by the collar of his shirt, spun him around, and pressed the gun against his temple just as the doors split open and a red-faced, slightly overweight security guard burst in, leveling a 9mm Beretta right at my face.

"Don't shoot, Jerry!" shouted Thornton.

The sirens were deafening now, underscored by screeching tires and slamming doors and lots of voices.

Two Secret Service agents appeared in the study doorway, both of them aiming guns at Jerry.

Two more came into the study, aiming their guns at me.

Three more suddenly smashed through the study windows. I didn't notice who they pointed their guns at.

"I think we're in trouble," I whispered to Thornton.

Then Gayle—perky, cheerful Gayle—came running into view with Agent Conan right behind her. She took one look at me and said, "Please tell me that's not a real gun, Mr. Welles."

"It isn't," I said, dropping it to the floor and putting my hands over my head.

Now I know what flypaper feels like, because I was instantly swarmed by Secret Service agents who tackled me—and none too gently, might I add—to the floor.

First Lady Karen Ryan stroked Winnie's back and said, "Don't you think you overreacted just a tad?"

"I can't help it. I don't like it when people try to hurt my friends."

I was in a private and heavily guarded room at Georgetown General. I had three broken ribs, a fractured collarbone, several facial lacerations, a dislocated knee, and two—count'em—two broken fingers on my left hand.

I bet Secret Service agents would make great football players.

"I'm so sorry, Karen," said Marian for the umpteenth time. "But Dr. Kleinman assures me that Winnie is fine. She just needs rest and extra medical care for a few more days." Winnie had lost a lot of weight in the past month but it was easy to see her strength was coming back.

Karen blinked and said, "I faded there for a minute, Tim. Run it by me again."

"It was what Rodney Anderson said about Winnie being 'bony.' As soon as he said that, I suddenly remembered the apron Tom Morrish had been wearing back at Marian's shop. At the time I'd thought it was too heavy to be just a grooming or painting apron, and I was right. Only a steel-lined apron is that thick. And only someone who spends time around an X-ray machine would have cause to wear something like that."

"Jesus," said Karen.

"There's not only an X-ray machine on the third floor of the shop," I said. "There's a whole laboratory. You should have seen the look on Kleinman's face when I kicked open that door."

"I thought he was still in Geneva."

"He came back into the country almost ten months ago. I'm not sure if he had the FLT–82 with him then, or if he and Morrish hired people to smuggle it in earlier, but it's here. A lot of it. And Kleinman's been manufacturing more in that lab." I leaned forward. "The stuff does exactly what the Swiss claimed. It completely cures FeLV in *any stage* of the disease! If Marian hadn't switched cats, Kleinman never would have tested Winnie. She'd be dead by now."

Karen looked at Marian. "Why *did* you test her?"

"I told Tom that if I went along with this, we'd test every cat brought into the shop. So far we've only detected

FeLV in five of them. I, uh . . . I talk to the owners so they'll help us keep the lab a secret."

"If you think I'm going to thank you for stealing our cat," said Karen, "then you've been sniffing flea dip for too long."

"I know what I did was wrong," pleaded Marian, "but you . . . you not only hurt me as a friend, you insulted my professional integrity."

I put my good hand on Marian's shoulder. "Once it's known that FLT–82 is here and that it works, you and Tom Morrish will be heroes to cat lovers from coast to coast."

Karen sighed. "I can't believe that Charlie Thornton would have let Winnie die."

"Believe it, because that's exactly what he intended to do, and then blame it on the drug. The treatment requires that the cat be given a series of ten shots over a five-week period. Winnie had two more to go when Rodney Anderson stole her."

"Oh, God," said Karen, her voice nearly cracking. "Does that mean that—"

"No," said Marian. "She was cured by the time she received the eighth shot. But Thornton believed that if she didn't get the last two, she'd die."

I said, "He knew there were more than enough people opposed to the bill who'd take his word that FLT–82 was a failure, and he'd have the First Family's dead cat to prove it."

Karen nodded her head. "Then it would just be a matter of exposing the existence of the lab and pointing the finger at Tom Morrish and however many of his supporters helped him put the plan into action."

"You got it," I said. "He'd all but single-handedly kill the bill, thus keeping the president's promise to the animal rights people, who would probably nominate Thornton's fat ass for sainthood."

"How did he know about the lab?"

"Rodney Anderson broke into the third floor one night. He didn't have to use a tire-iron to do it, either. The reason he was put in the outreach program in the first place was because he'd been arrested for attempted B&E three times—a crime he's well suited for; his dad's an unemployed locksmith."

Karen stared down at Winnie. "The very drug he vows to keep out of the country saves his cat's life. This'll put Jim in one hell of a bad position." Winnie snaked out of her arms and onto the bed, rubbing against the cast on my left arm.

"Do you think he'll get them to postpone the Senate vote so he can go public with this?"

"I can't answer for him. I can only tell him what we know." She smiled as Winnie crawled up and started licking my nose.

And then First Lady Karen Ryan's eyes got very, very narrow—a classic "Hold-The-Phone-I-Just-Got-An-Idea" look. "Can you still have Winnie ready for the opening of the show tomorrow afternoon?"

I help up my cast. "Three guesses."

"I could help you," said Marian.

I looked at Karen.

"All right," she said. "Both of you work on her. Tim, I'll arrange for your release tonight, but you'll have to be guarded by Secret Service agents. You're still officially under arrest. The two of you go back to the hotel and make Winnie a stunner, understand?"

"What are you going to do?"

"Open the D.C. International Cat Show." She stared directly into my eyes. "I'll be rewriting my preshow breakfast speech, naturally. I think all those cat lovers will be interested in what I have to say."

It took a moment for the full impact of her words to sink in.

"You wouldn't?"

169

A smile. "I would. I'll tell Jim about it first, of course."

"Beautiful," I whispered.

"Isn't it?" said Karen. "If Jim were to make the information public, he'd be bringing a storm down on his head. If I do it, I'm just being the too-aggressive, outspoken, and always-controversial First Lady the press has pegged me to be."

"You're gorgeous when you're righteous, you know that?"

"You're pitiful."

"And you're a viper."

"Felon."

"Shrieking harpy."

"Dirty Harry wannabe."

"I love you, my friend."

She started at that one. "Hold on, that's not the way it's supposed to go."

"This whole trip's kind of been that way."

She came over and put her hand on my forehead. "For someone who looks so harmless, you can sure start trouble when you want to."

"You're really gonna tell everything?"

"If I want to continue to sleep nights, I'll have to."

I grasped her hand. "I know you hate the idea of how many cats died because of the tests, and so do I. But like it or not this is a case of the end justifying the means. The tests may have killed hundreds of cats but FLT–82 is going to save the lives of thousands."

"I know." She kissed my swollen cheek. "I hope I can keep you out of jail."

"Yadda-yadda, warden."

"I've heard that routine. Lenny Bruce does it better." She smiled at Marian. "Thank you for helping to save Winnie's life." Her voice definitely cracked on the last two words and one thin tear slipped down her cheek. Winnie climbed up and started licking at her face.

"Well," I said, pulling myself upright and looking around for my clothes, "we should get going. I'm supposed to be a groomer, y'know."

"You'd better be good," said Marian.

"Don't start with me."

"Worried that I'll best you?"

"Watch it. Catnappers should know who their friends are."

"Don't be a jerk."

"Don't be pushy."

"Ass."

"Debutante."

"Hick,"

I looked at Karen. "I think I found a third partner for the act."

And we all laughed, good and long and loudly, enjoying every second. By this time tomorrow I'd either be a hero dining at the White House or a felon on his way to the Big House. Either way, I'd be famous and Winnie would be safe and healthy.

And I'll bet you thought a groomer's life was dull.

Cat and Canary

•

William J. Reynolds

The townhouse was a handsome three-story brownstone in
Georgetown, midway down a line of similar turn-of-the-
century structures that hearkened to a time when Washington, D.C., was in fact something of a backwater. A hundred
years ago, these houses were built for people of means, but
people whose names likely would be unknown across the
Potomac, let alone across the continent. Today the townhouses were occupied by individuals of no lesser means,
but individuals whose names, reputations, and faces were
beamed into the world's living rooms almost daily, thanks
to the efforts of Ted Turner and his minions. These narrow,
picturesque streets were home—at least temporarily—to influence brokers, lobbyists, government officials, and others
who hold the reins of power. Yet it occurred to Alexander
Grimm, and not for the first time, that although the city was
more sophisticated, perhaps, and certainly larger than its
hundred-year-old antecedent, it was no less parochial and
insular. Factor in such mutations as were the inevitable result of the ebb and flow of political parties' fortunes, and
you pretty much always saw the same people at these
quasi-official, quasi-social functions. The functions, too,
seemed always to be pretty much reruns of all of the other
functions.

172

Or so it seemed to Alexander Grimm. Though he would be quick to admit that he had never been invited to one of these functions before, and probably never would be again, and probably would not accept if he were.

Grimm entertained these thoughts as he stood in the spacious entrance hall of the townhouse, nursing a small glass of champagne that had started out near room temperature and was growing rapidly warmer, as was the room itself. The rise in temperature was owing to the fact that the hall was filled beyond capacity with various VIPs, functionaries, and hangers-on—Grimm figured he would have to number himself among the last—all presumably the invited guests of former Ambassador Thomas Barring Foyle and Mrs. Foyle. They were here to give witness to the return of the Canary.

The crowd was thinner in the library, just off the entrance hall, and so Grimm drifted in there. The Smithsonian had sent up a small display, consisting of a large color portrait of the Canary of the Tungus, a cutaway section of the globe showing the location of the newly reemerging nation of Altai, and one of those museum-type placards which purports to explain everything in five paragraphs or fewer. Grimm waited for a midwestern senator and his wife to give the exhibit their thirty seconds' worth of attention, and then bent to study the display.

The Canary of the Tungus is the primary national treasure of Altai, a Balkan nation in the former Soviet Union. The Canary, a 250-carat piece of amber (fossil resin of ancient trees), has existed in its current form since at least the mid-1400s, held by the traditional ruler of Altai, the Suzerain, on behalf of his people.

For most of the past 200 years, Altai has been under the dominion of a succession of foreign powers, most recently the Soviet Union, yet her people have maintained a fierce spirit of independence, a spirit which came to be embodied in the Canary of the Tungus.

In the early part of this century, a time of great economic and political turmoil, the Canary vanished. In the years that followed, and the world-shaking events those years brought—world wars, the Russian Revolution, global depression, the Cold War and the descent of the Iron Curtain—the people of Altai and her exiled Suzerain had neither the time nor the resources to search for the gem. However, with the disintegration of the Soviet Union, the reemergence of Altai as an independent nation, and the restoration of the Suzerain to his familial throne, efforts were made to locate the Canary and arrange for its return.

Eventually the gem was found among the vast estate left by Col. E. L. Barring, a British explorer, archaeologist, and museum curator. How the Canary came into Colonel Barring's possession is open to speculation; the Colonel died in 1956, at which time control of the estate and its assets passed to Thomas Barring Foyle, the Colonel's grandson and a former United States Ambassador.

Upon being informed that he unknowingly possessed the long-lost national treasure of the People of Altai, Ambassador Foyle immediately insisted that the Canary of the Tungus be returned to its traditional custodian, the Suzerain.

"Kind of brings a lump to the throat, doesn't it?" a voice murmured in Grimm's left ear. He turned, and looked up into the face of Michael Barrett, who stood a good head taller than Grimm. In fact, at a glance there seemed nothing in common between the two men. Michael Barrett was thirty-four but seemed younger; he was tall, curly-haired, and as slender as a number-two pencil. Alexander Grimm was compact, solidly built, with iron-gray hair and a demeanor that made him seem older than his fifty-eight years.

What they had in common was the police department, and the five years in which they worked together, Barrett as a member of Grimm's "special squad," an elite unit that handled kidnappings, terrorist acts, serial killings, and other such major crimes—crimes which became less and less "special" every day, Grimm frequently reflected. Although Grimm had retired nearly two years ago, the two men remained close friends. Grimm had expected to see Barrett this evening: the younger man had signed on as part of the security detail, a bit of moonlighting the likes of which cops everywhere undertake routinely, police salaries being what they are.

"It is a trifle ... heavy-duty," Grimm said, referring to the placard. "But no doubt politically correct. Well, you appear to have kept the lid on things so far—no one's been assassinated yet, as near as I can tell."

Barrett laughed softly. "No, but when I saw the pictures on the news last night of that scene down by the legation, I began to wonder if my cush gig was going to be so cush after all."

Grimm nodded, recollecting the violent demonstration that had led the local newscasts the previous evening. "Yes, it does appear that some of the suzerain's people would just as soon he remain in exile—and the Canary remain in hands other than his. But I didn't see any sign of them on the way over, and security up and down the block looks formidable."

"We tripled it after yesterday's little scene. But everything's been quiet this evening. Maybe they got it out of their system."

"Sure," Grimm said brightly. "The Tooth Fairy probably sat them down and had a do-better talk with them."

Barrett grunted, and nodded toward the large portrait on an easel just beyond the Altai diorama. The photograph depicted the Canary nestled in a crush of purple velvet, the light dancing artfully upon its many elaborate facets.

Grimm was surprised at the gem's yellowness, enhanced by the purple background and who knew what photographic embellishments; like most people, he thought of amber as being only golden in hue. "Impressive, huh," Barrett was saying. " 'Course, it's like the jewelry ads in the paper: the picture makes it look the size of a grapefruit, but in fact it's only about as big as a cough drop, give or take. I caught a glimpse of it this afternoon when they were rehearsing the presentation."

"As they say, size isn't everything." Grimm looked up as a buzz near the library doors indicated the appearance of the suzerain and his entourage. The suzerain himself was a slender, middle-aged man with dark hair liberally sprinkled with white; in his understated evening clothes, he looked like somebody's uncle. But somebody's uncle probably would not be ringed by half a dozen ceremonial guards in bright scarlet-and-blue uniforms, nor command the attention of every set of eyes in the house. With the suzerain was a tall, blunt-featured man whom Grimm recognized as the host, Thomas Barring Foyle. Foyle was well into his seventies, Grimm knew, but he had the powerful bearing of a man thirty years his junior, and the shock of white hair that fell across his forehead would inevitably be described as boyish. Foyle appeared to be directing his guest's attention toward the display, and Grimm and Barrett stepped discreetly to one side.

Foyle glanced at the men, nodded, then looked back again at Grimm. Smiling, he said to the suzerain, "Your Highness, I am honored to present one of our better-known authors, Mr. Alexander Grimm."

Grimm was slightly surprised that Foyle knew him, and even more surprised that he introduced him to the suzerain. Uncertainly, he extended his right hand. The suzerain, for his part, looked at the hand as if it were a tentacle, managed a slight inclination of his head in Grimm's general direction, and then turned his attention elsewhere. Grimm glanced at Foyle, whose eyes suggested a repressed grin. "Mr. Grimm—formerly Inspector Grimm—wrote a fascinating book about the search for a serial killer. I'm not big on true-crime books, but when my wife brought home *The Killer Inside*, I glanced at it out of curiosity and couldn't put it down. My wife and Mr. Grimm are old friends," Foyle went on. "When Perris found out you were in town, she insisted on inviting you—not that you aren't welcome anyway. Have you seen her yet?"

"No, I only got here a few minutes ago . . ."

"And she's probably still down in the family room with her nieces and nephews." Foyle frowned, and seemed about to say something else, then caught himself. "I'm forgetting my manners. I should also introduce Ms. O'Connor of the State Department"—Foyle indicated a studious-looking black woman who had come in with the entourage—"and General Korsov, the suzerain's chief of staff." Korsov was a poker-faced mustached man in the uniform of the Altai Guard; he nodded stiffly upon being introduced. "Oh—I'm Tom Foyle," Foyle added, laughing. "I recognized you from your picture on the book, but I guess that doesn't mean you know me."

"You've had your picture published here and there yourself, Mr. Ambassador," Grimm said. "This is my friend Lieutenant Michael Barrett, part of your security team."

"Lieutenant," Foyle said. "I was just going to show the suzerain this lovely display, which will move over to the Smithsonian next week. And then it will be about time for the ceremony . . . Say, I've got an idea: how would you like to go scare up Perris? She'd love to see you for a couple of minutes before kickoff, and you'd stand as good a chance of dragging her up here as anyone. Follow that corridor through there, the family room's at the far back of the house."

Nodding, Grimm murmured a word of departure to the others, and moved away. Barrett caught up with him near the library doors. "So that's how you wangled an invite," he said. "The old friend-of-the-ambassador's-wife bit, eh?" He waggled his eyebrows.

Grimm gave the younger man a look, and handed him his empty glass.

Perris Foyle was nearly twenty-five years younger than her husband, and one of those rare women who can look every bit her age and yet be thoroughly beautiful. Perris was much as Alexander Grimm remembered, small and slender, with alabaster skin and ebony shoulder-length hair, deep, gray eyes, and an intriguing set of dimples that appeared when she smiled, which was often.

Grimm paused in the family-room doorway and watched her for a moment. She wore a long jade green sequined dress, which spilled around her as she crouched on the carpet playing some kind of game with five kids. Grimm didn't know the game. Marbles went in at the top of a tall plastic tower, then down and around through chutes and sluices, tripping flags, flaps, and doors as they went. It was meaningless to him, but the kids seemed to get a charge out of it. So did the longhair cat that sat amid the circle of kids, occasionally pawing at a flag or flap as it sprang up. And so, for that matter, did Perris Foyle, who laughed like a child herself.

After a few seconds, she noticed Grimm standing in the doorway, and leapt to her feet. "Alexi!" she cried, and he noted that her Balkan accent had diminished considerably since he had last seen her, not quite fifteen years ago. Perris and Grimm's late wife had become friends through their mutual church, and for a time the Grimms and Perris and her first husband had seen a lot of each other. But people have a habit of moving away and losing touch, and the years have a habit of passing—and of falling away at times such as this. The two old friends embraced, and kissed, and took each other in deeply. "You look wonderful, Alexi," Perris said. "That gray hair—so distinguished!"

"You look even more wonderful, Perris. And not a gray hair in sight."

"Only her hairdresser knows for sure," Perris said, and the dimples appeared as parentheses around her small mouth. "I suppose my husband—you met Thomas, yes? Good—I suppose he sent you to fetch me, tell me to put on my big smile and my gracious hostess manners, and come hand over the Canary of the Tungus to that dictator who I must have as a guest in my home." The dimples were gone by the time she had finished speaking.

Grimm paused as they strolled up the long corridor, and looked at her appraisingly. "I thought you were Estonian," he finally said.

Perris smiled again, this time ruefully. "Obvious, am I? My father was Estonian. My mother was Altain. For most Americans, there's no difference—it's all just 'Russia'—or it was."

"Ah. And I take it you're among those Altains who aren't too thrilled about returning the Canary."

"Returning the Canary to Altai, fine," Perris said. "But to the suzerain? If people had any idea what that man's family did to the people of Altai . . ."

"But, Perris, those were the suzerain's ancestors. I admit the current model is a little short on the common touch, but he's never had a chance to lead; maybe he can do something for his people."

"*His* people," Perris echoed with disgust. "After spending most of this century under someone's thumb, you would think that Altai would be due for a taste of democracy. But no, as soon as the Soviets pull out, the military takes over and brings that dictator in from exile."

"Military types usually prefer dictatorships: they're easier to deal with. Democracy is messy."

"To just hand over the Canary to that . . . *person* is an in-

179

sult. I wish Thomas had told that man, General Korsov, that he didn't know what he was talking about when Korsov approached him about the Canary. He *didn't* know what Korsov was talking about, in fact: Thomas's grandfather left a huge estate, and it took nearly six months to verify that, yes, the Canary was among it. I wish Thomas had told Korsov that the Canary wasn't there, and told him to go away."

"But he wouldn't have. The Canary is important. As you say, it legitimizes the suzerain."

Perris made a noise. "I would rather take a hammer and smash that bit of amber into atoms than give it to the grandson of the man who— Well, Alexi, I could tell you stories, stories my mother told me about life in Altai under the suzerain, before the war. Suffice to say that the people welcomed the Nazis—*welcomed* them, Alexi—when they invaded. Never mind: Let's just have this done with."

The cat had followed them from the family room, and had been figure-eighting between their legs as they strolled up the corridor; now Perris scooped it up into her arms, and the cat rubbed its head affectionately against her shoulder. As they neared the main part of the house, Thomas Foyle met them. Perris raised her voice theatrically. "Oh, Alexi, it's my husband! Act nonchalant!"

Foyle smiled, and shook his head tolerantly, and kissed his wife on the cheek. "You found her, then," he said to Grimm, and then looked into his wife's face, his eyes serious but kind. "Ready, dear?"

"No," Perris said. "But let's get it over with." She smiled bravely if not sincerely.

"All right. You know the drill: You and I and General Korsov will go upstairs and remove the Canary from the safe."

"Yes, yes, then we bring it downstairs and you will formally present it to the tyrant."

"Please, dear," Foyle said, a pained look crossing his

craggy features. "His Highness prefers to be called a despot." He wiped his brow with a blindingly white linen handkerchief.

"I'll be sure to apologize to him later," Perris said. "Thomas, are you all right?"

"Just warm—so many damn people in the place. Let's take care of the handoff, then I'll step out for a bit of air. Mr. Grimm, I look forward to talking with you more later." By then they had emerged into the entrance hall, which was even more crowded than when Grimm had arrived. The Foyles continued on ahead; Grimm paused, and took a glass of champagne as it passed by on a tray. He didn't really want it, but holding it gave his hands something to do. He watched as the Foyles made their way through the throng of people to the foot of a curved staircase, where General Korsov and Ms. O'Connor of the State Department waited. No sign of the suzerain; Grimm presumed he would make an entrance when the Foyles returned with the gewgaw.

Michael Barrett drifted over to this friend. "How was the reunion?" he asked innocently.

"Shut up," Grimm said pleasantly. "Foyle doesn't look too good."

"It's a big night," Barrett said, "and he's not a young man. Built like a brick precinct house, though."

After a quick conference, the Foyles started up the carpeted stairs, followed by General Korsov. Perris put down the cat, which bounded on ahead of the trio. Ms. O'Connor remained at the foot of the stairs, checking her wristwatch. Grimm found that amusing: after all, the Canary had been missing for nearly a thousand years, what did a few minutes one way or another matter?

Yet there was an undeniable aura of expectancy in the crowded hall, and despite his best attempt to be aloof and cynical, Grimm felt it too. He caught himself looking at his own watch, and glanced rather sheepishly at his friend.

"The big buildup," Barrett said, grinning.

And then General Korsov was at the top of the stairs. Alone. Grimm and Barrett knew instantly that something was wrong; there was something in the man's face, despite the fact that he had been trained not to give in to panic. In moderately accented English the general called down, "A doctor is needed. Ambassador Foyle is ill."

The medical profession being as crowded as it is, and the house being as crowded as it was, several physicians, representing several specialties, were on hand. Two of the nearest rushed up the stairs; they and the general ducked into the room at the top of the stairs, which was Ambassador Foyle's study. Ms. O'Connor kept her post at the foot of the stairs, assuring the congregation that this was only a minor delay and asserting her certainty that the ambassador was fine and that the proceedings would be under way in a few moments.

"They always say that," Michael Barrett murmured to Alexander Grimm. "Why do they always say that?"

"Wishful thinking, probably."

The paramedics arrived within twelve minutes; presumably the doctors had phoned from upstairs. Ms. O'Connor went up to show the paramedics the way. Everyone else milled around, trying to pretend that nothing was amiss. Such phrases as "he's not a young man anymore" and "you know he had a heart attack four years ago" kept making their whispered way to Grimm's ears.

Eventually the paramedics descended the staircase, this time with their patient on a stretcher between them. A plastic oxygen mask obscured much of Foyle's face, but what Grimm could see of it looked distressingly gray. Perris Foyle and the two volunteer doctors brought up the rear. The housekeeper brought Perris her coat. Perris said a few words to the woman who was in charge of the catering, then moved toward the door through which her husband was being taken. One of the doctors told his wife that he was going to tag along to the hospital in case the ER doctors, or Foyle's own physician, had any questions.

Perris Foyle had reached the parquet in front of the door when General Korsov bolted from the ambassador's study and fairly vaulted halfway down the curved staircase.

"Stop that woman," he ordered. "She has stolen the Canary of the Tungus!"

Two of the Altai Guard stepped forward, probably in automatic response to their leader's bellow. Then they hesitated, perhaps because it occurred to them that they were not in Altai, or perhaps because Perris Foyle rose up to her full five feet four inches and fixed upon the guards a dark look that seemed perfectly capable of reducing diamonds to black ashes.

"I beg your pardon," she said placidly. "My husband is ill, and I will accompany him to the hospital."

She turned again toward the door, which was standing open.

"This woman has stolen the national treasure of the people of Altai," Korsov persisted, as if reading from a book. "It was in its case when Ambassador Foyle opened his safe: he showed it to me and Mrs. Foyle. He closed the case, then said he is not feeling well. He sank to the floor, and I came out to call for a doctor. Since then, I am being in the room the whole time. Now I retrieve the case from under a chair, where I presume the ambassador has dropped it when he fell ill. But the case is empty—rather, it contains only this." He held up his left hand to display a small bluish object: a kid's marble.

Grimm looked immediately at Perris. She sensed his glance, and made eye contact with him, but he could read neither her face nor her eyes.

Ms. O'Connor now came out of the study and descended the stairs. Korsov looked at her; she shook her head. Then she scanned the room, and spotted Barrett. With a cant of her head, she invited him to join her as she crossed over to Perris Foyle. Barrett looked at Grimm, and shrugged, and Grimm rightly took that as an invitation to tag along.

The two women and two men stepped out into the cool night air; on the street below, Ambassador Foyle was being lifted into the ambulance.

"This is outrageous," Perris began. "My husband has suffered a serious heart attack, and that miserable excuse for a general is only worried about a hunk of old tree sap—"

"Mrs. Foyle, I'm very sorry about the ambassador, but this is an extremely serious situation. The Canary is missing. You are the only person who was alone with it, for those few seconds, you're the only person who could have . . ."

"Yes," Perris said heatedly. "If what Korsov says is true. But what if the damned Canary was already gone when my husband opened the case, and Korsov is lying?"

Ms. O'Connor caught her breath. "Is he?"

Perris seemed to look through her, past her, and into Alexander Grimm's eyes. He returned her gaze as she presented it: steadily. His face was as immobile as that on the statue at the Lincoln Memorial.

"No," said Perris.

"Mrs. Foyle. I'm sorry. If you took the Canary—"

"You might call your lawyer, Perris," Grimm said quietly.

"—if you took the Canary," Ms. O'Connor persisted, "well, I think if you were to give it to me now, that would be the end of it. Certainly anyone would excuse a certain amount of . . . confusion at a time like this."

Perris looked at the other woman. "Confusion? I am not confused. But I *am* in some hurry . . ."

"Lieutenant Barrett," Ms. O'Connor said with a small sigh, "this is a delicate situation. We have no formal relationship to speak of with Altai; this is essentially a private matter between the Foyles and the suzerain. For that reason, I'm not sure the government has any real jurisdiction here. I think you're the ranking officer in attendance . . ."

"Yes, ma'am, I understand," said Barrett. With a slight glance at Grimm, he turned to Perris Foyle. "Mrs. Foyle, I'm sorry to have to ask you, but did you take the Canary?"

Perris looked at him as if he had been speaking in tongues.

"Perris, please," Grimm said. "Where is the Canary?"

She turned to look at him. "Alexi, I have no idea at all where the damn thing is. Lieutenant," she said, looking again toward Barrett, "am I under arrest?"

Barrett looked at Ms. O'Connor, then back to Perris. "I have no grounds to arrest. Hell, I'm not even sure a crime was committed even if you *did* pocket the thing; you hadn't turned it over to the suzerain yet. But I can't let you leave until the situation is at least a little clearer."

"Then you will not permit me to accompany my husband, who has had a serious heart attack?"

Barrett sighed heavily.

"Mike," Grimm said. "Perris. How about this: If Perris would agree to be searched—"

"In order to leave my own house?" Perris said indignantly.

"—and I accompany her to the hospital, you can be virtually assured that the Canary must still be in the house." He looked long at Perris, who finally nodded.

"All right," Barrett said unhappily. "Ms. O'Connor, please take Mrs. Foyle somewhere private and stay with her. There's a police officer named Anita Sanchez working the party; I'll find her and send her. Please stay with Mrs. Foyle while Officer Sanchez searches her."

"Of course," Ms. O'Connor said, and the two women moved back into the house.

"I have the feeling I'm kissing my pension goodbye," Barrett said to Grimm. "Hope you're happy."

"Far from it," Grimm said. "There's no way in blazes she *didn't* take that blasted rock."

He went down the steps to tell the ambulance driver to go ahead without Mrs. Foyle, and to collect his car.

Officer Sanchez was back in less than ten minutes. She looked at Barrett and shook her head. Barrett shrugged. "All right, Anita, thanks. You can help out with the search of the premises." As the officer moved off, Barrett looked at Grimm, who waited near the front door.

"Then it must be in the house somewhere," Grimm said.

"Unless she handed it off to someone."

"Who? After coming downstairs she dealt with no one except the housekeeper and the caterer. To pass it to either of them would mean a prearranged plan, with the other party's collusion, and I just don't buy into that. If Perris took it—and I'm forced to say she must have—then it was a spur-of-the-moment act. She probably had the marble in her pocket from when she was playing with the kids. When she found herself alone with the Canary, she saw the chance to do the suzerain a bad turn. If the gem isn't on her person, then she must have stuck it in a potted plant or something. It'll turn up."

"Spoken like someone who isn't seeing his career flash before his— Wait a minute. What if she slipped it to her husband, without his knowing it?"

"Then it'll turn up at the hospital."

"Yeah, like nothing ever disappears from those places." He gestured to one of the cops who was searching the house. "Get on the horn, get someone over to the hospital and make damn sure that everything in Foyle's pockets is accounted for, and I mean the lint too."

Perris Foyle emerged, looking positively regal. "Am I permitted to go to my husband now?"

Barrett sighed, and indicated the door.

"Will you drive me, Alexi?"

"My car is outside," Grimm said. "But first . . . Perris, I know how you feel about the suzerain. But don't you think you've made your point? You've embarrassed him; certainly you have no interest in the Canary beyond that. Eventually, it will turn up. So why not make things easy for all of these people and just tell us where it is?"

She looked at him coldly. "I told you before, Alexi: I do not know where the Canary of the Tungus is. Do you believe me?"

Grimm pursed his lips and looked deeply into Perris's eyes. They were dark, unfathomable—as always. "No," he said eventually. "I don't believe I do."

"I see. In that case, I will take a taxi to the hospital. Excuse me."

She turned her back on the men and went to use the telephone.

Ambassador Foyle's condition had been stable when he was admitted; the preliminary diagnosis of myocardial infarction was confirmed. A full recovery was expected. But shortly after midnight the Ambassador suffered the first of several more small heart attacks. He died on the operating table at 2:19 A.M. The Canary of the Tungus had not been among his possessions when he was admitted.

By two-thirty, the Foyle house had been thoroughly searched, beginning in the most likely place, the ambassador's study, and working out and down. The Canary was not found. The search team began working its way back up from bottom to top.

The Suzerain of Altai formally protested to the State Department, which formally apologized and sympathized; State in turn appealed to Mrs. Foyle, who did neither.

Three weeks after Thomas Barring Foyle's funeral, Alexander Grimm read in the *Post* that Mrs. Foyle was leaving for Europe, where she planned to stay "indefinitely." A State Department spokesman said the department had no plans to interfere with Mrs. Foyle's intentions. Which Grimm took to mean that the federal government, like everybody else, couldn't think what to do about it.

Despite people's best efforts, the earth orbits the sun, the moon orbits the earth, and time passes. Not quite eight months after the ill-fated reception for the Suzerain of Altai, Alexander Grimm sat with his back to the bustle of a K Street coffeehouse, making notes to himself for another book he planned to write, when a familiar voice sliced through the background clatter. "May I join you, Alexi?"

Grimm looked up into Perris Foyle's serene face. "I can't imagine the circumstances that would prompt me to answer 'no' to that question," he said, rising.

"Really," Perris said pleasantly, seating herself across from him. "Not even the circumstances of our previous meeting—and parting?"

Reclaiming his own seat, Grimm smiled. "I confess, I never expected to see you again after that night."

"Nor I you," said Perris. "But I am far from displeased that I was wrong." Those intriguing dimples appeared, almost as alluring as her dark, wide eyes.

"Same here. But I thought you had gone to live in Europe."

"Yes. I've only just returned. It was very tedious here, you know. After that night, I was under constant surveillance, almost a prisoner in my own home. I complained to the State Department, to the Justice Department, but they denied everything: watching my house, following me and my guests, tapping my phone, all of it—which I found more annoying than the surveillance itself!"

"Maybe they were telling the truth; maybe they weren't watching you."

"Someone was. I am not paranoid, and neither are the men who check my telephones twice a week." She saw his surprised look. "Yes. Thomas always had this done, and I

saw no reason to cancel the contract when he died. Someone was tapping my phones—State Department, Justice Department, FBI—"

"Or the Suzerain of Altai."

"Or the Suzerain, yes." Perris sighed, and waved away
the waitress who had arrived with a pot of coffee and a
laminated menu. "Nevertheless, it was tedious. So I left.
We had a small house in Ireland, you know; Thomas loved
it, it is so very remote and rustic. I had thought perhaps I
would live in Ireland for a while. Thomas and I had
planned to retire there . . . not that he would ever have retired. For a few months I read and painted—did you know
I paint? Watercolors; sometime I will show you—but, it's
funny, after only a few months, I was bored. I wanted to
come home. I had never really thought of Washington as
my home; I only lived here because this is where Thomas
lived. But when I felt as if I had been driven away, *then*
this was my home, and I wanted to come back. And so I
did, just a few weeks ago."

"And the surveillance?"

"In two days, I see they are back like before." She set
her jaw defiantly. "Well, fine. I say let them spy on me and
my friends. Let them tap my phones. Let them deny it. I
don't care."

Grimm smiled at her resolve, and sipped his coffee.
"You know, Perris, there's an easy way to end all of this.
Give back the Canary."

She looked at him, her dark eyes bottomless, unreadable.

"Stick it in a box and mail it to Ms. O'Connor at State.
Anonymously. She wouldn't care, as long as they got it
back."

Perris shook her head, and the light danced in her black
hair. "I told you before, Alexander: I do not know where
the Canary is. Nor do I care."

Grimm contemplated her. At length he said, "By God, I
almost believe you're telling me the truth."

Perris nodded solemnly. "Always, Alexi."

"But if you didn't take the Canary . . ."

A guilty half-smile sprang to life at the woman's full lips. "I always tell you the truth, Alexi, but not always the *whole* truth. I said I do not know or care where the Canary of the Tungus is. That is true; it was true the night of the reception, when you asked me. But . . ." She gave him a strange, contemplative look, while the half-smile stayed in place. "If I were to tell you, Alexi—*if*, mind—that I did indeed take the Canary, what would you do—what would you feel obliged to do?"

"An interesting way of putting it," Grimm said meditatively. "Well, I'm retired from the police department, so my obligation would be the same as any other private citizen's: If I know of a crime, I should report it. But you would simply deny having ever told me anything, and we'd be exactly where we are right now: Everyone certain you took the Canary, no one able to prove it. So I suppose there wouldn't be much point in my reporting it in the first place."

"Just so," Perris said with a laugh. "Then I will tell you: I did take the damned Canary of the Tungus. But I neither know nor care to know where it is now. Have I excited your curiosity?"

"At least," Grimm replied.

Perris Foyle smiled, and settled into the vinyl upholstery of her chair. "Good. Well, to begin at the beginning . . ." Her countenance grew serious and almost dreamy. "I had no plan to steal the Canary, Alexi. You know that it was nothing to me. I would have preferred it remain forgotten in that bank vault, with all of the other curiosities, artifacts, and treasures that Thomas's grandfather, the great archaeologist, pilfered from all around the world, back in the days when the English thought everything belonged to them."

"But it wouldn't remain forgotten. The suzerain wanted his national treasure back."

"Yes, the suzerain," Perris said with poorly masked contempt. "Well, you know my feelings about that man, and everything he and his 'royal house' stand for. I had tried to convince Thomas not to give him the Canary, just out of spite. But of course Thomas wouldn't hear of that, and I suppose he was right. As I told you that night, I wished I could think of something to do about it, but I couldn't. My only thought was to get through the damned presentation as quickly as possible, and get that man and his filthy people out of my home!

"This is what was in my thoughts when I went upstairs with Thomas and that General Korsov person. As Korsov said, Thomas took the case from his safe and opened it, for 'one last look' at the Canary—that was Thomas's joke, since he hadn't even known he owned it. He closed the case and we started to come back downstairs. But then he said he didn't feel well, and then he sank to the floor. I told that idiot Korsov to call for a doctor, and he went out to the landing. And in that moment, it suddenly occurred to me that I had the means to frustrate the damn suzerain, if only for a time."

"You snatched the Canary and replaced it with the marble from the kids' game."

Perris nodded. "I hardly even knew what I was doing—it was almost as if I were watching someone else doing it, swapping the marble for the Canary, then sliding the case under a chair ... Isn't it strange," she continued in that dreamy voice, "my dear husband collapses, and my first thought is not of him but of that damn stone."

"I think Thomas would understand."

Perris brightened. "Do you, Alexi? So do I, actually. Well, there you have it, anyway."

"There I have what? You still haven't told me where the Canary went."

Perris smiled, and after a long moment realization dawned on Grimm. "The fool cat," he said.

Perris laughed and nodded. "The fool cat, yes—

Josephine. When I took the Canary from its case, I realized right away that it would be missed almost immediately, and that I certainly would be searched. So would the room, the entire house. Thomas, no—but the gem would be recovered from his clothes as soon as he reached the hospital. I didn't want the thing for myself, you know, but if the suzerain was going to get it back, I didn't want him to get it easily. And then, Josephine appeared as if by magic, curious as always. I grabbed her, opened her mouth, and popped the Canary down her throat as if it were a big pill of medicine; it's easy to do if you know how.

"When I let go of Josephine, she ran off, of course; cats always do when you've injured their dignity. No one paid any attention to her. Why should they? They tended to poor Thomas . . . My only real regret is that I wasn't there to see Korsov's face when he opened the case. Or the suzerain's when they told him the Canary had been replaced with—I think it was what they call an aggie. Or, for that matter, the look that would be on his face if he ever knew that his precious Canary had ended up in a housecat's litter box . . ."

"Wait a minute," Grimm said, frowning. "You are seriously telling me that the Canary of the Tungus, the national treasure of the people of Altai, for which wars have been fought, dynasties built and destroyed, lives and fortunes sacrificed—this priceless five-hundred-year-old gem got *thrown out with a load of cat shit?*"

"Or coughed up in a furball," Perris said solemnly. "And sometimes Josephine slips outside, you know, so there's really no telling where the, er, event might have occurred. The point is that the Canary is gone, and probably for good. You believe me, do you not?"

"I don't know what to believe," Grimm confessed. "It's absurd . . ."

"You think like a policeman," Perris said, frowning. "Forgive me, Alexander, but it's so. If I tell you that I stole the Canary, smuggled it out of the country, and sold it for millions on the European black market, *then* you will believe me, because that is how a policeman thinks. But if I tell you that I stole the Canary not for profit but so that the suzerain would not have it, then you disbelieve me."

"Ah."

"Yes, ah. Now you begin to understand, Alexi? I have no interest in the Canary of the Tungus: it is the symbol of a world that died long ago and should be left to rest in peace. I could not keep it for myself even if I wanted to, not with men watching my every move. I could not sell it, with every police agency in the world on alert."

"Not that you need the money in any event."

"No: you must know that my husband left me rather a wealthy woman, Alexi. So, as I say, I have no interest in the Canary itself."

"Only in keeping it out of the suzerain's hands."

Perris nodded. "Or, failing that, having it come into the suzerain's royal hands after it has either been spit up or defecated out by an ordinary nonroyal house cat."

Grimm laughed. "You amaze me, Perris."

"Yes? To be truthful, sometimes I amaze myself, too. I could never have thought of a scheme like that, and yet when the opportunity arose ..." She shrugged philosophically. "Well, there it is, Alexi. The Canary of the Tungus is gone—for good, I hope. I hope the rest of the suzerain's reign goes as well for him."

"I had no idea you were so vindictive a woman," Grimm said in mock amazement.

Perris smiled and shrugged. "There must be much about me that you don't know. But now you know about the Canary. And what will you do?"

Grimm considered the question. "Someday," he finally said, "I will tell Lieutenant Barrett about it. He will appreciate it—not now, he won't, not yet. But someday. In the meantime, there's really only one thing to do about you, Perris."

"Oh?" The dimples were there.

"Find out if you have plans for dinner tonight."

Enduring as Dust

•

Bruce Holland Rogers

I drive past the Department of Agriculture every morning on my way to work, and every morning I slow to a crawl so that I can absorb the safe and solid feel of that building as I go by. The north side of Agriculture stretches for two uninterrupted city blocks. The massive walls look as thick as any castle's. Inside, the place is a warren of offices and suboffices, a cozy organizational hierarchy set in stone. I've often thought to myself that if an H-bomb went off right over the Mall, then the White House, the Capitol, the memorials and the reflecting pools would all be blown to ash and steam, but in the midst of the wreckage and the settling dust, there would stand the Department of Agriculture, and the work inside its walls would go securely on.

I don't have that kind of security. The building that houses the Coordinating Administration for Productivity is smaller than our agency's name. The roof leaks. The walls are thin and haven't been painted since the Great Depression.

That I am here is my own fault. Twenty years ago, when I worked for the Bureau of Reclamation, I realized that the glory days of public dam building were over. I imagined that a big RIF wave was coming to the bureau, and I was afraid that I'd be one of those drowned in the Reduction In Force. So I went looking for another agency.

When I found the Coordinating Administration for Productivity, I thought I had found the safest place in Washington to park my career. I'd ask CAP staffers what their agency did.

"We advise other agencies," they would say.

"We coordinate private and public concerns."

"We review productivity."

"We revise strategies."

"We provide oversight."

"But clearly, clearly, we could always do more."

In other words, nobody knew. From the top down, no one could tell me precisely what the administrative mission was. And I thought to myself, I want to be a part of this. No one will ever be able to suggest that we are no longer needed, that it's time for all of us to clear out our desks, that our job is done, because no one knows what our job *is*.

But I was wrong about the Bureau of Reclamation. It hasn't had a major project for two decades, doesn't have any planned, and yet endures, and will continue to endure, through fiscal year after fiscal year, time without end. It is too big to die.

The Coordinating Administration for Productivity, on the other hand, employs just thirty civil servants. We're always on the bubble. With a stroke of the pen, we could vanish from next year's budget. All it would take is for someone to notice us long enough to erase us. And so, as I soon learned, there was an administrative mission statement after all: Don't Get Noticed.

That's why we never complained to GSA about the condition of our building, why we turned the other cheek when FDA employees started parking in our lot and eventually took it over. That's also why no one ever confronted the secretaries about the cats named Dust. And above all, that is why I was so nervous on the morning that our chief administrator called an "urgent meeting."

I sat waiting outside of the administrator's office with Susana de Vega, the assistant administrator, and Tom Willis, Susana's deputy. "I don't like this," Tom said. "I don't like this one damn bit."

Susana hissed at him and looked at the administrator's secretary. But Roxie wasn't listening to us. She was talking, through an open window, to the cat on the fire escape. The cat was a gray tom with the tattered ears of a streetfighter. He backed up warily as Roxie put the food bowl down. "Relax, Dust," she said. "I'm not going to hurt you."

It was January, a few days before the presidential inauguration, and the air coming in through the window was cold, but nobody asked Roxie to close it.

"When has Cooper ever called an *urgent* meeting?" Tom continued in a lower voice. "Hell, how many times has he called a meeting of any damn kind? He's up to something. He's got to throw his goddam Schedule-C weight around while he still has it to throw."

Throwing his weight around didn't sound like Bill Cooper, but I didn't bother to say so. After all, Cooper was a political appointee on his way out, so whether he threw his weight around or not, Tom's underlying point was correct: Cooper was a loose cannon. He had nothing to lose. Intentionally or not, he might blow us up.

Roxie waited to see if the cat would consent to having his chin scratched, but Dust held his ground until the window was closed. Even then, he approached the food warily, as if checking for booby traps.

Susana told Tom to relax. "Two weeks," she reminded him. "Three at the outside."

"And then god only knows what we'll be getting," Tom said, pulling at his chin. "I hate politics."

Roxie's intercom buzzed, and without turning away from the cat she told us, "You can go in now."

I followed Susana and Tom in, and found Cooper nestled deeply in his executive chair, looking as friendly and harmless as he ever had. His slightly drooping eyelids made him seem, as always, half asleep. He waved us into our seats, and as I sat down, I realized how little he had done to personalize his office in the twelve years of his tenure. Everything in the room was government issue. There weren't any family pictures or the usual paperweights made by children or grandchildren. In fact, there wasn't anything on the surface of his desk at all. It was as if Cooper had been anticipating, from the day he moved in, the day when he would have to move out.

There was *some* decoration in the room, a pen-and-ink drawing on the wall behind Cooper, but that had been there for as long as I had been with the CAP. It showed an Oriental-looking wooden building next to a plot of empty ground, and I knew from having looked once, maybe fifteen years ago, that the drawing wasn't just hung on the wall. The frame had been nailed into the paneling, making it a permanent installation.

"People," Cooper said from deep inside his chair, "we have a problem." He let that last word hang in the air as he searched for what to say next.

Susana, Tom and I leaned forward in our chairs.

"An impropriety," he went on.

We leaned a little more.

"A mystery."

We watched expectantly as Cooper opened his desk drawer and took out a sheet of paper. He studied it for a long time, and then said, "You people know my management style. I've been hands-off. I've always let you people handle the details," by which he meant that he didn't know what we did all day and didn't care, so long as we told him that everything was running smoothly. He tapped the sheet of paper and said, "But here is something that demands my attention, and I want it cleared up while I'm still in charge."

And then he read from the letter in his hand. The writer represented something called the Five-State Cotton Consortium, and he had come to Washington to get advice on federal funding for his organization. He had taken an employee of the Coordinating Administration for Productivity to lunch, picking her brain about the special appropriations process as well as various grant sources. The woman had been very helpful, and the letter writer just wanted Cooper to know that at least one member of his staff was really on the ball. The helpful staffer's name was Kim Semper.

At the sound of that name, I felt ice form in the pit of my stomach. I stared straight ahead, keeping my expression as plain as I could manage. I knew some of what Cooper was going to say next, but I tried to look genuinely surprised when he told us what had happened after he received the letter.

"I wanted to touch base with Ms. Semper and make sure that the citizen hadn't actually paid for her lunch. You people know as well as I do that we don't want any conflict-of-interest cases."

"Of course not," said Susana. "But I don't see how there could be any such conflict. We don't actually make funding decisions."

"We don't?" Cooper said, and then he recovered to say, "No, of course not. But you people will agree that we wouldn't want even the *appearance* of impropriety. And anyway, that doesn't matter. What matters is that in my search for Kim Semper, I came up empty. We don't have an employee by that name."

Trying to sound more convincing than I felt, I said, "Maybe it's a mistake, Bill. Maybe the letter writer had the name wrong, or sent the letter to the wrong agency."

"Hell, yes!" Tom said with too much enthusiasm. "It's just some damn case of mistaken identity!"

But Cooper wasn't going to be turned easily. "I called

the citizen," he told us. "No mistake. Someone is posing as an officer of our agency, a criminal offense."

I said, "Doesn't there have to be intent to defraud for this to be a crime?"

Cooper frowned. "The citizen did buy lunch for this Kim Semper. She benefitted materially." He shook the letter at me. "This is a serious matter."

"And one we'll get to the bottom of," Susana promised.

"I want it done before my departure," Cooper said. "I don't want to saddle my successor with any difficulties," by which he meant that he didn't want to leave behind any dirty laundry that might embarrass him when he was no longer in a position to have it covered up.

Susana said again, "We'll get to the bottom of it."

Cooper nodded at Tom. "I want a single point of responsibility on this, so the personnel director will head up the investigation."

With Cooper still looking at him, Tom looked at me expectantly, and I felt compelled to speak up. "That would be me," I said. "Tom's your deputy assistant."

"Of course," Cooper said, covering. He turned to me. "And you'll report to him." Then he added, "You aren't too busy to take care of this matter, I assume."

"It'll be tight," I said, thinking of the Russian novel I'd been wading through for the last week, "but I'll squeeze it in."

Outside of Cooper's office, Susana patted Tom's shoulder, then mine, and said with complete ambiguity, "You know what to do." Then she disappeared down the hall, into her own office.

Roxie's cat was gone, but Roxie had something else to distract her now. She was reading a GPO publication called, *Small Business Administration Seed Projects: Program Announcement and Guidelines*. She didn't even look up when Tom hissed at me, "Sit on it!"

"What?"

"You know damn well what I mean," Tom said through his teeth. "I don't know what this Kim Semper thing is all about, and I don't want to know! This is just the kind of problem that could blow us out of the goddam water!"

I said, "Are you telling me to ignore an assignment from the chief administrator?"

I could see in Tom's eyes the recognition that he had already been too specific. "Not at all," he said in a normal voice, loud enough for Roxie to overhear if she were listening. "I'm telling you to handle this in the most appropriate fashion." Then he, too, bailed out, heading for his own office.

I found my secretary, Vera, trying to type with a calico cat in her lap. The cat was purring and affectionately digging its claws into Vera's knee.

"Damn it, Vera," I said, surprising myself, "the memo specifies feeding only. Everybody knows that. You are not supposed to have the cat inside the building!"

"You hear that, Dust?" Vera said as she rubbed behind the cat's ears. "It's back out into the cold with you." But she made no move to get up.

"Hold my calls," I growled. I went into my office and closed the door, wishing that I had a copy of the legendary memo so that I could read chapter and verse to Vera. It was bad enough that the secretaries had distorted the wording of the memo, issued well over twenty years ago, that had allowed them to feed a stray cat named Dust, "and only a cat named Dust." It seemed like every so often, they had to push beyond even the most liberal limits of that allowance, and no manager was willing to make an issue of it, lest it turn into a civil service grievance that would bring an OPM investigation crashing down around our ears.

I didn't stew about the cat for long. I still had Kim Semper on my mind. It took me a few minutes to find the key to my file cabinet, but once I had the drawer open, there weren't many folders to search through before I found what

I wanted. I untaped the file folder marked PRIVATE and pulled out the letter. It was addressed to me and sported an eleven-year-old date. "After failing to determine just who her supervisor is," the text began, "I have decided to write to you, the Director of Personnel, to commend one of your administrators, Miss Kim Semper." The story from there was pretty much the same: a citizen had come to Washington looking for information, had stumbled across the Coordinating Administration for Productivity, and had ended up buying Semper's lunch in exchange for her insights on the intricacies of doing business in the Beltway. Though he had been unable to contact her subsequently, her advice had been a big help to him.

After checking the personnel files, I had called the letter writer to tell him that he'd been mistaken, that there was no Kim Semper here at the CAP. Maybe, I suggested, he had gone to some other agency and confused the names? But he was sure that it was the CAP that he had consulted, and he described our building right down to the tiny, nearly unreadable gray lettering that announced the agency's name on the front door.

In a government agency, a mystery, any mystery, is a potential bomb. If you're not sure of what something is, then you assume that it's going to blow up in your face if you mess with it. At the CAP, where everything was uncertain and shaky to begin with, the unknown seemed even more dangerous. So I had buried the letter.

Now maybe it was coming back to haunt me. I wondered if I should cover my tail by xeroxing my letter and bringing Cooper a copy right now. "Hey, Bill. I had to check my files on this, to make sure, but would you believe . . ." Maybe that would be good damage control.

But maybe not. After all, Cooper seemed to think this was an urgent matter. I had known about it for eleven years and done nothing. And my letter was so old that I probably didn't have to worry about it hurting me if I didn't bring up

its existence. By now, the writer himself might not even remember sending it to me. Perhaps the man was even dead.
If I kept my mouth shut, it was just possible that no one
would ever know about my Kim Semper letter. And if that
was what I wanted, then it would help my cause to do just
what Tom had urged: To sit on the investigation, to ignore
Kim Semper until the executive-branch resignations worked
their way down, layer by layer, from the new president's
cabinet to our agency, and Cooper was on his way.

Either option, hiding the letter or revealing it, had its
dangers. No matter how I played it out in my mind, I
couldn't see the safe bet. I returned to what I'd been doing
before the meeting with Cooper, and I should have been
able to concentrate on it. Napoleon was watching this Polish general, who wanted to impress him, trying to swim
some cavalry across a Russian river, but the horses were
drowning and everything was a mess. It was exciting, but
it didn't hold my attention. I read the same page over and
over, distracted with worry.

At the end of the day, there was no cat in Vera's lap, but
there was a skinny little tabby begging on the fire escape.
At her desk, Vera was pouring some cat food into a bowl
labeled, "Dust."

"Sorry I snapped earlier," I said.

"Bad day?" Vera said, opening the window.

"The worst," I told her, noticing the stack of outgoing
mail on her desk. "Is that something I asked you to do?"

"Oh, I'm just getting some information for the staff library," she said.

I nodded, trying to think of something managerial to say.
"You're self-directed, Vera. I like to see that."

"Oh, I've always been that way," she told me. "I can't
stand to be idle." She opened the window to feed the cat
and said, "Here you go, Dust."

Cooper called another meeting for Thursday of the next
week. It was the day after the inauguration, and he must

have felt the ticking clock. Before the meeting, Tom called me.

"How's your investigation coming?" he said.

"Slowly."

"Good. That's damn good. See you in the old man's office."

For once there wasn't a cat on Roxie's fire escape. Cooper's door was open, and I walked right in. Susana and Tom were already there, and Cooper motioned me to a seat. Cooper didn't waste any time.

"What have you got?"

I opened my notebook. "First, I double-checked the personnel files, not just the current ones, but going back twenty-five years." I looked at Cooper grimly. "No one by the name of Kim Semper has *ever* worked for the Coordinating Administration for Productivity."

"Yes, yes," Cooper said. "What else?"

"I called over to the Office of Personnel Management. There is not now, nor has there ever been, anywhere in the civil service system, an employee named Kim Semper." I closed the notebook and put on the face of a man who has done his job well.

Cooper stared at me. I pretended to look back at him earnestly, but my focus was actually on the framed pen-and-ink behind him. If I had to give it a title, I decided, it would be, *Japanese Shed with Empty Lot*.

At last Cooper said, "Is that all?"

"Well, Bill, I haven't been able to give this my full attention."

"It's been a week, a *week* since I brought this up to you people."

"And a hellish week it's been," I said, looking to Tom for help.

"That's true," Tom jumped in. "The inauguration has stirred things up. We've had an unusually, ah, unusually heavy run of requests." Cooper frowned, and I could see

Tom's hands tighten on the side of his chair. He was hoping, I knew, that Cooper wouldn't say, "Requests for what? From whom?"

Susana saved us both by saying, "I'm ashamed of the two of you! Don't you have any sense of priorities? And, Tom, you're supposed to be supervising this investigation. That means staying on top of it, making sure it's progressing." She turned to Cooper. "We'll have something substantial next week, Bill."

"I don't know, people," Cooper said. "Realistically, something like this is out of your purview. Maybe it calls for an outside investigator."

Cooper was almost certainly bluffing. Any dirt at the bottom of this would cling to him like tar if we brought in the consul general's office. He wanted to keep this internal as much as we did.

Even so, Susana paled. She played it cool, but it was a strain on her. "Why don't you see what we come up with in seven working days? Then you can decide."

Minutes later, in the hallway, Tom said, "So what now?"

"Don't look at me," Susana told him without breaking stride. "I pulled your bacon out of the fire, boys. Don't ask me to think for you, too." Then over her shoulder, she added, "You'd just better appear to be making progress by our next little get-together."

Before he left me standing alone in the hallway, Tom said, "You heard the lady, Ace. Let's see some goddam action."

In my office, with the door closed behind me, I finished another chapter of the Russian novel and then got right on the case. I cleared space on the floor and laid out the personnel files for the last eleven years. It made sense to assume that "Kim Semper" was an insider, or had an inside confederate who could arrange her lunchtime meetings. And I knew that Ms. Semper had been working this free-lunch scam since at least the date of my letter. I figured that

I could at least narrow down my suspect pool by weeding out anyone who hadn't been with the CAP for that long.

Unfortunately, this didn't narrow things much. Even Cooper, by virtue of three straight presidential victories for his party, had been with the CAP for longer than that.

So what did I really have to go on? Just two letters of praise for Kim Semper, dated eleven years apart. The letter writers themselves had met Kim Semper, but there were good reasons for not calling them for more information. After all, I wanted to keep my letter buried to preserve my plausible deniability. And Cooper's letter writer had already been contacted once about Kim Semper. If I called again and grilled him, he might resent it, and I could use up his goodwill before I even knew what questions to ask. Also, he might get the impression that the Coordinating Administration for Productivity didn't have its act together, and who knew where that could lead? I didn't want a citizen complaining to his congressional rep.

What I needed was another source, but there wasn't one. Or was there?

I arranged the personnel files on the floor to look like an organizational hierarchy. If someone were to send a letter praising an employee of the CAP, where might that letter go?

To the top, of course. That was Cooper.

And to the Director of Personnel. That was me.

But what about the space between these two? What about the Assistant Administrator and her Deputy? That is, what about Susana and Tom?

Outside of Susana's office, her administrative assistant, Peter, was preparing to feed a black cat on the fire escape. Almost as soon as he opened the window, Peter sneezed.

"Susana in?"

"Yes," Peter said, "but she's unavailable." He set the cat bowl down and closed the window. Then he sneezed again.

"If you're so allergic," I said, "how come you're feeding the kitty?"

"Oh, I like cats, even if they do make my eyes swell shut." He laughed. "Anyway, feeding Dust is the corporate culture around here, right? When in Rome . . ."

From the other side of Susana's door, I could hear the steady beat of music.

I watched the stray cat as it ate. "I'm surprised, with all the cats on our fire escapes, that it isn't just one continuous cat fight out there."

"They're smart animals," Peter said. "Once they have a routine, they stay out of each other's way."

I nodded, but I wasn't really paying attention. Over the beat of the music, I could hear a female voice that wasn't Susana's counting *one-and-two-and-three-and—*

I went to her door and put my hand on the knob.

"I told you," Peter said. "Susana's unavailable. If you want to make an appointment . . ."

"This can't wait," I said. I opened the door.

Susana was in a leotard, and I caught her in the middle of a leg lift. She froze while the three women on the workout tape kept on exercising and counting without her.

"I told Peter I wasn't to be disturbed," she said, still holding her leg up like some varicolored flamingo.

"This won't take but a minute," I said. "In fact, you can go right on with your important government business while we talk."

She stopped the tape and glared at me. "What do you want?"

"To get to the bottom of this Kim Semper thing. And if that's what you really want too, then you can't be throwing me curve balls."

"What are you talking about?" She pushed the audiovisual cart between two file cabinets and threw a dust cover over it.

"I'm talking, Susana, about sitting on information. Or

call it withholding evidence. I want your correspondence file on Kim Semper."

Susana circled behind her desk and sat down. Ordinarily, that would have been a good gesture, a way of reminding me that she was, after all, the assistant admin, and this was her turf I had invaded. But it was a hard move to pull off in a leotard. "Just what makes you think I even have such a file?"

That was practically a confession. I fought down a smile. "I'm on your side," I reminded her. "But we've got to show some progress on this. Cooper is on his last official breath. Dying men are unpredictable. But if we hold all the cards, how dangerous can he be?"

She stared over my head, no doubt thinking the same thoughts I had about my own Kim Semper letter. How would Cooper react to knowing that she'd had these letters in her files all along?

"You've got the file where, Susana? In your desk? In one of those cabinets? If I close my eyes," I said, closing them, "then I'll be able to honestly tell Cooper that I don't know *exactly* where my information came from. It was just sort of dropped into my lap."

It took her a minute of rummaging, and then a folder fell into my hands. I opened my eyes. The three letters ranged from two to ten years old.

"Read them in your own office," she said. "And next time, knock."

On my way out, I noticed that Peter was reading something called *America's Industrial Future: A Report of the Presidential Colloquium on U.S. Manufacturing Productivity for the Year 2000 and Beyond.* A thing like that wouldn't ordinarily stick in my mind, except that Tom's secretary, Janet, was reading the same report. She was also holding a mottled white-and-tan cat in her lap. I didn't bother to confront her about it—that was Tom's fight, if he wanted to fight it. I just knocked on Tom's door and stepped into his office.

He swept a magazine from his desk and into a drawer, but he wasn't fast enough to keep me from noting the cover feature: THE GIRLS OF THE PAC TEN. "What the hell do you want?" he growled.

"A hell of a lot more than I'm getting," I barked back. "Damn little you've done to help this investigation along, Willis. Enough bullshit. I'm up to here with bullshit. I want your goddam Kim Semper correspondence file."

"Like hell." Tom glowered, but a little quiver of uncertainty ran across his lowered eyebrows. He wasn't used to being on the receiving end of such bluster.

"Cut the crap, Tom. This goddam Semper bullshit will toss us all on our asses if we don't give Cooper something to chew on. So give."

A little timidly, he said, "I don't know what you're . . ."

"Like hell," I said, waving de Vega's letters. "Susana came across, and I'd sure as hell hate to tell Cooper that you're the one stalling his goddam investigation."

He bit his lip and took a file-cabinet key from his desk drawer. "Jesus," he said. "I've never seen you like this."

"You better hope like hell you never see it again," I said, which was probably overdoing things, but I was on a roll.

As I read it in my office, the first of Tom's letters cheered me considerably. One was twenty years old, which altered my suspect list quite a bit. From my array of files on the floor, I removed anyone who hadn't been with the CAP for the last two decades. That left just myself, Tom Willis, and Tom's secretary Janet. I picked up Janet's file and smiled. Kim Semper, I thought, you have met your match.

And then I read Tom's other letter, the most recent one of all, excepting Cooper's. It praised *Mr.* Kim Semper, for *his* dedication to public service.

No, I thought. This can't be right.

Unless there was more than one Kim Semper.

I sat down behind my desk. Hard. And I thought about the cat named Dust, who came in a dozen variations, but who, by long tradition, was always Dust, was always considered to be the same cat, because the ancient memo had allowed for the feeding of a cat named Dust, "and only a cat named Dust."

I picked up the phone and dialed the number of the man who had written to praise Mr. Semper. "Mr. Davis," I said when I had him on the line, "one of our employees is in line for a service award, and I just want to make sure it's going to the right person. You wrote a letter to us about a Mr. Kim Semper. Now, we've got a Kim Semple on our staff, and a Tim Kemper, but no Kim Semper. Could you do me the favor of describing the man who was so helpful?"

As lame stories go, this one worked pretty well. It sounded plausible, and it didn't make the CAP look bad. And it brought results. Davis was only happy to make sure Semper or Semple or Kemper got his due. The description fit Peter to a T.

I tried the next most recent letter, but the number had been disconnected. The next one back from that—I changed Tim Kemper to Lynn—brought me a good description of Roxie. The third call, the one that cinched it, paid off with a description that could only be my own Vera.

That's when I buzzed Vera into my office.

"I want a copy of the cat memo," I told her.

"The cat memo?"

"Don't fence with me. If you don't have a copy of it yourself, you know how to get one. I want it within the hour." Then I lowered my voice conspiratorially. "Vera, I don't have anything against cats. Trust me on that."

She had a copy in my hands in five minutes. When I looked at the date, I whistled. Dust the cat had been on this officially sanctioned meal ticket for more than forty years, much longer than I had supposed. The memo also named the secretary who had first started feeding Dust. After a phone call to OPM, I was on my way to Silver Spring, Maryland.

The house I stopped in front of was modest, but nonetheless stood out from all the other clapboard houses on that street. There were abstract, Oriental-looking sculptures in the garden. The white stones around the plum trees had been raked into tidy rows, and there was a fountain bubbling near the walkway to the front door.

A white-haired woman holding a gravel rake came around the side of the house, moving with a grace that belied her eighty years.

"Mrs. Taida?" I said. She looked up and waved me impatiently into the garden. As I opened the gate, I said, "I'm the one who called you, Mrs. Taida. From the Coordinating Administration for Productivity."

"Yes, of course," she said. As I approached, she riveted me with her gaze. Her eyes were blue as arctic ice.

"You are Janet Taida, yes?"

"You expected me to look more Japanese," she said. "Taida was my husband's name. Sakutaro Taida. The artist." She waved at the sculptures.

"I see," I said, then reached into my pocket for the photocopied memo. "Mrs. Taida, I want to talk to you about the cat named Dust."

"Of course you do," she said. "Come inside and I'll make some tea."

The house was furnished in the traditional Japanese style, with furniture that was close to the floor. While Mrs. Taida started the water boiling in the kitchen, I looked at the artwork hanging on the walls. There were paintings and drawings that seemed vaguely familiar, somehow, but it wasn't until I saw the big pen-and-ink on the far wall that I knew what I was looking at.

"There's a drawing like this in the administrator's office," I said when Mrs. Taida came into the room with the teapot.

"A drawing *almost* like that one," Mrs. Taida said. She waved toward a cushion. "Won't you sit down?" she commanded. She poured the tea. "That's a Shinto temple. It has two parts, two buildings. But only one stands at a time. Every twenty years, one is torn down and the other is rebuilt. They are both present, always. But the manifestation changes."

"The drawing at work shows the other phase," I said, "when the other building is standing and this one has been torn down."

Mrs. Taida nodded. A white long-haired cat padded into the room.

"Dust?" I said.

Taking up her teacup, Mrs. Taida shook her head. "No, there's only one Dust."

I laughed. "But like the temple, many manifestations." I unfolded the memo. "This memo, the Dust memo, mentions you by name, Mrs. Taida. You started it, didn't you? You were the administrator's secretary when the secretaries received their sanction to keep caring for, as it says here, 'a cat named Dust.' "

"Once we began to feed one, it was very hard to turn the others away. So I read the memo very carefully."

"Mrs. Taida, cats are one thing, but . . ."

"I know. Cats are one thing, but Kim Semper is far more serious, right?" She lowered her teacup. "Let me explain something to you," she said. "The Coordinating Administration for Productivity was commissioned over fifty years ago. They had a clear wartime purpose, which they completed, and then the agency began to drift. Your tea is getting cold."

She waited until I had picked it up and taken a sip.

"A government agency develops a culture, and it attracts

people who are comfortable with that culture. After its war-time years the CAP attracted ostriches."

I opened my mouth, but she held up her hand.

"You can't deny it," she said. "For forty years, the CAP has been managed by men and women who wanted to rule over a quiet little fiefdom where nothing much happened."

She sipped her own tea.

"Do you have any idea what it's like to be a secretary under conditions like that?" She shook her head. "Nothing happens. There's too little to do, and the day just crawls by. You can't have any idea how hard it was, at the end of the war and with a Japanese husband, to get a government job. And then to have to sit on my hands all day, doing nothing . . ."

"Mrs. Taida . . ."

"I am not finished speaking," she said with authority, and I felt my face flush. "As I was saying, working at the CAP was like being a sailor on a rudderless ship. Have some more tea."

I held out my cup, as commanded.

"What endures in a government agency?" she asked as she poured again. "The management? The support staff? Job titles shift. Duties change. But the culture remains. It's like the tradition of a secretary feeding a stray cat at ten in the morning. The secretary may retire, but another will come, and if there's a tradition of feeding the stray cat at ten, then the person who takes the job will likely be some-one who likes cats anyway. The cat may die or move on, but another will appear before long. The feeding goes on, even if who is fed and by whom changes over time."

She put the teapot down. "Administrators come and go, but the culture endures. And Kim Semper endures. When a citizen calls the agency for help, he isn't referred to management. No one at that level knows anything. No, the citizen is referred to Kim Semper. And for the pleasure of the work itself, of knowing things and being helpful, the secretaries do the job of the Coordinating Administration for Productivity. And they do a very good job. How many of those people who are helped by Kim Semper bother to write letters, do you suppose? And how many of the letters that are written actually end up in the hands of CAP administrators? Kim Semper provides good answers to hard questions about productivity and legislative action. I gave the CAP a rudder, you see. It operates from the galley, not the bridge."

"There's the question of ethics," I said. "There's the matter of lunches paid for by citizens, of benefit derived by fraud."

She looked at me long and hard. It was a look that said everything there was to say about collecting a GS-13 salary working for an agency where the managers were fuzzy about how they should fill their days. She didn't have to say a word.

"Well, what am I supposed to do then?" I said. "Now that I know the truth, what do I say when the administrator asks for my report?"

"You didn't get to where you are today without knowing how to stall," Mrs. Taida said. "You do what you do best, and let the secretaries do what *they* do best."

"What about *after* Cooper is gone?" I said. "This is a bomb just waiting to go off. This is the kind of thing that can sink a little agency like ours."

"The Coordinating Administration for Productivity is a fifty-year-old bureaucracy," Mrs. Taida said, "with a little secret that no one has discovered for forty years. You're the only one who threatens the status quo." She picked up our teacups and the pot. "If you don't rock the boat, I'm sure the CAP, along with Dust and Kim Semper, will endure for time without end. And now, if you don't mind, I have things to do."

I drove back to the office slowly. I knew what I had to do, but I didn't know exactly how to get it done. At least, not until I got as far as the Department of Agriculture. There, I pulled into the right lane and slowed to a crawl.

Size, I thought. The thing that comforts me about the Department of Agriculture is its size. It is big and white and easy to get lost in. That's what safety is.

I drove back and got right to work. It was a big job. I enlisted Vera and Roxie, along with Janet, Peter, and some of the secretaries from downstairs. I didn't explain in great detail what we were doing or why it was important. They understood. In a week, we had generated the very thing that Bill Cooper had called for.

"Results," I announced, shouldering between Susana and Tom to drop my report onto Cooper's desk. It landed with a thud. Cooper blinked slowly, then opened the heavy white binding to the first page. *A Report on Personnel and Operational Dislocation at the Coordinating Administration for Productivity,* it read. "Everything you need to know about Kim Semper is in there."

Cooper nodded. "It's, ah, impressive. You people really knocked yourselves out."

"Yes, sir," I said. "I can't take all the credit. Susana and Tom were instrumental, really."

Neither of them looked up. They were still staring at the report.

Cooper began to scan the executive summary, but his eyes began to glaze when he got to the paragraph about operational location as a time- and institution-based function not contingent upon the identity of the individual operator. "So can you summarize the contents for me?"

"Well," I said, "it's a bit involved. But you can get the gist of it in the summary that you're reading."

Cooper kept thumbing through the summary. It went on for ninety-three pages.

"To really get a complete sense of the situation," I said, "you'll need to read the complete report. Right, Susana?"

She nodded. "Of course."

"Tom?"

"You bet your ass. It's all there, though. Every damn bit of it." He said it with pride, as though he really had made some contribution.

"It took a thousand pages to get it said, Bill. And it really takes a thousand to make sense of it all. So, you see, I can't just give it to you in a sentence."

"I see," Cooper said, nodding, and he was still nodding, still looking at the four-inch volume, when Susana and Tom and I left the room.

"You're a goddam genius is what you are," Tom said. And Susana told me, "Good work."

And when Cooper cleared out for good, he left the report behind. It's there still, taking up space on his successor's desk. Sometimes when I see it sitting there, I think to myself that a bomb could go off in that room, and everything would be blown to hell but that plastic-bound, metal-spined, ten-pound volume of unreadable prose. It wouldn't suffer so much as a singed page.

It gives me a safe and solid feeling.

[faded text from facing page bleeding through, partially legible]

Code Red: Terror on the Mall!

•

Bill Crider

[CHAPTERS FROM AN ABORTIVE TECHNO-THRILLER]

REFLECTIONS AND RECRIMINATIONS

Shawn and the FBI man, Porter, were standing in West Potomac Park, just across 17th Street at the head of the reflecting pool.

Porter held up the nail. "This is it, the thing that did them in. Just an ordinary galvanized roofing nail. Made in Korea. This one's from a batch that was shipped to this country only two months ago, all bought by Discount Handyman stores throughout the nation. This particular nail was sold by store number 26 right here in D.C. and was bought as part of a lot sold to Triple X Roofing. We're virtually certain that a Triple X truck on the way to a roofing job in Alexandria drove down Constitution Avenue this morning at approximately 8:05. The dispatcher couldn't 'nail down' the time exactly.

Porter allowed himself a small smile at his pun before continuing. "The nail dropped off the truck and fell into the street, where it lay until the terrorists drove over it."

Shawn took the nail from the FBI man and held it in the

sunlight, admiring its dull corrosionproof finish, produced
by a new process just perfected by the Koreans. After reading an article in an obscure trade journal, he had invested
heavily in the stock of the U.S. company that had come up
with the process, and he thought the stock would split
within a month, bringing him a tidy profit. *Sometimes being
a foreign-trade expert had its advantages.*

"What kind of tires did they have on their vehicle?"
Shawn asked. The tree the car had swerved into was being
inspected by the forensics experts, but the car had already
been towed away by the time that Shawn arrived on the
scene; otherwise he would have examined the tires himself.

Porter looked contemptuously toward the monument
where the terrorists had taken shelter. "Just the standard
manufacturer's rubber—P195 steel-belted radials."

Shawn and the FBI man shared a laugh over that. If the
terrorists had only known, they might have taken advantage
of the new iridium-belted tires, which would be on the market in a few months but which could already be obtained
through the right channels. These tires were impervious to
anything short of a railroad spike driven by a nine-pound
sledge. If they'd had those tires on their car, the terrorists
would have been in New York by now. Shawn had the tires
on his own car, and of course he had long since invested in
the company.

But the two men's laughter was short-lived. The problem
at hand was much too serious to be taken lightly.

"How many civilians did they kill?" Shawn asked.

"None," Porter said. "The monument wasn't open yet.
Too early. The custodian on duty was taken hostage, of
course, but he's a member of the Park Service."

The implication was clear: The custodian was a pro. He
would have been briefed about possible terrorist attacks,
and he'd be well aware of the fact that there would be no
negotiations for his release.

"There was a line of people outside, however," Porter

continued. "Waiting to get in. And the terrorists did shove one woman down. She received multiple contusions, and we've coptered her to Johns Hopkins. She was eighty years old."

"The fiends," Shawn said. *First cats, then an old woman. They had to be stopped.*

"I have a cat myself," Porter said.

Shawn looked at the FBI man without interest. The truth was that he didn't much like cats, and he thought that the president was just a little bit of a wuss for owning one. Not that Bush's dog had been much better, but at least it had been a dog. But it had written a book. What kind of dog was that? *Why didn't anyone own REAL dogs anymore, like Irish setters?* Maybe that was what was wrong with the country.

"Just who are we dealing with here?" he asked.

"The Bloody Swords of Allah," Porter said. "It's an extremist Shiite group that even the government of Iran disavows. Its members think that the Ayatollah was too easy on Salman Rushdie."

"What do you think of the Rushdie affair?"

Porter tugged at his earlobe. "I believe in freedom of speech, and I believe it should be a worldwide freedom, just like every other right-thinking human being believes. To suggest that a man should be killed for something he's written, well, it's just unthinkable."

Shawn smiled. A lot of the American public would be surprised to hear an FBI man make a speech like that, but in Shawn's experience, most of the feds were actually quite liberal in their thinking.

Just then a long black car drove through the cordon of soldiers that surrounded the Washington Monument. It came to a stop, and the driver jumped out, raced to the rear door, and opened it. The president stepped out.

In one hand he was carrying an M16 rifle, capable of firing up to 900 rounds per minute on full automatic. In his other hand he had a 40mm grenade launcher that he was awkwardly trying to attach under the rifle's barrel. When used by a skilled rifleman, the grenade launcher could hurl its deadly package over a thousand yards with considerable accuracy. A canvas bag holding the grenades was hanging from the president's shoulder.

Porter rushed over to the president. "You shouldn't be here, sir. This isn't your fight."

The president brushed by the FBI man angrily. "That's my cat they've got up there. It's up to me to get him back."

Shawn knew what was going on in the man's mind. Shawn had felt the same way once, when his own wife and son had been attacked while on a family vacation in Europe, an attack that came in retaliation for Shawn's interference in delicate trade negotiations between the U.S. and a Middle-Eastern potentate who had cornered the date market. Shawn's knowledge of the impending development of a synthetic date substitute by Monsanto had swung the balance of power to the U.S. in the dealings, and the potentate had never forgiven the analyst for his cleverness.

He walked over to the president and put a hand on his arm. "It's not your fault, sir."

The president was cool now, his momentary anger under control. He was a good man in an emergency.

"I understand what you're trying to do, Shawn." The president smiled to show that he meant it. He and Shawn were frequent jogging partners on their early-morning runs in the District, and they shared a passion for Big Macs and Razorback football. "But this is something I've got to do. You—well, you don't have to prove anything. You're a Marine."

That was true. Shawn had served in the Corps, and when you'd done that there was just something about you that other men recognized. An aura, almost. They could tell that you were among the best and the brightest as surely as if the hand of God rested on your shoulder.

"I didn't serve in 'Nam, sir," Shawn said.

"I know you didn't, and I don't hold that against you. I suppose it's generally known that I didn't serve in 'Nam, either."

It's generally known that you didn't serve anywhere, wuss. "Yes, sir. It's known."

The president brandished the M16. "That doesn't mean that I can't use this. I've shot many a squirrel in Arkansas."

Shawn stared at him.

"Let me rephrase that. I've killed a lot of wild game back in the hills. I can use a rifle."

"I never doubted that you could, sir."

That wasn't true. It would be almost impossible, considering that there were only eight small windows at the top of the obelisk, and those windows were covered with extra-thick glass.

"But what if you did? Think of the cat."

"The cat?"

"Supposing you do lob a grenade into the monument. You might kill some of those bastards. But what about the cat?"

"Hair on the walls," Porter said. "Cat hair."

The president's shoulders slumped. The presidential cat was a lot more popular with the nation as a whole than the president himself. It wouldn't do for him to kill his own cat.

"Buck up, man," Shawn said, his voice sharp.

The president's head jerked up. He wasn't used to having anyone talk to him that way, at least anyone outside his immediate family.

"It's not your fault they got the cat," Shawn said.

"But it is. I was the one that insisted she be walked on the grounds. I was the one who insisted on the extra-long leash. I—"

"Stop it!" Shawn said. "You did the best you could

221

under the circumstances. You did all that any man could do. You stopped them from getting your wife and child."

"That's true," the president mused. "But it'll be awhile before my wife forgives me for shoving her into that rose-bush." *And longer than that before she forgives me for jumping in on top of her.*

"Don't worry about that, sir," Shawn told him. "We'll get that cat back for you."

The president straightened. "Not without my help, you won't," he said, and smiled.

STAIRS

There are 898 steps on the iron stairway that goes to the top of the Washington Monument, which is 555 feet 5⅛ inches tall, including the fifty-five-foot-high pyramidion that tops the structure. There are landings at ten-foot intervals, and there are memorial stones positioned at each landing, stones donated by states and organizations. Shawn and the president were on the thirty-foot landing, where Shawn was reading the stone from Delaware, which declares that Delaware was the first state to ratify the Constitution and will be the last to desert it. The president was more interested in the memorial stone from Arkansas, which was on the same level and which Shawn supposed was only natural.

The president had been relieved of the M16. He was now carrying a Walther P–88 with a four-inch barrel and a fifteen-shot clip. It weighed 31½ ounces. The best thing about the pistol, from his point of view, was the fact that it was extremely well adapted to use by a left-hander. The gun was in a holster at his side.

Shawn was carrying a Sig/Sauer P–225, a shorter, lighter version of the P–226. It weighed 5½ ounces less than the president's weapon. The 225 had customized wooden grips; Shawn didn't like plastic. Both guns fired 9mm cartridges, though the magazine in Shawn's held only eight rounds, and both men carried extra clips.

"I still don't see why you had to come," Shawn said.

The president was still panting slightly. The thirty-foot stair climb had winded him, despite his jogging, and there were forty-seven more landings to go. "I've explained that," he huffed. "I had something to prove."

Shawn might have said something about the Secret Service men whose bodies littered the ground near the monument. He might have asked what they had to prove, but he didn't. They'd sworn to guard the president, and they'd known the risks. Under the withering fire rained down by the terrorists, it seemed impossible that anyone had survived. But there was no time to dwell on that now.

"Time to go on," Shawn said.

The president looked up at the stairs, thinking no doubt about the Big Macs with fries he'd had that morning and that he now wished he'd passed up.

"Right," he said.

Frank Tovar, the only American member of The Bloody Swords of Allah, saw that his plan to kidnap the president and his family had gone horribly wrong. He had been stupid to attempt it. He wondered whether his brain could have been softened from listening to too many Cat Stevens recordings.

"Fool," Ali taunted him. "We will die in this stupid shrine to a man with wooden teeth, and it is all your fault."

"Don't break discipline," Tovar said, glancing at their two companions, Nabib and Habib, who stared at him with open hatred. Plainly they agreed with Ali.

"Suppose we die?" Tovar said, trying to hearten them with a display of courage. "What does that matter? We do not have to die ingloriously."

He reached into the knapsack that lay at his feet and removed a thick package wrapped in brown paper.

223

"Plastique," he said. "Enough to blow this monument into the sky like a rocket ship. If we die, we'll take the shrine with us." He looked over at the black-and-white lump that lay on the floor, its legs tied with leather thongs. "And the cat will die, too."

The cat whined pathetically.

"It is well," Ali said.

The memorial stones were nothing more than a blur as Shawn ran past them up the stairs. He ignored them all, even the one from the Pennsylvania Sons of Temperance.

But he still couldn't catch the president, who seemed to have gotten his second wind somewhere about the twentieth landing and was now running well ahead. Maybe he was thinking about his daughter and how she would feel if the cat were to suffer. Or maybe he was wondering what the nation would think of a president who let his pet be murdered by terrorists. It didn't matter. For whatever reason, he was fairly flying up the stairway.

Neither he nor Shawn was making any noise, however. Both men had kicked off their shoes at the bottom of the stairway and were in their stocking feet. The president was wearing plain black Gold Toe ribbed socks, the over-the-calf design. But Shawn was wearing white running socks that were made of cotton bonded to a miracle fiber that drew perspiration away from the cotton and allowed it to dry on the outside of his foot. His investment in the miracle fiber had allowed him to add the fifty-two-inch TV set to the den in his twenty-room house near Baltimore, and there would be more goodies to come. If he survived the day.

The miracle fibers didn't help his speed, however. He still couldn't catch the president. Maybe it was his old bullet wounds. He'd been in the body shop more times than he liked to count, and the doctors had never been able to remove that bullet lodged near his spine. He hoped it didn't move and immobilize him. He couldn't afford that. Not now.

Ralf Johnson was trussed up just like the cat, but he had been working on his bonds for three hours. He had just about freed his hands, which just now were sweating considerably because he was watching the man called Frank fit the radio fuse to the plastic explosive. If only he could get free, he might be able to pull the fuse out.

Or he might not. He continued working on his bonds.

The cat whined. One of the terrorists kicked it against the wall.

"Don't harm the cat!" Frank said, looking up from the explosive. "It's our most valuable hostage."

Ralf didn't like the sound of that very much. His hands were sweating even more, but that helped him slip them in the ropes. He thought that the right one was just about to come loose.

But then it didn't matter. Frank stood up and shoved the plastic through the window.

Ralf was sure they would all die in seconds. He closed his eyes and clamped his teeth together. He didn't know why he closed his eyes. It wasn't going to make any difference when the explosion blew them to bits.

But they didn't die, and there was no explosion. The sudden stop five hundred feet below didn't cause the plastic to detonate. Ralf relaxed a fraction, but Frank still had the detonator. He could activate the fuse anytime he chose.

The terrorist also had a cellular phone, and now he punched in a number.

"Porter?" he said. "This is Frank Tovar. I'm giving you five minutes to call off your men. If the area isn't clear in that time, I'm blowing up the monument. But first I'm going to shoot the cat and throw it out the window."

He listened for a moment. Then he said, "I don't care. I want those tanks and rocket launchers gone. Five minutes.

And then I want a helicopter to fly me and my men out of here. Otherwise, the cat gets it. The monument, too."

Porter was still talking when Frank slapped the phone shut.

The president paused on the forty-ninth landing to pull his pistol from its holster. He was careful, but he wasn't used to handling firearms, so he wasn't quite careful enough. He clanked the barrel against the iron stair railing.

Ali heard it.

Shawn heard it too, and he cursed under his breath. He wasn't sure he could get there in time.

He slipped his own pistol from the holster and flipped off the safety. It made a barely audible click, but Shawn knew that noise didn't matter any longer.

Ali looked into the stairwell and saw the president charging toward him. He shrieked an indecipherable warning to the others and loosed a burst from his AK–47, which, including its wooden stock, measured 34.21 inches and weighed a mere 11.31 pounds with its thirty-round magazine. The 7.62mm bullets whanged off the stairs and the railings and knocked large chunks of stone from the wall.

The president tried to make himself small, no easy task, as the bullets flew around him, all thirty rounds being expended in less than six seconds.

Remarkably, the only wound he sustained was a cut from a chip of stone that sliced out a crescent under his left eye.

While Ali was slapping in another clip, the president brought up the Walther and pulled the trigger three times.

Shawn was almost there when he slipped on the stairs. The miracle fiber had wicked the perspiration away from his foot, but the outside of the sock was so wet and slippery that Shawn lost his equilibrium. When he stumbled, he cracked his chin on the stairs, and for a few seconds his head spun and his eyes would not focus.

Just at that moment, the shooting began. Luckily, Shawn had considered what the noise would be like in the tightly enclosed space. He had equipped both himself and the president with soft plastic earplugs, but even with them in place the noise was almost deafening. Some of the bullets ricocheted around Shawn, but he was untouched.

He shook his head in an attempt to clear his vision, but by the time he could see, it was very quiet in the monument. He went on up the stairs.

Now or never, Ralf thought. His hands were free at last, and when the shooting started, he jumped for Tovar. The two men fell heavily to the floor and rolled over on the cat, which squalled and tried helplessly to claw them. Tovar beat at Ralf's head with his Type 59 automatic, the Red Chinese version of the Russian Makarov, which was in itself a larger version of the Walther PP.

Ralf tried to get his hands on the detonator that Tovar had slipped into a pocket.

Habib and Nabib looked in horror not at their leader but at Ali, who staggered back into the room with three red holes in his chest. Clutching their own assault rifles, they lunged toward the doorway.

Shawn saw the president sitting on the steps, staring upward. Then he saw the two men hit the doorway, where they stuck momentarily before doing a little Alphonse/Gaston routine and coming through with their rifles blasting.

Shawn's pistol fired all eight rounds and the bullets volleyed off the walls and stairs around him. He could see flame spit from the barrel of the president's gun as well, and then the two terrorists were tumbling headfirst down the stairs.

DANGER IN D.C.

One of them came to rest on the landing at the feet of the president. The other's momentum carried him right on by, and his body somehow made the turn to pitch forward again and then jam sideways on the stairs in front of Shawn, who by that time had ejected the Sig/Sauer's magazine and slapped another in place. He gave a cursory glance at the body and saw that the man's head was a red ruin before stepping over it to join the president.

When Shawn got to the landing, the two men embraced without shame, drawn to one another by the bonding felt only by two men who have, together, looked death in the face and have not let the moment of their greatness flicker.

When the brief interlude was over, Shawn checked to make sure that the president had inserted a fresh clip in his Walther. Then they went up the final steps together.

The cat had been waiting her chance. When the two men rolled over her, her bonds came loose. She stopped her squalling and pounced.

Shawn and the president heard the appalling screams. Then a man exploded through the doorway.

God, Shawn thought, *that's the worst toupee I've ever seen.*

But it wasn't a toupee. Frank Tovar was wearing the cat, which had its front claws sunk into his eyeballs. Its amazingly puffed tail was sticking straight out behind.

In their momentary shock, Shawn and the president were bowled over by the terrorist, who simply flattened them as he ran blindly past.

Tovar tried to tear the creature from his head, but he was unable to do so, and, being unable to see, he missed the first step.

It was a long way down after that.

* * *

Ralf helped the president to his feet as Shawn got up slowly under his own power. They could hear Tovar bumping and screaming as he fell.

"Don't worry," Ralf said. "He's not gonna blow the place up." He showed them the detonator that he had wrested from the terrorist.

"To hell with him," the president said, wiping blood from beneath his eye. "Where's my cat?"

"Meow," the cat said, strolling nonchalantly into the room. Sensing that Tovar was tumbling toward his doom, the cat had leapt from his head on the fiftieth landing. Now it looked at the men briefly and then sat down and began to groom, first licking its fur and then brushing its whiskers with its front paws.

The president knelt down beside the animal and stroked its head. The cat began to purr.

"Still think you have something to prove, sir?" Shawn asked.

The president looked at him, his eyes full.

"Not a thing, Mr. Shawn," he said.

Indiscreet

·

Wendi Lee

Dolores Mendez must have been watching from a window because the door was open before Louise reached the bottom step that led to the Georgian-style home. Eyes red and cheeks streaked with dried tears, Dolores's iron-gray hair was not in its usual neat bun, but instead hung in careless strands around her motherly face.

"I'm so sorry," Louise said, giving her friend a gentle hug. "I'm going to miss Celeste."

"First Celeste, then Miss Kitty."

"Miss Kitty's died as well?" Louise asked as she followed Dolores down the hall that whispered its elegance in dark wood and muted wallpaper. For some reason, this news alarmed her more. Maybe it was the idea that the murderer had gone to the trouble of killing Celeste's pet as well as Celeste.

Dolores led her into the kitchen. Two cups of hot tea were waiting for them at the table. "No, she disappeared."

"For how long?" Louise caught sight of her reflection in the shiny chrome finish of the refrigerator. Although she was tall, model-thin, and black, she was just a caramel-colored blur dressed in black and gray to the indifferent appliance.

Dolores stirred sugar in her tea. "It's funny, but ever

230

since I found Celeste's body, I didn't think about Miss Kitty. Until this morning when I called you. But I don't recall seeing Miss Kitty since the murder."

Louise didn't have to ask for details. As soon as she heard that Celeste Knapp had been found dead in her bed yesterday morning, she called in a favor with an old Georgetown University classmate who was now a sergeant in Homicide. He had provided information that Louise would not have otherwise been able to get—Celeste had been strangled in her bed with a garrote. "Sounds premeditated," Louise had said. "Probably a pro," the sergeant had speculated.

Louise brought her mind back to the current problem—Miss Kitty. "So she could have disappeared at any time, starting when Celeste was found yesterday morning."

Dolores nodded, a tear sliding down her weathered face.

Celeste Knapp had been the madame of a high-class brothel well known for its high-powered clientele and hush-hush discretion. Louise had been introduced to Celeste when she was assigned to do a series of articles for her paper on prostitution in the nation's capital. As a journalist, she knew she would have to put aside her preconceptions and prejudices to write an unbiased look at the profession. It had been difficult at first, but Celeste Knapp had proven to be an eloquent interviewee, revealing the human side to prostitution. Louise became more comfortable in the presence of Celeste, Dolores, and their prima-donna cat, Miss Kitty, and the friendship had continued long after the series of articles ran in the *Washington Sun*.

"Have you talked to any of the girls?" Louise asked.

"Rachel's still sedated and Holly's with her boyfriend at Georgetown University, but Sarah's been here for me. She's gone to the drugstore to get a prescription for me." Dolores ran out of breath. Her face scrunched up in pain.

Reaching across the table, Louise gave Dolores's hand a squeeze. "What do you want me to do?"

"Help me find Miss Kitty." Miss Kitty was a Maine coon feline weighing in at a massive eighteen pounds. She had a beautiful tortoiseshell coat with white legs and underbelly. In a certain light, she looked a bit like a crazed raccoon. She had probably slipped outside during the commotion right after Celeste's death. Despite Miss Kitty's size, Louise wondered if the pampered pet would take care of herself. She had no doubt that if the feline could find her way back home, Miss Kitty would be found on the back doorstep, begging for that canned gourmet cat food.

Louise sat back in her chair and crossed her legs. "You might as well ask me to find Celeste's killer." The moment it left her lips, she knew it was the wrong thing to say. Now that it was said, she decided to pursue the subject. "By the way, have the police narrowed it down to a single suspect?"

"You know how it is with us working girls," a voice drawled from behind Louise. Tall, lithe, blonde Sarah joined them, a mug of coffee in her hand. "We don't rate a thorough investigation."

As cool and elegant as she appeared with her clients, they rarely got a glimpse of Sarah when she was angry. Louise found Sarah's icy anger frightening and refrained from contradicting her. She knew that the D.C. police were overworked, especially in the homicide division. If the suspect wasn't immediately apparent when the witnesses' statements were taken and the evidence was gathered at the scene of the crime, chances were good that the case wouldn't warrant much attention. There were too many people being murdered in their beds every day to try to solve every case.

Louise changed the subject. "So what's going to happen to the house?"

Sarah and Dolores looked at each other, then back to Louise.

"For the moment, business will go on as usual," Dolores said. Behind Dolores's back, Sarah made a face at Louise to show just how thrilled she was about working so soon after Celeste's death. Louise recalled that during an interview with Celeste, the madame had affectionately said that Dolores had eyes in the back of her head. In this case, Dolores turned slightly toward Sarah and pointedly said, "We have to keep clients happy in order to pay the bills, you know."

"Who did Celeste leave the house to?"

Sarah spoke this time. "Celeste's will was interesting, to say the least."

"And very generous," Dolores added.

"She had specified that those girls who had been with her for five years or more would share in the profits as equal partners with Dolores, who will continue to run things."

Louise raised her eyebrows in surprise. It was an unusual way to dispose of a business, but then it was an unusual business. This clause meant that Sarah and Rachel would share in the partnership, since they were the only girls who had been with Celeste for over five years. Louise wondered briefly if one of the two women might have offed Celeste in order to gain the profits of the brothel, but it didn't seem likely. Both women were close to Celeste and shared her serious approach to the business. And as far as Louise knew, Sarah and Rachel had no bad feelings toward Celeste. Besides, they would have had plenty of opportunity over the years, and better ways of orchestrating Celeste's death without raising suspicion.

Dolores spoke up again. "So will you do it?"

In her pensive mood, Louise had lost the thread of the conversation. "Do what?"

"Find Miss Kitty."

Even Sarah's forehead puckered a bit. "That's right. I haven't seen the little monster all day. Come to think of it, I don't recall seeing her yesterday, either."

Dolores recounted the saga of the missing cat to Sarah.

"I wouldn't worry too much about Miss Kitty, Dolores," Louise said. "She'll find her way home. You have much bigger problems right now."

The three women drank their tea and coffee in companionable silence. "This must be hard on everyone in the house," Louise finally said. "Where was everyone when Celeste's body was discovered?"

"I was sleeping in," Sarah replied distractedly. "I hadn't been feeling well the night before and Celeste let me off work early."

The door opened once more and Holly slipped into the kitchen. "Hi, guys."

Even with Celeste's death, Holly could not be subdued. She wore sloppy grape-colored sweats and had made an effort to tie back her untamable red hair. Louise figured she was grieving in her own special way, the way young girls do when they think they're immortal. Although she looked barely eighteen, Holly had been with Celeste for three years. The older customers preferred the less flamboyant and more sophisticated call girls, but Holly was very popular with the younger customers, especially those in the foreign embassies.

The door opened once again and Rachel entered, her usually sleek, dark hair plastered against her skull on one side. Her patrician nose was red from crying and her blue eyes were still glazed over from sedatives. She made no attempt to hide her grief. Dolores got up and went over to her, one motherly arm sliding over Rachel's thin shoulders. She guided Rachel into a chair and sat next to her, one hand protectively covering Rachel's right hand.

Louise turned to Holly, who had just sat down at the table with a can of Coke. "So, it must have been a shock," she said.

The youngest prostitute slouched in her chair and slurped some soda before answering. "It was awful. I mean, I didn't discover the body or anything, but after the detective took my statement this morning, I had to go over to my boyfriend's apartment just to get away. It still gives me the creeps to think that Celeste was killed in this very house." She shuddered visibly for effect, then turned to Dolores with an imploring look. "Dolores, do we have to work tonight? Can't we take a night off? You know, out of respect or something?"

Dolores stiffened, then let her shoulders slump. She shook her head. "I wish we could, Holly, but there are some customers who have standing appointments and they won't understand why we've closed down." Louise realized that Dolores was referring to men from foreign embassies who couldn't be reached by phone. If Dolores turned them away tonight, they might take offense and take their business elsewhere.

Holly turned back to her Coke and pouted.

"Holly, where were you when Celeste was killed?"

She turned to Louise and widened her eyes. "I'm not even sure when she was killed."

"The coroner has estimated the time of death to be between three and five this morning."

Holly rolled her eyes. "I was sound asleep, silly."

Rachel spoke up for the first time. "You weren't sound asleep, Holly. I heard you walk past my door about three-thirty."

Holly's amiable manner evaporated and she suddenly looked nervous. "Well, I . . . I guess I had trouble sleeping, so I came down to the kitchen for a glass of milk." She finished off her soda and abruptly stood up, tossing her empty can into the trash. Louise noticed that Holly's face had closed down like shutters over a window. "Well, it's been nice talking to you all. I've got to take a shower." She left quickly.

Silence settled in once again.

Rachel finally spoke. "For what it's worth, Louise, I'm an insomniac, so I spent the night reading in bed."

"How did you know it was Holly who walked past your door?"

Rachel fought a glimmer of a smile. "My room is next to Holly's, and her room is the last one in the east wing."

It was no secret that the two women were opposites in every way. Serious Rachel had little patience with flighty Holly and the feeling was mutual. When Celeste was alive, she had managed to keep them in balance. With the madame gone, Louise wondered what would happen to the cathouse. Dolores was a good woman, but she didn't have the necessary diplomatic skills that Celeste had picked up from her work with the embassies.

Dolores stood up, her face troubled. Signaling Louise to follow her, they went out into the hall.

"It slipped my mind when the detective was taking my statement," Dolores began in a low voice. "I can't tell you what time it was because I was just drifting off to sleep, but I'm certain I heard the front door opening and closing. I made a mental note to oil the hinges in the morning."

"You'd better call the detective," Louise said. The missing Miss Kitty crossed her mind and she wondered if that was how the cat had gotten outside. It almost certainly was when Celeste's killer had slipped in or out.

Dolores hesitated, then shook her head. "I'm not sure what good it will do."

"Does Holly's behavior strike you as odd lately?"

Dolores frowned. "Well, she seemed a little nervous, but we're all a little on edge."

"Has she done anything out of the ordinary?" An idea was beginning to form in Louise's mind, but there were too many pieces of the puzzle missing.

Dolores thought. "She visits her boyfriend an awful lot, sometimes for only an hour or two, like she did today. But that's not unusual for a young girl who's in love." Louise went back into the kitchen, leaving Dolores to make her call. The phone rang a few minutes later, then Dolores came into the room, a puzzled look on her face.

"Are you okay?" Sarah asked.

"It's probably nothing."

"What?" Louise prompted.

"I just talked to Holly's boyfriend, Tom. I told him she was in the shower and I'd have her call him back. Then I teased him about not being able to live without her for more than an hour." She paused and sipped her cold tea.

Rachel prompted her. "And?"

"He asked me what I was talking about and I said, 'Well, wasn't she just over to your apartment this morning?' He said he hadn't seen her for two days."

"What did you tell him?" Louise asked, leaning forward.

"That I had probably jumped to conclusions. He was upset, probably thought she was cheating on him. I had to calm him down."

Louise's eyes narrowed. "Dolores, how often does Holly go to Tom's place?"

She pushed back a strand of gray hair and shrugged. "Quite often. Several times a week. She stays overnight on her days off, but will usually visit him for just a couple of hours at least once during her workweek."

Sarah jumped in. "Louise, you surely don't suspect Holly of anything like murdering Miss Celeste. She doesn't have enough brains to pull off something like that."

"Maybe she's not guilty of murder," Louise said, "but she might be involved."

Two pieces of the puzzle were beginning to fit, but Louise still couldn't see the whole picture. She knew she was on to something, but it was nothing that could be brought to the police yet. There was no evidence, nothing concrete. Still she had a plan. Leaning over the table, she talked to the other three women.

* * *

It was close to a week later, Louise heard from Dolores. She was in her office and it was a few minutes before noon. "Louise? She told me that she's going over to see her boyfriend."

"See if you can delay her for five minutes. Ten minutes would be better. I'll be there as soon as I can." Louise hung up, grabbed a camera from the bottom drawer of her desk, and left.

It was a lucky coincidence that the brothel wasn't far from Louise's office. Five minutes later, she was standing across the street watching the front door when Holly walked out, bouncing down the steps two at a time. Dolores stood in the doorway, barely glancing in Louise's direction.

"Be back here by five," she called after the retreating Holly. "You have an appointment at six."

"Yeah, yeah," Holly's voice bordered on irritation. Louise followed at a discreet distance until Holly got into a taxi. There was a moment of dismay when Louise thought she might lose her, but she was able to flag down a cab almost immediately and say what every driver longs to hear: "Follow that cab."

The driver grinned and complied, keeping a car length behind Holly's cab until they reached Jefferson Drive on the Mall. Throwing a few bills at the cabby, Louise climbed out in time to watch her quarry disappear into the Hirshhorn Museum and Sculpture Garden. Holly had never struck Louise as an art lover. She remembered once mentioning Manet in passing and Holly had asked if he had invented mayonnaise.

After paying the entrance fee, she caught sight of Holly across the room, passing into the sculpture garden. Louise walked over to the windows that faced the court and kept her quarry in sight. With so many magnificent sculptures surrounding her, Holly sat on a stone bench and stared blandly into the reflecting pool. A short, swarthy man with a large mustache sat down on the other end of the bench.

He wore the muddy green short-sleeved polyester shirt and brown pants of a tourist. Louise raised her camera and began taking pictures.

They didn't talk to each other. In fact, it was all over in a few seconds. The man got up, leaving behind a small, white envelope. Holly sat there for another few moments, then casually slid the envelope into her purse and made a beeline for the exit. Unlike Holly, the man was a professional. He spent a few minutes pretending to study the garden sculptures before departing the museum. Louise followed him.

There was no doubt about it—this man was good at what he did, whatever that was. Instead of hailing a taxi, he caught a bus. Public transportation was the best way to get lost in D.C. Louise sat in the front of the bus and surreptitiously watched him until he got off on 22nd Street. From there, he walked to R Street. She walked on the other side of the street, occasionally snapping a picture here or there, trying to look like a tourist, not someone who was interested in swarthy little men with bad taste in clothes. When he turned into the walkway of a large white Federal-style building, she focused her camera and began clicking. Crossing the street, Louise got a look at the sign on the front gate: Embassy of the Socialist Federal Republic of Yugoslavia. Her fingertips started to tingle. All her newshound instincts told her that this was very important material. But Holly, a spy? At first it was difficult to believe, but as Louise started to think about it, things began to make sense.

On her way back to the office, Louise began to wonder what the connection might be. As Celeste told Louise in their interview, she had always considered her establishment as neutral territory, much like Switzerland. She considered herself and her girls to be like priests. Whatever a client told a working girl was never to be repeated or discussed with anyone. Even among themselves.

Yugoslavia was in the midst of civil upheaval and there

were a number of things that an unscrupulous spy for the Bosnians might want to get from the United States—things that couldn't be gotten through the normal channels. Besides, the Bosnians weren't in favor with the United States—in fact, they weren't much in favor with anyone at the moment.

Although Holly wasn't a call girl with the older, more powerful client base, she was a favorite among the younger men, many of whom were assistants to men in power such as senators, cabinet members, and diplomats. And they were usually in their bosses' confidences. Maybe Holly had cut a deal with someone here at the embassy to sell information that she had acquired from her clients.

When Louise got back to the office, she put a rush order on developing her film. While she waited, her editor called her into his office for another assignment.

"I can't go to a press conference right now," Louise said.

"That's what we pay you for." Carl Ringwald, the editor, leaned back in his office chair, folded his hands behind his head, and stretched. "Hillary Clinton may make an appearance. Bring your camera."

"I'd be happy to, but I really can't. I think I'm onto something big." She proceeded to tell him what had occurred, giving him just enough information about the events and how they might tie into Celeste's death to whet his appetite.

Ringwald relented. "You're not going to do anything stupid, are you?" He had returned his chair to its proper upright position and was straightening papers on his desk, belying the fact that he was excited about the prospect of breaking a hard-hitting news story about blackmail and politics. "You could be in danger. I'd like the story, but I don't want a dead reporter on my conscience."

"I've taken a defense class," Louise said lightly, although butterflies were doing a dance in her stomach. She was aware that there might be some risk involved. Investigating a murder was one thing, investigating a murder with possible political intrigue was a whole new experience for her.

"You're going to the police with this, right?"

"Eventually," was all Louise would promise. She left his office and picked up the photos.

Fifteen minutes later, she was sitting in the parlor with Dolores and the other girls, the photos spread on the coffee table in front of them. "Have you ever seen this man with Holly?"

Dolores picked up one of the pictures and frowned. "He doesn't look like one of our clients. I don't think so."

The doorbell rang and she got up to answer it.

Sarah examined a photo and shrugged. "It's hard to imagine Holly with this guy."

"He's certainly not her boyfriend," was Rachel's observation. Louise was feeling slightly disappointed, but she still had another place to show her photos. It just might be more dangerous, though.

Dolores returned with a tall black man. Louise thought he looked a little like Wesley Snipes, the actor. He wore a crisply pressed gray suit and his small goatee was neatly trimmed.

"This is Detective Sergeant Dean Griffith from Homicide," Dolores said.

His smile was serious, and she could feel him studying her as if he were wondering if she was a working girl. Suddenly she was self-conscious about her association with Dolores and Celeste.

"Uh, I'm a reporter for the *Washington Sun*," she said, much to her shame. Then she straightened up and added, "And a friend of Dolores here, and the deceased."

When he shook her hand, Louise found herself looking for a wedding ring, which made her blush. Dolores told Griffith that Louise was trying to help them find their missing cat. Griffith's eye strayed to the photos that Louise had tossed onto the coffee table. He picked one up and studied it.

"Where did you get these?" he asked in a sharp tone.

Louise examined where and why she had taken them. She couldn't help asking, "Does that man look familiar?"

Griffith smiled enigmatically without answering. She noticed that he didn't put one of the photos back down on the table; instead, he slipped the photo of Holly and the mysterious stranger sitting together in the museum courtyard into his inner jacket pocket.

When the homicide detective pulled out prepared statements for Dolores and the girls to sign, it was a good time for Louise to leave. Although she started to drive back to her office, she decided to turn around and head for the embassy. She had the pictures, maybe she would get lucky and be able to attach a name to the face. Showing the photo around the Yugoslavian embassy was risky, but she had a cover story prepared.

Louise entered the embassy only to discover that the guard was away from his window. A plate-glass wall separated the lobby from the cramped vestibule where the security guard questioned visitors about their intent. Louise peered into the embassy's lobby, which appeared impressive at first glance, but upon closer examination it had a shabby elegance. The red velvet upholstered chairs looked lumpy and gold paint was flaking off the chair legs and arms. The chandelier was missing a few crystals and some of the bulbs were burned out.

"Yes? What can I do for you?" The man's voice was laced with a heavy Slavic accent. She turned to face a solemn man in a guard's uniform. He laid a clipboard down on his desk and gave her his full attention.

"I was looking for this man—" Louise was interrupted by a high-pitched meow. A plumed tortoiseshell tail floated across the line of the guard's desk, seemingly of its own accord. The guard turned.

"Excuse me," he said, stooping to pick up a large cat who resembled a raccoon.

Louise managed to choke back her surprise and recognition, and forced herself to smile. "What a beautiful cat!"

The guard smiled back, the first sign that he was human after all. "She appeared at our embassy the other day," he explained. "I had come on duty at eight o'clock yesterday morning and she was inside the lobby."

"You've never seen her before?" He shook his head. Louise chose her next question carefully, not wanting to raise suspicions. "Is it possible that she belongs to someone here at the embassy?"

"No, I've asked and no one has ever seen her before." He shrugged and scratched her ear. Miss Kitty complied with a loud purr of contentment. "She is probably a stray." The guard paused. "For a moment, it looked to me as if you recognized her." He was sharper than she had given him credit for.

"I'm not sure," Louise put just enough doubt in her voice, "but she does look an awful lot like an acquaintance's cat."

The guard put Miss Kitty down and brought the conversation back to business. "What did you come here for? You said something about a man?"

"Oh, yes," Louise said, trying to sound as if she was distracted. She fished the photo of the man out of her purse. "I'm a reporter and I was taking pictures of the Hirshhorn for my newspaper earlier today. This man was in some of the photos and I thought it would be an interesting sidebar to get his impression of the museum. A foreigner's view and all." She hoped the story sounded plausible.

The guard frowned as he studied the photo. "Why did you not ask him at the museum?"

"I lost him when I ducked into the ladies' room, but he had dropped a calling card with this embassy's name on it." Louise knew that embassies sometimes gave their low-level employees generic business cards because the turnover rate was so high. She hoped this guy wasn't high-level. Studying the guard's face while he examined the photo, she didn't see any flicker of recognition.

"May I see the card?" the guard asked, looking up at her.

Louise made a pretense of looking for it in her purse. "I'm sorry. I seem to have misplaced it. But I was certain it was this embassy."

The guard shrugged. "He does not look familiar. We have so many people working here. Sometimes I only look at the badges and not the faces. If he is from our embassy, he may not wish to be interviewed. Some of our officials speak very poor English."

"Then this would be a chance for him to practice," Louise said brightly. She took the photo back and handed the guard her business card. "If you find him, please give him my name and number."

She left the building. It was hard to leave Miss Kitty there, but she seemed content enough.

Louise went back to the office for another hour of work, then stopped at a takeout Vietnamese restaurant around the corner from her apartment. It was after six when she opened her door and entered the vestibule; there was something ominous about the quiet of her dark apartment. Before she could flip the light on, a strong arm dragged her away from the entry and the door slammed shut. Although she was frightened for a moment, anger took over and so did her self-defense lessons. She jabbed her elbow into the intruder's ribs. He gasped and staggered back a step, but maintained his hold on her.

She stepped back with him and brought her heel down on what she hoped was his instep. He grunted and she felt his hold on her weaken momentarily. By now, her eyes had adjusted to the dark and she could make out the outline of her attacker's free arm in front of her, a knife in his hand. She bit the wrist of his constraining arm. He yelped, drawing his arm away. Louise took advantage of the moment and yelled to startle him and maybe summon help, then she dropped to the ground and used her legs, aiming vicious kicks at his knees. She could hear him muttering unintelligible curses when her kicks connected with his legs. When she felt him grab one of her ankles, she screamed again.

Suddenly, there was the sound of cracking wood. Light spilled in from the hall and men were shouting. Someone turned on the overhead lights, causing Louise to squint and blink. She fell back onto the floor, exhausted, and watched as plainclothes cops surrounded the intruder. It was the man from the museum, Holly's contact.

A firm hand helped her off the floor. "You!" was all Louise could say as she stared into the dark handsome face of Detective Sergeant Griffith. "How did you—?" But she already knew the answer.

"After you left, Dolores told me that she was worried that you might do something foolish," he replied, a mixture of amusement and annoyance in his voice.

"So you had me followed to the embassy. You did know who this guy was, didn't you?" Louise said, rubbing her throat where her attacker had had a choke hold on her.

"Well, it didn't hit me until I showed the photo to my supervisor. His name is Yevgeny Medjovic and he's a Bosnian sympathizer who has been suspected of trying to find an arms dealer now that the Russians are no longer a reliable source. I think he was hoping to make a deal with someone in the Pentagon. Holly was being paid for information that would lead Medjovic to a contact."

Louise watched with some satisfaction as one of the undercover cops clapped handcuffs on her attacker. She grabbed her camera, hoping she had enough film left in the camera, and snapped a couple of shots.

"Hope you don't mind, detective, but it's my job."

Griffith nodded. "I wish we could tie him in to Celeste Knapp's murder."

"You can." As Louise explained Miss Kitty's disappearance, Griffith's eyes mirrored growing admiration for her.

When she was finished, he shook his head. "My, that's some story."

"Are you going to have any problems putting Celeste's murderer behind bars because of his diplomatic status?"

"My guess is that the embassy will deny any knowledge of his actions and throw him to us as a gesture of goodwill."

Several weeks later, Louise sat in the kitchen of the cathouse with Dolores. This time, she was there for dinner. The smell of chicken and wine permeated the room.

"Imagine," Dolores said as she took the roasting pan out and basted the simmering chicken with the wine sauce. "You not only found Miss Kitty, but you caught Celeste's murderer as well." She put the pan back in the oven and straightened up to face Louise. "How can I ever thank you?"

Louise grinned. "I think you already have. That chicken smells wonderful. And the one who really deserves the attention is Miss Kitty. If she hadn't followed Medjovic back to the Yugoslavian embassy, Detective Griffith would never have been able to link him to Celeste's murder." She felt a small regret that after her statement had been taken, she hadn't seen the handsome detective again. "I have to say, Detective Griffith has been very much the gentleman with this case."

Dolores agreed. "I'm used to being treated with contempt by the police. He told me that he didn't have anything against places like ours. He said he's strictly Homicide and doesn't meddle in the other departments." She opened the lid of a pot and stirred something fragrant. "It's too bad about Holly," Dolores added gently.

"She's in for a long stretch, if she's convicted. Don't feel too sorry for her," Louise replied. "She was passing along sensitive information to anyone who would buy. Medjovic was just one in a long line. When Celeste found out, she was about to throw Holly out on her ear *and* go tell one of her more powerful clients. Medjovic couldn't have that happen because Holly was close to handing him an arms contact in the Pentagon. It was easier to kill Celeste than to find another cathouse and another call girl who was willing to become a traitor." Louise poured two glasses of wine and handed one to Dolores. The kitchen door opened and Dean Griffith walked in.

Louise's eyes widened, then she looked back at Dolores, who was beaming. "I forgot to mention that he's been invited to dinner as well." Dolores handed her glass to him, poured herself another glass, then raised it. Louise and Griffith followed suit.

"To Miss Kitty," Griffith said. Their glasses clinked.

"To Miss Kitty," Dolores and Louise solemnly intoned.

An insistent meow could be heard from a corner of the kitchen. Three pairs of eyes turned to watch Miss Kitty march back and forth in front of the oven, guarding the chicken.

Dumb Animals

•

Peter Crowther

Sonny Curtis didn't know anybody who had died in Vietnam. Didn't know anybody who had even been.

But he still found himself leaning against one of the big, black sections of the Vietnam Veterans Memorial, the one with all the names printed on it, looking around the edge for anybody who might have followed him. There was nobody.

And even though Sonny hadn't lost anybody in that war there were still tears in his eyes and, as he leaned back against the cool stone, the tears made the parkway and the trees shimmer. For a second, it reminded him of New York, like seeing the buildings through the steam drifting out of the manhole covers around Times Square. For that one second, it was like he was back in the Apple. But he wasn't.

This was Washington, D.C., and Sonny was a long way from home. It was cold and dark, the dead days of a new year. Not a good time to be away from the things that were familiar. He ran a hand down his shirtfront, his favorite shirt, a heady mixture of ocean blues and meadow greens, swirls of corn stalks and patches of soil, triangles and many-sided structures and shapes, all depicted in bright hues and thoughtful pastels ... and his hand touched the wetness. Sonny had blood on him. Blood on his best shirt.

248

He pulled it out from his body and looked down at it. The blood looked black in the glare of the solitary lamp, black and glistening, like oil or just plain dirt, swirling amongst the swirls already there, covering and dripping over and through the shapes, weaving its way into the cotton.

The only good thing about the blood was that it wasn't his.

Beside him, Frank's cat mewled in its basket, complaining at being jostled so much and at not being able to get out and roam around. Sonny moved his head back so the top of it rested on the stone and stared at the stars.

He had ducked out from the smoky bar on Henry Bacon Drive, left hand tightly holding a mess of bills and Frank's cat basket, right hand still gripping the long stiletto shiv . . . legs going full tilt, listening to the voices echoing after him
'You come back here!'
'Hey, he knifed Troy . . .'
'Get him!'

The accents of those voices, now replaying in Sonny's head, were deep and yawny. They lacked the characteristic drawl of the capital and its slow, long vowels and short, slurred consonants. They were Southern voices, he now realized. As foreign to the town itself as they were to him.

He had hit the street on a run, grateful of the darkness, and ditched the shiv behind some garbage cans outside back of an eatery on the corner of 21st Street, listening to the sound of its clatter fade only to be replaced by the lonesome pounding of his own shoes, running down the empty street. *Troy,* he had thought as he ran, pulling in air whenever he could, then holding it in so's he could hear if anyone was following. What kind of a name was that? Sounded like something off of one of the daytime soaps. And he had been unable to stifle a small, throaty chuckle . . . and equally unable to recognize it for the hysteria it was.

Sonny had arrived in Washington, D.C., in the late afternoon, when the light was dying, on a Greyhound which let him off with the other seven passengers at a depot on New York Avenue. He hadn't intended to come to Washington. Hadn't intended to come anywhere. Sonny had just wanted to get out of New York. He hadn't intended to hurt anybody. He had just needed some money. The story of his life.

What was it Bill Clinton had said just a few days earlier? Sonny had watched the inauguration on the television at Frank's place, back in New York. He had watched the new president refer to 'this beautiful capital' and he had felt a sudden kinship when the man had gone on to criticize the people there for being obsessed by 'who is in and who is out, who is up and who is down.'

That was him, Gerald Jerome Curtis—'Sonny' to his friends and other people who knew him—out and down. Sonny had never felt much of a kinship with anybody before, let alone a president. But he had felt it then. Maybe that was why he had picked the Washington bus, picked it out without realizing why he was doing it.

Anywhere would have been fine. Anywhere but New York. There were people in New York who wanted him.

Sonny had heard Frank on the telephone. Frank had thought he was asleep, crashed out on the sofa in front of the television with the cat, but he wasn't. He was too worried about creasing his shirt. And while the forty-second president of the United States was telling everybody that people deserved better . . . and that 'in this city there are people who want to do better,' Frank was telling people where Sonny was. Telling them to come round and 'get the lousy queen' out of there. Telling them to come around quick.

And so he lifted the serrated knife that they had used to cut up the tuna and anchovy pizza Frank had ordered from the shop around the corner and then sneaked up on Frank. And while in the room behind him Bill Clinton told America that the era of deadlock and drift was behind them, Sonny had pulled Frank's head back and sawed right through the neck in one sweep. Then he had let the body drop and said *Fuck you* into the mouthpiece—three times— smashed the bloody handset on the cradle until it shattered and then kicked the shit out of Frank Ryerman's still-warm corpse while he figured out what to do next. On the sofa in Frank's room, the dead man's cat watched with a casual disinterest, torn between the picture on the television and the action in the room.

While Sonny thought, the president was still speaking. Sonny had listened a moment and then walked back into the room and switched off the set. He had since read that the inaugural speech had been fourteen minutes long. Will Rogers had said all the same stuff more than a generation earlier and used only fourteen words: 'There ain't but one word wrong with every one of us,' Rogers had said, 'and that's selfishness.'

He had to go. He had to get out of that room . . . out of that city . . . somewhere where they wouldn't find him. The cat licked its paws and watched him as he watched it.

Sonny grabbed his jacket from the floor and knelt beside Frank's body, checking his pockets for money. There were a few bills plus a handful of change—twenty-seven dollars and sixty-three cents. Sonny looked up at the cat, then caught sight of the basket on the window ledge behind it. *There ain't but one word wrong with every one of us . . .* Sonny stood up quickly and moved across to the window ledge. He grabbed the basket and then the cat, dropped it inside and fastened the latch. Then he ran out of the room, ran along the corridor, down the stairs and out into the early morning streets, feeling the wind in his face and listening to the sirens caterwauling, sometimes in the distance, some-times like they were pulling right up alongside him.

And so it was that, on a particularly grimy sweat- and piss-smelling seat of the Port Authority Greyhound terminal, Sonny Curtis had gone for Washington. Gone to be near to the president of the United States of America.

Two men on the bus had been talking loudly about the new president. "We gonna see a new beginning now," the first man had said, said it proudly as though he was going to do something himself. "We gonna see some fairness now."

The other man had shaken his head while Sonny watched. "No way," he'd said. "Way I see it, this ain't no new start. Ain't no new nothing. All we done is we've gotten ourselves into bed with the last guy in the bar. That's all."

Sonny had wanted to butt in right from the start, but he had waited, held his silence and stared out at the early morning countryside. He knew diddly about Bosnia and Serbs, knew even less about unemployment—it had never done him any harm had it?—or inflation or gross national product. But even his lack of knowledge couldn't keep him quiet forever, not when they were bad-mouthing the president for crissakes. It was a matter of pride, of keeping the flag flying.

Sonny had leaned forward, resting his right arm on the seat in front, and called to the men. "Hey," he had called, soft so's he didn't wake the old woman who slept across the aisle, muttering to unseen gods or demons as her head slipped on the seat-back with the movement of the bus, first one way and then the other. "Hey, you can't say that about the president," Sonny had said.

The men had looked around at him. "And who're you," one of them asked, "his fucking bodyguard?"

"Hey," the other had said, "maybe it's Kevin Costner."

"Jee-suss H. Christ," the first one said then, pointing at Sonny's chest. Sonny looked down at himself but couldn't make anything out. "Is that a shirt?"

"Holy shit," the other added. "That ain't no shirt, man, that's . . . that's—"

"That shirt's like to've made Picasso puke, man."

The second guy slapped his knee, shuffled himself around so his knees stuck right out in the aisle.

"Whassamatter, man . . . you lose a bet?"

"I know who he is, man! He's Captain Bad Taste."

And they had giggled like a couple of high-school girls.

Sonny had wanted to pull the stiletto out of his Levis boot and thrust it forward so the point could draw just a single droplet of blood from one of the bulbous sacks of skin beneath the first man's eyes. *This is who I am,* the knife would have whispered around the redness, *who the fuck are you?* But, instead, he clenched his hand, made a fist. "I'm a citizen of the United States," Sonny had said over the drone of the bus's engine. "And I say that any man who cares about a cat can care about a country."

Sonny had read somewhere that Mr. Clinton had called in psychiatrists to look after his cat, Socks. Seems that all the pressure of being photographed and bustled around had upset the animal—The First Pussy, the magazine had called it. Ray Dringling had said, while nursing a beer in The Stopover bar down on 41st Street, that the magazine had got things confused. 'The first pussy is curled up inside of Hillary Clinton's pants,' he'd said and Sonny had wanted to slap him right in the mouth, had wanted to stop Ray's hysterical giggle and knock him clean off his stool. But he hadn't.

He gripped his shirtfront tightly.

Hillary Clinton had style. She would like his shirt, Sonny thought. She was a new woman . . . she was going to repeal the law that said to be good you had to be dull. Like Georgette Mosbacher said, 'If you're blonde, you're dumb. If you wear mascara, you can't read. If you use hairspray, your brain has atrophied.' That was how Washington used to be. But not any more. Not now the Clintons were in the White House. Now it would be style, not eccentricity. No more Barbara Bush in her puff-sleeved frocks and trainers;

no more Margaret Tutwiler and her Popeye the Sailor dresses; no more Laura Ashley blouses or velvet hairbands; no more, even, Eleanor Roosevelt-style fox furs or Mamie Eisenhower big-skirted frocks and white glove ensembles; not even any more of Jackie Kennedy's pillbox hats.

Sonny had seen Hillary Clinton and Tipper Gore out on the campaign trail, all Donna Karan bodysuits and tight-waisted jackets, and Ralph Lauren trouser suits in pin-stripes. They would set the fashion standard for the working woman. They would set the fashion standard for the country.

Camelot II: this time it's funky! Sonny recalled the line from the *New York Times* and smiled. It would happen . . . no point in getting all hot about it. He relaxed his hand on his shirt.

And on the bus, when the first man had twirled a finger at the side of his head, making the other man laugh, Sonny had sat back and put a hand on the top of Frank's cat's basket. Watched some more scenery drift by outside while he listened to the woman across the aisle beg with somebody called Herman to let Miriam be. Slowly, moving gently to the movement of the bus, Sonny fell into a shallow sleep and a dream. In his dream Sonny caught the two men years later in a little town just north of Mexico City, and he pulled their pants down and cut off their balls and fed them to Frank's cat.

Remembering his thoughts on the Greyhound, while sitting crouched down in the chill air of the nighttime capital, and with Frank's cat mewling beside him and blood streaked down the front of his best shirt in all the world, Sonny realized what might be troubling the animal. He knelt down and unfastened the basket's catch, lifted the cat out. It struggled and tried to scratch his hand but Sonny held on tight. "There," he whispered, "there now. Whassamatter, huh?" He stroked the cat's back, felt it arch beneath his hand. "You hungry? Is that it?"

Sonny glanced up at the park. Sure, that was it. Why hadn't he thought about it before? The cat must be starving. He hadn't given it anything to eat since they'd left Frank's place and that was almost twenty-four hours ago. Come to think of it, Sonny hadn't had anything either.

"Hey," he said. "You like my shirt? Huh?" The cat shuffled and tried to break free. Sonny held it tight and lifted a paw to his shirtfront, wiped it in the bloodstain. The cat settled for a moment and licked its paw. Then it jerked backwards and it was all that Sonny could do to stop it jumping from his lap and running off into the trees.

He dropped the cat back into the basket, trying not to listen to its frantic whining, and secured the catch. He had money now, money to buy something to eat. He shuffled over to the edge of the monument and peered around at the streets beyond. Nobody in sight. "Come on, cat," he said, getting to his feet, "let's go get us some food."

He had gone into the bar to get something to eat, too, he remembered. Maybe a sandwich, maybe a slice of pizza. Anything really. And three guys playing pool had seen him standing at the bar holding Frank's cat's basket. He had seen them notice him. It was like a second sense to him, honed over so many years of having to watch in every direction at once.

And the biggest of the three guys—the one whose name was Troy, he discovered later—had come up to him and pulled open his jacket, whistling. "Hoo-EE! I want it. I want that shirt."

Sonny had pulled his jacket closed and shrugged. "Ain't for sale."

"But I want the shirt." The man had looked around at his friends and pursed his lips. "Figure it make me look real fine," he added. "But I don't figure it make me wanna fuck cats." He looked down at the basket and scrunched up his nose like he was smelling something bad. "That yours?"

Sonny fastened his jacket and said nothing. The man was

thickset and very handsome, a rugged tuft of blond hair curling over his ears and a cigarette which had been jammed behind the left one. For a second, Sonny felt attracted to him and strangely proud that the man should want his shirt.

"I said, is the cat yours?" he said again.

"Maybe they on a date," one of the other men shouted.

Sonny looked around the bar, taking in who was where.

"That right? One of your friends tell you you oughta get yourself some pussy so you went right out and picked up this . . . this fucking dumb animal?" the first one had asked.

"Cats ain't dumb animals," Sonny had said. "By the year 2000 there'll be sixty-nine million cats in the United States."

The man's eyes had opened wide and, just for a second, the fact had interested him, had kindled the almost dead, infinitesimally small light that still smoldered in the dark recesses of the man's brain. But only for a second. "Would you like to be there to see it?" he said softly.

Sonny frowned.

"Would you like to be there to see all of them fucking dumb animals?"

"Look, I ju—"

"Sell me the shirt."

"Hey, I don't wan—"

"Sell me the shirt and you can walk outta here."

Sonny had glanced around at the man behind the bar, down the far end of the room. The man turned around and made like he was tidying some bottles on the shelf behind him. Sonny looked back at the man. "How much?"

The man had smiled. "That's more like it." He turned around and laughed at the others. "That's more like it," he said again, louder.

Sonny had bent down, put the cat basket on the floor beside him and lifted his pant leg just high enough to pull the shiv out of his Levis boot. When he stood up the man was holding a handful of bills, pulling them back and starting to count. Sonny had grabbed the bills with his left hand and slid the shiv into the man's gut with his right, sweeping the blade up towards the ribs, grunting. Feeling it catch on bone, he pulled it out.

Time had stood still then . . .

the men at the pool table watched, open-mouthed
the man in front of Sonny looked down at his stomach
the barman leaned on the bar . . .

. . . and then it had started again.

The man grabbed his belly with both hands and howled, sinking to his knees, the cigarette dropping from his ear in exaggerated slow motion. He was no longer attractive.

Sonny bent down and hoisted up the cat basket with his left hand, still clutching the bills, dropping a few on the floor.

And he had turned around and run.

You come back here—
Hey, he knifed Troy—
Get him!

Sonny closed his eyes. "What?"

"I said, what can I get you?"

He shook his head and stared at the woman like he was coming out of a dream. On the wall behind her were lots of pictures of hamburgers and packets of fries, milk shakes and cartons of soda. He had walked down to a fast-food place without even thinking about what he was doing. He pulled his jacket tight around the bloodstained shirt and considered the menu. "Gimme a Big Mac, side order of fries, a Coke and . . . and a Captain Nemo." The woman nodded tiredly and turned around to the dispensers behind her.

Sonny knelt down in front of the serving area and whispered into the cat basket. "How's that sound, huh, cat?" he said, wishing he could remember the cat's name.

He paid the woman with a twenty and watched nervously

as she held it up to the fluorescent light to check it wasn't a forgery. Then he walked across to a window seat and placed the basket next to the glass.

Feeding bits of the fish sandwich into the basket, Sonny watched the street outside. Just as he thought it might have been an idea to take a seat at the back, away from the window, a pickup—yellow or white, he couldn't make it out—drifted by and slowed right down. He leaned over against the glass and watched the pickup drift in front of the McDonald's and pull across to his side of the road, pull into a parking bay.

Sonny looked around at the people behind the serving area. They were talking about something, laughing, paying no notice to him. He looked along the back wall for another exit. There wasn't one. Over to his right there was a man wielding a wide cloth-covered broom along the floor. Two booths in front of him sat an old man staring into a mug of coffee.

Tap, tap.

The noise startled him at first, and then he realized what it was.

Sonny turned to the window, turned to the smiling face beyond the glass, saw the big hand tapping the window, watched the hand unfurl a single finger, saw it beckon to him to come outside. He turned back to the counter and saw one of the pool players from the bar, hands thrust deep into jacket pockets . . . but there was more than just hands in those pockets.

"You ready?" the man called over to him.

Tap, tap, insistent now. Sonny looked back at the window. The face nodded, still smiling, the head jerked backwards, telling him to come on.

Sonny stood, put down his Big Mac, suddenly realizing he had been holding it all of the time, and got to his feet. He reached over and picked up the basket.

Outside, the men greeted him like an old friend.

They took his arms and walked him along the road and across the street towards the Lincoln Memorial.

Then they crossed over into the park, towards the Vietnam Veterans Memorial. Nobody said anything.

When they got to the two black walls they stopped. "Put the cat down," the big man said.

Sonny did as he was told. "Are we going to talk?"

One of the other men laughed. " 'Are we going to talk, mithter?' " he said, singsong, mimicking Sonny's voice.

"Now take off the shirt," the big man said.

"It's cold," said Sonny. "I'll catch cold."

"It's the least of your worries," one of the others said.

He started to unbutton the shirt, slowly. "Look," he said, "I didn't mean anyth—"

The man slapped him across the face. "I didn't say talk to me, you little faggot, I said take off the fucking shirt."

Sonny tried to ignore the sting on his left cheek and continued with the buttons.

"Jacket."

"Huh?"

"Take off your jacket."

Sonny took off his jacket and laid it across the basket. Then he finished the shirt buttons and took it off, held it limply, looking across the men's faces, trying to make eye contact. All of them avoided his eyes except the big man. There were four of them. Too many.

"Give it to Earl."

A swarthy man chewing gum stepped into the light and smiled at him, held out his hand. "Thankth, mithter," he said, as Sonny dropped the shirt into the hand, watched it move away from him.

"Why . . . why d'you want my shirt?"

"Troy," Earl said.

"I—I thought Troy was dead."

Earl glared at him. "He is," said one of the others, stepping forward so Sonny could see him. "Gonna bury him in it."

Sonny looked around at Earl, holding the shirt out away from him like it was infected with something. The thought of that shirt—his best shirt in all the world—being put into the ground filled Sonny with horror. "Look . . . I said I was—"

"Gonna teach you a lesson," the big man said. He turned around and muttered to one of the men. The man pulled something out from under his jacket and handed it to him. When the big man turned back to face him, Sonny saw that it was a cushion. The man then pulled a gun out of his pocket. Sonny watched in fascination, trying to identify the model. Hands held each of his bare arms and someone jammed the cushion up against his stomach. "It's nothing personal, right?"

"No," Sonny said, looking from one to the other. "I didn't do nothing." Then he remembered. He had done plenty. "He made me do it," he corrected.

"Thay pleeth," Earl said, and, just for a second, Sonny saw the chewing gum, gray and teeth-marked, turn over on his tongue.

"Plea—"

The big man jammed the gun into the cushion and pulled the trigger. Twice.

Sonny was pushed backwards, hard. He felt the wall of names cold against his back. Then it seemed to get warmer. Just for a second.

The big man held a finger to his mouth and looked round the side of the wall at the street. Freed from the arms that had held him, Sonny slid down the wall and sat roughly on the grass at its base. He tried to move his hands up to his stomach but they wouldn't respond. His stomach felt like it was wide open, the wind blowing into it, blowing all the insides down across his pants. He closed his eyes, tried to speak. "P-please . . ."

The shots had not been loud, more like a branch snapping. The big man nodded to the others and put the gun into his pocket, then the four of them stepped across Sonny, the gaudy shirt that one of them carried flapping in the late-night breeze.

There was no pain. Sonny opened his eyes and watched them go, heard the cat mewl. "Please . . ."

The big man turned around and started back.

"Where you going?" one of the others asked.

The man didn't answer, just stepped over to Sonny and knelt down beside him. He pulled the gun out again and held it up to Sonny's temple. "Need another?"

Sonny moved his head slowly, side to side.

"What then?"

"Th-the cat. Let . . . go."

The man returned the gun to his pocket.

"What? What the fuck?" The man called Earl had come back and was standing behind the big man, watching Sonny's face over the man's shoulder. "What are you doing?"

"Letting the cat free."

"It's just a fucking cat, leave it," hissed Earl.

The big man had reached the basket and was unfastening the catch. He looked over at Sonny, made eye contact. "Have a heart," he said to them, keeping his eyes on Sonny as the cat pounced out of the basket and dashed towards the trees.

Sonny listened to the sound of their feet on the grass, growing distant. "Any man who . . ." he whispered to the darkness, ". . . can care for—"

Then both he and the night were silent again.

Talk Shows Just Kill Me

•

Billie Sue Mosiman

Buddy lay in his prison cell late at night, wide awake. The tiny radio earphones buzzed like wasps in his ears. He was a talk-show addict and his favorite man was Larry King. Sometimes, if Larry had on a boring guest (Clarence Bigwig, author of *How To Make Money Selling Real Estate In A Down Market*), Buddy tuned in Tom Snyder. But Tom was going off the air. Ratings must have been low or something, and that pissed Buddy off. Tom was a good guy, his voice over the radio deep and silky as wild honey, his strange sudden laugh like a strangled goose sounding from the bottom of a wooden barrel. He'd miss him.

Once in a while, Buddy turned the tuner and picked up a couple of talk-show guys out of Chicago, and they chattered on about entertainment trivia. The first movie Gary Cooper starred in. The color of Scarlett's dress in the scene when Rhett told her he frankly didn't give a damn. Silly stuff. Never kept Buddy interested for long before his fingers twisted the dial, searching for another show.

Buddy knew them all. The late-night crowd on the radio. Preachers begging for donations. Some British-sounding New Age guy who gave out moral advice. Psychiatrists who had little patience with the slobs overmedicated on psychotropic drugs who called in wanting to know why

262

they had to drool, was it a side-effect or were they losing their minds for real?

Buddy even knew about ole Rush Limbaugh, but he was daytime radio, and in the daytime Buddy had more important things to do than listen to a talk-show host rant about those "liberal bleeding hearts." For instance, Buddy had to stay alive. An iffy affair in prison. Any prison, but especially this one stuck in the heart of East Texas where the inmates would stick a shiv in you just for giving a crooked look to the wrong person.

So it was, that fateful summer night, when Buddy lay in his bunk, earphones pressed deep into each ear canal, his head full of voice, when Larry King announced his guests for the next two weeks, one of whom was to be Roger Spenser. Roger! The man who had come into Huntsville Correctional Unit with a notebook in one hand, a tape recorder in the other, and picked apart Buddy's brain. Picked it cleaner than a buzzard on a coon carcass, then made himself a name by fictionalizing and sensationalizing Buddy LeFevre's true and real-life pain.

Larry King's announcement of the guest he'd have on for two hours Friday after next, *Roger Spenser, author of* Dying Kisses, *a novel of suspense that has been on the* New York Times's *best-seller list for four months,* caused Buddy to jerk upright, eyes widening, mouth falling open.

That son of a bitch. Buddy knew Roger did it. Knew about the book and the fame. He even knew, when he was being endlessly interviewed, that Roger Spenser was going to write a book—he had admitted that from the very outset. But what Buddy didn't know was that his *real* story, the *truth*, was going to be mangled all to hell and back, his life was going to be made to look like a dumping ground for any stupid psychosis Spenser could fantasize, and Buddy was to be the victim of a piece of crap book pretending to be hot new fiction.

Naturally, the "novel" made a big hit. Of course the

country reacted to the story. It was made of blood and guts, brain and intestine, heart and soul. It was a Buddy LeFevre casserole, events and people so mingled and cooked, you couldn't tell hamburger from broccoli, fact from fiction. In places it rang so authentic, you had hairs standing up and walking down your arms. Other times the scenes caused you to close your eyes and wince with empathy. It wasn't that Roger didn't write a good book. He just wrote one scraped together out of Buddy's pitiful existence.

"What's doin'?" Georgie asked from the top bunk.

Buddy barely heard his cellmate. He pulled one earphone out and said, "Huh?"

"Whassa matter, you get a nightmare?"

"Naw, forget about it. I just heard something on the radio."

"Oh. Okay. You bumped my mattress so hard, I thought you wuz jackin' off or something down there."

Buddy laughed because it was just too obscene an image that flashed to mind for him not to. He'd jack off, all right. He ever got his hands on the great Roger Spenser, he'd jack him so hard, his head would spin right off his shoulders.

He lay down again, and withdrew the other earphone from his ear. Larry was introducing the night's guest, a feminist who had changed her mind and thought women ought to be women, donchaknow, women in dresses and stockings and high heels, the kind of women men liked to take to bed. *Vive la différence!*

To hell with that. Buddy wanted a woman, sure, but his most pressing need was altogether different. Hate, anger, betrayal burned in his chest like the pain signaling a myocardial infarction. He had trusted Roger. He had opened his heart to Roger. He thought Roger was going to write a book vindicating him, a book that would explain to the world how he was not really responsible for his life of crime and violence, it wasn't *his* fault, he'd been made rough by circumstance, starved for affection and acclaim,

despised and ridiculed for looking like a dumb Sumo wres-
tler, wrongly imprisoned when he should have gone to one
of those cushy mental hotels where they doled out Prozac
and let you loose when the funds ran out.

Three years ago Roger came to the prison and got permission to have ongoing sessions with Buddy. Roger was
so understanding. With his pale blonde hair and wire-frame
glasses, his hunched shoulders, thin and bony beneath his
starched white shirt. Roger listening, probing, asking questions. Letting Buddy ramble, spewing forth every vile and
sick thought he'd ever had, every terrible deed he'd ever
done, every vain hope he'd ever harbored for help and a
better life.

"You'll write it down like I told you, won't you?" Buddy
asked, signing the release papers for his life story. "You'll
tell them how it was, right?" He knew he wouldn't be paid
for the book, not since the Son of Sam ruling, but if Roger
just wrote the truth, that would be something.

Roger hovered like one of those long-legged Texas cow-
birds that follow cattle to pick at hot manure. "Sure, sure,
Buddy, you know I will. I'll tell it just like it was."

The lying son-of-a-bitch bastard.

Buddy read the book. He got it through the prison library
system as soon as it was published. He sat for three days
during free time reading. Blanching, going white as book
paper. Feeling the tornado of fury swirling inside.

Dying Kisses claimed Buddy (named Brody in the book
and what kind of pussy name was that?) was a psychopath
of the worst sort. He had no conscience. He was raised like
an animal and lived like one. Killed like one. He was so
dangerous the prison authorities should never let him out to
see daylight.

Buddy killed, all right, but Roger made it look bad, he
told it all wrong. Buddy killed the woman he loved because
she messed around on him. She knew better than to mess
around on Buddy LeFevre, what was a man to do? He had

robbed, stolen, and lied to take care of her. He would have given his right arm to keep her in cigarettes and Wild Turkey whiskey. But that wasn't good enough. She walked, took up with a pimply twenty-year-old who had a crack habit costing him three hundred bucks a day.

Buddy let the air from his lungs escape through pursed lips until all of it was gone, until he was an empty sack lying beneath the sheet on the bed, the little earphones in his left palm, buzzing like captured flies. He took in a new breath and again let it out slowly until it was all gone. This wasn't exactly meditation, not with his mind racing round and round. It did, however, serve to calm him so he could think again.

In two weeks Roger was going to be in Washington, D.C., on the Mutual Radio Larry King talk show. On Monday Buddy came up for parole.

If he got out, Roger was in serious trouble. Bigtime, losing-his-life trouble. A man who prospered from another man's heartache did not deserve to live. In fact, he had more to die for than Buddy's old dead girlfriend. Lots more. Screwing around with a man's *life* was the ultimate treachery.

Buddy sweet-talked his way out. He had been a good boy. For a period of ten years his behavior had been monitored and found acceptable.

With the money he had earned while in prison—not much, a couple hundred dollars savings—he bought a bus ticket from Huntsville, Texas, to Washington, D.C. It was summer, hot, the streets of the capital city steaming like short-order grills.

Once in town, Buddy blended in with the night people and found a place to stay with some heads in a crack house. He didn't do drugs, but he wasn't against selling them if it kept him from sleeping in doorways or on park benches. The heads didn't much like him. He was fat, they were skinny. He had been fed on prison food until he weighed in at a smidgeon over three hundred pounds, while they smoked poison and weighed no more than a pile of bones. Also, he didn't smoke the stuff, didn't shoot any dope, and he was much too alert for their liking. Still, he fit in merely because he knew the life and he wouldn't rat them off. And who was going to throw him out? It would take a legion of crack heads to lift one of his concrete-post legs off the ground.

He asked around about Mutual Radio. Where was it? Which building?

One head who had in the distant past been a college professor (of philosophy, what else?), something that didn't surprise Buddy, still knew enough about the world he lived in to supply the information. "The Larry King show isn't broadcast out of Washington," he said.

"No? That's funny. They always say it's coming from Washington, D.C."

"Well, they don't really."

Buddy began to wonder if the head had already smoked so much he didn't know his ass from his elbow. "Okay, where do they broadcast from then?"

"Crystal City."

"What the hell's a Crystal City?"

The head pointed south. "It's a subdivision of Arlington, Virginia. Right across the Potomac from D.C. You take the infamous 14th Street Bridge."

"What's so infamous about it?"

The head gave him a squinty look. "Oh, yeah, you been in the joint. Maybe you don't get the news there. The 14th Street Bridge is where that Air Florida plane crashed in 1981. All those people died. The river was iced over. Terrible thing."

Buddy nodded, storing the information. "You know what building in Crystal City? You know what story the show is on?"

"Couldn't tell you. Never been there. I thought once maybe I'd be on radio and TV. I wrote a book, you know, but my colleagues were jealous and kept it from being published. Professional disagreement. Called my research faulty. All a put-up job 'cause they didn't want to see me succeed."

"Bad luck."

"You're telling me. It might have made me a fortune. I might have gotten tenure."

"No doubt."

"Now look where I am." He swept a skeletal arm around the street and almost knocked down a whore from her high perch on black shiny spike heels.

"Hey, man, watch what you're doin', or I'll havta bust you in de teefe."

"Sorry, ma'am." The head stepped back, and tipped an imaginary hat.

Buddy said, "This is better than being in a jail cell. Try to stay out of them if you can."

The head brought a pipe to his lips and cupped the bowl from the breeze in order to light the crack inside it. He took a puff and swayed on his feet.

Buddy walked off, hands in his pockets. In just about two minutes the head wouldn't even remember talking to him.

Buddy needed a car if he was going to Crystal City. He had until Friday to find one. Two days. Plenty of time. Stealing cars was child's play.

Buddy sat in the two-year-old Lincoln (the same kind of car Larry King preferred to drive) with the windows rolled down. He smoked Marlboros, one after the other. He had picked up an alley cat that hung around the crack house, scraggly little white bitch with torn ears. He liked her, liked the way she walked, tail high, though she was starving, her hipbones poking from her back end like tepee poles. He took charge of the feline, feeding her cans of tuna, giving her dishes of milk. She adored him. At the moment, she lay curled in his lap below the steering wheel. Sleeping for all she was worth, belly full, safe from harm. Occasionally he ran his hand over her fur and felt her purring, the gentle vibration soothing to him. She was the only cat he had ever known that liked riding in cars. He had taken her everywhere with him the past two days. He carried her in his arms until he found the car. She slept nestled in his arms. He called her Cat, and when he was alone, he told her what he was going to do to the man who had stolen his life.

"Cat," he said, "this guy is a lowdown individual. He pried all my secrets out of me and then he made them into a lie. He called me names. He said I was too dangerous to live. And that was the only thing he got right in the whole goddamn book that's made him a rich man."

He listened to the radio. Larry King had on Roger Spenser and seemed to like him. You could always tell when Larry liked the guest. He'd laugh at the jokes. He had a tone in his voice that came out over the air waves to signal to the audience, *hey, this guy's all right, he's fine, he's a lot of fun, folks.* And he defended him.

When a couple of boffos called in to heckle Roger, Larry cut them off with his famous retort, "Rest well, sir."

Buddy had been dialing the portable car phone for over an hour, trying to get through. They didn't screen the calls on the Larry King show. You got on, you got to talk until Larry pushed the button to sever the connection.

The phone on the other end was either busy or it rang and rang. Buddy lounged in the seat smoking, petting Cat, and dialing the show.

Suddenly he was on the line, connected. They asked where he was calling from. He lied, said Washington. Not more than a minute later Larry's deep voice said directly into Buddy's ear, "Washington, D.C., hello."

Buddy froze. Smoke plumed out his nostrils. His hand stilled on Cat.

Larry said, "Washington, go ahead. Do you have a question?"

Buddy thawed, his brain ticked over like a toy wound too tight and now on the roll. "Uh . . . Larry?"

"Yes, go ahead." You could hear the exasperation in his voice. He didn't like callers fooling around. Wasted time. Created dead space on the air.

"Roger?" Buddy said, finally in control of his runaway heart.

"Yes."

"*Go ahead,* caller." Larry was a millisecond from punching another button for a different caller on hold.

"Roger, you had no right to make up those lies about me."

There was genuine dead space over the radio now. Buddy couldn't even hear Larry's breathing. He thought he might have been disconnected, that Larry had actually snuffed him for daring to say such a thing.

Finally, in a weak, whiny voice, Roger said, "Is that you, Buddy?"

Larry interrupted. "What, is this the convict you interviewed for your book? The one you based the story on?"

"I think it is. Buddy, is that you?"

Now Buddy felt swallowed by his own smile. It engulfed him. He had Roger scared and Larry off-balance. No caller in North America could have done that but him.

"Yeah, it's me, Roger. What I want to know is, why'd you do it? These people out here reading your book think you're some kind of hotshot writer, but me and you know what you done, don't we? We know how you took the truth and turned it upside down. How you made me look the chump. How you lied to me about writing my life story and then turned it into lying *fiction.*" He spat out this last word with all the vehemence he could muster.

270

"Why don't you tell the good people, Roger. Tell them how you conned me. Tell them what a thief you are."

Larry had control again. "Are you saying that Mr. Spenser didn't write your story the way you wanted?"

"The way I wanted!" Buddy let out a belly laugh. "He wrote it to make money. He made me into a monster, which ain't true, and got himself on the best-seller list that way. He's nothing more than a cheap pimp."

"Uh ... what do you have to say to this, Roger?" Larry asked, sounding intrigued by the call. Controversy. Nothing better to glue an audience to the radio than controversy.

The smile had all of Buddy now. Cat felt the electricity in the air and stood on his lap, arching her back, the hair standing along her rigid spine of knotted bone.

"Buddy?" Roger sounded like a man getting real sick to his stomach. "Buddy, now you understood that I was going to fictionalize your experiences ..."

"That's bull and you know it," Buddy said. "You promised you'd tell the real story, the whole story. You'd let readers know how a man winds up a criminal, what leads him into the life. You were going to tell them how Phadre walked out on me and how I just momentarily lost it. But instead what do you do? You make up all kinds of crimes I never committed and you make me out to be something I ain't. You call me *obese* and lacking self-esteem and *below average intelligence*. You make me into a Saturday cartoon, Roger. And what do I get out of it? I get laughed at. If people met me and knew I was Brody in *Dying Kisses*, they'd spit in my face. That's what you did, you lowlife, sniveling, co ..."

And then the connection went dead. The dial tone stung Buddy's ear like a slap. He threw the car phone across the seat. The violence made Cat screech and jump onto Buddy's shoulder, digging in her claws.

Buddy breathed out slowly, exhaling all the evil and all the pain. He reached up and took Cat into his big wide hands. "There," he said, rubbing behind her battle-scarred ears. "There now. It's over now. I won't yell no more."

On the radio he heard Larry King go, "Whew! That was something. Are you afraid this guy might seek revenge?"

Roger said, in a steady, but dismal voice, "I don't think he can. He's in prison in Texas."

"But that call was from Washington. He's right here in the city."

"Maybe there was a mistake," Roger said. "I know he's in prison for murdering his girlfriend."

"What you don't know," Buddy whispered. He glanced up at the building housing Mutual Radio offices and that smile that earlier took over his entire body came back bigger than ever. Bigger than even the world.

Buddy waited until the part of the show was over with the guest and Larry went to Open Phone America where people were allowed to call in and talk about anything on their little minds.

He saw Roger come out the door and down the walk to the parking area. He saw him enter a limousine, waited until it cleared the drive, and move down the street for the 14th Street Bridge. He followed behind it at a distance. When it turned into a hotel in the city of Washington, Buddy drove on past and parked down the street.

He was very good at waiting. He had had plenty of practice.

It was nine in the morning before he saw Roger exit the hotel front. Buddy's eyes were made of grit and Cat was hungry. But it had been worth it.

He watched Roger cross the street, weaving through traffic, and head off down the sidewalk like a man with a purpose. He probably wanted to buy his wife a miniature of the Lincoln Memorial before he took a flight from the city. That was exactly the kind of thing he'd do. Or maybe he'd buy her a mink or a diamond. After all, he was a wealthy man now.

Pushing Cat aside, admonishing her to stay, Buddy was out of the car and crossing the street. He affronted Roger two blocks from the hotel, just as he was about to enter a swank department store. He had him by the arm and leading him down the sidewalk before the smaller man could make a croak.

"Buddy!"

"The very same."

"I don't want you to be angry."

"I just bet you wouldn't. Maybe you should have thought about that before you wrote your book."

"I've got money, Buddy. Lots of money."

"Made it all off me, too, you piece of shit. Took my story and sold my blood."

"I can pay you. How much you want? Ten thousand? Twenty?"

"I read in the papers your advance was two point three million. You offer me twenty grand."

"Okay, all right. I can give you a hundred thousand. I don't have all that money from the advance. There's taxes and . . ."

"Oh, yeah, why don't you tell me your sob tale? How you spent some of it to buy a couple of houses. One in the Florida Keys maybe or a villa in France. How you spent some more for a cruise with your wife and kiddies to Europe. How those new cars set you back, and the college funds for your children, and the house you bought your old mother, I guess. Why don't you just *cry about it, you lousy little creep!*"

"Buddy, don't do this, don't be this way. I thought you knew I was writing a novel. It couldn't be just like you told me or it wouldn't have made sense!"

That pulled Buddy up sharp. He dug his fingers deeper into Roger's upper arm. Passersby glanced at them then looked away, avoiding conflict. "Wouldn't have made sense? My life makes no sense? Is that what you're saying, Rogerino? The days I lived were senseless, the crime I committed came out of nowhere and had no reason, the prison term I served was nothing but a cakewalk at the prom dance?"

"I didn't mean that, Buddy, honestly, I just mean real life has no real . . . solution."

"Oh, and I guess the plot meanders and the characters are cardboard stereotypes, is that it? You think I give a shit about your writing problems, Roger? You think I'm gonna stand here and feel sorry for your creative *muse*?"

Buddy jerked him forward and turned him left into an alleyway. There were empty packing crates and overflowing garbage cans. Refuse littered the area. It smelled like something big and full of blood had died there. A long time ago.

Roger shook all over, stricken with palsy. His feet stumbled and he was talking complete gibberish. Flecks of saliva clung to his thin lips and his eyes were crazed. Buddy began to feel sorry for him. He tried not to. But the guy was such a waste. He couldn't get a perfectly straightforward story right, he couldn't defend himself, he couldn't even talk himself out of trouble.

Buddy slammed him up against the brick wall of a building. He heard the air whoosh out of him. His blood drained to his feet, leaving his face colorless.

Buddy spread apart his big feet and put his fists on his wide hips. He could hear traffic sounds and horns from the far street they had left. He could hear a frightening mishmash of words in his ears, the way he would when he woke in the mornings with the earphones still in his ears, swimming up from sleep to the sound of demonic voices from the radio.

"I ought to kill you. You know that's only right," he said. "I could do it with my bare hands. Take your stupid neck and wring it tight."

He thought Roger was saying something like *please, please, I'm sorry, please . . .*

"I meant to do it. You ain't nothing but a walking idiot who robs from the poorest of us to further your own aims. The world should be shed of you."

Please don't, please forgive . . . please . . .

"But I think what would be much more interesting is to have you take me to live with you. Wouldn't you like that, Roger? I thought about it all night long. What your life must be like now you're a famous author. What a celebrity you are. I can tell you more stories and you can write them up any way you please and we'll share the profits. Your wife will be my wife and your children my children. We'll travel together. You'll take me on the talk shows with you, I'll even get to meet Larry King. You can buy me a car and give me a nice room with a great big bed in it. You ever call in the cops, I simply take a knife and rip you and your family to itty-bitty pieces, what you say? You think that would be fair payment for what you've done? Don't you think so? Huh?"

Buddy stood over Roger where he had slumped down onto his haunches, holding his head in both hands.

"You want to live or you want to die here, lie with the rats, Roger? It's up to you, my friend."

After some minutes, Roger raised his head, lifted his red-eyed gaze, and nodded in agreement. "You win," he said.

"And ain't it about time?" Buddy asked, helping the poor man to his feet so they could leave the alley and enter the bright sunshine of a new day.

"You know," he said, swaggering a little now as he walked beside Roger. "I think I'd like to have one of those new Lincoln Continentals, just like Larry King drives. Those don't cost too awful much, do they? And I've always wanted a hot tub. Right outside my own room. You got a cook and a maid? We'll need 'em. I want my food served to me, steak, potatoes, the works. Your kids play Nintendo?

I've always wanted to play one of those games. How about a wide-screen TV? You got one? We'll get one. Biggest one the Japanese make. Here, stop a minute, I have to get my cat. She's no trouble. Your family should love her. I'm sure this is gonna work out fine. I've always admired writers. They're so ... accommodating, that's the word, isn't it, Roger, accommodating?"

The two men strolled back to the hotel, one as huge as a bull elephant, and cocky for all that weight, cradling a mangy white cat in his arms. The other one was small, dwarfed, better dressed, rather artistic looking, but not quite as happy as his companion. From up close it appeared he was not a happy man at all. Even Larry King, who had met him the night before, probably wouldn't have recognized the celebrated author of one of America's most popular best-sellers.

Freedom of the Press

•

Barbara D'Amato

Iwalked into the office of Representative Peggy Nicklis at 1:55, for a two o'clock appointment. Then I stopped and stared.

She saw my face and started to laugh. When she was done chuckling, she said, "You're Cat Marsala?"

"Yup. Thank you for seeing me, Ms. Nicklis."

"And you expected a much grander office." She was still half laughing.

"Well, I didn't expect—uh—exposed heat pipes, cracked linoleum, a sloping ceiling, two small rooms—I suppose this outer room is for your secretary?—furniture that looks like it was retired from the Library of Congress, and a window the size of the Elvis stamp." In addition there was a slightly off-center bookcase crammed with books, several reasonably adequate bookcases visible in the inner office, some empty cartons, an old desk in the reception room and an old desk in the inner office. Three phones and an answering machine on each desk. Two very large metal wastebaskets. A plush blue cat bed and a litter box in Nicklis's inner office. And a cat. Everything in both offices was tidy; everything was neat and straight and clean, but the place was definitely shabby. Nicklis watched me, smiling.

"It's a matter of seniority. You get better and better offices the longer you're here. Washington is all about how important you are. This is definitely a starter office. Plus, this isn't the only thing," she said. "The nearest bathroom for women is *seven flights* of stairs away from here."

"Jeez!"

"And not just seven flights," she giggled, "but down three, then *up* two, then down two."

"They weren't prepared for you women."

"Well, it also makes you feel sorry for two hundred years of secretaries, dashing for the far-off water closet."

I had recognized her right away, of course, from a zillion photographs and television interviews. So she seemed like an old friend. She acted like one too, showing me into her office and sitting down next to me in a corner where she had two overstuffed chairs. The cat came over, swept its body across my ankle and told me it wanted to be stroked precisely twice. Cats know exactly what they want. After graciously accepting this homage he allowed Peggy to scratch his ear, then he stared at each of us in turn, collecting admiration.

I asked, "Who is Mr. Cat?"

What I thought she said was:

"His name is Mugum."

"Mugum?" I looked at the tawny, lithe cat. He went to his big, plush cushion and lay down. He lifted one hind leg in the air to inspect it. Apparently decided it was an excellent leg. He put it down and rolled onto his back.

"Mugum is a very unusual name."

"It's spelled 'MGM.' Pronounced Mugum. He's named that because he looks like the MGM lion. MGM is a ginger tom, aren't you, baby?"

"Did you get him after you moved here—"

"Oh, Lord, no! I've had him all his life. He's seven now. We've moved to D.C. together, haven't we, tough guy? MGM goes everywhere with me."

MGM curled up and went to sleep.

Peggy Nicklis was slender, with dark hair cut blunt. An easy-care style. She wore a suit and flat shoes that would be easy to get around in. My mother would have said, "She doesn't do a lot for herself." Peggy also wasn't what United States culture in the waning days of the twentieth century considered especially beautiful.

Peggy Nicklis certainly wasn't the first woman to serve in the House of Representatives, but she was the first from an extremely conservative district just northwest of Chicago. She had received a considerable amount of media attention because she had won without being particularly flashy in her statements or striking-looking in her photographs. The word for Peggy was businesslike, and she had received the trust of the voters, rather than catching their fancy.

Hal Briskman at *Chicago Today* had said to me:

"What we want is a story about how she's settling in, now that she's been in Washington three weeks. Is D.C. intimidating to her? How does she like her office? Are rents breathtakingly expensive? Does she feel like one of the gang yet?"

"That's not very pithy, Hal."

"We don't want pith. Readers are fed up with pith. Don't talk budget deficit with her, Cat. That's not what we want right now. Don't talk health care. Don't talk education priorities. Do a fluff piece."

"Fluff! I don't do fluff."

"Fluff is good for the soul."

"Not this soul. But I *will* do the interview, if you want."

"And do it the way I want. Keep in mind: you play, we pay."

"Oh, very well."

He said he'd pay for the tickets, meals of course, and two nights at a hotel in D.C., which adds up. And pay for the article, of course. Well, that's the business I'm in. I'm freelance, which is always a precarious way to live. And while some of the stories I've done have been big, and my byline is noticed by an occasional reader, I'm not famous.

Being famous would be nice.

Peggy answered my questions straightforwardly. "Well, yes. Rent here truly does take your breath away. For what you'd pay in Chicago for a medium-sized apartment with a Lake Michigan view, here you get one and a half rooms looking out at a fire escape and the brick wall of the building next door ten feet away."

"You're saying we aren't really keeping our legislators happy?"

She smiled. "I wouldn't think of saying that. Anyway, I'm planning to spend most of my time here in the office. I go home mainly to sleep. That way I figure I'll earn more time back in Chicago, too. My folks and my friends are there."

"How about new friends here?"

"I'm meeting a few people. It's slow, though."

"You probably don't have much time to socialize. You have a lot of work and catching up to do."

"Yes. Still, there are parties galore. The White House had the so-called freshmen, the new guys, to dinner. That was exciting. I've been to several special-interest dinners, and a Democratic Party bash in honor of the newcomers. A couple of embassies. My father's family is Polish, so I got asked to their embassy party, of course."

Peggy's secretary came back from late lunch, stuck her head in the door and waved. Peggy introduced her as Annie Boyd.

Peggy said to me, "Could we continue this tomorrow?" To Annie she said, "It was two o'clock Monday and Tuesday, wasn't it?"

In the outer office, Annie nodded her head, yes, it was Monday and Tuesday at two.

The interviewee is always right. I said, "Sure, and

thanks." However, it was supposed to be Monday and Tuesday two to three, and this was only two-thirty. Peggy realized that.

"I know we're stopping early. But let me make up for it tomorrow. I'm still backed up with work and I'm barely unpacked."

Well, who could fault a person for that? The last time I moved, it took three months of my life and three years off my life.

Washington was cold but bright Tuesday, and I spent the morning walking. I strolled the Mall, went into the National Air and Space Museum and the National Gallery, and finally walked up Delaware to eat at one of the fast-food places in the underground mall at Union Station. It was truly fast, served coffee in cups as big as soup bowls, and it let me watch the noon news on an overhead TV. There was trouble in the Middle East, fighting in central Europe, and a newsman for United Press International, Lee Chesterton, whom I knew slightly, had driven off the Frederick Douglass Bridge last night and drowned. It was thought alcohol was involved. He was well known here, and it was a big story with a lot of the usual Washington speculation.

After lunch, the Smithsonian beckoned, but a person needs a week to do it justice. No point right now. I strolled through the National Sculpture Garden instead.

A minute or two before the hour, I arrived at Peggy Nicklis's office. Her secretary Annie simply waved me through. No pomp here. Peggy looked tired and the ginger tom was out of sorts too. He hissed at me, then stalked over to the window, jumped up to the ledge and prowled back and forth.

"I heard about Lee Chesterton's accident on the noon news," I told Peggy. "I'd met him a couple of times when he covered a story in Chicago."

"It's a terrible thing to have happened. He was a nice person."

"Yes, terrible. You dated him a couple of times, didn't you?"

She looked up, surprised. "Two or three times. How did you know that?"

"People think reporters just wing it. That must be why they think the job is all glamour and no work." She gave me a lopsided smile. I said, "I always research people I'm going to interview. You were photographed, I think by the *Washington Post*, at a party with him ten days ago or so."

"Yes. It's a shock."

The cat stared at the back of Peggy's neck. He jumped from the windowsill to the desk, and from there to the floor. Peggy got up and shut the door to the outer office. The farther door to the hall was open and she didn't want the cat to get out. The cat stalked past the bed, sheared away, and prowled around the wastebasket as if it were some sort of prey.

I said, "I'm sorry. It must be especially hard for you, so soon after moving in, losing one of the few friends you've met here."

"It is. Although maybe if I'd known him longer it'd be worse." She said this calmly, but there was a lot of sadness in her eyes.

I felt extremely sorry for her. At the same time, I was excited and tense, which made it harder to look relaxed and in charge of a chatty interview. The ginger tom crouched, then sprang forward and ran under the desk. I felt like a cat myself, waiting to spring at a mouse.

"Apparently the investigators believe he'd been drinking," I said. "They're reporting ethanol in the blood."

"He did drink. I asked him not to once, because he always drove his own car. Not like a lot of Washingtonians, you know. They seem to think being chauffeured is proof that you're a real success. Anyway, he didn't like it when

I asked him not to drink too much, and I didn't want to upset him, so I just dropped the subject."

Didn't want to turn him off, probably. Unfortunately, Peggy was not a person who would be surrounded by men asking her out.

She said, "Washingtonians drink too much, almost all of them."

I went on. "They think there was somebody else in the car with him. Several cars on the bridge stopped when they saw the Porsche crash through the guardrail. A witness said two people swam away."

"I heard that."

"It looks like they both got out safely. The car floated for a while, and they crawled through an open window. Whoever was with him could swim. But he was a very weak swimmer."

"Unless she—unless whoever it was drowned too."

"Well, no. There was a call from a pay phone reporting the accident. Asking for help. Almost certainly the passenger. I guess she hoped the rescue people might save him."

"I guess."

"I shouldn't have said 'she hoped.' The caller whispered and the news report said the police didn't know if it was a man or woman."

"Yes, I heard that too."

"She has good reason not to want to be identified."

"Yes. The way it is, she could be anybody."

I was profoundly conscious that this could be the scoop of my career. Carefully, I went on.

"Whoever it was, he or she would be guilty of leaving the scene of an accident."

"And that's a crime," Peggy said, placing her hands together, folding the fingers and squeezing.

"Leaving the scene of a fatal accident. I think it's a felony."

She didn't respond. We sat looking at each other for at

least half a minute—a *very* long time in polite social discourse. The ginger tom slipped past me, skirted the blue cushion, jumped to the top of a bookcase, and paced back and forth.

Finally, Peggy said:

"Are you going to report that it was me?"

I hesitated too. From feeling excited, I had gone to feeling sick. Some decision had been made viscerally without my brain being involved. It had to do with how I would feel about this six months from now. What I was about to do was foolish. After all, I had my own career to take care of, didn't I? All right. It was my life. I was free to do what I chose. I was going to be foolish.

I said, "No. You've suffered enough."

"What—?"

I pointed to the cat. "He prowls constantly. He's restless. He won't lie down in that bed."

Peggy wrapped her arms around her chest.

I said, "How else would I have known? MGM went everywhere with you. No wonder you're tired. How many pet stores and animal shelters did you have to go to this morning before you found a tom with exactly that coloring?"

Strays

•

Kristine Kathryn Rusch

i

It happened during Clinton's first hundred days. D.C. was
a changed town. Arkania was in. So were strong women.
Wife No. 3 had left me just after the inauguration, and Secretary No. 45 quit, vowing to file a sexual harassment suit.
She was a great girl, with legs that wouldn't quit, and I was
sorry to see her go. The secretary, that is. Not the wife.

My fancy-schmancy office was cold and empty without
her. I no longer needed the front room with its oak desk,
cool blue walls, and indoor-outdoor carpet. The phone system was too complicated for me to use, so one afternoon I
pulled it from the wall, and reverted to my black rotary. The
commissions I got from the Bush people for staking out
Democrat parties vanished on November 4, and since Wife
No. 3 cleared out half the savings, I couldn't hire Secretary
No. 46. I spent January looking for new digs, and February
advertising in the *Post*'s classifieds because I couldn't break
the lease I had. The cases were few and far between. The
money even scarcer. I followed a Democratic senator's wife
for three days before he found out I used to work for the
Bush people. The commission wasn't bad, but it didn't make

the rent. I scoped out a bunch of women for Senator Packwood, but that job ended when the press got wind of it.

I was reduced to insurance claims investigation when the call came in. Woman's voice, very concerned. Address fell in the middle of an upscale brownstone neighborhood in McLean. Lots of money, well hidden. Real money that didn't need the parade of wealth to prove it was rich. Bush country. Home.

I drove my silver Thunderbird on the George Washington Parkway, glad the car at least was paid off. Can't be a dick without wheels. Still, they don't make T-birds like they used to. No pickup in the new models, and the design looks like Sports Cars for Suburbia. The baby had speed though once it got going. Sometimes I needed speed. Along the way I passed lots of nondescript blue sedans, most with vanity plates. I stared at one, DAN 1996, all the way into McLean. Some folks never gave up.

The brownstone was in a tree-lined neighborhood that had a hush so deep it seemed like all the occupants had died. I knew they hadn't though. Curtains moved all over the block when the T-bird parked in front of 1256 (lettering neogothic, no name beneath the script). I felt like a cop in a whorehouse: couldn't see a thing, but knew lots of folks were seeing him.

The door chime was three soft tones designed to echo through the house without disturbing the occupants. The dame herself answered the door. Surprised me. I expected a genteel male butler with a voice as soft-spoken as the chimes.

She had been a looker once. Still was, if truth be told. Mass of silver hair, expertly styled to curl and fall in a dignified way around her face. Her figure was trim, her undergarments firm so that her breasts poked out like an eighteen-year-old's. Her legs put No. 45's to shame. Her skin had that papery look brought on by age and good nutrition. She didn't look so much old as softened.

A white cat wound its way around her legs, peeking through at me like a flirtatious child. "Mr. Ransom?" the woman said. "I'm Beverly Conner."

I took the offered hand, felt the knobby knuckles that indicated arthritis, and did not squeeze. I stepped inside. The entry was done in browns, a deacon's bench by the door, a hand-carved mirror near the coatless coatrack, and a Rembrandt sketch—original, judging by the framing—near the closet. The faint odor of cat piss seemed out of place.

She led me through the hall to a kitchen that was made of windows. Sunlight dappled in from the garden, and the warmth enveloped me. The oak table was clean except for the German tea service waiting on the tabletop.

"Please sit," she said.

I sat.

Her obvious wealth didn't impress me as much as the cats. They watched like small sentries from the most unlikely of posts. A calico sat on top of the refrigerator. A black one slept on the chair opposite me. I had noticed another curled on the back of the couch as we passed the living room. She must have kept housekeepers employed full-time just mopping up the cat hair.

I thought only poor old ladies kept a zillion cats. Guess I was wrong.

"What do you need, ma'am?"

She plopped a newspaper clipping in front of me. I recognized it. It had run in the *Post* just the day before, and I had read all the way to the end, even though it gagged me. The *Post*, bastion of the Washington elite, had run an obituary on page one.

Of a cat.

Granted, it was a famous cat, even by D.C. standards. Bob, the Weather Cat, who had paraded in his cute little weather outfits—yellow rain slicker for rain, sunglasses and Hawaiian print shorts for heat waves—on Fox 5 every night during the five o'clock news. Bob put up with it with an amazing dignity—he was a cat after all—but folks watched to see if this week Bob would rebel. He hated the snow parka, and bit it off during a two-day storm that dumped five feet on downtown last winter, and he destroyed the rain slicker after a particularly bad stretch of showers by, you guessed it, peeing on it.

Bob, D.C.'s favorite contrary character, had been brutally murdered. His obit, on the front page of a paper that put the deaths of first-term congressmen in the Metro section, read with a seriousness usually reserved for presidents. Memorials were to go to the D.C. Chapter of the Humane Society. Seems our pal Bob had started life as a stray. Something else he shared with most of Washington's power elite.

Murdered. And I was sitting in a houseful of cats.

I had a bad feeling about this.

I shoved the paper back to her. "Yeah. I seen this."

"Bob lived next door," she said. "He isn't the first cat to die in this neighborhood."

"Cats get murdered all the time," I said. "Poisoned meat, hit-and-runs, steel traps. No one thinks it's any kind of conspiracy."

She blanched. "Perhaps you're not the man for the job, Mr. Ransom," she said primly.

A tabby wound her way between my legs, motor running. A white cat jumped on my lap in a flurry of fur. A black kitten meowed from the top of the microwave. They looked like the guard for a South American *junta*—charming on the surface with a bit too much animal underneath. "I usually do political jobs," I said.

"Well," she said, crossing her arms and turning her back on me, "this job is just humoring an old lady."

She walked over to the window and petted a graying black tom. He chirruped with pleasure and rolled onto his back, nearly dislodging the plastic screen covering a wealth of African violets.

Something in her movement suggested a loneliness that

she couldn't completely hide. I had noticed no pictures of children when I walked in, no too-small wedding ring embedded into her left hand. This lady lived for her cats, and they seemed to love her.

My lack of employment was making me too sentimental.

"Okay," I said. "I'll humor you."

She turned. Her smile was radiant, transforming her elderly face into the face of a girl.

"For a five-hundred-buck retainer and a hundred bucks a day expenses," I said.

She didn't even flinch. Should have charged her my political rates in which everything got multiplied by ten—and even that was cheap by government standards.

She reached for her billfold which sat by the grocery-list pad on the counter. She picked it up, took a gold Cross pen out of the Sigma Delta Chi mug next to the pad, and came over to the table. As I watched, she wrote a thousand-dollar check in perfect cursive then handed it to me.

"You undercharge, Mr. Ransom."

Didn't I know it. It never was more clear than at that moment.

"Okay," I said. "I know about Bob. Give me the poop on the other murders."

She pushed her billfold aside and folded her hands on the oak tabletop. "I beg your pardon, Mr. Ransom," she said. "But I don't think you do know the—poop—on Bob. The papers didn't report it all. It was too horrible."

She shuddered, a dainty movement that made me think of romance novels and debutante balls. (The things a man sees in my profession . . .) She grabbed the teapot for support.

"Tea?" she asked, her voice shaking.

I nodded. She poured into two small, wafer-thin cups, then set the pot down and opened the sugar jar. "One lump or two?"

"None," I said, taking my cup. My thumb nearly dwarfed

it. I took a sip and drained it. I barely had a chance to taste it. "Bob?"

She nodded, flung the tea back like a strong brandy and poured herself another cup. "He was tied between four bushes in my garden like vets do when they spay, gutted from stem to stern, and his heart was removed. He was shaved before they strung him up, and the police say he was alive when he was gutted."

Vets. Vets. For a moment, I thought she meant Vietnam vets. Then I realized. Veterinarian.

She belted the second cup back, and poured a third. I stuck my teacup under the pouring spout wishing for something strong. No wonder she was upset.

"The other cats, were they killed the same way?"

She shook her head. "Baggins was a victim of a hit-and-run. Seemed like an unfortunate accident, but he was shaved too. Then there was Sophie, whose throat was slit; Ridicio, who was hanged; and Rin Tin Tin, who was nailed to a tiny cross." She sighed and buried her head behind a wrinkled, ring-studded hand. "The police think some crazy is on the loose, but they don't have time to look for him. They just want me to keep my babies indoors." She dropped her hand. Her mouth was a thin line, her blue eyes flashed. "I want him caught. No one should be allowed to menace innocents."

I had my doubts about whether cats were innocents—I'd seen more than one torture a mouse—but I wasn't about to let my opinion tamper with a much-needed commission. I had almost made that mistake once today. "Who's the on-site officer?" I asked, and the case officially began.

ii

The precinct smelled like old, wet tennis shoes. The concrete walls had a layer of grime over them from poor heating systems and summer dampness. I sat on an ancient green office chair with springs missing in the middle, sipping lukewarm watery coffee, and waiting for Lieutenant Thornton to get off the phone so that he could talk to me. He had been gesturing and swearing into the receiver for the last fifteen minutes. From what I could tell, he was dealing with a call from home.

Three transvestites in black fishnet were cuffed together and being dragged through by a female police officer. An elderly woman clutched her right arm and looked down as she spoke to a burly man at the desk beside me. She had been mugged and lost her Social Security check, all her identification, and the fifteen dollars that was going to carry her through the month. The officer was polite, but bored. He had seen it all before.

So had I.

I made it a practice to look away.

Thornton slammed the receiver down. "Stupid bitch," he muttered. I had been right. Wife. He leaned forward. "Long time no see, Ransom. I thought they were sending you home with Ronnie's boys."

"We'll be back in four more years," I chanted.

"Yeah, right." He leaned back and lit a cigarette with the filter broken off of it. "At the rate our friend Bill is screwing up, probably. What can I do you for?"

I set my paper coffee cup on the only bare spot on Thornton's desk. "Bob the Weather Cat."

He laughed and leaned back, smoke coming out of his mouth and nostrils. "Lord, how the mighty have fallen."

I grinned. "Hey, I'm not a big-city cop who is handling a case outside his jurisdiction. The McLean homeboys sent me over to you. How come D.C. gets to handle a Virginia case?"

Thornton rolled his eyes. "McLean department is small. We usually take the famous as a favor to them. I guess that includes famous animals. So who hired you? The station or that crazy old bat next door?"

"The old bat."

He nodded. "She calls every day. I don't have the heart to tell her that the case is way down on our priority list— like below the subbasement."

"She knows. That's why she hired me."

Thornton took another long drag off the cigarette, then stamped it out in the full ashtray near the phone. "She just needs to keep her precious babies inside. Then they won't get gutted by the neighborhood Satanists."

"You know that, and I know that. But if I can pin a face and a name to Bob's murder, then I get a five-thousand-dollar bonus."

Thornton gave me a half-smile. "Seems to me that was a starting fee once upon a time."

"Yeah, well, the gravy train has retired to Kennebunk-port."

Thornton stood up and stretched, his beefy arms straining against his regulation tee. "You should work for the district, man. Same old shit at the same old pay, but you don't have to worry when the rubes come to town."

"Maybe I like holding the hands of little old ladies."

"You just weren't smart enough to rig the election when you had the chance."

I ran a hand through my thinning hair. "I thought Gennifer Flowers was a good move."

"Maybe, if you were trying to trap a Kennedy. People expect a man with a wife like Hillary to get some on the side." Thornton took out another cigarette and pounded it against the desktop. "I'll get you the files on our friend Bob."

"Thanks."

He disappeared into the back. The old lady next to me burst into tears, her voice finally rising above the general din. "But how will I *live* for the next month?"

The cop was shaking his head. "You have to talk with the Social Security people."

"But I don't even have enough for dinner tonight!"

I stuck a hand in my pocket and fingered the crisp

twenty I always carried there for emergencies. The woman stood and wiped her eyes with a crumpled handkerchief. Then she stuck the handkerchief back in her sleeve. "That's not your problem, is it?" she said to the officer. "I'm sorry."

I stood too, and blocked her way. She was tiny, about four feet nine, and weighed less than a hundred pounds. The kind of woman I would expect to have a cat-filled house that smelled of piss. "Lady," I said, "I overheard. Can't do much about the mugging, but I can help with tonight."

I shoved the twenty at her. She stared at it for a moment. "I don't take charity, young man," she said. She handed it back to me, and walked around the desk, hunched and clutching her arm.

"It's not charity," I said, but she didn't turn. It *was* charity—we both knew it—but she didn't want it. So much for trickle-down economics.

Thornton came back with the file. It was thick, filled with publicity stills of Bob in life and ugly shots of Bob in death. The cat's limbs had been stretched out of their sockets. The cat must have put up a hell of a racket while he was being killed. Someone had to have heard something.

But who paid attention to a howling cat?

Other than the details of the death, the file was useless. I took a sip of my now-cold coffee. It tasted like colored swamp water. "Hey, Thornton! What about the other deaths?"

Thornton frowned. He was lighting one cigarette from another. I noticed a white band of skin on his left finger— where his wedding ring used to be. "What other deaths?"

"The shaved hit-and-run, the cat nailed to a cross, all those?"

He shrugged. "No one called us on 'em. We only heard about them after the Weather Kitty bit it. Of course we're going to watch any other deaths, but the old ones just don't factor."

"Did you interview any neighbors?"

"For chrissakes, Ransom. It was only a cat—a famous cat, mind you, but still a cat."

He had a point. In a city with the highest murder rate per capita, where little old ladies got mugged at bus stops, where mayors thought nothing of sticking candy up their noses, one cat didn't matter a hell of a lot.

To anyone except a rich woman with too much time on her hands.

And me, because she was paying me.

I photocopied the report on the station's in-house copier. Black streaks marred the paper, but at least I could still read it. I thanked Thornton and left.

Two blocks away from the station, I saw the little old lady, walking as if her feet hurt, head bent, hand clutching that useless arm. I pressed the window button and the passenger window rolled down. I leaned across the leather upholstery. "At least let me drive you to a hospital."

She looked up. A bruise had started to form on her left cheek. "What are you so worried about me for?"

I couldn't answer that, not even to me. Maybe I saw myself in her shoes not too many years away. Maybe I had a soft spot. Maybe I wanted to focus on something else beside dead cats. Maybe I wanted to believe that in her youth she had great tits. I shrugged. "I was a bad man in a previous life. The angel Gabriel met me at the pearly gates and told me they would be locked forever unless I did one good deed. You're it. Now get in."

She smiled, revealing a mouthful of bad teeth. "You don't expect me to believe that, do you?"

"Do I look like the kind of guy who would be kind for the hell of it?"

"No." She pulled the car door open with her good hand. "When I saw you upstairs, I pegged you for a Republican."

I dropped her at Washington General, helped her with the admittance forms, and promised to talk with the Social Security people. I also got the details of the mugging—in broad daylight near the Jefferson Memorial (and the lovely tourists stood around and *snapped pictures*)—and promised to keep an eye out for the creep. Muggers had a pattern, and if Dolores fit into that pattern, well then maybe I might clean one speck of dirt off the city streets.

Damn. Dems in office and everyone becomes a bleeding heart.

I was back in McLean by midafternoon. Fortunately for me, feminism is a token word there. Women of Beverly Conner's status did not work. They stayed home and baked cookies, in Hillary parlance. Of course, that would change by '96, but we were still feeling the effects of Reaganism.

Thank god. Otherwise no one would have been home.

I parked on a side street and canvassed the neighborhood on foot. I learned early in my career that to say I'm a private dick in D.C. was tantamount to getting a door slammed in my face. In this town, everyone had a secret. Even people who didn't have secrets liked to pretend they had one. The more secrets a person had, the more powerful. And the more they hated investigators.

They didn't mind the police though. Cops kept the neighborhood safe and were notoriously poor at closing cases.

I had some pretty good fake ID. Had to. The folks in this town were also paranoid.

In each house, I got coffee and a sob story about poor Bob. The first three houses had an empty dog run in back and a kitten playing on the floor. The things people did to be trendy. Socks had made D.C. into a cat-person's heaven. Dogs were suddenly pets *non grata*. I didn't learn anything until house No. 5.

DANGER IN D.C.

The woman who answered the door was considerably younger than her neighbors. An adult Siamese perched on her shoulder. She was slight and near the end of a pregnancy. Her T-shirt, which read BABY with a large red arrow pointing toward her stomach, was too tight.

I told her my spiel. She introduced herself as Suzanna Blackwell, and let me inside a house filled with children's toys, family photographs, and warm brown tones. A house she had decorated herself, obviously, but the first one I had walked into that actually felt lived-in.

She sat me at the kitchen table (Formica that looked like faked marble) and wiped it off. Then she gave me a plate of cookies and offered coffee or milk. When I discovered that all she had was instant, I took the milk.

"I heard it, you know," she said. She had to push her chair away so that her distended stomach wouldn't brush the edge of the table. "About six in the morning, some cat was yowling. But it sounded like it was in pain, not in heat." She reached up and petted the cat on her shoulder. Its slanted eyes watched me with a cool appraisal. "I looked out the window and saw nothing. Then the yowling stopped and a man ran through my bushes, covered with blood. That's when I called the police."

"You called?"

She nodded. "I used to let Whiskers here go out, but not anymore. Too many deaths in the neighborhood. We got him for the kids, but he's really closer to me."

Obviously. I had never seen a cat content to ride on someone's shoulders before. Especially shoulders as small as hers.

"Can you describe the man?"

She nodded. "He was wearing dark clothing, and he was white. He had a regulation haircut—looked almost military—and he was about . . . taller than six feet because his head brushed that tree limb out there."

"The investigating officer didn't talk to you?"

Suzanna smiled and pulled the cat off her shoulder. She

rubbed her chin against the top of its head. "He didn't think it all that important."

"You did tell him you saw a man, not a boy?"

"Oh, yeah," she said. "But he was so convinced that it's some gang that he wouldn't even listen to me. Now Whiskers doesn't go outside at all, and I don't even let the kids play in the yard after school. I hope you catch this guy because my husband is talking about finding a place outside the Beltway. I don't want him to make the commute from the White House. The drive is long enough now as it is."

Suddenly all my meters started ticking. "Your husband's a political appointee?"

She shook her head. "He's actually detailed from State. He's been at the White House since '86. He's not an appointee so Clinton's people don't want to mess with him. They can't even fill the seats they're supposed to fill. No sense adding a few more—at least for a while."

"Does everyone here work with the government?" I meant the comment as sarcasm, but she seemed to take me seriously.

"Sure. Except Mrs. Conner, and it seems to me her husband used to work for CIA."

"Her husband?" I had seen no evidence of a man's presence in that house.

"Oh, he's been dead for years. They say he died doing some work in Vietnam in the late sixties, but my husband says that Mr. Conner was actually in Red China when he died. All very hush-hush, even now." But clearly something she enjoyed gossiping about.

"But everyone else works for the government."

"Oh, yes." She bit the head off a gingerbread man and talked around the food. "Willis, next door, is Treasury. The Sanderses just moved in. He's with HHS. I could go on."

"What about Bob's owner?"

"Oh, Julie! I forgot about her!" Suzanna bit off the gingerbread man's torso. "She just moved in a few months ago.

She trains animals for local stunts and stuff. The house used to belong to Senator Symms from Idaho. He sold it to a new woman appointee from Washington State, but she didn't like the neighborhood—too chichi, she said—so Julie got it."

I frowned. Old habits died hard. "How many Clinton people in the neighborhood?"

She laughed. "Too many, according to my husband. I think three-quarters of the houses turned over at the turn of the year."

That explained the dog runs and the cat-filled households. Not political chauvinism but new owners reflecting the president's bias. Cat people, all of them.

"And no one is upset about the cat deaths?"

Suzanna shook her head. "Willis spoke to us all about gangs the other day, saying that they're not neighborhood-oriented any more, that they go where the money is." She sighed. "You just have to put up with things living in the big city. I can't wait until my husband retires and we can get away from all this. Of course, by then, I probably won't think anything of living in fear. I hate it now though." She patted her stomach. "Doesn't seem right somehow."

"No, it doesn't." I said. I stood, having had my fill of gingerbread and milk. "Thanks again, Mrs. Blackwell."

She trailed me to the door, which didn't give me time to study the photographs. Some of them, I noted, were of a skinny man in a suit posed with Bush, or Reagan, or several better-known congressmen. The rest were snapshots of two towheaded boys, going from smiling babies to gap-toothed children. Twins, it looked like, and at her size, she could be carrying two more.

Amazing the things pictures told about a family and its values. I said my goodbyes and was walking to the next house before I remembered.

Snapshots.

How could I have been so dumb?

The rest of the neighborhood proved a wash. Cool reception and even cooler interaction. Bob's owner, Julie, wasn't home, so I made a mental note to contact her later.

I had to clear my mind from the cat garbage. I went to my local information sources and left messages for any tourists with pictures of that day's mugging at the Jefferson Memorial, promising to pay top dollar for a clear shot. That kept me from spending cash on the development charge, and also gave me a way out so that I wouldn't have to spend money on the naïfs who would photograph a crime instead of stop it.

I stopped at Washington General on my way home to see Dolores. She was asleep when I got there, her skin a faint china blue against the crisp white sheets. Her bones looked brittle. Her right arm was in a cast and an IV was feeding into her left. I went and found the duty nurse who told me that Dolores would have to remain for a few days because her malnourishment made her injury more serious than a broken arm and a few cracked ribs would normally be.

"We see lots of this," the duty nurse said. "They can't afford to pay all their bills on Social Security, so they only eat a meal a day and even skip that at the end of the month."

I frowned. "I thought the government was supposed to cover her expenses."

The nurse laughed, a bitter sound. "The government probably won't even cover her hospital bill, since she waited a few hours before coming in. I think we're the only medical workers in the city who support Clinton's health-care reform ideas. Maybe then we'll actually get paid for the work we do."

She trudged off, her well-worn heels squeaking against the linoleum. Her legs were on a par with No. 45's but the shoes did her no good. Didn't matter though. She kept trim by working crowded hospital corridors. Number 45 used an overpriced exercise bike.

I found the nurse's legs much more appealing.

V

The phone woke me up at 6:00 A.M. Beverly Conner sobbing into the line, "Please come, right away!"

As I turned on the light and rolled out of my waterbed, sliding on the black satin sheets, I wondered which one bit it: the little kitten mewing on top of the microwave? The big tom by the window? The white cat that twined its way around my ankles? I kicked aside piles of unwashed clothing, slid on a pair of jeans, a sweatshirt and stuffed my wallet in my back pocket. I hurried through the living room, narrowly avoiding all the electronics equipment which I too rarely used, and grabbed my raincoat off the credenza Wife No. 3 did not want. Then I hurried out the door.

I had forgotten that the GW Parkway was full this time of the morning. Commuters in their Beamers, car phones pasted to their ears, trying to be the earliest person in the office. That would change in the middle years of the administration, when everything became routine, and change back just before the election in case Clinton managed to squeeze a second term out of the voters. Fortunately, I was heading *to* McLean. My side of the GW Parkway was nearly empty.

I pulled up behind the Virginia police. They had two squads sitting in the middle of the road, lights flashing. Faces peered through curtained windows as they had done on my first visit. I strode up the stone steps to Beverly's house and knocked.

Her face was puffy and her eyes bloodshot. "Mr. Ransom," she said with such relief that I was tempted to put my arms around her. She stood aside to let me in.

The faint odor of vomit covered the scent of cat piss. But the house looked tidy as ever. Half a dozen cats watched

300

warily from the hallway. Another four sat in the picture window, tails twitching.

"What happened?" I asked.

"I found another one, tossed in my rosebushes, shaved. Lieutenant Thornton thinks it is some kind of gang—"

"Let me go talk to him," I said.

I slipped out the back door and joined the three policemen huddled around the rosebushes on Beverly's well-manicured lawn. Clumps of black-and-white hair covered the dew-coated grass as if the shaving had occurred right there.

The cat's body looked naked and pathetic on its bed of thorns. "Anyone know who the cat belongs to?" I asked.

"The Reeds down the street," Thornton said, his hands stuck in his back pocket, the cigarette in his mouth unlit. "They've had the cat for two years. They're pretty broken up about it. I think they're even going to let their little girl stay home from school."

"Reed?" I said. "That a name I should know?"

"Doubt it," Thornton said. "They're old Friends of Bill. He was going to give Mrs. Reed a political appointment, but had to settle for a Schedule-C. That nanny thing again."

"How old's the girl?"

"Chelsea's age. Goes to Sidwell Friends, the same school."

I frowned. "You know, Mrs. Blackwell next door saw a man go through her bushes after the last murder."

"Murder?" Thornton said. "You're beginning to sound like the bat."

"Shhh." I glanced over my shoulder at the window. Six cats had crowded onto the sill, but there was no sign of Beverly. Thank god. "She said the man looked military. He sounded more Secret Service to me."

Thornton nodded. "I'll check it out."

I left the site. Something about that cat, discarded and pathetic in death, made me think of Dolores, lying in the hospital bed and pasted to an IV she couldn't pay for.

I went back inside. Beverly was sitting at her polished dining-room table, looking lost. I couldn't tell if she had overheard Thornton's burst of sensitivity or not. "How'd you get all these cats?"

She smiled, then. It was a sad smile that accompanied a glance out the window. "Most of them were strays," she said. "Dumped by former owners, or lost, or abandoned kittens. Funny thing about cats. They don't beg, no matter how hungry or injured they are." She swallowed hard. "I keep thinking about that. I didn't hear the little guy cry out. I didn't hear anything. I just imagine him trying to maintain his dignity while they were removing it . . ."

Her voice trailed off. I sat down across from her, trying to imagine how she had lived over the years. Husband with the CIA, always gone, always focused on work. No children. The cats were her life. They were her babies. A cat's death was the same to her as a child's.

Then it all went rocket clear. "Let me see that picture of Bob again."

She frowned, but stood, obviously relieved to have something to do. She went into the study and came back clutching the newspaper clipping. I studied the photograph for a moment.

"How many children are on this block?"

"I don't know. Quite a few. They all play together."

"Young children?"

She shook her head. "Young teenagers. Mostly girls. One of them got invited up to the White House last week. It was quite a big deal." She pushed an orange cat off her chair and sat down. "What do you want with the picture of Bob?"

I showed it to her. "Does he look like anyone to you?"

She took it, then pulled a pair of half glasses out of her breast pocket and stared at it. "There are an awful lot of cats that look like Bob," she said. She glanced outside. The latest victim had shared Bob's coloring and general body shape. She glanced back at the photo. "Oh, my god," she whispered. "He looks just like Socks!"

vi

The pound had a small herd of black-and-white cats. I took the friendliest one, who reached out at me through the little triangular holes in his cage each time I passed. The pound let me have him for free. Fortunately, he'd already had his nuts chopped off, or I would have had to wait a few days. I didn't have a few days. I was afraid Mrs. Conner would change her mind by the time I got back.

She hadn't. She had a room specially designed as a cat isolation ward. I guess she used it when a cat was pregnant or seriously ill. Socks II: The Sequel went into that room for the night, and I bunked down on the floor with my watch alarm set for 4:00 A.M. At that time, Sequel and I would hit the streets.

Mrs. Conner went to bed at nine. I watched the end of the third Indiana Jones movie on Channel 20, then joined Sequel in his little room, watch-alarm set. I woke up at midnight with the cat sitting on my back, nuzzling its nose in the hair at the nape of my neck, purring like a souped-up V-8 engine. I pushed him off and got him to settle, only to wake up an hour later as a scratchy tongue rubbed a hole in my chin. Finally I grabbed him, wrapped an arm around him (as much to hold him down as to give him comfort) and tried to sleep again. When the alarm went off at four, Sequel had one paw across my chest like a lover.

What was it Thornton had said? Some cliché about how the mighty had fallen?

He had no clue.

I had fixed a little homing device to Sequel's collar just in case. Then I picked him up and carried him to the back door. Together we went out. He prowled and I followed.

The sky was faintly pink at the horizon. The air had an

early-morning chill and dew had already formed on the grass. By the time Sequel had done his personal business, my tennis shoes were soaked.

I had never trailed a cat before. He didn't have a care for sidewalks, streets or the other amenities of civilization. He crawled under bushes and leapt over fences, ran around houses and hid behind drainpipes. I followed as quietly as I could. Once I lost him when he hid for forty minutes under a rosebush tracking a mouse. I scraped my finger on barbed wire, and stubbed my toe on a hidden brick. By midmorning, Sequel was camped out on Mrs. Conner's backyard, snoozing in the sun. I was crouched in the bushes, trying to stay out of sight while dislodging the thorns I had picked up from the neighbor's rosebush.

The only thing I had learned all morning was that my fingernails were too short to act as tweezers. That, and the fact that cats led dull little lives enhanced by their overactive imaginations. If people had that much fun doing mundane tasks, factory workers would be whistlin' while they worked.

Fat chance.

I was no better. I had gone from trailing Ted Kennedy in the predawn hours to following a black-and-white cat who looked like Socks. Of course, if Sequel had still had his nuts, the job wouldn't be all that much different.

vii

It took three days, two pairs of tennis shoes and fifteen cuts to the right hand alone before I hit pay dirt. Sequel and I headed out at our customary 4:00 A.M., and I marveled at the neighborhood. I had been prowling through bushes and climbing over fences for days now, and not a soul had called the cops. No wonder the upper class needed security systems. Anyone with a different social standing was beneath their notice—whether that anyone looked like a thief or not.

The morning was foggy, and the only way I could tell dawn was approaching was because the mist took on a Stephen King/end-of-the-world pink glow. I had discovered a hole in a trellis big enough to hide me but with enough view through the leaves to allow me to keep Sequel in sight most of the time.

Sequel had chased a squirrel under his favorite rosebush when I heard a car door slam a few blocks away. A chill ran down my back. Leather shoes clicked against the asphalt bike path. The wearer either belonged to the neighborhood or had learned what I did about the so-called Neighborhood Watch program.

He came out of the fog like a movie commando bursting through a haze of smoke. He looked just the way Suzanna Blackwell had described him: Over six feet, broad shoulders held with military precision, haircut so perfect it looked glued on. His clothing was invisible Washington blue and his tie was knotted so tight I wondered how he could breathe. He clutched a tape recorder in one hand and a dish in the other. With a flick of his thumb, he turned the tape recorder on. It made a funny whirring sound that I could almost identify.

Sequel perked up his ears, squirrel forgotten.

"Here, kitty, kitty," the man said, voice soft.

Sequel ran toward him like the man was God himself. The man shut off the tape recorder and crouched, putting the dish on the ground. Half a beat too late, I realized what the sound was.

A can opener.

The man had recorded the sound of a can opener opening a can. Sequel approached, friendlier than I had seen him with anyone but me. Tail twitching in anticipation, yowling like he was about to get a great treat.

The food was probably drugged.

I burst out of the bushes, twigs scraping my thinning hair, trellis tottering, and launched myself at the man. Sequel screamed and darted for his rosebush as I caught the man in the middle. The dish went flying and landed with a crash that echoed in the fog-shrouded street.

The man was all muscle and as solid as the Lincoln Memorial. He landed on his back and grunted as the wind left his body. Lucky for me I had the element of surprise or I never would have taken him. I shoved a knee to his groin and put my whole weight on it as I yanked my cuffs off my belt.

"Stupid son of a bitch," I said, "what are you doing picking on cats?"

Then I looked down at him and knew. One of Quayle's men. They all had gone their own way when Danny returned to Indiana—loose cannons without a brain cell among them. It had been charming in their boss, scary in men with bodies like Arnold Schwarzenegger. With a grunt, the man shoved me off him. I rolled away in time to push Sequel from the plate of overturned food.

"Beverly!" I cried. "Call 911! Beverly!"

I tucked Sequel under one arm and deposited him near the house as I ran after Mr. Macho. My tennis shoes gave me the advantage of silence, but his training gave him speed. He made it to the nondescript black sedan parked half a block away, slipped in and drove off.

But not before I saw the license plate.

DAN 1996

Dream on, asshole. With folks like him working on Quayle's reelection campaign, Bill and friends would have to be real incompetents to lose.

I stood in the middle of the street wheezing like an eighty-year-old with one lung. Sequel twined himself around my legs, licking the remains of canned food off his whiskers.

"Great, buddy," I said, picking him up. "Now we got to get you to a vet and pump your stomach."

At that moment I knew it was too late. I had become a cat-loving bleeding heart with conservative aspirations.

Another Clinton Democrat.

I guess it had only been a matter of time.

viii

Thornton tracked our man and brought him in. They don't know what they'll charge him with yet, but they'll make it a felony so the guy will have to spend some time behind bars.

Turns out Mr. Macho had worked for Quayle (my memory was as good as I thought it was) but had been fired for being too stupid—and acting on those harebrained ideas during the 1992 Bush reelection campaign. Too stupid to work for Uncle Danny. I had been in Washington too long. I had finally seen everything.

This harebrained scheme was right up there with Dan's speech about canals on Mars. Mr. Macho decided to terrorize the little friends of Chelsea Clinton, killing the Socks look-alikes in hopes that word would get to Chelsea, and she would think Washington a horrible place. The pressure would wear on Bill and he would decide not to run in '96. Or something like that. The ultimate goals of the plan were as foggy as that last morning. Apparently Mr. Macho was not too good at future planning.

What a surprise.

I had more good news. My little messages left at strategic places had turned up several good prints of Dolores's mugging. The cops even knew the guy, a former informer for the DEA, cut loose after the Marion Barry deal. He was behind bars now. Dolores didn't get her purse back, but Justice Was Served.

Me, I go over to Beverly's house twice a week for tea

and conversation. My apartment has the faint odor of cat piss, thanks to Sequel, and my secretary's legs are for shit. But Dolores needed work and before her marriage in the early forties she used to be LBJ's personal secretary, back when he was an unknown congressman from the Great State of Texas. She's a ball-busting, no-holds-barred Democrat with a long memory that has served me well on at least two occasions. Amazing how many sons in positions of power will work hard to keep their fathers' memories unscathed. Amazing how many senator fathers have senator sons. And then some.

I work for the Dems now. Scoping out H. Ross Perot isn't as much fun as going after the Kennedys—the little man with big ears doesn't have quite the appetite for parties that Ted has—but it is work that pays well. Lord knows I'll need the money if Hillary's VAT tax goes through.

But I shouldn't complain. I'm an official FOB now, with a photograph behind my desk to prove it. But it's not the picture of me and Clinton that is my prize possession. It's the gift from Beverly—a political cartoon clipped from the *Washington Post.* It's a picture of Socks walking down the street surrounded by cats in suits, obviously Secret Service. The cutline reads: "Socks Goes to Washington." Beverly stuck a photo of my face over one of the security cats with "My Hero!" scrawled on the side. Sappy sure. But someone has to make this city safe—even if it is for a small subset of the population.

Besides, compassion is in these days. Compassion for cats is even better. Ever since the news broke, my phone has been ringing off the hook. I'm the only D.C. detective to get his photo in *People* magazine—right next to a picture of Bob, the Weather Cat, of course. But who's complaining? He's the one wearing the ugly yellow rain slicker.

Like footsteps in an empty alley or screams in the dead of night, cats and mystery fit purr-fectly together in these collections of cat tales by modern masters of mystery.

CAT CRIMES 1, 2, AND 3
all edited by MARTIN GREENBERG and ED GORMAN

Published by Ivy Books.
Available in your local bookstore.